playground
zero

playground
zero

a coming-of-age novel
set in Berkeley

SARAH RELYEA

Published 2019
Printed in the United States of America
ISBN: 978-1-63152-889-7
ISBN: 978-1-63152-888-0
Library of Congress Control Number: 2019919051

For information, address:
She Writes Press
1569 Solano Ave #546
Berkeley, CA 94707

She Writes Press is a division of SparkPoint Studio, LLC.

For Robin Epstein

contents

Part I

a wandering moon

chapter one

The Raysons: Alice

COMING FROM THE yard, where a willow swayed and the fence hung heavy with damp honeysuckle, a long-legged girl appeared in the doorway. Willow and honeysuckle, grass and stone bench: soon gone. She would remember them, of course—how she and a neighbor girl had overpowered the bench under the willow one school-day afternoon. They'd never imagined they could, and so they'd pushed and pushed, and then, in one impossible moment—chaos! Though alarmed by the heavy thud, she'd been enjoying the success when her mother appeared. Running for the gate, the other girl snagged a honeysuckle frond and then was gone, leaving a fragrance over Alice and her mother, willow and dismembered bench.

She would remember the Mall and the monuments and the spring cherry blossoms from Japan.

She'd been on peace marches. Ten and nearly grown, soon she'd be by the dock of the bay, California dreaming.

She would remember summer lightning bugs—how she'd chased them with her brother; how fugitive they were!

Weaving a honeysuckle frond around her head, Alice came through the door. Glancing up, she could feel the empty room eyeing her: long bangs held in place by the frond, pouting mouth and somber, almond-shaped eyes, like her mother's—no changes there. Mornings, she resembled her mother; by noon, her brother. The long arms and legs were slender and hers alone.

She would remember the honeysuckle frond and the empty room on moving day.

The movers had come and gone. She should be folding her sleeping bag. Dragging the heavy bag, Alice passed through an abandoned mesh of hanging beads; as she cleared the beads, they clacked in a rush of swaying rhythm. The sound always made her imagine a caboose passing by.

The unseen caboose rounded a bend and was gone. Under her palm the glossy door frame was cool, though the day was already muggy—June in Washington.

They were bound for a new land. She must go knowing nothing of the place, whether good or bad.

Her parents had gone there scouting the land. They'd gone farther than the spy who crossed through Indian country during the Revolution—she'd read about him in her brother's book—and brought back encouraging news of a place where the weather was always warm and the forests wild with vegetation. Her mother spoke of the new house as a castle in the shadow of the Berkeley hills—so large, so gloomy with heavy redwood beams in the local manner. Then, in a moment of fancy, her mother had snapped up a couple of regal chairs as furnishings; she'd bought them and, eyes aglow from the buying spree, brought them home in the car on her own, no asking Tom. They were Shakespearean props for *A Midsummer Night's Dream* or maybe *Macbeth*, her mother had laughed, as she arranged the blood-red thrones by the fireplace, where Alice and her brother were playing an idle game of King and Queen on them when the movers came.

Her mother was calling from the yard. The moment had come. Gathering up the sleeping bag, Alice passed through the front doorway, seeing once more the layers of peeling paint, then through crocuses to the car, where her family paused under a humid sky.

Her father approached holding a map, colored as though of the Holy Land, a heavy forefinger marking the route. They would soon be crossing dangerous lands that had lured rough men and runaways, cowboys and covered wagons, through wild grasses, deep waters, and oak-maple jungles to lonely deaths. She would reap the reward: roads and jukebox restaurants, suspension bridges and Grand Canyon overlooks, a new ocean, sandy beaches. They would journey; they would be happy.

Folding the map, her father headed for the house.

He was closing up the house when a baby-blue Rambler rounded the corner. Alice had wondered if they would really come: but Kathy's mother had promised, and here they were.

Kathy jumped down from the passenger seat, her eyes red. Oh, she'd been crying! They could be close, as they had been for nearly a year, if only the Raysons were staying. The anger suddenly gone, the quarrels forgotten, they approached each other by the curb as Kathy's mother leaned from the Rambler.

"Marian," she purred in a deep, playful growl, waving over Alice's mother. "Come here. I have something to tell you."

The mothers were close, and they'd become closer as Kathy's father—a defenseless man, an oyster in need of a shell—was leaving. Though Kathy adored him, she bragged one day how her mother had hurled the frying pan. There were other confessions on the way home from school; and once Kathy added, in seeming condemnation, "Your parents never argue, do they?" She'd come to the Raysons' house often enough to know. "They're repressed," she murmured, rubbing it in. Even so, Kathy was fun and loyal, or had been before her father made plans to go. That was when she suddenly found something else to do.

Now those problems were gone, and for a moment they were together. Alice was fumbling for words when she heard a booming command.

"Kathy!"

The mothers were done.

"Kathy, hurry up!"

"Well, goodbye. See ya." Alice found the same phrase as always.

Kathy fought back her tears. "See ya."

Soon the cars headed off together along the avenue. Then Kathy's Rambler rounded a corner and the parade was over. The Raysons' old Chevy Delray sped down the avenue, a hand waving from the rear window.

"Off we go," Marian summed up, turning and offering the children an encouraging smile below her sunglasses.

Blonde and casual, she wore a sleeveless paisley dress and sandals; her shoulders were smooth and pale, her features pleasingly angular. Tom had sandy hair, heavy shoulders and a square jaw; he too wore sunglasses.

"Well, I'm sorry to go. It's been a good home," Marian sighed, wiping her cheek. Then she added, "Can we go by the Lincoln Memorial, Tom?"

"Along the Mall?"

"Yes, we should see the Poor People's Campaign before we go. Can we get through?"

"We'll see."

"Barbara says we should go."

Barbara was Kathy's mother, a geyser of news. Alice had been stung to learn of the move from Kathy, who'd heard from her mother and come up on the playground, chummy and sorry she'd been mean. As usual, the Raysons had preferred to keep the plans among grown-ups. They'd informed the children only when there was no longer anything to conceal or much chance to complain.

Now there would be summer in Berkeley, a place near San Francisco; Alice would need new pals.

Curt glanced over at her. Though he was two years older and a boy, they'd played together before Kathy, who was always arguing with boys.

"How come her mother bought that Rambler?" he murmured in a confiding tone, though the eyes were teasing.

No one responded.

"I mean, why choose a lousy car?"

Curt remembered car models and design features, baseball games and earned run averages; he always had something to do. But why should Alice care about such things? The world of cars and sports and grown-up concealment was passing, and something new was beginning.

Her mother glanced back. "No squabbling," she commanded. "We're going to see the civil-rights people. No one seems to remember the message anymore, but we can honor Dr. King's memory by keeping peace among ourselves." Then she paused and murmured, "Tom, no going down where the trouble was."

Her mother was referring to the shopping corridor along 14th Street, where they'd always gone for shoes. Now the shops were closed; they'd been smashed and looted in days of outrage after the killing of Dr. King. Only her father had seen the damage as he passed through every day on the way to work and back. Surrounded by houses and lawns, the others had been far enough away for the mayhem to seem unreal.

Curt leaned forward. "The Senators are playing Oakland at two o'clock. Frank Howard's up against Catfish Hunter. Can we hear the game?"

As everyone knew, Howard was Washington's home-run hero, while Hunter was the up-and-coming Oakland player who'd thrown a perfect game back in May.

Tom glanced back at Alice. "And you?" he asked blandly. "Any requests?"

She made no response.

"What's that song of yours?" her father pursued. He was referring to the song he'd found her blaring in the basement playroom a few days before. The song was new to her, part of the Top 40 countdown. The Top 40 was also new to her, something other than baseball.

Tom reached forward and sound flooded the Chevy: "White Rabbit" in full swing. He glanced at her in the mirror. "Loud enough?"

Through the window she was enjoying the tangled trees of Rock Creek Park. They often passed the park, because it was on the way downtown. The song pulsed through a crescendo and ended. Tom turned off the radio.

"Well," she heard her mother saying, "we've chosen a good moment to go to San Francisco."

Soon they were passing Adams Morgan and P Street, where they'd gone for dinner on Saturdays. Kathy's mother had recommended the restaurant, Luigi's. The Washington Monument could be seen ahead, far away yet always there, as though a new heavenly body had been hung in the sky.

The Chevy came through a tunnel and emerged among apartment blocks and government buildings. The facades were shadowless, since the day was cloudy. As the Chevy paused for the red light by St. John's Church, Alice saw the rearing horse and rider of Lafayette Square. A dampened White House lay beyond; the monument, larger now and lower, reminded her of a chimney capping the Johnsons' house—soon someone else's.

She would remember the church on Easter Sunday, though they'd gone just once.

The Chevy rounded Lafayette Square and passed the White House and the Ellipse. Soon they were under the monument. Looming up and up, the thing could be seen mingled with cloud —a planet for the Raysons' wandering moon.

The Chevy neared the monument and broke away, heading west along Independence Avenue. Peering through the trees of

Ash Woods, they saw a shantytown fanning out in rows. Then the Poor People's Campaign was hidden by a leafy camouflage.

The marble figure in the Lincoln Memorial reposed in shadow as the Chevy passed the site's southern end. Alice had seen the statue of Lincoln up close; one summer evening, her mother and Barbara had taken the girls there after a peace rally under the Washington Monument.

She would remember the dead man's presence. The peace marches had been solemn, if informal—government on the grass. Now a shantytown had sprung up in the muddy park, as monuments glimmered under a cloudy noon.

THE RAYSONS HAD been on the road for days. They'd passed the Blue Ridge Mountains and Kentucky forests and hundreds of miles of farmland and plains and Ozark plateau. Now they were traveling alone through a no-man's-land. During the morning much had changed, the dry plains of the Texas panhandle becoming red-green with scrub as mesas appeared here and there. Then they found a place for lunch, a hamburger restaurant near Tucumcari.

"It's a big country," her mother sighed as they crossed tar and gravel through waves of heat.

Alice straggled, her eyes scanning south where a huge mesa rose from the surrounding plains like a flat-topped volcano. Clouds were moving from the south; a scorching gust fanned her bangs and reached through her boy's shirt—an old, oddly elegant one handed down from Curt. She was longing for lemonade, but her father would refuse. Water was free, she knew; yet all morning in the car, contemplating a vast, unknown landscape, she'd been longing for lemonade. Now, as she dawdled under an azure sky, ignoring the others, there sounded her mother's cry, loud enough for everyone to hear.

"Why, there she is—in the burning sun!"

She'd been caught. Up and down the road, there was red-green scrubland as far as the eye could see, and then the mesa. She longed to go there. Even so, she headed slowly for the door, contemplating a "Tucumcari Tonite" ad by the road.

"Can I have lemonade?" she asked, though she was wondering something else, something harder to say.

"Ask your father."

"Maybe in Albuquerque," came her father's response.

The family dawdled over lunch, hearing country songs on the loudspeaker. Then they passed through wilting sun to the car.

"A hundred and seventy-five miles to Albuquerque," her father announced.

Soon the road was galloping by. Thunderclouds were massing in the southwest, even as a dry gale lashed through the open windows. Her mother was humming a hanged man's love song, pausing to recall the words from a folk recording she'd played in the living room in Washington. *They hung me in a lonesome grove from a sycamore tree.* Her mother preferred folk songs, though just before the move she'd purchased several new albums, all by San Francisco groups. Her brother preferred games, as long as he could win.

Now he was leaning over the chess board, focused on capturing Alice's king. In one taut and sweaty movement he grasped a bishop and purged one of the pawns that was protecting her king.

"Check." Curt's tawny head bobbed over the board.

She moved her king, wondering how long she could hold off. He swooped in with a knight.

"Check."

Again she moved her king, though really there was nowhere to go.

Curt reached for the bishop, leaned smiling, then blew a bubble. There came a pop as another pawn fell from the board.

"No gum," commanded her mother, pausing in her song and then resuming.

Alice made one final move, and Curt was aglow.

"Checkmate," he announced, as though reminding her of a foregone conclusion.

Suddenly her father slowed the car. The chessmen cascaded to the floor, a cornered squadron toppling from a cliff; she groped for them one by one, as the Chevy rolled onto the shoulder.

"What's happening?" Her mother sounded apprehensive.

"Thunderstorms up ahead," her father responded.

"Oh yes, look at the clouds!"

"C'mon," he urged, glancing back. "Let's get out and watch."

They climbed from the Chevy, leaving the doors open. The heavy clouds hung over the road ahead, dwarfed by the sky. Alice had seen the Washington planetarium; Kathy's mother had taken them. Now they were under a real heaven; she would tell Kathy when—no, if—she saw her. There was so much to tell; they'd seen Kentucky and Oklahoma—and the words were fun to say, long and unusual. There had been others: Tulsa, Amarillo, where they'd been this morning, Tucumcari and the mesa, and soon Albuquerque. Words for places that lay somewhere out there, beyond the borders of the highway.

She was facing west—the whole family was—when enormous bands of color began forming in the sky.

"Oh, there's a rainbow!" her mother enthused.

Her father made no response.

Colored bands were spanning the road, one pillar on the grasslands and one soaring from some mountains to the north. She'd never seen such a thing . . .

For weeks in Washington she'd imagined the journey to California, when she would see everything. And here was the land, everywhere, now. Lunar and barren, her mother had grumbled during lunch, as though there were no grasslands, no evening fire clouds, no bands of pure color.

"C'mon," her father commanded, jumping in the car, but the bands had faded before the Chevy could reach them.

"Well, that was something—a perfect rainbow," her mother sighed as the road wound through a canyon pass. "It's a big country," she added, as though unsure what she thought of it all.

The road dropped hard from the canyon pass, then branched and slowed. They were approaching Albuquerque.

Curt was drumming his fingers on the chess box as the canyon pass faded; a baseball glove hung over one blue-jeaned knee.

"Play another game?" he demanded.

"But we're almost there." Alice folded her arms. He was only two years older; even though sports were hopeless, she was nearly par in chess. She'd been looking at mesas and simply blown the game.

"You can play when we get there," her mother suggested, glancing back at them. "Only a few minutes more."

Soon they were in another motel, rounded up by a neon lasso. The game was nearing the end and close, but then her father brought the hamburgers and there was no more chess.

THE FOLLOWING MORNING the Raysons traveled up the mountain to Santa Fe.

On a bench in Santa Fe's old Spanish square, Alice was reading her mother's book. She'd just begun a new tale: a princess had gone to free her father from a faraway kingdom. Her mother was there, in sunglasses and sandals. The book was long, having many tales of talking animals, and spells, and dense forests and the children who wandered there. She'd begun reading in the car days ago in Ohio, and now as her father and brother searched for a store selling baseball cards, she read through the tale. As the men emerged around a corner, her mother removed her sunglasses.

"I'm glad you can enjoy long books. Maybe you could show your father how far you've read."

As her father approached, she jumped from the bench and held up the book. He grasped it and balanced the binding in one palm, opened at random, and began reading. She glanced up, perusing the sober face as he read. Then he lowered the page, heavy thumb pressed beneath the words.

"Read me that," he commanded.

"The Tale of the Needle and Four Threads." The tale was unfamiliar; she preferred reading of animals or brothers and sisters.

Her father closed the book and turned it slowly around, examining the cover. It was an old book belonging to her mother and having a small tear along the binding. He fingered the tear, frowning.

"Fine reading for someone your age—already ten." He handed over the book with a bemused shrug, as though it held small value. The unassuming eyes surveyed her; she was aware of heavy shoulders and forearms, her father's, and longish legs, her own. Her brother ran by, shoe laces undone; her father paused, glanced around, and then turned and demanded, resuming a familiar conversation, "How many people are there on the Supreme Court?"

During the journey he'd moved on to new subjects, but she remembered the old drill.

"Nine."

"And in the Senate?"

"A hundred."

He grunted approval. "And how about the House of Representatives?"

She could never remember that one. "Four hundred and twenty-five," she proposed. She knew the answer was wrong even as she spoke.

"No." He unfastened a sleeve, folding it slowly and carefully along the muscular arm, the faded and impassive eyes gazing beyond her now, to the mountains. "Was that a guess?"

"Four hundred and thirty-five?"

"You're sure?" He sounded calm but somehow surly. The only way to appease him was to fess up.

"No."

"Well . . ."

He continued gazing, measuring something behind her. She felt as though he'd caught her lying or even stealing. Wondering what there was to see, she turned and found the mountains, looming above the square as though from an enormous drive-in screen. It reminded her of an outdoor movie they'd seen one summer in the car: *How the West Was Won*. She was pulled back to the Spanish square by her father's deep, colorless tone.

"Don't you want to learn the correct answer?"

Though she no longer cared, there was no sense in saying so. She glanced at him and then away, appearing unconcerned.

"Four hundred and thirty-five. You had it, but you were guessing." As she turned to go, he remarked, "We'll be in California soon. Do you remember the name of the capital?"

Here was a new one; she would try to parry. "We're not there yet."

"Can you tell me anyway?"

"San Francisco."

He'd never asked before, so how could she remember? San Francisco was one of the few California place names she knew. Well, there was Los Angeles and the new name, Berkeley. But San Francisco made her think vaguely of gold and cable cars and lumber and hills, all the things a state capital should have, and then earthquakes; moreover her father, who worked for the government, would soon be working there. Yes, that made sense: San Francisco it was. Los Angeles had beaches and Hollywood, freeways and Watts, while Berkeley so far was only a name. Her mother had told them how her father had changed jobs—

though he'd be staying with the federal government—but not much else, only that a family they knew from Washington had lived in Berkeley for a year and found it wonderful, as lovely as Barcelona. Barcelona was far away, in Europe. They'd known the other family, but only casually. She was confused why her parents would choose a place on so random a reference; they were following someone else, it seemed. She wondered why her parents so often seemed to be following someone else, as though they had no preferred ways of doing things. She wondered if they would have to go around that way forever, with people they hardly knew telling them where to buy a house, where to go for Chinese food, and what to read—her mother always had two or three books that someone had loaned her, saying she had to read them.

"I told you in the car," her father was saying.

When had he told her? She must have been reading. "I forget."

"They call it Sacramento."

The word had an echoing sound, the name not of a city but of a lake or a monument in stone.

Before he could ask anything more she ran off, and soon she was with her mother on the shaded bench in the Spanish square.

"Well," inquired her mother, "was he pleased that you're reading such a long book?"

Alice slumped on the bench, dangling her legs. "What's the House of Representatives?" She and her mother had gone over these things before, she knew.

"Oh, that's one of the houses of Congress, the lower one. The upper house is called the Senate."

She'd seen the Congress building from the Mall in Washington, when they'd gone there for huge demonstrations. "Why upper and lower?"

"The lower house is closer to the people."

That was always the response, though the meaning was unclear. "Tell me what Congress does." Familiar as well, but she wanted to be sure.

"They make laws, honey, for the whole country."

"How many laws are there?"

"Oh my goodness, there must be thousands."

"Thousands? How can anyone remember them all?" Alice paused; the problem emerged, amorphous as the sunshine gleaming everywhere beyond the small globe of shade under the trees. "How can I learn all thousands of them?"

"You probably know many of the important ones already. Most laws cover unusual or specialized situations, and even your father knows only a part of the law."

She could never learn so many laws. It would use up all her time, just knowing whether Congress would be mad at her for demonstrating on the Mall, or pushing a boy in the hallway when he teased her, or jaywalking, or reading her mother's books when they made her father mad.

She abandoned the bench as her father approached, unfolding a map to show her mother a place called Los Alamos. As her mother turned away, frowning, her brother ran up with a handful of baseball cards, torn already from the wrapper. A few moments later, they were heading for the car.

Then came the narrow, swerving road up the canyon to a small town, so far from anything that it hovered there, a sandbar under the sky, surrounded by faraway swells of land. They passed fences of barbed wire, guarding seemingly deserted buildings. Her father meandered around, peering one way and then another as though searching for something he'd lost. Her mother rode beside him, scowling through her window, hands folded grimly in her lap.

The sun glared. The parched breeze rushed through the window, rubbing Alice's face sandpaper smooth. No one had told her why they were here, and she sensed there would be no response if she inquired. Maybe there was no reason; maybe they'd come only to see sandbar and sky, and then leave. They'd done so before, on summer beaches—why, then, was her mother so upset to be here?

Alice opened her book and began to read, but the canyon road had made her queasy and the words hovered, meaningless, before her eyes. She closed the book. She whispered to her brother, "Where are we?"

He shot her a glance. "Dummy, it's where they made the Bomb."

In the pause that followed, her father murmured inaudibly, and her mother groaned, "I just feel so ashamed . . ." Soon they returned as they had come, through the canyon toward Santa Fe and then beyond, reaching Gallup at dusk.

As they approached Gallup, her father reached an arm over the frayed seat cover and dropped a pack of baseball cards on her leg.

"You should have your own," he remarked, with a sidelong glance.

Later, in the motel, she tore the wrapper from the cards and pretended to study the numbers on the back, the way her brother would do.

"Who'd you get?" he demanded, eyes gleaming, urgent and chummy.

She showed him, slyly, as though flashing a poker hand.

"Trade ya," he cajoled.

Curt searched through her cards, humming to himself as he replaced a few with players he already had.

BY THE EDGE of the Grand Canyon, the Raysons gaped in wonder and shared a bag of apples. A warm breeze mingled the dust of eons.

Then they drove through hours of searing desert.

"After the unbearable heat, let's have a proper meal," her mother suggested as they began seeing signs for Las Vegas.

"That's why I recommended going through there in the evening," her father responded.

"Through the desert at night?"

"No more whining," he snapped, tossing a surly glance at the back seat, as though the challenge had come from Alice. "We're almost there."

"How much longer?" Curt demanded. He'd slept on a cot in Flagstaff and was feeling edgy.

"Please, dear," her mother soothed.

"I'm hungry," Alice complained.

Her father glanced around. "How hungry?"

She made no response as Curt glowered around at the moonscape, humming tunelessly, one leg bouncing with nervous energy. Alice slumped, knee pressing on the front seat where her father rode.

"Who's pushing on my seat?" he demanded.

She moved the offending knee. "Not me."

Her father glanced around. "Do you want any dinner?"

She made no response.

"No more tantrums from you, lady."

"Tom, you need a good swim," her mother murmured.

One evening the summer before, her father had rounded up Alice and Curt and herded them to the local swimming pool. Soon they'd begun swimming every evening after her father came home from work. There in the pool together, away from her mother, he swam underwater laps or had them jump from the high board. She enjoyed the pool, splashing with Curt and gliding submerged as long as they could in search of coins—or maybe pearls.

Alice wondered if they would swim in Las Vegas, as her glance followed a passing Joshua tree—a desert pine. A world of wonders was rushing by. "When are we—"

"Soon," her mother responded sharply, "very soon."

Her father glanced over one shoulder and changed lanes, then slowed, pulling up on the shoulder of the road. A truck passed close by, rocking the Chevy.

"Have the tantrum here," he commanded, bland and surly, one arm reaching over the seat as though he would go for her leg.

As she glanced away, he turned around and gunned the car.

Soon they reached Las Vegas. Her father found a large hotel with a family restaurant on the balcony level overlooking an enormous, bean-shaped pool with a small palm grove sprouting from an island in the center. As they waited in the restaurant to be served, a few sunbathers lounged by the edge of the pool, in the waning rays of day. Her mother and father were now smiling, while her brother rehearsed the rules for poker. There was even lemonade. She was sure her father would go down to the pool, for he disapproved of gambling, or so she'd been told, but when they returned to the room her mother glanced around, as though wondering something.

"Your father wants some fun," she told them. "I have no plans to gamble, but I can look around. Stay here and keep each other company. You've had a long day."

Her father was already in the hallway. Her mother closed the door; and Alice and Curt found themselves alone.

"Hey—" Curt was being chummy, but she'd had enough chess.

"I'm gonna read."

"You saw the pool. Wanna go?"

"She'll come back."

"Unh-unh. They're on a splurge."

"Where?"

"Gambling, dummy. Slot machines, poker, blackjack. Vegas has everything. People go for days, never see the sun."

"How do you know?"

He made no response.

"Mom and Dad never—"

"They are now."

Curt rummaged in the duffel and hauled up some navy-blue trunks. "You coming? Hurry up."

They changed in the room and headed for the lobby. The hall led around and around before they found an elevator; it was empty, as though reserved for them alone. Curt held the room key, large and brass, stamped with the number 729. In moments they emerged in the lobby, each bearing a towel slung over one shoulder.

"Look like you know where you're going," murmured Curt. He headed across the huge lacquered floor past the front desk, which was surrounded by a tour group. Beyond an enormous chandelier, raucous sounds flowed from the gaming rooms. She followed her brother, who followed some arrows. When they'd reached the end of the lobby, the pool lay beyond a small door.

The sun hung low, and few people were in the water. The island and palm grove had an abandoned appearance—there were four trees on supple stems, overhanging a phony beach and gray boulders. She shaded her eyes from the glare and approached the pool. The water was glassy and blue as the cornflowers in the yard in Washington. Curt shed towel and shoes and jumped in, splashing her. She plunged after, thrashing her way to the pool floor, colored a glimmering blue. A few bubbles escaped her mouth as she peered around through the water. When she could no longer hold her breath she crouched on the floor and sprang, soaring upwards. Curt splashed her as she surfaced. Gulping for air, she splashed and moved off underwater.

When she came up, her brother was nowhere to be seen. Then he surfaced, one hand holding up the room key. He waved, flashing the treasure.

"Race you," he called, and flung the key over the water. It

plunged, a quavering gleam. She followed, pushing her way down and along the blue floor, searching for the key. Her brother rose, returning to the surface; he'd won the race, it seemed. She came up gasping: there he was.

"Go ahead, toss it," he called.

"But you have it."

"Nope." He paused. "Uh-oh."

Together they swam down, scanning the blue depths. The key was gone.

There was no problem, he assured her. She should stay by the pool, he would go for another key, he told her. He headed for the lobby. She paddled around the area where the key had fallen. There on the blue floor something gleamed, and she dove down, sure of having found the key—but no, only a leaf. Nearby, beams of light surged from the depths of the pool.

She swam on. The beams were coming toward her, blazing in golden pillars from the pool floor, as though she'd swum through the darker bands of a rainbow to some purer inner core. She passed the beam, brushing the glass covering with her hand, as the water returned to a blue and darkening glow. Above the surface of the water glimmered a small sun, the hotel searchlight, sending up rays through the evening sky.

The pool widened ahead; she rose breathless to the surface and found herself near the small island. No one was there, only a pale stone statue of a boy, one arm hanging as though he'd just thrown a spear. From the hotel ballroom, across the pool, there came the sound of hunting horns played to a jazzy rhythm. Knowing she would never go there, she turned to hear. Then she climbed from the water and lay beneath the swaying palms.

Her face was dry, and her shoulders and arms. Once wholly dry, she would not choose to return to the water; so she dove, with a splash.

The water had grown cool. She peered through the murky glow; and there, on the floor of the pool, was a brass glimmer— a key. She darted down and grasped for the metal, which blew along the floor as she approached, like some living thing; then she came up gasping by the edge of the pool.

A man approached her. "Are you here alone?"

"Yes."

"You'll have to leave, then."

She held up her hand, showing the key. "My brother's coming back."

"No one under twelve in the pool area alone. I'm sorry."

The man watched her climb from the pool and followed her toward the lobby door, as if he supposed she would make trouble. There was nothing to do but leave; her brother would have to understand.

When she found the room, the door was open. All three of them were there.

"Here she is," her mother said, frowning.

Her brother lay propped on a plush bed, reading the sports news. He was damp and drowsy and wearing pajamas, as though he'd showered. "Told ya she was swimming," he drawled, yawning.

She heard her father's bland but somehow surly tone. "Well, lady, I was about to go and haul you from the water."

"Yes," her mother reprimanded, "there'll be no nonsense when we reach Berkeley. No roaming around, unless I say."

Alice was unsure what had happened, only that she'd been caught, while her brother had seemingly fooled them. He leaned over the newspaper, conversing with her father about a baseball game. "Howard's in a slump," she heard him say. "Howard only got a single."

Her mother was looking dismayed. "Now Bobby Kennedy's gone, along with King—and we're here in Las Vegas, of all places," she said, her face flushing in anger. "All this killing—can't we just stop?" She paused, shaking her head. "Please, no more news—I've had enough for now."

Her father scooped up the newspaper and folded it, seemingly lost in speculation.

Soon, Alice thought, imagining covered wagons coming in sight of a new ocean, sandy beaches, *soon enough we'll come to the wonderful place of gold and seagulls.*

Marian

THE MOVE HAD been Tom's idea. One day he'd come home from the federal agency where he was working on Johnson's civil-rights agenda and announced that he would be leaving by the end of the month. "I have a job in San Francisco—a big move up," he had informed her, without further ado, as though the summary could be counted on to convey all. To Marian, Tom's manner had seemingly implied that she could go or remain as long as she needed for herself and the children, though of course no such dilemma or referendum had really been proposed. Marian was happy in Washington—they'd been there several years, longer than anywhere else, and she'd made a good home among people she was pleased to know. The children had begun school and found a group of regular companions. The neighborhood was uncommon, somewhat daring, full of younger people like themselves who opposed school segregation and the war. There were black families and many people from New York, lawyers and academics employed by the government or by one or another program or research group. A new world was happening all around; she could now see herself as a member of an important group, along with others who demanded that something be done about civil rights and the war. She went with Barbara when they gathered for demonstrations on the Mall and marched on the Pentagon; they had plans for the schools, Congress, the South; everyone was reading something adventurous, by some black or left-wing author her parents would have snubbed, had the author managed to be found in a room with them. Now and then something had truly happened. A leader had been assassinated and a phone call from Barbara had come as she was napping. Someone had moved to the Maryland suburbs, usually for the schools. Then there was the summer Tom had strayed; in the aftermath, she'd found a gray tabby cat for her son, but he—the tabby—ran away and was never found. He'd chosen a new home—or so she reassured the children, to spare them fears of something worse.

Tom had refused to reveal any purpose underlying the California move, beyond the step up. As she now understood things, he would be second in command, with a chance of soon heading the regional office. That sounded good; but he'd never been a manager, and he complained of the Washington bureaucracy. Regardless, the move had happened, and fast. There had been days and days in the car, through lush familiar farmlands of grasses and trees and corn, followed by a sunburned moonscape, barren and dry. Tom had surprised her by gambling in Las Vegas, and by the appalling hour in Los Alamos. She'd never imagined he would drag her to the place where they'd made the atom bomb; as much as the death of Bobby Kennedy, it had cast a pall over the final days of the trip. Then one gleaming, sunny morning in mid-June she'd heard the cars by the motel in Berkeley and opened her eyes. The room was bare. Tom's duffel lay open on the floor, rummaged. The children were playing in the larger room; she could hear them squabbling together in low tones. They'd been roused by the sun, she supposed, for there were no shades in the room.

Marian groped under the pillow for her watch: nearly ten o'clock. Hardly surprising; she'd been fatigued for days. She pulled on a bathrobe and opened the hollow plywood door of her temporary bedroom. In the living room, the children's sleeping bags lay bunched on the floor. Curt was dangling from the couch, grouping baseball cards, while Alice was lounging on the floor, reading. They hushed as Marian appeared in the doorway. She was consoled to find them peacefully engaged—the room would be home for a month, until mid-July. She and Tom had rushed there from Washington to buy the house, choosing in a day a fine one near the campus. That part—the large, wood-shingle house near the campus—appealed to her; but she was unsure how she would manage for a month in such a cramped space. Tom would be very busy. As for the children, in September they would be entering seventh and fifth grades, and already they were losing what she remembered as an early companionship. Maybe sharing space would be good for them.

Curt glanced up from the baseball cards. Reaching for one of the sleeping bags, he unearthed a small portable radio and pressed a lever. Sound burbled in a steady stream as he arranged the cards.

"Are you guys hungry?" Marian asked.

Curt was nodding in rhythm to some barely heard song. "Had some cereal already."

"You, honey?" she added, turning to her daughter.

"We had the cereal."

"Well, then . . ." And she enclosed herself in the bedroom to prepare for the day. Tom had gone to the new job, across the bay in San Francisco. The place was a name to her, a photograph in a magazine. Nob Hill, Lombard Street, Haight-Ashbury, the

Golden Gate. Tom had planned to use the car, though only for today. She wondered how far she would have to go for shopping. Already she needed coffee and eggs and something for dinner and then more cereal for tomorrow. She hung the bathrobe on a hanger and unfolded a casual flowered dress from her luggage. Glancing in the long mirror on the door, she donned the dress, along with loafers she'd worn for the car. Fumbling for a brush in a small travel bag, she smoothed from her forehead and shoulders rumpled blonde waves and clamped to her ears small dangling pearls. Then she rubbed on her mouth a layer of barely observable gloss.

In the other room, Marian told the children to amuse themselves until she returned. She opened the door on the glaring sunshine of a parking lot and wandered over warm, oil-smelling asphalt to a shabby avenue of gas stations, motels, and liquor stores. There was nothing to help her know where she was, only the name, University Avenue—though there was no campus to be seen. She rounded a corner, coming upon small yards and bungalows, the grass already turning from emerald to dull gold. There was a balmy smell from the bay. The sun shed an odd charm on the dreary bungalows, the colors of pale faded blossoms. As she looked closer, she saw crumbling adobe and small unusable porches and tumbledown fences and abandoned cars. There were few people around, only some black men on the avenue, in what was seemingly a black neighborhood. So far she had seen only a small grocery, selling chips and beer, where an older man in shades leaned on the counter reading a newspaper. There she made a few purchases: a can of coffee, eggs, milk, and some English muffins.

As she ambled along the warm avenue, remembering the journey in a blur, wondering how they'd come to be here, she glanced up. The avenue sloped up and away from the bay, leading her eyes along until they found a range of hills, rounded and hung with clouds. They would be there soon, near the hills. She paused for a moment, remembering how unprepared she'd been.

Marian bore her purchases through the parking lot. As she passed one of the rooms, a boy appeared; though hardly older than Curt, he was coolly dangling a cigarette. He glanced at her, surly and unconcerned, and swaggered through the door of the other room, indistinguishable from her own except for its number and place in the row. He seemed as though he'd always been there, and she wondered: How many other families were renting these two rooms by the month? And who were they?

She passed along the row and through the door of her room. The children were there, more or less unchanged, Curt studying the baseball lineups and averages—would he follow new teams now?—while Alice continued reading. The sound from the radio had become louder, Marian thought, and more annoying. She'd heard them arguing as she approached, but now they were flung apart, ignoring each other's presence. She set down her purse and the grocery bag.

"Honey, could you turn that down? Someone could be sleeping."

Curt barely glanced up. He was chewing gum, "Now?" he wanted to know.

"Yes, now, when I ask."

"I mean them—they're sleeping *now*?"

He'd never approved of her sleeping in. Fortunately, Alice was undemanding and forbearing, able to amuse herself. The swimming in Las Vegas, though alarming, had surely been a fluke. Even as a baby Alice had played by herself on the floor while her older brother made havoc with the pots and pans: what a handful he'd been. If given leeway, he would soon overload the room they were all sharing. Marian would have to figure out how to manage them, fast, for she already knew there'd be no wandering around the neighborhood for them, through those deserted blocks with the bungalows. Even the avenue would be a problem; what was reasonable for her, a well-dressed woman no one would dare to bother, made no sense for young children. Tom should have found another motel in another neighborhood; she should have demanded it. But there'd been no leeway when they finally crossed the hills—yesterday, already evening, so lovely then to gaze on the darkened bay and glimmering lights, yet considerably waylaid. For once Tom had been the slow one, touring around Los Alamos and Las Vegas as though they were ugly Americans, delaying them for three whole days. Then he'd rushed to work in the early morning.

Curt had agreeably lowered the sound. Now he glanced up, infused with purpose, eager, smiling. She loved that look. He jumped up; he was no longer dangling from the couch.

"Can I go out?" he asked. He was already as tall as she was.

"Have some eggs," she offered. "I'm making them now."

"Had enough cereal." He paused, unsure whether he needed permission. "I'll go look around."

Her daughter had closed the book. "Can we see the house?"

"No, dear, your father has the car. Maybe tomorrow."

Curt was leaning through the doorway, looking up and down the row. Marian saw her son's halo of tawny hair, like young tiger fur; sometimes she imagined running a hand through it. He was ready to go, wearing the same polo jersey and jeans turned up at the hem—she bought the jeans long, though he always wore them out before he could grow into them. He'd even donned the leather school shoes; the laces, of course, had been hanging loose for as long as she could remember.

"Curt."

"Huh?"

"Please don't go wandering around."

"I'm just going for the newspaper. I need the box scores for yesterday's games."

"Then I'll take you for the paper when I've had my coffee. Or you can go with your father when he comes home."

Curt paused by the door as though stranded, then scuffed slowly to the couch.

Alice was also gazing out the door. Though less slovenly, she was beginning to seem more of a problem, in cut-off jeans and an old long-sleeved shirt formerly belonging to her brother. Marian had encouraged the hand-me-downs when her daughter was younger and had shown a preference for outdoor play; allowing the girl to wear her brother's old shirts was less objectionable than buying her brand new boys' clothing. That would have been a clear endorsement. Now, however, she was growing up, and some change was in order. Marian surveyed her daughter—more somber than herself, with her long eyes and a pouting, revealing mouth.

Through the screen Marian saw the unfamiliar boy saunter by, no longer holding a cigarette. He glanced through the door, waved at them, and then tore off toward University Avenue.

Marian gathered herself together. She would forgo coffee for now. From her purse she pulled *David Copperfield*, the book

she'd been reading to them in the car. "We could read together."
No one responded as she removed the bookmark. "Now where
were we?"

When Tom finally showed up, he had no time for the store.
He was in the bedroom, working.

SEVERAL DAYS LATER, when Tom had begun riding the bus and
no longer needed the car, Marian was able to show the children
the new house and neighborhood. They drove up University
Avenue and along some other streets, turning here and there.
Nearing Telegraph Avenue, Marian was forced to pause as a
throng of young people surged around the car, barely allowing
them through. A young man rapped on the hood of the Chevy,
then flashed a V-sign when Marian glared. Finally they reached a
shady street of lawns and London plane trees. Marian pulled up
by a looming wood-shingle house: 2928 Forest Avenue. She'd
told them the house was large and grand, and now she wondered
how it would measure up.

The children scrambled from the car.

"The house has much more room," she commented, following them.

Curt had been edgy for days. Now he seemed unhappy. "We
had enough room in Washington."

"Oh honey, there's a den and a sunporch and—"

"How about the yard?"

The yard would be good only for a flower garden. "We'll
come with your father and see the neighborhood," she reassured
them.

"Who gets the sunporch?" Alice demanded.

"No one. But maybe you can have the nearby room. Unless
your brother—"

"She can have it."

"Are you sure?"

"Dad asked us already—I want the room over the yard."

"As long as you're agreed." She was glad Tom had taken care
of something.

Then they drove up a road leading through the hill neighborhoods overlooking the bay. Though she'd never been there
before, she'd heard wonders; but the narrow, winding streets and

bold upgrades soon unnerved everyone. More than once she encountered a stop sign on the upgrade, as the hood of the car
launched toward the roofs and clouds. Marian could see her
daughter's nervous face as she ground the gears loudly for fear of
flying backwards down the hill. And she wondered how the
children regarded the elegant yards and fantasy homes; already
she wanted one herself.

The peak held new and awesome challenges: canyons plunging from the road, so that they seemed to be traveling through
the heavens, but for the blaring horns sounded by more rushed
and daring drivers. On her left, a vacuum; on her right, rock
and sand and clumps of grass, whirling round as they passed.
For a moment she glimpsed a promontory and Florentine villa,
seemingly perched on the bay, when suddenly a grove of unfamiliar trees rushed swaying toward her along the road.

"Oh my," she gasped.

The children were speechless.

As they descended, Marian chose less winding streets, hoping to bypass the plunging grades and curves, though soon the
road swooped down, down, like a fairground ride, tumbling so
far and fast that she feared burning the brakes and barreling
through the red glare racing up from the crossroad. The car
jammed through the red light over more level roadway and
slowed, sending up smoke and a foul stench of burning rubber.
As the car recovered unhappily by the curb, Marian and the
children regarded the stone walls and sloping gardens of the
neighborhood. Near the car rose towering walls of herringbone
stone and ivy, topped by a lawn of fern and then camellia, reveling in aggressive glory, bursting with red blossoms. They had
never seen such opulence. Marian was unsure where they were.

That evening they regaled Tom, making an amusing story of
the ordeal, but he would have none of it.

"Planning to go again, are you?" he demanded, as though
they'd been naughty.

Tom had heavy hands and shoulders, a broad forehead and
chin. As a boy he'd been almost redheaded, though no longer,
and he was closely cropped. He had pale eyes, the color of a
stormy sea surrounding a cavern or keyhole, through which he
observed the world. Marian often wondered what he saw, for he
would so rarely say.

"Why, Tom, I was only showing the children the house. And then, of course they wanted to see some other things."

Tom regarded the children, saying nothing.

Every evening, Tom was immersed in learning the San Francisco job, where he was the head lawyer managing local school and civil-rights compliance for a regional federal office. He'd begun dropping the names of new colleagues and the acronyms of federal programs, as though Marian had always known them. Marian found herself wondering if something was happening that he'd rather conceal, though of course there was nothing, only Tom's ways.

Tom

COMING WEST, HE'D seen many of the big things he'd wanted to see. The impressive part had begun in Santa Fe, when he'd consulted the map as Marian drooped on a bench in the old Spanish square. They'd been following Route 66—Tom had heard the song as a boy and imagined traveling west in his father's Ford—but a road was a road was a road. Santa Fe was Marian's call; he'd assumed she would be gushing over the adobe houses and shops peddling turquoise jewelry made by Navajos, but as soon as they got there, she made for a bench in the shade, saying she was feeling queasy. They'd just come through a gaudy canyon road—the land was huge and lonely and ungoverned, just what a man was looking for—and there she was, complaining on the shady bench in Santa Fe, when he read the name Los Alamos, another hour up the canyon. When he showed her the map, one thumb pressed under the name, she blanched. But he had resolve; he would see the place where Peach Street became Oppenheimer Drive. He would go there, the family be damned.

There had been other places he'd always wanted to see: the Mississippi River, the Grand Canyon, Las Vegas. Now he could say he'd seen them all. But he'd rambled and delayed; they'd barely reached Berkeley and found a reasonable room—a room Marian would regard as passable—soon enough for him to show up for the new job, Day One.

Now the journey was over and a job was looming. He would

finally be in command; and how would that go? That was the everlasting conundrum, dogging him for as long as he could remember. In the race he was running, there was no gun lap, no end —just a growing burden of things undone. On the other hand, the new role would be higher profile and more hands-on. In Washington he'd become a cog, codifying ever-changing policy demands, concerned mostly with fending off legal challenges before they could happen. Here the game, though fundamentally the same, would be played more from the implementation angle. The problems—school desegregation, welfare programs—were big and bureaucratic, but they had far-flung impact, and they were headline-grabbing.

On the morning of Day One, fog was on the bay. Tom suppressed any looming concerns and reveled in the breeze coming through the car window; in any case, there would be no more suffering through the Washington summers. The fog grew dense as he was approaching the Bay Bridge. Beyond the surrounding cars everything faded, vague and gray, so that the Chevy soared as though launched from a cannon. As he passed Yerba Buena Island and was descending the span, the fog cleared and the Chevy emerged under a cool fresh sun. Ahead lay San Francisco, rising from remnants of fog. There came a lurching in his spine as he imagined the days to come. He would forgo lunch and wander.

Tom found a garage by the Federal Building. He would be seeing the Regional Commissioner, Fred Mandelbaum, at 9:30, and as usual he was early. Tom was standing in the lobby, hearing the gal answer a call, when he found himself commandeered by a woman who was proposing to show him the floor.

"Good morning, Tom. Ginger Nyman."

"Good morning."

Tom supposed she'd been assigned to him. He would remember her eyes; there was something daring in them.

"How was your flight?"

"We came by car. We saw the Grand Canyon," he announced.

The woman's eyes sparkled as she surveyed Tom's drab government gray. "I hope the real thing measures up."

"And Los Alamos."

"Oh really." Her glance paused on the heavy hands and shoulders. "Come along, and I can show you around."

She was leading him through the lobby, showing her pumps and graceful legs, as the door swung open and Fred Mandelbaum appeared. In Washington, Tom had passed a couple of hours conveying a sense of urgency and command to Fred regarding the agency's role. Mandelbaum had impressed him as one of the new breed, informal and ready to get things done. Now on home turf the impression was confirmed; the man's flapping lapels and blooming tan made him appear incongruously youthful as, calm and collegial, he held forth a palm. Tom grasped the hand and pumped.

The woman was no longer there. Tom learned from Fred that she was a colleague on the floor, a young lawyer.

Tom was soon assigning work for the agency's legal staff. Ginger Nyman, along with Jim Kaczmarek, who was an old-timer in the department, and a lawyer and former caseworker named Claire Forsini, had been managing the agency's response to the report from Washington on the Hunters Point riot, September 1966, during the final weeks of Ronald Reagan's successful campaign for governor. The presidential commission blamed the unrest on high unemployment among the largely black population of Hunters Point, near the naval shipyards. Tom was annoyed that Jim—a hangover from the Eisenhower days—was heading the group. They had several working lunches in an Italian restaurant near the Civic Center. Along with the lasagna and salad, Tom had the house red, while Jim gulped a Martini. Ginger preferred lemonade, in a tall cool glass, and Claire ordered espresso.

Though Jim was disarmingly folksy, he soon dropped the easygoing manner and began probing Tom for agency rumors from Washington. Tom responded with admiring comments on the mountains surrounding Los Alamos.

Jim leaned back. "Go south from Denver some day. Now *that's* some country."

Claire narrowed her eyes. "You took your family there? With all the contamination?"

"I thought they should see the place," Tom responded blandly.

"I see you have an adventurous temper," Ginger concluded, ignoring Claire.

Tom was pleased to see a woman vying for him. Marian was always remarking on what a regular sleeper he was or how much self-control he had, as though she found him dull—but then, she could sleep all morning. No wonder, when she'd stayed up for hours sipping wine and reading novels. Then when he found a spare hour for something he enjoyed, such as playing ball or poker or working on the Chevy, she'd remind him that he was a Harvard man. Now in the new office, he was in charge and in demand. And he was away from some of the pressure; Congress and the commissioner were dampened rumors, something to jaw about over lunch.

Ginger had been in San Francisco only a year, but Tom could see she was already an old hand. She drove a royal red Mustang, and on Mondays she dropped remarks about her days exploring Marin County, north along the coast. Tom had no comparable amusements, for he had a job to learn and a family to appease, holed up and unhappy in a Berkeley motel.

Soon she found fun in spurring him on.

"Tom," she encouraged one day, as though prodding a straggling horse, "what about Lombard Street, Fisherman's Wharf? Have you been there?"

"No chance so far."

"Gosh, that's a shame." She paused over Tom's lapse, considering something. "By the way," she added slowly, "you'd enjoy the redwoods—hundreds of years old, taller than the Washington Monument. Your family's been on the road; go up north and see some."

"How far north?" Tom inquired.

"Far, I suppose—up by Oregon," she responded. "But there's always Muir Woods—you could be there in an hour."

Tom's imagination made a sudden curve. He'd never cared much for roaming before the journey west, but now he wondered how the redwoods would be with Ginger. Maybe the job would send them somewhere—Sacramento or even Washington. Then he could show her around, the way he was supposed to do.

ONE MONDAY MORNING, Ginger proposed having lunch at Fisherman's Wharf. So far Tom had gone nowhere, only the Berkeley campus with the family.

"Planning to join the hippies?" she teased.

"Would they have me?"

"You could always apply."

They had the rendezvous in the lobby, and no sooner had they emerged from the Federal Building than he was following her through the door of a cab. For all the years in Washington, he'd rarely used a cab. They found an outdoor table by the wharf. He should have the fish and chips and sourdough bread, she smiled, hardly bothering with the menu. A young man in navy seaman clothes rushed up, with much fanfare, and took the order.

Ginger wore pumps and a ribboned blouse beneath a tapered, pale-rose jacket. Tan and blooming, she had a long nose and fun but measuring eyes, and she was younger than Tom by several years; younger also than Marian.

She was telling him about herself. Tom learned that she was a farm girl from Michigan who loved horses. She'd found a horse ranch in Marin, north along the coast near a place called Bolinas, and on play days she drove there, over Mount Tamalpais. So far she'd been savoring her freedom, living month to month really, but she was used to riding and now she'd resolved to save enough money for a horse. The woman who ran the ranch would board a horse for less than Tom was paying for the garage downtown.

"I've been using the bus," Tom confessed.

She paused, as though making a plan; in her hand was some sourdough bread. "Well then, you'd have money for a horse."

He'd hardly ever seen a horse, but he'd be a damn fool for saying so.

"I'm also from Michigan," he remarked, just so she'd know they had something in common.

"Are you?" She glanced at him fully, taking in the heavy hands and shoulders. "You're no farm boy, though."

"Oh no, Dearborn."

She held her glance. "Never seen a real horse up close."

"Well—"

"You can always learn." She paused, tearing a corner of bread, dabbing casually but elegantly with the butter, as if she'd made it herself. "I suppose you went to Ann Arbor, then. Have much fun there?"

"I'm from Harvard."

"Oh my, Mr. Ford's grandson," she returned, right on cue.

Tom blushed and deadpanned, "You mean nephew."

She laughed approvingly, as the young man in navy clothes appeared, bearing plates of fish and chips. Tom was enjoying her company, but there was no cause for alarm, he supposed: she knew he had a family. She wanted to know all about the children. "They'll love California," she was saying. "They can play baseball all year round." Then she added, "You should show them the ranch, get them comfortable on a horse."

"Once we're in the house," he told her.

"They say the young ones never fall off." And her eyes sparkled with humor.

She laughed about her year in San Francisco and wanted to know why he'd made the move. He spoke vaguely of the land, the energy, the causes—how they'd been impressed by the Free Speech Movement back East. Then there was Washington, the sweltering summers and endless government gossip—he'd wanted a change. She spoke of her three years flying around the world for Continental Airlines, before she entered law school.

"Why, Tom," she teased, "are you one of those Michigan boys who's never been away from home?"

"Abroad, you mean?" he inquired. "Why, I've been to Canada."

"Oh, that hardly counts," she laughed. "I know, Tom, you saw Sault Sainte Marie."

He'd seen the falls and canal works, and he'd seen the St. Lawrence, too.

Ginger plunged on. "When I was flying, I traveled all over Europe. In Rome, three of us slept on the steps of St. Peter's. And then there was the Paris flight. You'd love traveling, Tom."

"I have a family," he reminded her. He wondered whether she could see him blushing.

"The kids can go along," she smiled.

After lunch, they headed up the hill through North Beach. Tom found the weather pleasantly cool for June. That was a good thing, for she turned up a daunting slope and then another. As she led the way he could see her shape. Now and then they paused and turned to gaze over the bay.

Soon they were passing below Telegraph Hill. Tom peered up at the tower rising from the top and then glanced away.

"Any longer and you'll be playing hooky," Ginger teased.

On the way to the Federal Building, she had the cab go down Lombard Street. Tom nearly laughed as the road unwound below them like a toboggan run looping down an Olympic slope. He had never seen such turns, such folds, such maneuvering as the cab lurched along, paving stones rumbling below. The driver was humming to impress them with his casual command. Tom glanced at Ginger, smiling shyly, wondering how he would have handled things, had he been manning the car. She leaned in as the car pulled around a final curve. He glanced up at a looming house and walled garden. In June, everything was in bloom. Beyond the rooftops rose another hill and then another.

As the cab returned to earth, Ginger told him about a horse show. It would be at the Cow Palace from Friday through Sunday.

IN THE EVENINGS, Tom returned to the motel. The family was bored, but he had a job to learn. He told Marian he would use the bedroom in the evening, and the three of them could read in the other room. When she complained, he reassured her that they would be moving soon. In the bedroom alone, he pondered the California shoreline. Ginger had told him of bluffs and sand and redwood canyons, saying they reminded her of Italy. Tom had never been to Italy. He had seen some museum paintings in Washington, with Marian, but they were old and implausible and far from the real thing, he supposed. For now the Bay Bridge was exotic enough—in the morning, as he drove in and could see the hills and towers of San Francisco, or on the way home under the evening color, coming on around the bay. San Francisco would be a good place for him, a place he could share with Ginger. Tom had been a good boy long enough.

On the job, Ginger had begun teasing him about the close-cropped hair. He'd always worn an army crew cut during the Washington summers, and so far he'd found no reason to change.

"You should grow it out, Tom," she said, laughing, "or they'll think you're a drill sergeant. You don't want it as long as the hippies—just long enough to spare you a sunburn up there, if you ever go riding."

"All in good time," Tom said.

Curt

Feeling edgy and keyed up, Curt imagined the inspiring scene: an incoming fast ball, a swing and a *crack!* followed by the soaring arc of the ball before it dropped, clearing the center-field fence. As usual, the game's hero was Frank Howard, one of the great sluggers. Even though the Senators were the American League dogs so far, Howard was having an awesome year, slamming ten homers in a single week in May. Before leaving Washington, Curt had been following Howard's season with buoyant interest, despite the team's dismal performance. Then for several weeks, he'd been feeling gloomy and lonely as Howard faded. Now, coming off a July slump with a single and a homer, the slugger was warming up the underdog cause again. The game had been close half an hour ago, but what was happening now? Curt was thousands of miles away, relying on a local announcer's offhand summary of the game. Along with everything else they'd dropped on him by moving away, the loss of Frank Howard was hard to endure.

Curt was feeling restless, though there was no sense in complaining. His mom was already in an excitable mood.

"That seemed a rather long month," she was saying as the family came along College Avenue in the Chevy, heading for the new house on Forest Avenue. The moving van would be there. They would have a home now; he would no longer feel he was always in someone's way.

"Really long," Curt agreed, sensing a chance to vent, "and really cramped." He'd had enough, beginning with ten days on the road, as he leafed through sports magazines, feeling numbed by the coming changes. Then the month sharing a motel room, hanging around while his dad was off working in San Francisco and his mom was reading or napping, appearing from the bedroom only long enough to complain about the ballgame he was following on the radio. What was he supposed to do? There was nowhere to go, other than a weedy yard in back of the motel, where there was no space for doing anything much, and some scruffy kids were always running around. He'd managed a few jokes with one of the boys, but as soon as the boy came wandering by the screen door looking for him, his mom would come from the bedroom to see what was going on. That scared the boy off.

Even so, the boy had bragged about playing baseball in a summer league. Searching the phone book, Curt found the league's number and made the call. Soon he heard from an upbeat-sounding coach who was in need of more players for the San Pablo Lumber team—so Curt was already warming up with the Lumberjacks, as they were known. They would be needing a third baseman, but he was hoping for something more challenging. He could see they were an underdog team, same as the Senators.

"Oh honey," came his mom's soothing response. "Here's our new house."

Edgy energy overwhelmed him as the Chevy slowed by the large wood-shingle house. The moving van lay open; the Raysons' belongings could be seen along the curb. Somewhere among them was the jersey with Frank Howard's number, 9. And somewhere was the bicycle he'd be riding to Lumberjack games.

In the Washington neighborhood, everything he needed had been nearby. Playing fields and Rock Creek Park and always enough boys for a game. A shopping center where he would buy *Superman* comic books and baseball cards, chewing the bubble gum on the way home before *she* could say, "No gum." And there was Joshua's house, where they would hang out eating corned-beef sandwiches and chips and boning up on the baseball stats. Why had the family gone and dumped such a good place?

Glancing up, Curt saw a shaggy young man emerge from the van, wheeling a familiar bicycle—his old 3-speed. Observing the mover's clothes and snarly curls—right out of *The Three Stooges* show, including the overalls—Curt was suddenly glowing; following weeks of mopey suspense, he was no longer restless but engrossed in the day.

Propping Curt's 3-speed by the curb, the shaggy man came up. "What's happening on Telegraph Avenue?" he demanded.

"Telegraph?" His dad's muscular arm leaned from the Chevy.

"Yeah, you passed by the campus, right? Are the cops still there?"

"The cops?"

"Tom—," came a warning.

"We're greenhorns," he announced, cheery and deadpan, "fresh from Washington."

The man laughed dryly.

"Tom, no fooling." His mom sounded alarmed. "There's something wrong."

The shaggy man nodded. "They're suppressing our Bastille Day by sending the cops. Our government's waging war on us, same as the French and goddamn de Gaulle. But the people have had enough."

There was no response.

"They're gassing flower people," the man fumed, as though the Raysons should be outraged.

Curt's dad merely opened the Chevy door, casting a cool, meaningful glance over the household belongings. "We have some work ahead of us."

"So we do," the man conceded, as they headed for the house.

Curt had already seen the area around Telegraph, overflowing with people and only blocks from the house. And back in Washington, on the evening news, he'd seen mobs rampaging and the cops gassing them. Those Washington mobs, defying the government's overwhelming power, had been fascinating and scary. But flower people fighting the cops sounded goofy, as improbable as a Rose Bowl parade.

Two more men emerged from the van, carrying the couch from the Raysons' den. Curt's dad came from the house, and the family gathered for a moment by the Chevy. The house had dark shingles, a gabled roof, navy-blue woodwork. The day was sunny, and it was cool for July. Curt dangled his baseball glove from one arm, glancing around the yard. A palm tree swayed over one corner of the house. He'd seen the house before—how had he overlooked something as crazy as a palm tree?

"Let's go in," his mom said, smiling.

Tossing his glove in the Chevy, Curt ran ahead, barely pausing on the porch. The wooden door was impressively heavy, with ironwork suggesting a fortress or even a dungeon; as he entered, the overwhelming impression was of wood and more wood, cool and shadowy—a musty forest.

"Let's get some windows open," his dad said, taking command.

As Curt sprang to comply, he saw Alice in the doorway. She glanced around the living room before heading for the second-floor bedrooms. Curt struggled for a moment with a jammed window, feeling growing frustration.

"Can I go and see my room?" he demanded, barely pausing for a response. He'd chosen a room he'd never seen, and what if he'd chosen wrong? Alice would never change her mind once she was in possession; she would seal the deal before he could challenge her.

Climbing to the upper floor, he could hear the movers assembling the bed frame in the master bedroom. He paused by a wooden pillar and then headed down the hall, passing another bedroom and a sunporch before reaching the rear of the house. There he found the room he'd chosen, facing south and overlooking the yard. Sun was streaming through the windows; he could see sky and neighboring yards. Feeling a rush of energy, he flung open a window and leaned gazing over the yards and fences.

Then he heard someone and spun around—but it was only Alice. She hovered by the door as though comparing rooms.

"You chose already," he said, with a shrug, cool and aloof. Why was she there, just when he was enjoying a moment alone?

"I know. I'm just looking around."

He glared. "You heard Dad. Go open some windows."

He'd been sharing space with her for weeks, hardly complaining; she was the complainer, whenever the game was on. He just wanted a few weeks of normal summer. He would go by the schoolyard tomorrow. Then, on Wednesday, he would be playing for the Lumberjacks. He'd show them how good he was.

He could hear his mom in the hallway, trying to appease Alice. "Well, are you glad we're finally in the house?"

"Sure."

"There's so much more space." Then, in a lower tone, "Your room's just as large."

"It is?"

"So your father says." And they moved on.

Curt glanced around the room, assessing the space. The bed could go by the window. He woke up early, like his dad; as day was breaking, he would enjoy surveying the world and hearing the Top 40, the sports roundup from the evening before, the morning news.

He emerged from the room, wondering where the others were. Then, going down, he found them in the living room, admiring the wood paneling and the ceiling beams.

"Here we are—at long last," his mom was saying, with a weary sigh, as though she'd moved everything herself.

His dad was carrying some bookshelves.

"Let the men do the heavy work, Tom."

She should know he was enjoying himself—he was more manly than the shaggy movers, in any case.

"Come, how about something cool? The men are having some beer."

"When we're through."

"There's only a few more things." She was glancing around at the furnishings, seemingly already arranging the room in her mind. "What was the man saying about Telegraph? We're very close by the campus."

"Someone had a Mardi Gras."

"Mardi Gras? Tom, are you sure?"

"There were some problems involving the cops."

"During the summer, when everyone's away?" She blinked, as though someone had broken the rules. "In Washington, we had mobs and the army and the whole place burning. What's happening here?"

"They gassed some flower people."

Her eyebrows rose in high drama. "Oh, yes! And the French —wasn't the moving man denouncing de Gaulle?" She shook her head. "But why gas them? They're so peaceful."

Curt was searching for somewhere to plug in the radio. "Who's peaceful?" he teased.

"Why, the flower people!"

"Oh, them." He paused. "Can I hear the score now?"

"Of course."

Sound burbled from an old Westinghouse speaker as he leaned in to hear.

"What are they saying?"

"Shhh!"

There was a hush, then the announcer's bland and maddening tone. "*The Senators are down one in a doubleheader in Chicago. Howard came off a July slump with a home run in the opening inning.*"

"Lousy underdogs," Curt mumbled, switching off the radio.

The family paused in the cool, dim, wood-paneled room, hearing the movers come along the hall, laughing together. One of the movers—not the shaggy *Stooges* guy in overalls but a beefy longhair in a Stanford football jersey—handed his dad a paper to sign. Then the man folded the paper and, calling "Have a wonderful day!" over one shoulder, followed the others through the door.

There was a pause, then a chugging sound, and the van roared away. The Raysons gazed on somber redwood beams. They were home.

chapter two

Marian

PERSUADING YOUNG CHILDREN had been easy, but no longer. More cajoling would be necessary. They'd been willing companions in Washington, playing in the house and yard, or heading off together for the playground. Now they were rarely found in the same room. Some real nudging would be demanded of her, if she would have an hour of freedom. And so she'd carefully prodded her daughter, reminding Alice of how welcoming her brother and the boys had always been, and suggesting how they would probably agree to have her along, if she'd only go. Her daughter's response had been less than eager—a glance through long bangs, a nod; but they'd finally gone off together, just as Marian was wondering why she was dreaming up plans now, during the summer, when they were around the house. Of course her plans were hardly real plans—in a new place, among new people, how could they be? Replacing her Washington group would be hard. She'd found companionship there among men and women who read everything, saw foreign films, enjoyed intellectual exchange. Things here were more open, colorful, and free. She could already see the challenge of blending in among the very young, who had the run of things in a college community. Even so, there would be a peer group for her. In the campus neighborhoods, everything was nearby. She and Tom could enjoy a cafe or a foreign film, folk singers, book readings. Of course Tom would be busy; but she imagined a shopping bag full of books and records, something new for the family. Though Tom would ignore such things, as always, her daughter would share them, and maybe her son, if only he could be persuaded. There was hope: he'd been a sparkling young boy.

When she was sure they'd gone, Marian donned her white

linen blouse, a new floral miniskirt—her only real purchase so far—and sandals. In the bedroom mirror, she brushed on some eyebrow liner and combed through her hair: she had good eyes and hair and had once been compared to Lauren Bacall. Then she grabbed her purse and headed for Telegraph Avenue. The place was a blur of alluring shops and nonconforming young people, and though she'd passed by in the car, she was dying for a closer peep.

As Marian passed along Claremont Avenue and then Derby Street, she could see the neighborhood changing as she neared the campus and the upscale homes and gardens gradually gave way, supplanted by faded wood-shingle houses. These would be the homes of young professors, she supposed, glancing along a row of unfussy places with large porches and tangled yards. Groups of gaudy young people passed by, clowning or murmuring among themselves. They were unhampered by any hangover from the '50s conformism she'd known, and flowing along so freely in male-female openness that one could hardly say if they were couples or mere groupings. She wondered if her daughter would someday feel the allure. Perhaps—when she'd dropped her tomboy ways. As for herself, having chosen already and found a successful Ivy League man, Marian could safely contemplate the downy candor of these boys and wonder how long the appeal would linger—for surely the appeal would fade, once the girls could no longer ignore the warning signs, the damning absence of a hunger for real accomplishment. She'd longed for a moody, expressive boy, though of course she'd chosen Tom, who had the other things—goals, focus, will-power—as they passed through the humdrum years together, moving up. That was why these random hours by herself were so pleasing, so lush; deeply happy, she could have forgone communal involvements, but Tom had grown aloof—he'd strayed and come back, leaving her angry, and her feelings yearned for more. Tom's fling had been only a stumble, a flare-up of waning youth, but it had made her own imagination rebel. These personal hours gave her a chance for daydreaming; they formed a psychological frame for the everyday world—the world she and Tom would always share.

On the corner of Telegraph Avenue, as the red light changed to green, Marian was overwhelmed by a surging crowd. So near the campus, she could feel the expressive energy, the flaunting of developing personality. Surrounded by the unwashed young and rudely aware of body odors, she was already mingling among them when she remembered how far she'd come from these downy adolescent beards. Turning in the eddy, pausing, leaning on a shop window as the throng flowed by, she found her pulse racing. Then, as she was calming herself, she became aware of pulsing designs, the shopkeeper's concept for luring customers. Sinuous shapes wove a mad geometry, as though posing an imponderable classroom problem or summoning up Freudian fears. Geometry had always dismayed her; though she'd managed her usual A's, she had a lingering memory of being summoned to the board by the teacher—a man she'd been dying to please—and languishing under his probing gaze, as proofs fled her mind.

Now in the noonday jumble of colorful rebels—extras from some Hollywood film, or several films, for such rags had never belonged in any one story—she imagined being summoned before the untamed young, who were no longer co-eds or even Beats but in some new phase, confirming her as middle-aged, beyond the confusions of youth: reclining figure with man and child, like a Henry Moore sculpture. She would never abandon herself to the fray, as some of these young women had clearly done, whereas they would regard her as square for never having smoked grass. Would they offer her some? Marian hoped they would. One should always choose how far one would go.

She approached a cafe. Through the glass a bearded man could be seen; he wore John Lennon glasses and a corduroy blazer, and he was reading. The place had the casual glamour of a Boulevard Saint-Michel cafe, or Les Deux Magots. The bearded man was immersed in a heavy volume—a philosopher, perhaps, reading *Being and Nothingness*. During Tom's fling, she'd found herself in a cafe with a Washington neighbor; he'd pressed her hand and she'd made no response, as though her hand lay unsensing—as though her hand were a thing. And what now, if the professor should press her hand? Would she do the same as before? She could only imagine. The professor was fingering a strand of beard. He adjusted the eyeglasses, glanced up—was he aware of her? Impossible to say, as he lowered his eyes—they were blue-gray—slowly drummed the table, and, turning the page, resumed reading.

Marian moved off, pondering. If she had a novel, she could linger for hours in a cafe, alone and unbothered by anyone. She would blend in; people would come and go; there would be loose unravelings of conversation, personal dramas. There were bookshops nearby, a good reason for coming here on a summer's day. She could buy a novel and spend an hour in the cafe. The children were playing safely on the playground, and here was her chance for some grown-up fun. Pausing over a shop's love beads and slogan buttons, she imagined an expanding world. Among the slogans were *Peace* and *Che*, a plea to *Free Huey*, a saw-toothed marijuana leaf. For a moment she conjured up Huey Long, the Louisiana demagogue, before remembering the confusing case of Huey Newton, the Black Panther accused of killing a police officer. If only Barbara were here.

She paused by a used-book shop, just the homey place she'd been looking for. As she was browsing the window, a plump man with graceful hands and heavy jowls appeared in the doorway, wearing jeans and a tweed jacket, leather sandals, and a beret. He paused, opening a large pocket watch; beyond him Marian glimpsed a room overflowing in books. As she delayed, her eyes scanning *The Teachings of Don Juan*, he closed the cover and moved on, cussing to himself.

Passing through the doorway, she found herself in a gloomy room smelling of tobacco smoke. The bookseller had abandoned the counter and cash register, leaving a cigar in the ashtray. A large clock hung over the counter. The clock had a swirling psychedelic face, and the large red hands—yes, they were hands, forefingers pointing—read just before noon. She could spend hours here! She glanced through the gloom and saw a lamp, an armchair, and a cafe table deep in one corner. Passing some bins of secondhand records—something for the family—she made her way toward the armchair and the glowing lamp. On a nearby shelf was a jumble of used paperbacks. There were dog-eared copies of *Leaves of Grass* and *Little Big Man*, Kerouac's *On the Road* and Marshall McLuhan, *To Kill a Mockingbird* and Margaret Mead. Norman Mailer rubbed shoulders with *Eichmann in Jerusalem*. Everyone in Washington had read the Eichmann book, but what of some of these others? There were Kesey and Ferlinghetti, authors she'd never read. How good would they be? As good as Kerouac, even? And she could only read him when she'd had some wine. There were books about psychedelic drugs and more *Teachings of Don Juan*.

On being and nothingness, what would Don Juan have to say?

Just before the tempting corner was a row of doors, suggesting dressing rooms or perhaps the casket scene from *The Merchant of Venice*. Though they were closed, one bore a sign saying "Open Me" in flowing colors. She glanced around, feeling vaguely foolish for succumbing to such a game, and grasped the knob. The door sprang open. As she fumbled for a light, something made her cry aloud—her blouse, aglow with uncanny light, as though under a foreign sun. Glancing up, she saw a handsome, longhaired man— a rock singer, no?—confronting her from a poster, the face in a lavender glow, the eyes boring deep. Softly closing the door, she was among the books once more.

Now the lamp and armchair caught her eye. The armchair was draped in green and purple cloth; and floating on the green and purple was a hardcover volume and a label commanding, "Steal Me!" The command was odd enough, but how about the lure? She stealthily removed the paper and found a faded copy of Aldous Huxley's *The Doors of Perception*. She'd read Huxley's *Brave New World* in her college days; one of the boys from her modern-novel class had urged her to, before leaving for law school. Opening the book to the flyleaf, she read "Augustus Owsley Stanley III—January 19, 1963." A gryphon crouched in a corner of the page, wings curled around its haunches. Mysticism, she would have supposed, or maybe psychology. Browsing some random pages, she found a psychedelic experiment, a closely rendered day—an opening up, a change in consciousness. Tom would make fun, she thought, smiling ruefully. She fingered the binding, imagining slipping the volume into her purse. Tom be damned—he ignored her books, anyway. Yes, she would have the thing!

The books lay in long rows, under the labels "Anthropology," "Psychology," and "Modernity." Pausing along the anthropological shore, she remembered Joseph Conrad's image of a man-of-war firing its cannons into the immense African continent. Then, rounding a corner, she nearly stumbled over a wooden ladder, where a young woman in jeans and sandals was reaching for Mead's *Coming of Age in Samoa*.

There was the sound of a canary, as the bookseller emerged from one of the doors, blowing some birdsong as if he'd always known how.

Marian searched through a bin of secondhand records and chose four. They would be for the family. The bookseller was now deep in conversation with a man bearing a bag of newspapers. Overhead, the clock's forefingers had seemingly paused on noon, under the full sun of forever. Glancing through heavy-framed glasses, the man rang up her purchases. Marian handed over a five, and he made change, gabbing amusingly. Then he tossed a free underground newspaper in her bag and nodded goodbye. As she passed through the door, she heard him paying homage to the Grateful Dead and someone named Owsley.

Young people thronged the block. During her sojourn in the bookshop, they'd become increasingly strange, now suggesting a crowd called up for the filming of a madhouse scene: the bearded boys, the slovenly girls, all in garments from some *marché des puces*—or rather fragments, for nothing added up. She wondered how many of these young people were in college, regardless of the clothing. Things would change come September, she hoped, when the dropouts would go away, across the bay to Haight-Ashbury.

She found her way to the cafe. The professor was there, reading; she took a nearby table and ordered coffee and a lemon cake.

She opened the underground paper and saw an alarming figure: a bloody-fanged rattlesnake. "BERKELEY COMMUNE: DON'T TREAD ON ME" read the headline. They'd found a memorable image; but what was the message?

The cake appeared, followed by coffee. She folded the *Berkeley Barb* and had a lemony morsel. A scruffy boy wandered through the room, panhandling. He was her daughter's age. Someone offered an apple; he grabbed the apple and ran, laughing, through the door. She followed the unfolding scene. The professor was glancing her way; feeling unsure of the norms and unable to gauge the man's response, she opened her book and began mulling.

She'd waded through the move seemingly alone, for Tom would demand results but then leave the planning to her. She'd chosen the house, even the neighborhood, though of course he'd agreed. They knew several people who'd been in Berkeley and recommended South Campus, though some preferred the hill neighborhoods—a stunning fantasy world well beyond Tom's government pay grade. In any case, Tom was grudging of extravagance and there was no sense in pushing him when the backup was so thoroughly pleasing, an upgrade for them. In South Campus they were near the shops and people. As for the schools, a new plan for desegregating the elementary schools would begin in September, following a plan already in place for the older grades. Though the house was near Curt's junior high, Forest Avenue was far enough from Alice's elementary school, in a nearby black neighborhood, that she would be going by bus. The plan should pose no problems in a suburban college town, and Marian and Tom had regarded Berkeley's progressive schools as another reason for moving there. She had no major concerns; after all, the school and neighborhood in Washington had been successfully integrated by a determined group of young families: black and white parents with professional jobs who'd sought out change, making common cause across the color line and encouraging the children to get along, as they shared classrooms and weekend games. After that carefully cultivated harmony, her children would be ahead of the others in knowing what to do, how to behave.

In the meantime, she was looking for groups where she could begin making new friends. A Washington neighbor had dug up some information on Bay Area peace groups; another had recommended the Lawyers Guild, in case Tom wanted to get involved in defending protesters; and someone's son had passed on the names of San Francisco bands—a sound more advanced, less folky than Dylan or the Beatles. Even before the move was confirmed, Marian had come home one day with her new albums and begun playing them. They had been helpful in persuading her daughter.

The professor was gone, replaced by a girl—too young for college, Marian judged—who draped her legs in a young man's lap. She was uncombed; he was unshaven; they had no shoes. The girl giggled as the young man massaged her foot.

Marian was grown up and grounded and would bypass much of the youth movement, though she wondered where she would have ended up, if college girls in her day had been more daring, less focused on manners and men. Though embarrassed by some of the bodily candor, she was eager to engage herself in a new world where young people had political commitments and personal styles and live-in lovers before marriage, where they turned on and made things—woven rugs, macramé, clay pots glazed and fired in a basement kiln. She'd never made rugs or pots, though of course she sewed; her own mother, immersed in housework, had made manual labor seem so unappealing. Maybe Marian had been wrong; maybe these things could be enjoyed. She and Alice would use a potter's wheel together. With her mother's encouragement, Alice would openly enjoy the mess, would learn the new rhythms and dance freely, spared the formal moves of the days before rock 'n' roll. As long as her young daughter was there, no one would censure the mother for coming along. Alice could become a folkie, strumming a guitar; they would work on that.

Marian opened the *Berkeley Barb*. Paging through, she ran across a blurb for the Folk Singer's Circle. Maybe Tom could be persuaded to give it a go. On the same page was a column on Black Panther Huey Newton, charged in the murder of an Oakland cop. Scanning the column, she learned that the trial had already opened—on July 15, hard on the heels of Bastille Day. Then as she paused, wondering who she would know in the coming years, she saw a reference to the Peace and Freedom Party and remembered having heard of them from her Washington neighbor. Tom would come with her, she was sure.

Alice

THERE WAS A school playground on the corner. She was enjoying having a playground nearby for the summer—so far a long and lonely summer. She could say she was going to the school and then wander freely, as they had in the old neighborhood, where they'd known everyone. Then there would be less concern from her mother. For her mother, school was the place to go, even in summer when no one was there, only some younger boys.

If only she had been happy in the house reading, there would have been no problems. Her mother approved of reading. Other things could be iffy.

The neighborhood was lush and blooming; there was something alluring in the yards they passed, reminding her of the land of Oz—when the changeover from Kansas came, and the scene glowed in Technicolor.

The school on the corner was only for the younger grades, K

through three, so she would be going somewhere else—Lincoln School on Ashby Avenue. Lincoln was far enough away that she would be going by bus. Her mother had promised they'd see the place before school began, but her mother was moody these days and so far there'd been no chance. So for the remaining weeks of the summer, there was the nearby playground, just down the block. Lincoln was far, even by bicycle.

In Washington, she'd gone off alone every morning, reveling in the few blocks of freedom. She could join a group or go alone. She could run, as the crossing guards flagged her on.

On the other hand, she'd hardly ever been on a bus—only a few times in Washington, with her mother and Curt. The school bus would be completely new. Because Lincoln and the bus were unfamiliar, she found a sense of freedom in imagining them. They were grown-up things. She would do as her father had done every morning for as long as anyone could remember; she would have a personal place away from the family. She'd been alone in a swimming pool in Las Vegas; now every evening before sleep she imagined the palm trees and the statue, the brass room key. Along with these images, a new world was forming; it hung low in the sky, a moon she'd never seen before.

Alice and Curt were heading for the playground. On summer mornings in the old neighborhood, they'd gone to the schoolyard together. There on the grass fields dampened by morning dew, a group of boys would be playing baseball. The boys were always there; like the weekly TV shows, the game would never end. For a season she'd had a place in the game as long as her brother was there. He was large and commanding—a leader. And so, because she had a boy's swing and could run, she could join in the game. From the outfield, where nothing much happened and no damage could be done, she could safely observe the boys, free from teasing and the struggle for belonging. Whenever a fly ball came her way, her brother would run up, waving her off; he would never have her losing the game for the boys. Now and then, demanding her chance, she'd caught a high fly, feeling a rush of glory as the ball dropped hard from the sky, nearly taking off her glove.

They reached the playground, where some boys were hanging around the jungle gym. Curt glanced around. He was dangling a baseball glove in one hand, a ball in the other.

"I'm going by my school," he announced. He'd already passed over the boys by the jungle gym, who seemed Alice's age or younger. "You can come, or—"

"Who's going to be there?" She eyed the faded jersey he always wore—Frank Howard's number, 9. Curt was becoming leaner and more muscular.

"Some guys from my team."

"Do you have a game?"

"No," he responded, glancing away. "The guys go anyway."

The junior high was a few blocks away, off Telegraph. Curt was there every day, playing baseball or hanging around. He had a group.

"Maybe you can find some girls here," he suggested, surveying the schoolyard through the fence, "though it hardly looks promising."

The problem was real enough—she should have her own group, but how?

"Or you could go by your school," he proposed.

"That's far."

"You have your bike."

"Mom says—"

He gave her a long glance. "She say when she's taking you?"

"No."

"So, go on your own," he said, shrugging.

"Mom says no."

"Mom always says no," he said sharply. He was daring her—she could join in and keep him from turning on her.

Maybe things could be easy. Contemplating breaking her mother's rules, she made no response.

A boy rounded the corner of the playground, gliding along on a skateboard.

Curt followed the boy's progress. "Mr. Henderson's moving me up," he bragged as they watched the boy push off, looping a figure 8. "If I go on playing well, I can be on a good team next year."

"What's wrong with the team you're on now?" she asked.

He glanced over her frayed collar, as if confirming something. As usual, she was wearing old stuff he'd outgrown. "Maybe you can play for them."

"They take girls?"

He laughed. "You're so dumb."

They were coming along the playground fence when the boy rolled up, fingers grasping the aluminum mesh, leaning, grinning, eyeing them through the links.

"That's your girlfriend?" he demanded of Curt. His black hair was tousled and curly, and his jeans were fraying.

"Who?"

The boy glanced her way.

"No, she's only my sister. Why?"

"Thought so." The boy swayed back and forth, fingers enmeshed in the fence. "She looks like you," he added, then deadpanned, "That could be good or bad."

"No good for her."

Alice moved off, wondering what was brewing. Some boys would let her tag along, while others refused. The clues were often confusing. The boy followed, gliding by the fence long enough to make her pause. Then he rolled back toward Curt.

"Where's your skateboard?" he pursued.

"At home."

Her brother was covering; skateboards were a California thing. She could have informed the boy; and so she was impressed by the way her brother coolly ignored her as he shrugged, idly tossing the ball—he was so sure of her. He was larger than many boys his age; he eyed the other boy, smaller than himself though probably in the same grade.

"You play baseball?" he inquired, tossing up the ball, barely moving as it dropped in his glove.

"Sure." The boy was enjoying the show. "Hey, I'm Sammy."

"Curt. Wanna play?"

Sammy glanced over the playground. "Here?" He was small and wiry and would never have enough power for baseball. Alice wondered if he'd rather do something else.

"No, the junior high. Willard."

"They're all playing summer league—"

"There's no game today. We're just having fun."

Sammy glanced around. "I'm going to Telegraph. I have other things to do."

"Oh, yeah?"

"Yeah. Say, are you new here?"

"We came in June."

"From where?"

"Washington."

"You mean Seattle?"

"No, Washington." Curt paused. "Frank Howard, LBJ."

Sammy pondered for a moment. "And what does everyone do there?"

"Same as here, I imagine."

"Funny guy." Sammy scuffed at the ground, smiling, then nodded toward Alice. "And what's her name?"

"Oh man, I forget."

Sammy pondered. "Pollyanna," he proposed.

"No."

"Cassandra."

"That's funny."

"Medusa."

Her brother guffawed. "How'd you guess?"

Sammy scooped up the skateboard. "Hey, Pollyanna, you coming with us?"

"Where?"

"Telegraph. We can see some bongs."

Her brother shrugged, as if bongs were vaguely boring. "Sounds okay."

Sammy surveyed him. "Ever used one?"

"Sure."

"In Washington? With LBJ?"

"Oh, man. You're funny." Curt was gazing impassively, ready for more information, but Sammy just headed for the playground gate, waving them along.

The boys ran ahead, Sammy's head bobbing by her brother's shoulder. Alice followed, enjoying the chance for a boys' adventure. After a few blocks, Sammy veered uphill, away from Telegraph. She ran after them, and as she caught up, he bragged, "I can show you a tree house."

"Where?"

Sammy waved vaguely toward the looming hill. "Up there, in someone's yard."

The lane wound one way and then another, ascending among older homes. The boys ran ahead; now and then Sammy turned, waving her on. There seemed to be no one around, only the homes, jutting from the looming hillside above the road or crouching below. Fantasy worlds, they had archways, redwood beams, tile roofs, dangerously steep driveways; leaded panes looked out on landscaped gardens of rose and tiger lily, palm and redwood and eucalyptus, vying for sunlight in the shady groves. Though no one could be seen, Sammy was creeping along as though he feared someone would hear.

They rounded a bend on the zigzag road. Four huge trees rose from a square of garden, overhanging the houses.

"Redwoods," Sammy said, with a touch of proprietary pride.

She gazed skyward.

"And up there—" He moved on, gesturing toward the gray-green trunks, the trees' lower branches swaying in loose, dangling fronds. "Those are eucalyptus."

As they leaned gazing, Sammy waved them along and headed up a footpath camouflaged among some houses. The path jogged and opened on an overwhelming flight of wooden steps. Panting, she followed the boys up the shady path.

The world of cars and level roads was falling away. Houses rose close by, looming above her shoulder and overlooking the steps. Though the houses were enclosed by fences and shaded by trees, here and there a room could be glimpsed, beckoning her through a window. She leaned peering through the window of a large shingle house surrounded by an iron fence, and found a cozy, wood-paneled bedroom. A wrought-iron gate opening on the footpath was the house's only entrance.

She paused, gazing up the steps. Just above where the boys were, a dog appeared and then a woman. The long-legged dog—lean, like a greyhound—had no leash and was bounding along. Graceful, purposeful, he glided weightlessly by. The woman was young and blonde and wore jeans. She jogged by unconcerned, her gaze focused in the descending sweep of branches, casually following her dog's free wandering. The day was balmy; the swaying branches soon enclosed the woman in gray-green foliage.

They could hear the dog barking for her. Echoing up the steps, the barking sounded eager and oddly close.

"Come on," Sammy urged, rounding a corner by another path. "There's the tree house, over there. Hurry up," he added, "before she sends the dog."

They had come to an overlook leading along the slope. Just below them lay backyards, and then the awesome world beyond.

Alice and Curt paused, gaping on campus and bay, as Sammy approached a yard enclosed by a redwood fence. Beyond the fence, reposing in the branches of an old oak, was a boy's very own one-room house: shingled roof, redwood walls, bamboo ladder. Unparalleled.

"So cool," Sammy said, sighing enviously.

"Uh-huh." Curt's glove was hanging loosely from his wrist. "Who's the lucky dog?"

"Boy from my school. They call him Tree Frog."

The boys guffawed.

"Hey," Sammy said, grinning, "who's going over the fence?"

The fence was high. She could imagine them going over and leaving her on the overlook, where the dog could come for her.

Curt was pondering. "She can go first," he suggested, cheerfully.

Sammy came up. "Hey, Pollyanna—"

"I'm not Pollyanna."

"You wanna go?"

"C'mon," Curt murmured, "leave her alone. She's scared."

"I'm going over," she said, steeling herself.

"Good. Lemme help you." Sammy crouched by the fence, fingers enlaced. The fence rose high overhead, but she would go over. Once she'd proven she could, Sammy would accept her.

In a moment of struggle, she clambered up and perched on the fence, searching for a way down into the yard. Grasping a ledge, she lowered herself slowly and jumped to the ground.

A sudden thumping sounded along the fence, followed by whooping. Her pulse jumped; the boys were fleeing around the corner and away, leaving her alone. Feeling mad and scared, she glanced around the garden where she found herself, wondering why she'd come. Of course: as in Las Vegas, she'd been fooled. Then she remembered the palm trees and the pool, the brass room key. There was no problem—there would always be a way home.

The bamboo ladder swayed as she grappled up the rungs. Scrambling through an opening in the floor, she was in a boy's playroom. In one corner was a globe of the moon; a telescope hung overhead. There were maps of the sky.

She was idly spinning the globe when there came the sound of someone in the yard below, singing to himself. Through the opening in the floor, she saw a gangly redheaded boy heading for the oak tree. He ran up, grasping the ladder, and she moved back—it was a shame to be found out so soon.

The boy emerged ruddy-faced through the opening in the floor. Peering around, he caught sight of her crouching by the globe.

"Who are you?" he said, glaring.

"I'm Alice."

"How'd you get here?"

"Sammy—"

"Sammy?" the boy scowled.

"He brought us here."

"Brought who?"

"Me and my brother."

The boy looked around. "And where's your brother?"

"They ran off."

The boy was pondering. "You tell Sammy—," he began, then paused. "Here's what. You can stay if you'll tell Sammy about the dog."

"What dog—the greyhound?"

The boy's eyes shone, as though he'd just remembered something. "No, the one in my yard."

"And what should I say?"

"He has huge teeth. He chased you up the ladder and nearly caught you." The boy's clear blue eyes were laughing as he surveyed her, though she could see no malevolence in them. He reached for a shelf and grasped a pack of playing cards.

"What can you play?" he asked.

"Hearts, gin rummy, war."

The boy brooded. "Gin rummy," he concluded, and began dealing cards.

THE SUN WAS high over San Francisco as Alice came running down the steps, heading home. Reaching the level road, she glanced right, remembering the route Sammy had shown them. Then she ran on through the leafy shade.

Throbbing sounds were coming through the door of her house. She pressed the handle and the door swung open on the foyer and red thrones; her mother's bag and a newspaper lay on one of them. Beyond the foyer, the living room was pulsing in bass and drums; she'd first heard the song, "Somebody to Love," in the playroom in Washington. In any case, there'd been no reason for running. Her mother would be in a good mood— she'd been on a spree.

Her mother's head was bobbing in the phonograph's blaring sound. Pausing as Alice appeared, she blushed as though she'd been found enjoying some embarrassing pleasure and was searching for a justification. Then as Alice came closer, she handed over the album cover with a conspiratorial smile and resumed her role.

"Where's your brother?"

"Playing baseball." There was no sense in worrying her mother.

"At Willard?"

"I guess so."

"Oh. I passed the playground on our corner. Were you there?"

"Yes."

"Somehow I missed you."

"I guess I was looking around the neighborhood."

Her mother paused, surveying her face for signs of something. The mood was new, as if her mother had been hoping for whisperings of change, an epiphany.

"I was hoping we could go to Telegraph together," her mother remarked, as the song galloped on. "I found you some new records, so when school begins, you'll already know what the others are enjoying. I'm sure you'll never be a square."

Her mother's words were cajoling in a new way. They suggested a confusing image—a square was someone who refused to go along, and so made no impression on others. If so, then her mother was saying she could become someone by going along.

The song churned from the phonograph, engulfing the room in rhythm. The large house was jumping, the throbs barely dampened by her mother's many books. There was a crashing crescendo, a pause in the fury, and then a wavering melody, as a new mood began.

Released from the frenzy, Alice remembered her own concerns. The boy who played gin rummy would be in Mrs. Whitman's class. Would she be in the boy's class, or somewhere else? There was no use in appearing overly eager or curious. Her mother would let her know whenever the assignment had been made. In any case, she hardly knew Tree Frog.

Her mother's glance was close and flushed. "We can go to Telegraph soon," she promised, as though reassuring Alice, "and I can show you the shop selling posters and jewelry. I'm sure my daughter will love those colorful designs."

Sammy had wanted to go to Telegraph—that must be why they'd run off. What were the boys doing there? Surely they had no need of jewelry.

"Psychedelic, that's the word," her mother pursued.

The word sounded new and vaguely chemical. Her mother was encouraging. "Another song?"

There was no way of leaving the room. Feeling cornered, she hoped there would be no more psychedelic songs. There was something compelling in the rhythms, and the singing had a vaguely menacing edge. The songs had alluring force and fury. They were new; they should be hers. So why was her mother playing them?

AFTER A SUMMER spent almost entirely alone, Alice was enjoying a surge of hope as she headed for school. She'd been feeling more perky just imagining the day; the school had placed her in Mrs. Whitman's class, along with Tree Frog. She'd always had her brother in the same school, so the thought of knowing someone, even a boy, was reassuring. Maybe they would play together; or maybe she would have a group of girls. She'd known black girls in Washington—Lori, her neighbor and classmate, had been a pal— and as her mother had been saying all summer, Alice should be a leader; having seen successful integration in her Washington school, she would be ahead of the others, who were only now learning about it. There would be no real problems, her mother was sure, as long as there were some who could show the way.

In her classes, where a grown-up was the leader, she'd always managed her boredom by daydreaming or doing more than the teachers demanded. Those things would remain the same; so the playground would be her place, if only she could find a group as she had in Washington.

The school bus chugged along. Some of her peers were jabbering; "Proud Mary" was blaring a rolling rhythm over the speakers. By the time they pulled up along the fence, she was feeling upbeat, ready for a challenge.

Crossing the playground, however, she found herself fending off gloomy feelings. The yard was large and unshaded, bleak; churning energy ran through the crowd. Some black boys were tussling, and though the scuffle seemed more in play than in anger, they were landing hard blows. A crowd had gathered around, goading them on; finally one of the boys broke away, cursing, as the crowd jeered and clamored for more. Fighting had been uncommon at her old school. Keeping clear of the bad apples—or so they seemed—she made her way alone. People were already forming teams: whites gathering in small groups as they came by bus from several neighborhoods, and blacks congregating in larger groups, for they were continuing in the same neighborhood school and already knew each other. Things were just beginning; even so, there was an unusual absence of mingling or even casual sharing of space that jarred her sense of the normal. Even boys and girls on a playground never kept so completely apart, unless compelled to do so.

The school bell rang. Pushing and shoving, the groups surged for the doors. As she struggled forward, Alice got caught up and pressed among a group of black girls. Nearing the doorway, sardined among the larger, all-encompassing crowd, she found herself squeezed against one of the girls.

"Don't push me, whitey," the girl commanded, shoving her hard.

"Ooooh, she goin' be sorry," another added.

They had her surrounded.

Back on the playground, a few groups were ignoring the bell, clearly in no hurry. Finally a black man appeared by the door, calling for order and rounding up the stragglers.

The group jammed through the doorway and suddenly eased. Clear of the girls but repelled by the ordeal, Alice found herself in a dreary corridor. The anger had been raw and demeaning. "Whitey"? She'd never heard that word from the black girls in Washington, when they met up on the playground or in a neighbor's yard. No, that was a new one—and out of bounds. There were words she should never say, so why should she hear "whitey"? There were informal rules here; they were in school. In any case, she'd only pushed the same as everyone else.

Approaching the classroom, Alice found some white girls—were they supposed to be her group?—hovering by the door, looking on, as though on the verge of leaving. In the room beyond were several black students, joking and laughing among themselves.

The front row, seemingly a no-man's-land, was occupied only by a shaggy white boy who slumped, arms folded, regarding the board. Two rows back, a black boy with flashing eyes was opening and closing a desk.

A chubby black boy entered the room, waving and smiling.

"We're in the same class!"

"Hey, Vaughan, come on over here."

"No, let's be by the window."

"Teacher gonna move everyone anyway."

"How do you know?"

"They always do."

Some black girls were flowing around the room, claiming desks and then moving off and choosing others. Alice had never seen kids running so freely around a classroom. Being unruly had always been Curt's role, but here were some unruly girls. That could be a good change. Even so, she enjoyed learning new things, mulling over the lesson, the teacher, her peers; how would she feel surrounded by so much random energy?

As Alice crossed the room, one of the black girls panned her up and down, surveying her burgundy corduroy dress, and then glanced away, coolly ignoring her. Moments later, the girl dashed from the room and a loud argument began in the hallway. No need for more warnings; Alice could see that these tough, wiry girls, slapping and sassing, were out of her league. How had they become so bold? Her mother would be shocked if she behaved so loudly and spontaneously. Alice's role was already crumbling—these girls would hold her in contempt. They were leaders already, and who would she be?

Comparing her shaky morning with her mother's hopes for the school, she was feeling unprepared and vaguely ashamed.

As the argument continued, the white girls crowded through the doorway together, claiming some desks, circling the wagons. Alice found both groups annoying—no one was doing as they should.

Among the black children, a few remained aloof from the

group: in the second row, a handsome, carefully dressed boy with close-cropped hair; near him, a girl with cool, observing eyes and a shiny permanent, similar to the styles in Washington; and, squeezed in a desk in the corner, a morose, pimply girl. Older and larger and shunning everyone, she pondered the floor, her eyes revealing a smoldering glare if anyone came near. Crossing the room, Alice passed the girl with the shiny perm and abruptly sat down, feeling proud of her bold move. She glanced at her neighbor: long-legged like herself, the girl was surveying the room with a knowing smile. So far she seemed more appealing, and maybe more helpful as an ally, than the group of white girls. Though congregating—even clinging—together, they were clearly strangers, for they were exchanging names. One was wiping away tears. Looking around the room, Alice wondered if she'd messed up in passing them by; but her mother had counseled her to be a leader. These separate groups were wrongheaded, even cowardly. Eyeing the white girls, now busy bonding by the door, she felt a pang. However embarrassing the unconcealed confusion was, she'd probably end up relying on them. Even so, where had they been? Her school and neighborhood in Washington had been integrated; though unusual, as her mother had commented over and over, that was what she knew. For months she'd walked to school with Lori, a black girl from her class. They'd gossiped together and gone to each other's homes—though that was rare; they'd competed over spelling bees and been scolded together for squabbling in class. Her mother would never approve of her playing with someone who got teary over sharing a classroom with some black kids.

The weepy girl was glancing her way, waving her over.

The black girl near her murmured, "Go on and move, if you want. She's saving you a place."

"I'm fine here."

"What happened—she was mean to you or something?"

The suggestion was sardonic and sly.

"No."

"Then go on—she's saving your place."

"I've never seen her before," Alice responded, as if defending herself, then added, "I just moved here."

"Ooooh." The girl paused; she finally understood. "Where you from?"

"Washington, D.C."

"You're far from home then." The girl assessed her closely but not unpleasantly. Alice was proud of her burgundy corduroy dress; the other girl wore a peach-colored blouse and skirt, and white patent-leather shoes. Before things could go any further, however, she leaned away, murmuring something to a black girl at a nearby desk. Then there was a flurry as another white girl—blonde and hardy, a leader—came laughing through the door and rushed for the seat Alice had just passed up. Alice was aware of an unpleasant feeling, a feeling of dismay.

"Teacher's coming!" a boy called from the doorway, the boy named Vaughan. He rushed across the room as a woman appeared. An eager "Good morning!" came from the hardy blonde girl, followed by guffaws from Vaughan and his companion. Then the group hushed, busy sizing up Mrs. Whitman. Alice found the woman's presence calming; Mrs. Whitman was her mother's age and vaguely beautiful, with long dark hair and warm eyes. The girl near her lowered her chin, surveying the woman from under her shiny bangs.

Following the teacher, just as the bell was sounding, came a gangly redheaded boy in beige slacks and long sleeves. Finally—Tree Frog. From the door he glanced over the group. Then he loped across the room, passing Mrs. Whitman's desk, and found a place in the second row.

Mrs. Whitman opened the roll book and commenced reading names.

Tree Frog's real name was Howard Singer—all wrong. The girl in the nearby seat was Jocelyn Clark, while the carefully cropped boy was Benjamin Forman. Among the girls by the door were Nora, the hardy blonde; curly-haired Debra; and Tammy, the weepy one. Tammy had cheered up; with long brown hair, she now appeared self-possessed in her frilly blouse and beads. Slumped under Mrs. Whitman's gaze was Jason; he had shaggy brown hair and long hands, as though he should play the piano. By the window, two black boys sat together, joking: Vaughan and Michael.

Mrs. Whitman glanced around the room and made some adjustments, moving Vaughan and Michael up from the back row. However, when she addressed the morose girl in the corner, the girl refused to respond, shifting only her eyes. There was an uncomfortable pause, as Jocelyn murmured under her breath, "Leave her be," and then Mrs. Whitman moved on, breaking up the group by the door by placing Nora on the other side of Jocelyn.

When the lunch bell rang, Jocelyn jumped up and ran to the door, where she fell in with some girls from another classroom. Alice joined Nora's group as they headed for the lunchroom. However, they were busy bonding and made no more moves regarding her. Finally Nora glanced her way.

"Do you play handball?" she asked, in a haughty tone.

"No."

"No?" Nora leaned in, amused.

"I play baseball, though," Alice added.

Tammy giggled. "Do you have brothers?"

"Yes."

"Oh, so that's why!"

They were a group, maybe—or would be. She would have to see.

BY THE THIRD week, the class was already becoming boring and slow. Mrs. Whitman seemed overwhelmed by the range of skills among her students, who were unable to follow lessons together, while Vaughan and Michael murmured and laughed all day long. In the beginning, Mrs. Whitman responded warmly and generously, hoping for some common goal, but there was nothing she could do. The boys were goofy and carefree, and they were increasingly sassy, playing her for a fool, vying to defy her. Whenever Mrs. Whitman was gaining control of the class, a challenge would come from Vaughan or Michael, so that Mrs. Whitman would feel compelled to respond. They could unravel the woman, and Alice, who had never seen such open contempt for a teacher, began to wonder about the power it gave the boys. They fed on her helplessness; when they weren't clowning and tormenting Mrs. Whitman, they slumped sadly, gazing through the windows. Alice had sympathy for them then.

Mrs. Whitman's warmth and the boys' demeaning rudeness made Alice feel vaguely ashamed. She was growing fond of Mrs. Whitman; but there was something uncomfortable in feeling for her, being moved by her during class. The woman's warm sympathy was confusing; her face was full of feeling, making the class vulnerable. Mrs. Whitman was suffering, the boys were angry, the class was floundering, and there was nothing Alice could do to help. On the playground, some of the boys were showing her the same demeaning contempt, commenting on her clothes, her body. Government people like her father had been carefully planning the whole thing. Why, then, was she feeling so uncomfortable? If she was unwelcome in the school, why would her father and the government demand her presence there?

Then there was Jocelyn, arms folded, coolly assessing the scene.

"My mother's a teacher," she murmured. "If they're scared of her, they'll do what she says," she added.

In the hallways, some black students looked through Alice, completely ignoring her. She was confused and discouraged by the loss of normal eye contact, for casual mingling was now impossible. Once, forgetting the new ways, she glanced at a passing girl. For a moment, something was exchanged. Then the girl scowled.

"What you looking at, honky?" she demanded, waving her hand in Alice's face as she passed.

A smaller group of black students glared or shoved, using ugly names, accusing Alice of being in the way. In the beginning, she wondered what she'd done wrong, but there was nothing—nothing she could change. They just seemed sure that whites belonged somewhere else. Coming on randomly, the clashes were scary and enraging, for there could be no pushing back. She was cornered.

These responses were new and menacing. Her mother's imagined harmony fled in a rush of anger and taunts. These kids wanted to move up in the world, she'd been told; apparently they would do so by pushing her down. In the classroom, however, many of them were way behind. The grown-up world would reward the learning, not the anger; but what could she learn here? In any case, there would be years of hassling, and the hassling would grow worse. The boys would become large, like her brother.

She became aware that rumors flew among her new peers. If she defended herself against one person, soon enough others would begin taunting and harassing her in revenge. She was in a dry prairie, and someone had already tossed the match.

One morning, as Mrs. Whitman was facing the board, eraser in hand, and Vaughan and Michael were engaged in the usual clowning, Howard Singer suddenly rose up, grabbed his desk, and hurled it upside down. Books and papers spilled over the floor.

"Enough!" Tree Frog hollered, red-faced and panting with rage. "I've had enough!" Then he ran from the room.

Scarcely a month had passed. Everything was new and wild. Though appalled, Alice was also jealous. Tree Frog would get away. She would never dare; her parents would never understand, they would simply be mad. They were in the program for the long haul, and so was she.

Leaving the classroom in rising chaos and the desk topsy-turvy, Mrs. Whitman abandoned the group, following Tree Frog. Once she was gone, the room hushed, as everyone brooded on the event. A few glanced shyly around, eyeing the damaged desk. For some reason, though the mood was gloomy, there was a coming together in trouble—they were the ones who would be coming back.

"So much for redhead," Jocelyn murmured to herself. "He's gone."

Tree Frog was oddly impressive. Who would have imagined he could be badder than Vaughan and Michael?

"Gone where?" Alice wondered aloud.

Jocelyn's eyes flashed in weary contempt. "Where do you think?"

Howard Singer never returned. Though they hardly knew each other, Alice was feeling a sense of loss as rumors bounced among the white girls. The others were openly pleased. "He brings down your grade," confided Tammy, who knew him from her old school. Nora summed up, "There's something wrong with him, of course. His mother's a psychologist." Soon he was simply gone.

Being together in the same school made everyone a member of one group or the other. Forced to be the person her appearance made her, Alice was becoming aware of her body as never before. She'd crossed some boundary she'd never heard of, and suddenly the playground had a menacing feel. Under a new dress code, she no longer had to wear dresses. Wearing pants gave her a sense of freedom. Maybe they would see her as tough;

maybe she could defend herself. So she began wearing pants. When she wore her jeans, however, someone—usually one of the black boys—would run up to her, demanding, "Are you a boy or a girl?" In the beginning, confused by the boy's seeming confusion, she responded, absurdly, "I'm a girl." Soon enough she saw through the charade. Once, when she demanded of a lean, agile boy, "And you—boy or girl?" the boy glared and shoved her hard. Maybe lying low would help; that's how other white kids were dealing, heads down, ignoring bullying—but so far, she'd refused. If they were cowards, things would only get worse. From her brother she'd learned that cowards deserved to be hounded. And from her mother she'd learned to manage problems on her own, for any problem among children surely involved shared blame. She began to envy Howard Singer, who'd found a way out.

Soon enough, Alice had a chance to see the principal's office for herself. Ben Forman had been teasing her ever since she'd begun wearing jeans. "How come you look like a boy?" he demanded. "Where's your dress?" From then on, he'd been following her around, remarking on her clothes. When she showed up in the burgundy dress, the only one she enjoyed wearing, he knew just what to say. "How come you always wear corduroy?" he pursued. "Your father, he's too poor to buy you another one?"

Ben's clothing was always clean and ironed. A good student, he'd been ashamed one day when he'd made a wrong response. Vaughan had laughed; Mrs. Whitman had ignored him as Ben coughed up another answer, the right one.

On the school bus, some of the girls from the Berkeley hills had fancy clothes, more costly than anything Alice had, though her family was doing well enough. She enjoyed wearing jeans, that was all.

"I wear what I choose," she told Ben, as he pursued her nagging and taunting by the girl's bathroom. He was more annoying than mean; but he followed her around so much that the other children had begun to comment, saying, "They be going together," and laughing. She would not have them saying that; she would never go with him.

Alice had lunch now with Nora and Tammy, the teary girl, who was more fun than she'd seemed that first morning. She made revealing comments on everyone and was amused by Ben.

"He's so churchy," she said, giggling. "He has to be good, always."

Alice began planning how she could make Ben leave her alone. Maybe if she called him a senseless name—nothing he could take personally—maybe then he would see how absurd the game was.

Then one day she was in the girls' bathroom when she heard someone come in. Before she knew what was happening, a boy —one she'd never seen before—came crawling under the door of her stall. The boy was on the ground, peering up and smirking; placing her shoe on the boy's forehead, she shoved as hard as she dared. The boy struggled for a moment, then he was gone. As she emerged from the bathroom, Ben came running by. She was burning with shame.

So when he approached her, murmuring, "Corduroy, corduroy," she called him a bad name.

The bad name she nearly used was the wrong one, beyond the pale; for years her mother had warned her. But there was another word in heavy use on the playground—one that made her angry, and so she flung it at Ben.

"You're a bitch," she told him, hoping he would be confused and maybe leave her alone.

Ben stared at her. "What did you say?"

"You're a bitch, you're a—"

"Ooooh . . ." He tore off across the playground. She had not supposed it would be so easy.

A few minutes later, a playground counselor approached her, Ben trailing behind, smirking.

"Principal wants to see you," the man announced. Hanging on him, Ben was bobbing with eagerness.

No one was supposed to squeal. That was really out-of-bounds, as Ben surely knew.

The principal, Mr. Boyd, was a small black man; he was wearing wire-framed glasses, a vest, and a pale-blue shirt. He had summoned her; he regarded Ben's charge as worthy. Ben had changed the rules and squealed, and now she was in big trouble. Mr. Boyd would blame her; he'd already formed a conclusion, for Ben had been allowed to go.

She was feeling numb and cornered as Mr. Boyd waved her to a wooden chair. He leaned before her on a large paper-laden desk, the kind her father would use. She hardly knew the rules anymore. The telephone rang, unanswered; Mr. Boyd was a busy man. She wondered whether he would lose his temper and yell, as Kathy's mother used to do.

"Now tell me," he began, calmly, "why would you call Ben an ugly name?"

Though embarrassed by the charge, she would never argue. That only made grown-ups angry. But maybe she could defend herself all the same. "He keeps bothering me."

"Bothering you?"

"Teasing. Something about my clothes."

"I see. Ben makes fun of your clothes." Mr. Boyd folded his arms, as if wondering what else she had to say.

She nodded.

"Do you make fun of him?"

"No."

"Do you regard Ben as a friend?"

The proper response was surely yes; how could she say Ben would never be her pal without offending Mr. Boyd?

"Well, do you?"

"I guess so."

"You guess so. You sound like you're not sure." Mr. Boyd seemed calm, reasonable; she would fess up and see what happened.

"He annoys me."

"I see. Usually we keep away from folks who annoy us. Maybe you should keep away from Ben."

"But he follows me around, he bothers me."

"Some boys are awkward. He means no harm."

There was a pause.

"What was the name you called him?"

She was very glad she'd suppressed the other name; even so, she was feeling embarrassed.

"You called him a 'bitch.'" Coming from Mr. Boyd, the word sounded bland, vaguely silly—even more so because it seemingly named her, rather than Ben. "If a person is pestering you, why not call him a pest?" Mr. Boyd gave a vague smile. He was more amused than angry. "Now, you remember what I say."

Alice made her way through the door. She was exasperated— no one had ever complained to the principal about her before.

Though Mr. Boyd was vaguely amused, he would remember her as a girl who'd done something embarrassing and wrong. Mr. Boyd seemed reasonable, but he was enforcing rules in an absurd way. Nearly every day someone called her names like "whitey" or "honky"; but Ben Forman should be carefully, squeamishly labeled a "pest"? All the same, Mr. Boyd was a calm and reasonable man; maybe she should run and tell him whenever someone called her a name. She would become a squealer; and soon enough she and Ben and Mr. Boyd would be pals . . . But how could she inform a black man that someone had called her "honky"? What would he say? Her mother would be no help; she'd never heard the word. No, Mr. Boyd would blame her, he already had. She was alone and would have to make her own way.

Marian

PEACE AND FREEDOM'S Berkeley chapter convened on Tuesday evenings, moving from house to house in South Campus. Marian would finally be meeting some neighbors. The woman she'd spoken with, Sabrina Patterson, had sounded eager and commanding on the phone, as though her name should mean something to the caller, as though she held an important place in the group. Marian had enjoyed the Quakers and Ivy League renegades she'd found in her peace group in Washington. So many had been employed by the federal government, though. She would feel more fellowship among university people. If only she were younger, she could have enrolled in a modern-novel class, maybe something in French. Tom had colleagues; she needed her own group. She would survey the grown-up scene and do something useful during the wrap-up to the murderous 1968 campaign year.

Sabrina's yard had red flowering trees and an overgrown juniper hedge; there was a hammock on the porch. Bearing homemade bread, her usual offering, Marian pressed the bell. A gong sounded, and the door was opened by a barefoot girl wearing torn jeans, whose cool, assessing glance combined uneasily with her manner—far more comfortable in her body than any thirteen-year-old girl should be. Marian wondered if her own daughter—growing up so freely—would soon be that way.

The girl scampered off wordlessly, as though she'd pigeon-holed the guest and found her undeserving of the usual courtesy.

Crossing the foyer, Marian paused in the doorway admiring the living-room bookshelves, much more impressive than her own. Among the books were many *objets*: wood carvings of women, jewelry made from shells, brass dragons. Someone had anthropological leanings.

The group was large, and so far everyone was white. Marian found that odd, after her Washington circle. There were men and women her age, though of course a few were very young. They were more casual than her Washington peers, the shaggy men in jeans and beards, the women in loose flowing garments or, if they were young, in jeans and dangling earrings. Surveying them from the door, Marian found the group more comprehensible, less vagrant than the Telegraph crowds—more grown-up couples than newfangled '49ers here. She was glad she'd worn her sandals and Indian-print dress; if only she had some dangling earrings, she would blend in.

Marian crossed the room, passing a long-legged man slouched on the floor. Leaving her bread on the food board, she found a folding chair near a wine cupboard.

Soon some of the younger men were carving up the bread, joking and passing a marijuana cigarette among themselves. They had the underfed look of young, uncoupled males—even the Party founder, Shel, who had just come in, causing a flurry among the men by the food. Full of energy and command, Shel had charisma and a brand image—black jeans, black jersey, a bomber jacket. Several years younger than Tom, he was dropping references to Cuba, Czechoslovakia, and Cambodia, where he'd reported on the war. She was glad that Tom, who would spar when faced with male competition, had stayed home.

Amused by the marijuana and the eager young men, Marian was planning how she would make a splash, what she would say. They were there for the same reasons, she assumed: the savage war in Vietnam; the assassinations of King and Bobby Kennedy; the bloody Democratic Convention—all had soured them on the two-party system. Johnson had made a damning compromise with the party's Southern wing, waging war as a payoff for support on civil rights, and Humphrey—Johnson's vice president, now the Democratic candidate—would pursue the same

strategy, if elected. Nixon, the Republican candidate, was pledg-
ing "peace with honor," but no one on the Left could forgive the
anti-Communist campaigns he'd waged in the late '40s and the
'50s. Now that American ground forces were seemingly losing
the war, maybe people would come around and support withdrawal. A long and undeclared war, assassinations, urban uprisings—if things continued, the country would become a phony
democracy. They'd assumed a reasonably ordered world would
always be there, regardless; how foolish they'd been.

A woman about Marian's age came from the hallway. In a
slim dress revealing bare thighs, she was glowing, expansive; she
wore long bangs swept back. Though she was white, the impression was of a woman from the era of the Pyramids in sudden
and graceful motion. She was followed by a man in Mayan garb
who leaned in, whispering something humorous in her ear.
Coming forward, the woman found a seat by Marian as the man
—presumably her husband—faded through the door. The barefoot teenage girl barged her way through the room just as the
woman was calling the gathering to order.

During the pause, she remarked, "You must be Marian."

"Yes, that's right."

"Sabrina. So glad you're here—we need volunteers. There's
the campaign, and Huey, and—"

They heard the sound of a door slamming.

"Oh, there goes Helen—my daughter," Sabrina murmured.
Then she rose and commenced reading an agenda. She had easy
warmth and aplomb, and the husband had a professor's manner,
regardless of the Mayan garb. Marian assessed them as former
Easterners, a good find.

Then Shel rose, removing the bomber jacket and limbering
up. There was a hush as he began speaking.

"An American jury has refused freedom for Huey Newton.
He remains imprisoned on false charges of manslaughter. Huey's
lawyers are planning an appeal of the case, and Huey needs your
support. Dan Dupres is organizing Peace and Freedom's 'Free
Huey' defense committee. If you can spare an hour, speak to
Dan."

The long-legged man on the floor waved an arm. He had a
rugged jaw, and he wore unlaundered jeans, army boots, a fringy
purple vest. He was handsome and flamboyant—more so than

Shel. There was applause, and an older woman began circulating a sign-up sheet.

Sabrina leaned in, confiding, "Dan's new—and very forceful."

"Now," Shel resumed, "a few words on the Telegraph uprisings. There was the Bastille Day uprising—some of you were there."

Marian remembered the day—the mover had demanded news of Telegraph Avenue and then denounced the cops. She'd been dismayed by the man's words—"gassing the flower people"—and confused by his vehemence. As she glanced around the room, wondering who had been there, she saw Dan nodding proudly.

"And there was Labor Day. All summer, the cops have been bashing heads on Telegraph—in our own South Campus neighborhood. We're learning what oppression means. For too long we've refused to condemn government assaults on our communities. Now we're seeing how the system works, what they're capable of. As the Panthers say, the cops occupy our communities like foreign troops. Huey, Che, Ho Chi Minh speak for oppressed people everywhere—black, brown, yellow, and white."

Marian wondered where the image had come from, for she'd encountered it somewhere in her reading: a black man coming to sudden awareness of himself as a full person, a man among men of all colors—black, brown, yellow, and white—a spokesman, a leader. The image had a humane appeal, a revolutionary flare. Such community was a challenge for the group in the room—a group that was, so far, entirely white. But it was becoming less improbable for the very young. Curt and Alice, who were already learning to be leaders in the change, would do more than she and Tom could; maybe she could learn from them.

Shel was gearing up. "Our movement needs everyone who's demanding real change. The Panthers' program has room for every black person in America. No one in North Vietnam is unemployed."

"They're doing the people's work," Dan murmured.

"Yes, and here's the problem," Shel said, nodding. "So far, we're a group of cerebral souls—philosophers, up-and-coming professors. Longhaired, dope-smoking streetfighters feel unwelcome among us. But if you've read Eldridge Cleaver's *Soul on Ice*, you know it's the longhaired streetfighters who are making personal change—and it's the ones making personal change who are gonna make revolution."

There were cheers, as a new energy flowed among the younger people. Marian was enjoying a sense of camaraderie.

"The Man has guns and gas—but guns and gas won't win a war. For that, you need the people."

Someone gave a war cry.

Marian glanced around the room, feeling a rebel energy that pleased her. Yet she was also leery—she'd been hoping for grown-up peers.

Dan began speaking, commanding the group from the floor.

"I have a proposal, people," he called out. "Something from the *Barb*. Something for the Berkeley City Council and its occupying army."

"Go on, Dan."

"A plan for our freedom. As things are, we have no land, no space we control, even on Telegraph—I know, because they gassed my jeans shop last summer. So here's a proposal: South Campus should secede from the gestapo madness of Berkeley, become a people's town. We can have our own cops, govern ourselves through real democracy. We can choose people rather than cars, parks rather than dorms. Berkeley's black community can break away at the same time. We vote for their thing and they vote for ours, and Berkeley becomes three towns." He paused. "Self-government. All power to the people. Black control of the black community. Our control of our community."

"And what happens to Huey?" Shel demanded. "What happens to the Panther program, when we're doing our own thing?"

"We need land—space for organizing," Dan responded.

Marian remembered the *Barb* cover: "BERKELEY COMMUNE: DON'T TREAD ON ME." So *that's* what they meant. The proposal was whimsical, even funny.

Now Shel began covering some background on the Panthers, headquartered in Oakland. He was professorial, summing up the major themes before moving on. In response to harassment by the cops, as rampant as anything in the South, the Panthers had formed patrols of Oakland's black community. Whenever the cops were harassing people in the ghetto, the Panthers would show up bearing shotguns. So far, the Oakland and Berkeley cops had responded by provoking armed confrontations with several Panther patrols. Shel regarded the patrols as necessary self-defense of the black community.

"Community patrols represent the power of an oppressed people," he concluded. "They're freedom fighters for an internal colony."

"America's Viet Cong," Dan muttered.

"And they need support from committed groups within the white community. That's where we come in," Shel added, nodding.

Marian was feeling ungrounded. She was aware of the Panthers, though barely. Of course she'd seen the "Free Huey" slogan everywhere and knew the Panther leader had just been found guilty of manslaughter in the death of an Oakland cop. Peace and Freedom was demanding Huey's release. Yet Marian had read confusing reports of the proceedings in the nearby Oakland courthouse—propaganda by the cops or the defense, depending. Then, on the heels of King's assassination, another Panther leader, Eldridge Cleaver, had apparently been ambushed by cops—or had ambushed them, though who could really say? The news reports were very conflicting.

Sabrina was leaning closer. "The Panthers have become a symbol, a vanguard," she was saying in Marian's ear, "and so of course the cops are gunning for them."

"Yes, I see. Things are changing," Marian responded ambiguously.

"That's why the schools are so important—by changing the young people, we change the system."

"I agree." Marian glanced at Sabrina, suppressing rising doubts. What were Curt and Alice—though her group was younger and presumably less aware—hearing from their black peers? And how would she help them understand? Though Marian had been following Huey's case in the papers, she was unfamiliar with the community patrols. She and Tom had been in Washington when the Panthers had appeared on the Oakland scene over a year before, in May 1967. Now she remembered having been alarmed by images of the group bearing guns into the California State Assembly to block passage of a law banning the carrying of loaded firearms in public. Marian would have preferred a world with fewer guns; but Tom, dry and lawyerly, had responded by running through some Second Amendment arguments. Even so, she hung back: Black Power was surging, and the Panthers, though aligned with Peace and Freedom, certainly had a Black Power image. They reminded her of H. Rap

Brown, who'd urged black people to burn a Maryland elementary school. She'd been repelled, but was the anger so surprising? In Virginia, whole counties had closed schools rather than desegregate. Though she'd support Peace and Freedom for its general platform opposing war, and though she'd support the Civil Rights Movement as long as desegregation was the goal, she feared what would come of more armed confrontations.

"The campaign, Shel," Dan urged.

Shel nodded. "As you know, Peace and Freedom will be campaigning for Eldridge Cleaver. Some in Peace and Freedom urged us to endorse Benjamin Spock, the baby doctor. But Cleaver's now free on parole, and he's already begun campaigning on the Black Panther program, with its demands for full employment and armed self-defense of black communities. By supporting Cleaver's independent campaign, we can strengthen Peace and Freedom and advance the Panther platform."

A shaggy older man called out, "I'm for Dr. Spock! Anyone who can govern America's babies can govern America!"

Marian laughed, wondering what office they were campaigning for.

Dan was pounding the floor. "We need a real leader—someone who knows the score!"

Shel resumed. "Some people are refusing to support Cleaver, saying he's a paroled felon and only thirty-three years old, below the minimum age for office. But Cleaver and the Panther program are drawing people into the Movement. We're already managing Huey's campaign for Congress; we're campaigning for Kathleen Cleaver, who's challenging State Assemblyman Willie Brown."

Sabrina leaned over and murmured, "Kathleen—Eldridge's wife, from a Quaker school near Philadelphia and then Barnard College."

"Willie Brown's just another black politician," Dan called out. "The Panthers can pressure him from the Left."

"That's right. And now Peace and Freedom is supporting the only meaningful movement in this country by running Eldridge Cleaver for President!"

There was loud applause.

Marian felt a jolt—she hadn't grasped what they were endorsing. But was Cleaver—ineligible on many grounds—really running for President? If so, they were gearing up for a purely symbolic campaign. She gazed around the room, wondering if her new group would really embrace a hopeless cause. Voting was a fundamental right; she'd never squandered her chance.

A motherly woman announced, "I could campaign for Catiline, the rebel who nearly burned Rome—that's how mad I am!"

As the cheers resounded, someone produced a baggie full of marijuana and some rolling papers.

Marian demurred, feeling she'd gone far enough for one evening. She bid Sabrina a warm but hasty goodbye and headed for the door, forgetting her bread plate.

THE FOLLOWING WEEK, as Marian was working in the Peace and Freedom office, she found the ruggedly handsome man named Dan Dupres already using her bread plate for an ash tray. Hoping for a chance to see Sabrina, she'd volunteered for a few hours among the smoke and mimeograph fumes, making phone calls, typing correspondence, and proofreading the Party newsletter. Unfortunately, Sabrina was there only in passing; though as she was leaving, she suggested meeting for coffee. Things were suddenly progressing.

As for the young Peace and Freedom people, they were amusing enough; but then, hearing from one of her Party colleagues some implausible phrase—"arming for the struggle," "freedom from the white mother country"—she wondered why she was there, among the comings and goings of the young.

Dan was on the phone, rehearsing the Panther program. As he spoke on, Marian heard a new demand and began to feel more misgivings about campaigning for such a program.

"The Panthers are demanding land and bread," Dan boomed, as though speaking from a balcony to a gathered crowd below. "They're demanding land, bread, housing, justice, education, and peace," he intoned, waving a cigarette. "Self-determination, Mr. Newsman, self-determination. That's all they're asking for. And here's one final demand—a UN-sponsored referendum to be held throughout the black colony to determine the will of black people regarding their national destiny."

Dan paused and fingered the pocket of his purple vest, embroidered with cannabis leaves. Frowning, he hung the cigarette from his mouth and dug a lighter from the vest pocket. The

long chin moved back and forth, reminding Marian of a horse
caught with a mouthful of hay.

"I dare you, Mr. Newsman!" he laughed and hung up.

Marian moved in on her bread plate. "Oh, there!" she sang,
sounding sharper than she'd meant.

Dan glanced around uncomprehendingly. "Are you manning
the grape table today?" he demanded, as though addressing a
tardy employee.

"Who, me?"

"Someone signed up for Sproul Plaza," he said, frowning,
"but they've gone AWOL. There's a grape strike—"

"Yes, I know." She'd just proofread a long essay on Cesar
Chavez.

"Then maybe you can help out at Sproul. Here, you'll want
some 'Free Huey' leaflets, too."

He seemed no longer aware of her presence as she headed for
the door, wondering if the children were home from school and
how long she could be away from the house. Was it her imagination, or were they sullen when she'd been out doing things?

She rounded the corner and found her car. Who was Dan—a
college man or someone who'd fled the defense plants? He was
very sure of himself. She was unclear, however, if he really knew as
much as Shel, who had degrees, who'd reported from abroad and
maybe even co-authored some of the Panthers' essays. And was
black America really a colony? What if the colony chose independence? Where would the new country be—Alabama? Oakland?

She found her way to Sproul Plaza, just beyond the border of
the campus. There she helped a young woman in jeans, sandals,
and dangling earrings gather signatures and hand out leaflets. The
young woman was auburn-haired and curvy; her breasts bulged
from a cowboy blouse. Marian found her bold and vulgar. The
place was busy, even raucous, for a university campus, where
everyone was supposedly studying. But no—there they were,
sprawled on the steps of the Student Union or gathered around
some bongo drummers. The young woman, Wanda, was vaguely
familiar; Marian had seen her before, probably at the meeting.
Wanda referred to herself, with grim humor, as a "mother-country
radical" and pumped Marian for information about Huey's trial.
Marian finally had to acknowledge that she knew only what she'd
seen in the papers.

"Oh? I thought your old man was working with Charles Garry," Wanda said with a frown, referring to Huey's lawyer.

"Oh no," Marian smiled, "my husband does practice law, but he's with the federal government."

"Bummer." Wanda furrowed her brow; then her face hardened. "So that's what he does for bread, huh?"

"Well, yes." Marian, who had been feeling condescending and motherly, was now chagrined, as if she'd been forced to reveal some awful compromise. She wondered what Wanda—or maybe Wanda's father—was doing for bread.

Wanda lowered her chin, scanning the plaza, pausing as her eyes came upon a group of unleashed dogs roaming to and fro. "I would kill for a world where you could use the law to make real change, rather than using it to *fuck people over*."

Marian concealed her annoyance. "And what are Huey's lawyers doing?"

"You know what I mean."

Later, as Marian rushed through her grocery shopping, she resolved to forgo grapes. Though the kids loved them, they could manage a small sacrifice. California was an overflowing orchard of strawberries, plums, pears, oranges, peaches, and avocados. There was more than enough, and anyway, they should be helping the grape workers. Or so she reminded Alice, who refused the plums and pears and pleaded for grapes.

AFTER PEACE AND Freedom meetings, Marian usually found herself talking with Sabrina, whose husband was a professor of anthropology. Michael Patterson had supported the students during the Free Speech Movement, and Sabrina spoke knowledgeably about Bay Area and California politics. They had two daughters—Helen, the older, barefoot one, and Maggie. Sabrina was taking graduate classes in her husband's department and wanted to know if Marian would be enrolling in any courses. Michael was usually too busy for Peace and Freedom. An authority on Franz Boas and cultural anthropology, he had been trained by Margaret Mead, at Columbia, and George Foster, at Berkeley. Now he was applying for a research grant to spend several months in South America with a colleague who was studying languages found in the Amazon. Michael was interested in the federal government's poverty programs and questioned Marian closely on Tom's work.

Marian began reading Boas and Mead, so she would have something to talk to Sabrina and Michael Patterson about. She wanted to get to know Sabrina and Michael, for she assumed they were more compatible than she and Tom and was hoping to learn how it was done. Sabrina was calm and humorous, confidently self-regarding for a mother of daughters, while Michael was comfortable with both himself and Sabrina. There seemed to be none of the subliminal resentments that contaminated her evenings with Tom. Michael was amusing and informative in conversation, rather than sparring, like Tom. At home, Marian began referring to the Pattersons, to gauge Tom's response. Though he'd met them, he showed no eagerness for more.

When she was alone, Marian found herself wondering about Michael. Would she have been happy with someone like him? It was becoming harder and harder to remember why she'd wanted Tom, why she'd been so eager to marry him. She'd been young, barely twenty-one. Now she was no less appealing than Sabrina, no less intelligent; though anthropology was new for her, it was no more foreign than law. Perhaps she even had some saving graces that a woman of Sabrina's confidence and self-regard could be assumed to lack. She would be less demanding: had she not remained loyal to Tom? She wondered how easy a man such as Michael would be—in any case, Sabrina seemed sure of him, even when contemplating his prolonged absence in South America. Tom had grown away from Marian as far as conjugal life was concerned; she could never be sure of him. Sometimes she sensed Tom moving closer, but never for long. Now the move west, though very unlooked-for, had opened up a new independence. A grand upheaval was engulfing her world, and during the Peace and Freedom Party meetings Marian found herself watching the young men around her, wondering whom she would choose had she world enough and time.

In truth her leanings had not changed; now she would have a place for exploring them. She was charmed by academic men, and among Sabrina's group, she was impressed by the whimsy and camaraderie buoyed by a rebel energy.

chapter three

Tom

ONE SATURDAY AFTERNOON, Tom drove the Chevy along Telegraph Avenue. He'd made some adjustments to the place, wearing jeans, a blue workingman's shirt, sandals. Now there was something he needed, something he had a hankering for. He'd agreed to go riding with Ginger the following Saturday and was searching for an accessory suggestive of horsemanship. Nothing flagrant; nothing the family shouldn't see. He was planning on using work as a cover, some project demanding weekend hours throughout the fall—the impact of housing discrimination on schools; a federal desegregation case in the Los Angeles area—anything Marian would go for. If she pumped him for information, he could always bluff; he was drowning in the stuff anyway.

Tom passed a shop selling leather goods. The place had appeal: there were bomber jackets, supple and smooth, suede jackets hanging with fringe, sandals and cowboy boots, rodeo chaps. These things were showy; he needed something less flamboyant—a cowboy shirt or gunslinger's heavy belt and buckle—just for mood.

Leaving the Chevy around the corner, Tom approached the shop, passing a scruffy boy who was demanding spare change.

"Good with horses?" Tom inquired.

"Huh?" The boy was lean, round-eyed, dumbfounded.

"Are you good with horses? Could you be a stable boy?" Tom demanded, deadpan.

"Go away, man."

Tom eyed the boy for a moment, as if confirming something, and entered the shop. The smell was overpowering: a warm, beefy odor, soured by the sharp reek of tanning and dyeing chemicals, close and musty as a locker room. Feeling engrossed in the work-manship, Tom fingered some rodeo chaps, remembering the movies he'd seen as a boy, then thumbed through a rack of belts. The buckle was the challenge—no trendy peace symbol, just a good Western design. He probed the hanging leather, comparing buckle designs, and chose a prancing brass horse. The leather was broad and deep brown. He was ready.

Climbing back in the Chevy, Tom dropped by a hardware store and purchased a caboose for Alice's electric train. It would come in handy.

WHEN HE REACHED home, he was already wearing the gun-slinger's belt.

"Oh, there you are!" came Marian's greeting, as though he'd been gone for hours.

Passing the dining room, Tom saw envelopes and "Free Huey" leaflets from her new crusade. He had enough meetings and entanglements and, as a federal employee, could not openly campaign for anyone. Though he had some rebel urges that made the Panthers appealing, the thought of Marian campaign-ing for Eldridge Cleaver was dryly funny. Even so, she was en-gaged in the world; that would take some pressure off him.

"How was the hardware store?" she pursued. She'd already begun preparing dinner.

Tom would play good boy. "I found something for Alice." He held up the paper bag with the caboose.

Marian glanced up. "Oh?"

"A new caboose." Tom paused, assuming a look of vague worry. Then with furrowed brow, he peered toward the dining room, where Alice was playing one of her records. "She's on the floor, doing nothing."

"Yes, she's been there for hours." Marian's words sounded vaguely reproachful. He knew her moods; she had some demand in mind. "Playing records, as usual."

He gave a grunt.

"You know, Tom, you should do something with her."

"Such as?"

"I've suggested the Singer's Circle, but you refuse. There must be something you can do together. She's your daughter."

"There's the caboose," Tom proposed, as though he'd just come upon a wonderful idea.

"There's so much to do here," she went on. "The redwood parks sound marvelous. Sabrina knows the good ones."

Tom nodded vaguely.

"Let's plan something for next weekend."

Tom was feeling calm; he would parry.

Then Marian's face clouded. "Damn—Sammy's going off with an older brother and wants Curt along. Well, we can see the redwoods anyway." She glanced closely at Tom, eyebrows up. "Are we sure of Sammy?"

Tom shrugged. "He seems harmless enough."

Raucous sounds were chugging through the house. Through the dining-room door, Tom could see the girl sprawled on the rug. He gave Marian a sharp glance.

"Alice!" she called. "Come here. We're making plans."

Alice leaned in the doorway. "Where's Curt?" she asked.

"Playing baseball. Why?"

"Just wondered."

Curt and Sammy were doing the right thing, Tom thought —becoming independent. Though Marian imagined the boys wandering Telegraph Avenue, her fears were unfounded. The junior high was on Telegraph, that's why they were there. As for Alice, she should be off playing as well. The neighborhood was full of young people—where was the problem? The sun was shining, the weather was great, the schools were embracing progress. Tom was enjoying being ahead of the game: Berkeley had headed off a federal compliance challenge by adopting a voluntary desegregation plan, and having a son and a daughter in the schools was a plus as far as the agency was concerned. He was demanding no more of others than he himself was willing to do. People would cling to neighborhood schools as long as they could obscure the underlying purpose—preserving de facto segregation. Only major demands by the federal government, enforced by the danger of losing funding, would make them budge.

The desegregation plan had placed Alice in a formerly black school on Ashby Avenue, barely two miles away—fifteen minutes by school bus. For all the busing furor coming from the urban North, the arrangement should cause her no problems in the long run. So far, however, she was responding by closing up. There could be many reasons for the change, and it would probably be a few weeks—or longer—before she could say what she was feeling. Though the current signs were ambiguous, she could handle school well enough to overcome any temporary adjustment problems.

Tom would delay the redwoods. The family was no fun; he always ended up feeling responsible for someone else's unhappiness. Marian would never go far in the woods, while Alice would keep to herself. And anyway, by then—presumably—Ginger would have shown him a whole world up in Marin.

Alice wandered off.

"Well," Marian sighed, "let's plan something soon."

Following the girl, Tom passed through the foyer and climbed to the second floor. Marian had completely missed the prancing brass horse; but then, she never imagined him buying anything for himself. Now he would have a look in the full-length mirror in the spare bedroom.

Coming along the second-floor hallway, he reached the spare room, just across from Alice's room. Beyond was the sunporch, where she would be. Closing the door, he eyed himself in the full-length mirror. He should have been taller than five foot nine. Nevertheless, the brass buckle gleamed, half-covered by a fold of workingman's shirt. Casual. Flowing. A lucky charm, a mascot.

Grasping the paper bag with the caboose, Tom crossed the hall and peered through the door of Alice's room. There on a board were her electric trains, the ones he'd been buying since she was four. She was ready for a new car. As he was gazing through the door, remembering the sounds of the train whistle near his boyhood home, Alice came through the glass doors of the sunporch. She saw him and paused, her face somber. He sensed her concealing something.

"How's the old engine?" he asked, unsure of her mood.

"Works good enough." She was wearing bell-bottoms, like the local girls; she glanced away.

Tom rephrased. "The engine can pull all the cars?"

"So far."

Tom swung the paper bag and caboose loosely in one hand. "Do you want to see the redwoods?"

"If you and Mom do," she said, with a shrug.

Tom had supposed as much: she was not pushing for the woods.

"Do you like horses?" he pursued.

"Do I *what*?"

"You know—*horses*?" The mimicry was easy and impromptu; he'd made her frown without meaning to do so. "You have a book—your mother gave you a horse book."

"I never read that one."

"Not interested?"

"I just haven't read it. Are you saying I should?"

"I asked if you liked horses."

"I dunno, I've never seen one." She paused. "Maybe we could have a cat."

Tom held up the bag. "Well, here's a new caboose. I bought it today." Approaching the bed, he placed the paper bag on it, then headed for the door. In the spare room, he opened a window and leaned out. Cool, damp air was coming in. It was early evening, already October. Hearing the whir and whine of an engine coming from Alice's room, Tom gazed over the roofs on a flaming Western sky.

Alice

THE DAY WAS sunny, but as usual her mother was napping as Alice headed for the nearby school, where her brother had met Sammy. The boys had become inseparable, leaving Alice to fend for herself.

The playground was empty. Pondering the tree house and Howard Singer, she imagined going there alone, climbing the steep and secluded path. Tree Frog had flamed through Lincoln School like a comet, leaving a trail of ash. Precocious and assured, he'd refused the boredom and bullying and won. But for her, things were getting worse. A few boys had begun making smacking sounds as she passed in the hallways; they were precocious in other ways. For some reason—confusion, anger, fear of being blamed—she was keeping her problems secret, especially since Mr. Boyd's scolding. Though she'd had no warning, such things would go on happening.

Pausing under a dense tree, she reached for a low-lying

frond. She was remembering a gangly, redheaded boy pushing over a desk. Amazingly, Tree Frog's parents had rewarded their son's mutiny. She imagined doing the same—but no, her father would never go along. He would blame her, saying everyone should have the same chance; he'd already suggested as much when she'd come close to revealing the hassles at school.

Tree Frog's parents were professors; when he was older, he would follow physics and psychology the way she followed underdogs.

Alice approached Bancroft Way, bordering the campus. She could see the Campanile bell tower; it reminded her of the Washington Monument, only closer, less intimidating. She would go there soon, but for now the energy was flowing toward Sproul Plaza, and so she followed, falling in behind a group of longhaired young people. Older than her and Curt but younger than her parents, they belonged to an uncanny category of strangers brought close by the faces she'd seen on album covers. Mingling with them, she passed the raucous drummers by the edge of Sproul Plaza and became one of the crowd. No one seemed bothered by her incongruous presence; no one suggested that she leave. Even so, the swirl of young adults, the hippies gathered on the steps of the Student Union, the leafleting longhairs made her feel that she'd crossed a border and was now trespassing. The campus buildings, too, like the federal buildings in Washington, had an unimagined purpose scarcely belonging to her. Yet she'd found her way here—it was as if she'd passed through a door in the Rayson house and found a hubbub . . . a merging . . . heaven or hell. If only she would dare.

The sun shone blindingly in her face. The space engulfed her as a Romanesque building blotted out the Campanile. A bearded man was coming through the crowd bearing an armload of papers, and as the Campanile bells rang a clumsy melody, he glanced up and rushed on. Following along the enormous length of the Romanesque facade, she rounded a corner and soon found herself in a small glade. Several people lay reading; a man was wandering barefoot. The barefoot man was bearded and bare-chested and had a suffering face, reminding her of a face she'd seen in a painting in the museum in Washington. He was blowing bubbles.

Leaving the glade, Alice wandered east, passing several older halls. The Campanile could be seen above the campus buildings. Soon she could see a slope rising beyond the border of the campus. She was far from where she'd come in and feeling very confused.

The Campanile was ringing noon.

She crossed a road and headed uphill. Howard Singer's tree house would be there, somewhere . . .

After a long climb, she emerged on a wooded hill above a Greek-style amphitheater. She was surrounded by golden grasses, whose feathery seeds were borne on the wind. Eucalyptus fronds, giving off pungent odors, swayed in the languorous air rising from the bay. Crescents of dry foliage formed a treacherous ground cover. She climbed slowly, using roots and bare earth for footing.

Approaching a eucalyptus tree, she fingered some bark that hung in parchment folds from the soaring trunk. Further up, the slope reached a road and leveled off. She was alone, overlooking the grove and, far below, amphitheater, Campanile, bay, and beyond. Wandering beneath the canopy, she was suffused with a sense of freedom.

Then, emerging from some hanging branches, came two men. They were coming up the hill. She moved camouflaged among hanging fronds as the men—in worn Levi's and wearing caps—waded through tinder-dry grasses.

Shoulder-high, the grasses flowed over the open spaces in sunburned waves of grain.

The men rose up the hill. Soon they were concealed once more by canopy. She could hear them now, laughing. Leaning on a eucalyptus trunk, cool as parchment, she surveyed the glimmering bay. Then she descended the path.

Tom

HE COULD WEAR jeans to work on a Saturday—who would say no? He closed the door of the spare bedroom, though Marian was asleep, her usual morning thing. He fingered a long white sleeve, then changed his mind and chose the rough working-man's blue. He'd be working, in a way. Pushing the rough cloth down the unfastened jeans and along his thighs, he closed the fly and buckled the prancing-horse belt. It pressed on him like a brand. He wondered what Ginger would say.

Marian could sleep for hours. He would be away for dinner, or so he'd warned her, saying he had a long day's work in San Francisco, though Sunday would be free. There was a World Series game each day; missing the Saturday game was bad enough, he'd complained, as though he had no choice.

Not long before, Marian had been amusing herself by demanding personal confidences from him. The game had been to make him reveal himself. So one evening he'd made up a story, something about a woodshed—there had been none—and masturbation. He'd been found by his mother, he told Marian, and rushed to a psychologist. Marian had smiled at the folly. "How old were you?" she asked. "I thought all boys do that."

"Seven."

"You were doing those things at seven?" Her tone was high and alarmed.

"Well, maybe more like eleven."

"Oh." She'd seemed reassured. "Women rarely have such stories."

"No?"

"Good heavens, Tom."

Ginger would help with the alibi—she would be good that way, he thought, as he imagined her teasing smile.

They had made plans over lunch, with Tom proposing dropping by her apartment and Ginger then naming the corner of Arguello and California, a few blocks away. They would be near an army base and in easy reach of the Golden Gate Bridge. From there, he would chauffeur them to the ranch in Marin. One of the horses was preparing for an endurance race, and Tom would be doing a favor by riding her, sparing the ranch hand a day on horseback. Tom had never supposed he would go so far by horse—over some low hills and then running on the beach. "Cassandra's used to greenhorn riders," Ginger had assured him, in her teasing tone. "She won't take advantage the way some horses do." Tom had scarcely seen a horse, much less been near enough for the animal to abuse an advantage. Even so, Ginger had her plans, and he would be ready. He'd been imagining the scene: though the ocean would be chilly for swimming, they could wade in the surf. There would be lunch by the shore, some galloping, maybe a shady grove. Surely the horses could amuse themselves for an hour.

Nearing Arguello, feeling a damp line developing along his jaw though the day was cool and dry, Tom could see the dome of a synagogue. Beyond the dome rose glimmering groves of eucalyptus, overhanging the bay and Golden Gate; the army base would be on the far slope, facing the ocean and the incoming enemy. Then, as Tom was musing, a royal-red hood loomed in the mirror, sporty and low: a Mustang. He heard the sound of Ginger's horn.

"I'm carrying the saddles," she was saying as she came up alongside. Her eyes were gray-green and archly commanding; her hair had a fresh wave. She wore a pale-blue cowboy blouse with ruffled cuffs; her glossy fingernails were posed on the steering wheel. "There's a parking space around the corner on Cornwall Street. You can leave your car for the day."

So, she was hauling her gear around. He wondered where the riding saddles would go in a San Francisco apartment—hardly the living room. Maybe she had a porch or a dressing room, or—who could say?—maybe the bedroom would do.

In any case, she'd planned on taking her car. Usually he would have maneuvered around such a plan, but Ginger left no room for that. "We'll have to hurry," she called as he leaned from the Chevy. "Fog's coming in soon."

Tom glanced up. The sky was a depthless blue, no clouds anywhere; but the autumn weather was unfamiliar.

As he lowered himself through the Mustang's passenger door, he heard her say, "Well, cowboy, I guess you're ready."

So, she'd seen the prancing horse.

Tom rarely rode in the passenger seat. They were passing through a neighborhood of elegant homes, grander than the ones they'd seen from the cab on curvy Lombard Street. Suddenly the car passed under a grove of eucalyptus.

"We're in the Presidio," Ginger said, smiling. "You'd never know it's an army base."

Tom was awed. They were surrounded by plunging canyons leading to the Golden Gate: here was no dreary Fort Leavenworth, where he'd done an army tour. As the road looped around and began descending, Ginger placed the car in low gear, her hand pulling lightly on the lever, her forefinger flexed as though for display. Tom glanced down, admiring her long and shapely fingers. When he looked up, a panorama lay before them of harbor and bay and far-off, foggy Marin. Soon they were on a freeway heading over the bridge. Though he'd been there for several months, Tom had never gunned the Chevy up and over the span. The cables hung tautly in the morning sun as the roadway curved up, coyly approaching. The glimmering bay in the east and ocean haze opening west announced endless morning: a whole day lay before them. They made the crossing under an easy lull, as though unaware of a changing mood. Soon a tunnel loomed ahead, enclosed by colored arches; passing under the rainbow, they were engulfed in a roaring mechanical light.

Tom could see how much Ginger enjoyed managing the day. As the tunnel receded and golden hills loomed, she gave him some background on the ranch, glancing over now and then to gauge his response. It was the familiar stuff of government planning. Several years before, the ranch and other farms in the area had been bought up for the state parks. The farmers had been encouraged to remain, leasing the land for a nominal fee, so the agricultural economy would endure. As for the ranch, the former owners had preferred to leave, and a woman named Julia had been found to replace them, maintaining the land and allowing some public access—such as boarding horses for folks from San Francisco.

Soon they abandoned the freeway for a winding lane passing through a suburban development. As the road began climbing, Tom glanced around on elegant woodland refuges surrounded by redwood and eucalyptus. Ginger was regaling him and laughing, and he supposed she was covering for some nervousness. That was a good thing, he thought, enjoying the sound of her giddy monologue.

The road wound through dry hills and then dropped down the western slope. Ginger drove them north along the shore, following a ribbon of sand and marsh and lagoon, a wild and lonely place separating ocean and rugged canyons. As they were leaving the lagoon, the land opened up. Soon they came upon a road leading west and south, along the far side of the lagoon.

Ginger glanced west. "There's a small peninsula and a village—Bolinas. Would you care to see?"

Tom nodded yes.

They drove along the peninsula. The road headed west past some houses and then a main drag—a bar, a cafe, a general store.

"Bolinas was a boom town years ago," Ginger informed him. "Then the lagoon filled in and they closed the port. Now people come here when they're running away to a rural place. The area is unincorporated—no local government, no police force."

"And no making hay," Tom joked.

"No, but they can get by cheaply. Some end up in Bolinas because welfare pays more here than in San Francisco." Her eyes scanned the porch of the general store, pausing on a scruffy threesome. "Some people sure can work the welfare system—others have family money, though you'd never guess."

Tom nodded. During his forays along Telegraph Avenue, he'd wondered how many of those young people were sponging on government programs for the poor. What everyone was calling "the counterculture" was hardly more than another unforeseen spinoff from Johnson's war on poverty. The random idleness bothered him more than the urban revolts. He wondered how well a person could get by on sponging out here—or in San Francisco.

Ginger flashed a smile. "You remember what the Commissioner had to say—'A great plumber is more admirable than an incompetent philosopher.'"

Tom pondered. "And?"

"Well, maybe these folks should go ahead and be plumbers, rather than imagining they're philosophers."

A bedraggled young man wandered toward the car, followed by a dog. Ginger slowed to let them pass.

"That fellow there," Tom said. "I say he'd be a bad philosopher and a bad plumber, too. There should be some way of determining if he's a good dropout, eh?"

Ginger gave a knowing laugh. They wound through a lane and headed back toward the coast highway.

"Ever see these problems back home?" he asked her.

"We have farm workers, rural poor—but they're real people. Helping the genuinely poor is one thing. The government should be doing that. But the ones here—"

"Surely a small group, no?"

"Why, Tom, they're all over Telegraph Avenue."

"How many—a few hundred?"

"More. And have you seen Haight-Ashbury?"

Tom glanced over, feigning offense.

"I never go there," she added. "But last summer, people poured in by the thousands. They came for the 'Summer of Love' in Golden Gate Park, and now they won't leave."

"How long can they keep going?"

"For years, if they're on the dole. And now they're everywhere—San Francisco, Berkeley, even up here." She paused. "Look over there, Tom." Following her gaze, Tom saw a deep meadow leading to a farmhouse and a red barn, something from a postcard or a children's jigsaw puzzle. "We're here."

"Oh my."

Ginger headed up a long gravel driveway through some dry stubble. As they reached the fence, she stopped the Mustang.

"How about opening the gate, Tom?"

He climbed from the car, then jogged up and fumbled with the latch. The wide aluminum gate swung open in a pendulum arc. As the car purred through the gate, he heard her calling, "Make sure it's closed all the way."

While Tom was closing the gate, she pulled around and parked by the barn. The farmhouse rose nearby, as though watching over them.

Ginger dragged a saddle from the trunk, leaving the other for Tom. Halfway to the barn, she called over her shoulder, "Hurry up, Tom, fog's coming in!"

Leaning in and grasping the other saddle, he saw a pair of shiny black riding boots and a lady's silver-handled whip. The boots conformed closely to the shape of the calf; reaching above the knee, they lay in mid-gesture, like the legs of a mannequin. They reminded him of the fox-hunting Englishmen Marian had shown him in one of her museums. He gazed toward the barn, wondering if Ginger would be using the boots and whip. While he was mulling over the problem, she emerged from the barn.

"Tom, would you bring my boots?" she called.

Balancing the saddle on one arm, he grasped the boots. Lifting them from the trunk, he lowered his hand on the hood and slammed it closed. Then, dangling boots and stirrups, he approached the barn door, where she lingered, eyeing him; in one hand and over her shoulder looped a tangle of leather straps. Tom could already smell the horses. There was the heavy stench of manure; then as he came closer he encountered a warm, humid smell, enclosed and musty like a locker room, the press of many working animals in a small space. Hanging over it all was the sweet, pungent odor of hay.

Ginger led him along a row of stalls, passing the rumps of horses. Above each stall hung a small board branded with a name. As she paused under one of the boards, Tom looked up and read "Haley." Over the edge of the stall leaned a long nose and jaw, chewing methodically through a mouthful of hay. The saddle was slung over a nearby trestle.

"Well, hello, Haley," sang Ginger, as one would speak to a baby or perhaps a dog.

The horse's ears responded to her sounds even as the jaw persevered in the chewing. Ginger drew a carrot from her pocket and, laying it in her palm, brought it toward the horse's mouth. The enormous jaw went on chewing for a few moments and then, in a grasping gesture that made Tom flinch, scooped up the carrot, crunching loudly, and recommenced chewing.

Ginger headed back along the row and through the low door of a shed, and Tom found himself alone among the horses and the smells.

He'd made only one other jaunt to a farm. He was a boy, and they were going all the way to Columbus to visit his grandparents, old people he'd never seen, stopping by a farm on the way for peaches and apples. While his mother was looking over the peaches, Tom had wandered through the door of a cavernous red barn. In the gloom, he'd passed along a row of stalls among overpowering smells and, turning a corner, found a stable boy grooming a horse. He'd been dumbfounded by the animal, and as he was backing away, something leaped and clung to his pant leg. Then he jumped, and a large thing bounded away and through a hole in the floor. He'd run crying from the barn and been scolded for trespassing.

Ginger came from the shed wearing sleek English riding pants and the black riding boots. She'd slung a saddle pad over her shoulder. "You can help me saddle up Haley, and then we can show you Cassandra," she said, her smile promising an alluring surprise. Tom was feeling like a rookie; even so, he was ready. "How about handing me the saddle," Ginger prompted, as she placed the pad on the horse.

Tom handed over the saddle and observed her hands as she leaned in, adjusting the horn high on the horse's shoulders and pulling a leather thong around the taut bulge of the belly, then looping the thong through two brass rings.

"You want it snug but not tight," she commented as she worked. Tom was feeling eager as he heard her saying, "C'mon, let's see Cassandra."

Cassandra was around the corner, near the equipment shed. Ginger showed him just where to place the saddle and how to fasten the thong. Tom eyed Cassandra's mouth as Ginger put on the bridle, clamping the bit between the horse's teeth. Thankfully, he was not asked to feed her carrots.

They led the horses from the barn. Before Tom could see how she'd managed the maneuver, Ginger had mounted her horse and sat, gazing down on him from the saddle. Tom grasped Cassandra's reins; she jerked her head, then tugged stubbornly, already heading for the gate. Tom braced himself for a tug-of-war with an animal several times his size.

"Want some help?" Ginger's eyes sparkled as she glanced down her long nose.

Tom enjoyed a good challenge, and she'd been sure to arrange one. "Yes," he responded simply.

"C'mon, cowboy, you're supposed to be watching."

"You're just too fast for me, lady." The word popped up, warming his face.

"Steady her, Tom. Get your foot in the stirrup—there, that's it—grasp the horn, and boost yourself up. Grab her mane if it helps. She won't mind."

In a moment Tom found himself swinging one leg over the horse, as she gave a stomp. Cassandra was a handsome mare—a red dun, Ginger called her—and larger than Haley. Now that Tom was in the saddle, the horse paused calmly while he fumbled for the stirrups.

"She won't give you problems," Ginger was saying. "She has a good temperament. And you were a football player, right?"

"Yes, a safety." Though strong, he was small for college ball, even at an Ivy; he'd quit after sophomore year. But he'd played all the same.

"Then you're ready for anything. Look, here's how you hold the reins." She held up her palm, extending thumb and forefingers as he'd seen her do before and laying the reins across. "Keep them loose. No need to pull—she understands commands. And if she's slow, tap your heels. Cassandra won't take off; but if she does, just grab her mane. But don't worry, she's a good girl—aren't you, Cassandra?"

The horse wagged her head, as though shaking off a fly.

"The rules sound easy enough," Tom said. "Now let's see if I can follow them."

Ginger led them around the farmhouse and through a gate. Beyond the gate was a line of rolling green hills. The land appeared to be pasture, but Tom couldn't be sure. He murmured about how pleasant the place was, as if he'd always yearned for a rural retreat; Ginger responded by naming some wildflower plants—blue blossom and coffeeberry, coyote mint and golden aster, though only the aster was in bloom—and giving him riding tips. "Heels down, Tom. No grazing—let her know who's in control."

Tom followed Ginger's commands as well as he could, but Cassandra showed a stubborn eagerness for the bushes by the path, especially the blooming aster. Swaying and bobbing her muzzle as they passed, she grabbed at the plants, dragging on the fronds and then, with a yank, tearing them loose. Rendered superfluous by the grazing animal, Tom was forced to clamber down and, bracing and pulling hard on the reins, haul her jaws from a coffeeberry bush. The enormous brown eye glared sullenly as he struggled. When she'd finally been strong-armed from the coffeeberry, her head gave a wild, snorting shake as her rear hoof landed in a petulant stomp, before she regained her calm and stood, ready to resume, the unreadable eye staring into Tom's. He mounted and they continued along the path.

The path led across the road. Tom heard a clopping sound on the asphalt, and soon they entered the woods, heading west toward the beach. The path was narrow—no fire road, as he'd expected; it wound along a streambed, then turned up through coastal hills. Climbing, the horses broke into a slow run, and Tom soon found himself fending off low-hanging branches. He rode with one hand loose on the reins—Cassandra ignored any commands he gave—and the other over his forehead, as a shield. More than once, he had no chance to fend off the approaching branches and was forced to duck. Ginger rode ahead, glancing back now and then to make sure he was keeping up. When the path opened in a small clearing, she dropped back alongside him. "Go on ahead, Tom. She's dragging her feet. Usually the lead horse will keep a good pace."

The climb continued, now with Tom in the lead. Cassandra was moving with greater force and willingness.

"Let out the reins," Ginger called. "She knows the path."

The reins slid through his palms and then, like the rolling of a wave, the horse gathered up her hind legs and bolted into a run. Tom was flummoxed. Branches were hurling by. He pulled hard on the reins and nearly fell, before grabbing the horn and regaining a semblance of balance. In that way, he reached the top of the ridge; a long, gently sloping path opened up below.

Tom wondered how closely Ginger had followed, but there was no chance to turn and look as they began the descent. Finally he gave up and dug his hands in the horse's mane. Cassandra was running down the gradual slope at a smooth and easy gallop, and in a mile or so, with a final push they emerged from the forest on a broad, sandy beach. There they came to a halt, Cassandra panting as a warm damp smell of barn rose from her. She gave a loud snort; moments later, Haley appeared, tossing her head and prancing through the sand. Ginger was flushed and smiling.

Now that the ordeal was over, Tom was feeling charged up. "Someone let the horse out of the barn," he called.

"I never thought she'd run away with you. Were you able to manage?"

"Oh my, yes. We had a good run."

Tom looked along the beach. He assumed they would dismount and leave the horses; he would prefer being alone with Ginger. Along the edge of the woods the land rose in a sandbar; and from the sandbar the beach sloped down to the ocean surf. Haley and Ginger led the way through the deep sands. The waves were high and crashing. As Cassandra lagged, nosing some seaweed, Haley waded through waterlogged sand for a hundred yards and then, tossing her mane, cantered back toward Tom.

"We've gone four miles," Ginger called. Tom had supposed more; it had been hard to tell. "Ready for lunch?"

"Oh yes, very ready."

"I should say so, after that run."

They rode toward a grove of low wax-myrtle trees by the border of the woods. When they had dismounted, Ginger showed Tom how to fasten the reins to a branch. Then she untied a bag of sourdough and salami from her saddle. A large driftwood log lay nearby. Perched on the log, Ginger opened a Scout knife and began slicing some salami and bread. Tom had brought a small flask of brandy, and he wondered whether he should offer some to Ginger. Though he thought she would probably refuse, he wanted some for himself. He pulled the flask from a jeans pocket.

"Brandy?"

"Why, Tom, you know I plumb forgot the lemonade."

"Have some then."

"No—you go ahead. I'm making the sandwiches."

When they were done, they sat sharing the flask, looking across sand and ocean. A wind was gusting offshore; Tom supposed it would be going on two o'clock.

"That horse enjoys a good run," Tom remarked.

Ginger laughed. "I told you she's an endurance horse."

"So she thought I was an endurance rider?"

"She thought you'd go along."

"I see."

"A few more days in the saddle and you'll do fine."

"Oh my, a real Californian."

"I bet you were bored by those stuffy people back East," she teased.

"I sure was."

"People here go away on weekends," she continued. "They have things to do."

She leaned away to put the wrappings back in the saddlebag, and when she'd finished, seemed to come in closer. The beach was cool and windy, ending in a steely blue. He wondered if there were any sheltered areas but, glancing around, thought probably not. Suddenly he held her hand and she allowed him, though seeming hardly aware of the touch.

"How about a walk down the beach?" she suggested.

They left the shaded log and wandered toward the surf. He'd never learned how old she was but supposed somewhere near thirty. He wondered if she'd been seeing someone—how else would she know of so many places to go?—and why she was pursuing, if that was the term, a family man. Maybe she'd had no man in her life; would she know how to have a simple affair? Or would she demand that he free himself from Marian? But that was getting ahead of things.

Tom suddenly grasped her arm, pulled her to him, and kissed her hard on the mouth. She yielded for a moment and then moved away.

"Can't leave the horses alone for long," he heard her say. Then she added, "We could have dinner before we go back. There's a place in Bolinas."

So, she was in no real hurry. They'd just had lunch; the sun was high over the water. Near them by the water's edge three seagulls followed the receding surf, darting around clumps of seaweed. Another gull was hovering overhead. Tom and Ginger passed surf-borne branches, bleached and smelling of rotting seaweed. Along the shallows the stuff lay in rubbery vines, held afloat by vegetable fins and air bladders. Tom had removed his shoes during lunch; he was enjoying the feel of wet sand underfoot. He'd never camped on a beach, even as a boy; surely the sounds and smells would make all the difference. Ahead of them to the south was a fog bank, concealing the meeting of land and water. Tom slowed down and glanced toward Ginger.

"My, my," he remarked.

"It's lovely."

There was a pause, and she moved away.

Tom followed, aroused, but Ginger was already leading him back. They were heading for the grove of trees, the horses, the run through the woods. As they approached the horses, he could see Haley's ears moving around. Nearby, Cassandra was tearing at the lower branches of a wax-myrtle tree. Tom came up on her left, sensing her steamy, pungent heat, and found himself looking over the sopping haunches into Ginger's eyes. Her cheeks were flushed from wind and sun, her eyes an ocean color, gray-green and flecked with brown. Behind her the woods lay in shadow. They would be soothing after the beach and the gleaming sun, unforgiving as the stadium lights during an evening game.

FOR DINNER, THEY had beer and fish and chips in a Bolinas cafe. Then they followed the road unfurling like an idle ribbon bordering the narrow lagoon. Beyond the lagoon the western ocean lay illumined, like a vast and vacant stage beneath the gloaming of a candle. Wooded hills rose to the east, where the moon shone nearly full above the trees. Ginger parked the car by

the side of the road and they got out. Tom heard the murmur of
a stream flowing through a culvert under the road and into the
lagoon, spreading before them in a liquid plane, a stagnant expanse choked by reeds and the broad floating leaves of water
lilies. Shadowy light gathered on the dull surface, as though the
moon lay imprisoned in the depths below. Tom heard the cry of
a seagull overhead, followed by the soft lapping of water. He
looked out across the lagoon to the far shore darkening in an
elemental streak, sands and foam stretching forever forth. Tom
glanced at her face, illumined by the same moon that shone dully
in the watery mass. The seagull sounded its cry, dropping in
slow arrow's flight along the water's rim.

"Peaceful, isn't it?" Her voice sounded in the warm, breezeless
air, like a penny tossed into a tranquil pool far below a waterfall.
"They say folks used to raise ducks here for the San Francisco
market."

When they were back in the car, Tom rolled down the window and looked out across the dimming lagoon.

"If you come again, you can ride Champion."

He turned and saw her profile against the dark, massy woods
across the road.

"That's the palomino stallion they've got. He rode dressage
when he was younger."

Tom murmured a vague reply; he could not remember having
seen the stallion. They had passed the lagoon and were entering a
wooded, winding stretch of road. The headlights glided among
trees like the beams of a search-and-rescue party, illuminating a
halo of low trunks and smudges of hillside. Tom remembered the
path and the galloping horse beneath him. From time to time he
could make out the contours of the ground or the leaves of a
bush, gleaming into life and then gone. He wondered what lay
beyond the foreshortened headlights.

The road was now passing canyons. Near the dead center of a
sharp curve they had slowed, nearly stopped, when Tom saw a
boulder glaring suddenly on the outer rim of the road. It hung
there; then it was swallowed by darkness and matted underbrush.
Through the trees came shuttered flashes like a porch lamp seen
through a picket fence, and then an oncoming car sped toward
them around a bend, followed by two others coming close on.

The cars passed on; they were once more alone.

"In the old days, they had beef and dairy ranches and a ferry to San Francisco," Ginger was saying. "Up by the ranch, there were a hundred Jersey cows only a few years ago."

"Oh my."

"There was even a copper mine. During the war, some army men came over to keep an eye on things. There were rumors of Japanese, wearing blue denim and passing as farmers. Trying, anyway."

"You mean there's more than blue denim involved?"

"There sure is."

The road had reached another canyon, crossing a stone bridge and plunging through a blur of fog, dense and glowing, illuminating itself alone. The car jerked to a halt. Ahead in the blur Tom saw two shiny spots, like silver dollars gleaming from the bottom of a sunny pool. As he stared, they seemed to blink and then swivel to one side before vanishing in the darkness. "Deer?"

"Could be. Or maybe elk."

She waited for another deer or elk, and when none came, slowly started up. The road was climbing along the other wall of the canyon; as Tom turned, he saw that the fog had thinned and he now gazed upon a wide expanse sloping toward the sea. Low fingers of fog snaked among the hollows of the hills. Tom was gazing from the window on the slope, mysterious and immense, when the road careened around a curve and dropped down among a grove of trees, where it wandered for some ways before ascending again and emerging upon an open summit.

Ginger found a pullout and parked the car. Bare and unadorned except for patches of shrub laurel, the earth fell away from the road. Tom smelled damp dust. Fog hung in the canyons below, as they stood together in the windless hour of night among the secrets of the ridge. Tom took her hand, drew her to him, and kissed her.

Then he stood, hearing the soothing hum of far-off surf and thinking of farms and villages nestled far below.

"Seems awfully dry for farming."

"Only in late summer and autumn." She paused. "I used to love seeing the stars on the farm."

Tom was surprised to find them there, in vast numbers, though he'd rarely seen or thought about them. But Ginger, it seemed, had always remembered them.

Before long, they approached the bridge crossing, and soon they entered San Francisco, passing through the Presidio. They reached the corner where Tom had parked the car.

"See you on Monday, Tom," she chimed as he opened the door.

"Oh yes."

She sped away.

Soon he was heading for the Bay Bridge, passing through the clogged streets of Chinatown. Paper lampshades hung from awnings. Barrels loomed in doorways. By the curb, men unloaded goods for a wholesale noodle company. From the seeming chaos, some form of synergy emerged as they worked. Soon the Chevy was passing Joy Long Garden, where some boys ran among the crowd. Glancing through the doors of Joy Long, Tom saw large family groups and maroon-clad staff. Through the doors emerged an elderly couple, then some women and girls, followed by a man and a young boy. The man was spare and wispy, in loose-hanging trousers; the boy hung back by the curb, eyeing the goods on a woman's cart. People were the same everywhere, Tom thought, as the lane began moving. By the Dragon Palace, he saw a white couple passing the doorway, the woman in furs and blonde cascade. Then the paper lampshades gave way, edged out by photographs of pinup girls under flashing red and white lights.

Traffic was flowing smoothly up the ramp and over the Bay Bridge as Tom followed an Oldsmobile wagon carrying some boys in back. He would manage things. Ginger was good, he would hang on for more. Her gray-green eyes rose in his mind, teasing and close over the horse's back. She would lead, as she'd already done. So far there was no hurry. He was enjoying the suspense of seeing where things could go, if only he could hang on and ride.

He glanced down: nearly nine o'clock. Ginger had been so engaging, the ranch and landscape so real, that he'd forgotten about an alibi. He'd dream up something by morning. In the meantime, he could drop comments on the day. They'd ordered sandwiches on sourdough, of course. Among his colleagues, only Jim Kaczmarek, from Cleveland, had complained about missing the game—no one else was cheering for the Tigers or the Cards. Claire knew only that her husband was a Dodgers fan, a Brooklyn guy who never gave up. And Ginger? Tigers, presumably, but she was working in another area these days . . .

Tom was passing bungalows along Ashby Avenue, with stubble lawns and old Fords by the curb. Soon he saw an empty schoolyard, the building looming in the background—Alice's school, Lincoln. A woman ambled by the high fence, a girl hanging on her hand and a boy straggling behind. Beyond the fence, as the traffic signal changed to green, he slowed by a liquor store. A Coors logo shone in the window. Three black men in jeans were leaning against the plate glass; above them the Marlboro Man rode a bucking bronco.

Tom had been there before. Three years ago, he'd begun an affair with a friend of Marian's, but before long the woman had messed up and let something drop. He'd done damage control but there'd been no going on. He and Ginger would be more careful; they would handle things.

College Avenue was dead, closed up for the night. Tom was nearly home and should be resolving on a course. For now, though, he could always sow confusion. The children, for example, had begun evading house rules by wandering around alone. Take Alice—for she would be home. She'd begun wandering all day, going off on her bicycle. She must be leaving it somewhere—on campus or near Telegraph.

He parked the Chevy by the house. Someone was on the couch, probably reading, and the windows glowed. So, Marian was enjoying an evening alone. Alice, of course, would be in her room playing the phonograph. Good—he would bring up her wandering far from the house, he would show annoyance and concern.

Tom paused on the lawn, glancing up. From Marian's aimless pose, one hand propping her head, he supposed she was deep in one of her imaginary worlds. That was just as well, for he'd planned poorly—the muddy pants, the horsey smell. He should have brought a change of clothes in the car. Moving away from the window, he examined his jeans and found sand and mud. Bending over, he cleaned the cuffs as well as he could with his stubby fingernails. Then he rubbed his fingers in the grass. As for the sneakers, they were old and already thoroughly worn. He was damp under the arms, but that was no problem as long as he could change before Marian came close.

Tom entered the house. Peering from the foyer, he saw Alice's somber eyes looking at him from her mother's place on the couch. Ah well, she would be easy to manage.

"My, my, you're still up." Tom spoke evenly.

"I'm reading."

"Where's your mother?"

"In the bedroom, I guess."

Tom moved back from the doorway, away from the lamp. He was already heading for the stairs when he heard Alice.

"I was wondering . . ."

Tom paused in the foyer, hoping she would hurry. He needed to go up and change before anyone came close.

"Yes?"

"Could we see the park tomorrow?"

"The park?"

"Yes, the one in the hills."

"Why?"

"I've never been there." She paused for a response, then glanced away. "Some girls from school go there."

"Are you going only because other girls do?"

"No."

"What does your mother say?"

"She says I should ask you."

"I'm planning on watching the game."

Aware of giving off a horsey odor, Tom hung on, assuming she would soon concede. Then he could go up and change in the spare room. Glancing up, ready for the escape, he found himself caught as Marian appeared on the landing, wearing her day clothes. She was coming down.

"Oh, Tom, you're back."

"Why is she demanding we go to the park?"

"Who's demanding?"

Tom gave a nod.

"I thought she'd gone to bed."

"I'm reading," came Alice's cry.

Then in the ensuing confusion, Tom moved away as Marian passed through the foyer.

Responding to the brewing unhappiness, Marian barely glanced at him. Tom slipped away; he was safe.

Alice

ALICE LOOKED UP, feeling abashed—they'd interrupted her mother's reading.

"So, was there a response?"

"Yes."

"Well?"

"He's planning on the game."

"And your brother's with Sammy." Her mother came from the foyer, her mind seemingly elsewhere. "I knew your father would want to see the game. The Tigers haven't won a World Series since—oh, ages ago. I remember my father following the winning game on the radio. Men surely do love baseball." She smiled at Alice as though sharing some secret of human nature, and then changed gears. "What do the girls do in the park?"

"I don't know, Mom. I've never been there."

"You and I could always go."

Alice looked down at her book, wondering why her mother was always proposing things she never meant to do.

"What have you got there?" her mother inquired.

"The one you gave me." It was about a white man who'd made himself appear black, to see what people would do, how the world would change. He was having an adventure, in a sense, though far from the scary *Fellowship of the Ring*. Even so, she wondered how the world would change, if she could be somebody else—a boy, for example.

"Do you suppose he's coming back down?" her mother wondered. "Has he had any dinner?"

"How should I know?"

The phone rang in the kitchen. "When he comes down, would you please ask?" And her mother headed for the back of the house.

Soon she heard movement and her father came through the doorway. He'd gone for a pipe, and he'd exchanged jeans and blue workman's shirt for even more casual shorts and T-shirt. She was sorry he'd changed: now that he had more hair, the jeans gave him a Marlboro Man look that made him seem young and cool.

Her father found a place on the couch. Letting himself down in a slouch, he propped his legs on the coffee table.

"Can you get there on your bike? The park?"

"No." What was he suggesting? She'd thought the subject was closed.

"Oh? Why not?"

"It's too far and too steep."

"You seem to enjoy some very long rides."

Alice sensed a trap but was unsure where it lay: the park, the bike, making him go somewhere, going somewhere on her own . . . "I took a walk today."

"Oh? Where?"

"Around the campus."

"You enjoy walking, do you?"

Her father unfolded the newspaper and began leafing through it. She could see the bare legs and feet; the pipe was propped nearby. She was sure he had something on his mind, but what?

"About the park," he began. Then rumpling the paper, he scanned some headlines. "Who's going to win the game tomorrow, eh?" he asked, closing the paper and leaving it in his lap.

"Dunno. The Tigers?"

"Could be . . ." He appeared to be contemplating the odds. "Well, I'm planning on watching the game. If you want to go to the park, your mother's going to have to take you." He reached for the pipe.

"I don't have to go."

"You seem awfully eager."

"I suggested it, that's all."

Clamping the pipe in his mouth, he fingered a match, scraping it along the box so that it flamed. Alice was no longer reading, or feigning to do so; she made no move as, holding the flame over the bowl, he inhaled and glanced up, blowing smoke.

"Where do you leave your bicycle when you're on Telegraph? In one of those racks?"

"I don't go to Telegraph."

"Mmm?" Smoke curled from his mouth.

"Mom told me not to go there alone."

"I know."

"So—"

"Are you doing as your mother says?"

"I wasn't on Telegraph," she repeated, annoyed.

"Oh? Just the campus?"

Her mother appeared in the doorway. "Are we still arguing about the park?"

"No, Telegraph."

Her mother had a ready response. "You're way too young for that scene. Unless you're with one of us."

"Yes, I know."

"Then why are you bothering your father?" Suddenly absorbed in some grown-up problem, she turned to him. "That was Sabrina. There was a Peace and Freedom caucus today. They've amended the platform."

Her father made no reply.

"They've resolved to include the Black Panther demand that the Oakland Police Department be banned from the ghetto and replaced by men from the community."

He glanced up. "Are they so wrong about that?"

"I was hoping you'd go to a caucus and have some words with those young men. You're so much more informed about the law than they are. If someone like you refuses to show them the problems with so-called community policing—groups of young men with guns settling matters among themselves—then who will?"

"'Support your local police,'" her father intoned, mouthing a Party slogan. "That's what they say in Alabama. And if community policing's good enough for Alabama, it's good enough for black people in Oakland. Anyway, it's one more formal resolution meaning nothing—"

"But Dan and Shel are so thoroughly persuaded," her mother argued. "They demand withdrawal as if referring to an occupying army. Does that really make sense to you?"

"Well, call them what you want, but there's an appalling use of force," Alice heard her father respond with unusual feeling.

"So you support those young men?"

"No, but they're responding to a real problem."

"I know that, Tom, but I'm concerned about the way they're responding."

"Then you should have spoken up," he countered sharply.

"But you have the knowledge of the law. You're with the federal government, after all. They would hear you before they heard me."

Sparring had begun. Though Alice was unfamiliar with what they were discussing, the tone had clearly changed. Now she felt her mother's eyes on her and glanced up. Her mother looked away.

"Tom, would you mind opening some wine?"

He rose and took a heavy bottle and two long-stemmed glasses from a cupboard. The household had few rituals; for that reason, Alice enjoyed the one that was unfolding. Usually something fun would ensue.

Her father fumbled in a drawer, then glanced inquiringly at her mother, who had taken a place on the couch.

"I suppose it's in the kitchen."

He headed for the hall.

"On the counter, Tom," she called.

On the couch, her mother began leafing through one of the magazines she'd brought home from the Party headquarters.

"Do you suppose your father's seen these photographs in *Ramparts*?" she mused. "If so, I wonder what he has to say," she added, glancing at Alice, as though seeking support.

Soon he reappeared, bearing glasses of red wine. Alice saw her mother glance at him, then place the magazine on the coffee table. She was clearly pondering something.

"You know, Tom, I'm having some qualms. So is Sabrina— that's why she called." She shook her head. "I'm annoyed to admit it, but I'm feeling . . . bamboozled. Can we really have groups of armed men threatening lawmakers? Here's an essay by one of the Panther lawyers, defending the armed march on the California State Assembly." She paused. "Well, that's the lawyer's job, I suppose."

He had been ignoring her, but now he perked up. "Can we really have groups of armed police imposing their will on an unarmed populace?"

"No, but the way the Panthers are choosing to respond is rather inflammatory."

"Oh?"

"My God, Tom." She turned to Alice. "Shouldn't you be thinking about bed? It's nearly ten o'clock."

"She can stay," her father responded. "She needs to understand these things."

Unsure whether to stay or go, Alice took refuge in her book. Her father continued in a reasonable yet somehow taunting tone.

"The law never says where one may bear arms, only that one may do so. It says nothing regarding the intent in carrying a gun, unless it can be shown that the gun has been used in a crime. Since the Panthers merely appeared on the floor of the Assembly, we have no grounds for asking why they were bearing arms. They bore arms because they had a constitutional right to do so."

Her mother appeared increasingly confused, even angry. Alice looked from one to the other. Was her mother wrong? She'd confirmed as much; she was always saying he was a lawyer, he would know.

"Yes, Tom, Second Amendment and all that. But the encouragement of armed uprisings is a grave matter—a crime, if I'm not wrong."

"Where was the encouragement?" he demanded, though it seemed clear enough, even to Alice.

"An armed force intruded on the Assembly for the purpose of preventing lawmakers from passing a popular law. I regard that as encouragement."

"And what if a group of nude people came to the Assembly to lobby against a ban on nudity?"

Alice was glad she had her book, because the idea, coming from her father in a dry and humorless tone, nearly made her laugh.

"Nude people are hardly a threat," her mother responded with marked sarcasm. "Rather the reverse, I should imagine."

"Many things have harmful uses, but no one says they should be completely banned. Guns, like cars or nude people, have good and bad uses, and it's the bad uses that should be outlawed, not the guns themselves."

"I see what you mean, Tom, but what we're really talking about is a symbolic armed assault on our government and lawmakers."

"A symbol has substance only in the mind of the beholder."

"Oh my—what's happened to common sense?"

"The senses are less common than personal."

"Oh for crying out loud."

Her father's reasoning, though obscure to Alice, had clearly annoyed her mother, who paused, then recommenced in a condescending tone.

"Tom, when a group appears in a room openly bearing guns, the danger is symbolic or real, as you please. But had you been there, you would have run for cover along with everyone else and we wouldn't be having so absurd an argument."

"Why should the symbolic danger to lawmakers carry more significance than the danger felt by black men stopped by the police?"

"I don't suppose it should." Her mother paused, face flushed. "But as we both know, there's a presumption in favor of those who are responsible for maintaining public order."

"Yes, and you see how that holds up whenever cops enter a black neighborhood."

As the sparring ceased for the moment, Alice closed her book and made her way from the room.

As soon as she was gone her mother resumed, though in lower tones Alice was not supposed to hear.

"Be careful around her, Tom. She's too exploratory as it is."

Marian

TOM HAD MANEUVERED around her. Even so, she was sure the problems of policing in black neighborhoods would not be resolved by an armed gang of young men storming the government with an array of demands. That was not democracy. However, Tom's arguments conjured another image even less compatible with her concept of democracy: that of government forces rounding up unarmed members of an oppressed race. Tom had never held dangerous opinions: on the contrary, she'd always thought of him as reasonable, thorough, careful—to a fault. In Washington, he'd always spoken in lawyerly terms of federal enforcement of voting rights in the South, where state and local governments had long barred black people from the polls. He'd supported sending troops to enforce federal law, if necessary, and he'd been angered by the refusal of Kennedy and then Johnson to do so. He was even more angered when the same administration that had refused to impose order on the South had agreed to send American forces halfway around the world to impose order on Vietnam.

Tom rose from the couch and moved to the door. Marian heard him go up, presumably to bed—though he seemed headed for the study. Surely not now, after a whole day at the office?

She leaned over her copy of *Ramparts*, regarding the photograph. There were the Panthers, marching in formation onto the floor of the California Assembly. She'd heard of the armed appearance back in Washington—though barely, as something happening far away. Now she made common cause with people who regarded the Panthers with urgent sympathy. Though conceding the need for self-defense, she'd been dismayed by the armed posturing, the photographs of men and women in leather jackets and berets, posing with rifles, flaunting the image of an urban guerrilla army.

Now, in the flush of wine and exasperation as she took in the photograph, she began to find the image amusing and wondered how she would have responded had she been there as an observer. Assuming that no guns were blazing as they entered—and none were—would she really have been so alarmed by these men in leather and Parisian berets? The men were comely, in a sense, if one saw them simply as men, similar to the platoon leaders in a scene from a World War II film, the faces stern, as though to signal a seriousness of purpose. She turned the page and found a photograph of Bobby Seale, who'd led the Panthers into the State Capitol. Of course, it was Newton who was more of an intellectual, who'd read political theory somewhere and was supposed to have formulated the Panthers' ten-point program, though there was also Cleaver, who'd just published a book of essays and was somewhat literary, one of the prison intellectuals, like Genet, the men who taught themselves to read in the prison library and, if the sentence was a longish one, ended as authors. And hadn't Newton learned to read in prison by poring over a copy of Plato's *Republic*? It was an apocryphal tale, she was sure, but still . . . It seemed the *Ramparts* group had found Cleaver while he was languishing in prison, even before the Panthers had formed, and had rushed him into print on the heels of Che Guevara . . . She gathered that Cleaver was not as impressive as some of the other black writers, not yet, but she'd had no time to read the book and couldn't really say.

She turned the page and encountered another image: Huey Newton seated on a wicker throne, holding a rifle and an African spear. Now, that was clever symbolism, calling to mind some form of pan-African cultural bond. All those images of men with guns, men with spears, men with bows and arrows and bazookas and what have you, were so pervasive that it was hard to sustain the argument she'd just been making. Was that why Tom had seemed annoyed? She closed the magazine and finished her wine. With Tom, it was so hard to tell.

Part II

occupy

chapter one

Alice

AS THE MORNING dragged on, Alice was feeling low. She'd raced through her reading assignment before anyone other than Tammy and Debra and now, overhearing them giggling together as though they were on the way home from summer camp, she found herself brooding. Classroom neighbors, Tammy and Debra had become playground pals, but Alice's classroom neighbor, Jocelyn, had her own group of black girls from another class and a cool, uncomprehending gaze, if Alice was foolish enough to go anywhere near. Early on, seeing Alice coming up, one of the group had demanded, "What you want with us?" as another jeered, "Go away, white girl." Jocelyn's eyes were flushed with scorn and spurning as she murmured, "She's in my class," and the girls moved away laughing. Back in the classroom, an ugly mood hung over them, flaring up now and then.

In response, Alice had been forced to rely on her other class-room neighbor, Nora—until the handball dust-up. Back in September, Nora had passed every lunch hour playing handball with the other white girls, and for a while they enjoyed the game. Blonde and energetic, Nora shepherded the group through the lunchroom and around the playground, keeping them close, fending off taunts. She was regal—generous and temperamental, as she pleased—and the others were her followers. Even so, Alice was an up-and-coming challenger, for handball was a girl's game and, free of her brother's domineering control, she was feeling unleashed.

In the beginning, Nora always won, persevering over the other girls in turn, while her good humor and easy dominance gave the games a deeper purpose. Tammy and Debra enjoyed losing, it seemed, for that way they could show they were girls. Rough play was for boys and Nora. They regarded Alice, the only real challenger, as an amusing renegade until one day, when she landed the ball in a corner, beyond Nora's easy leap. Sure of trouncing her in the end, Nora laughed and complimented her adversary, unaware of how keen Alice was on winning for once, after losing among boys for so long. And so, to the girls' annoyance and chagrin, Alice replayed the move throughout the lunch hour, riding roughshod over everyone else's feelings, defeating Nora and then doing away with the others, as if she had something to prove. The strategy was flawless—as gloating and dependable as cheating. As far as everyone else was concerned, it was worse than cheating—galling but not glaringly wrong. Nora was good-humored in defeat; it was Debra who, by flouncing off the court before her game was over, announced Alice's blunder.

The following morning, Tammy, carelessly aloof from the playground squabbles, caught Alice by the classroom door. "Don't you know, Nora always wins," she confided, covering her mouth with one hand as though she'd just revealed someone's crush. Tammy was confusing; though she'd gone teary in class, somehow that no longer seemed embarrassing. For the moment, Alice was aware of unusual feelings, refusing to shun a girl she would have shunned before—and even admiring her.

Following her loss, Nora dropped the handball games and began leading the group to some benches on the playground, where she would brag about her summer camp in the Berkeley hills and how she'd gone kayaking on a lake.

Soon after, Alice had gone to her mother with a problem: she was hoping to get to know one of the girls in her class, but Tammy's house was far away. She was wondering how arrangements could be made; she could go by school bus, if Tammy offered, but getting home would be a problem, and so she was hoping her mother would agree to come for her, if anything happened.

"Are you sure Tammy's eager to play?" her mother probed.

"Eager?"

"If she were, you'd know."

Alice was feeling overwhelmed by school problems and unsure of anything.

"There must be some girls nearby," her mother went on. "Why is Tammy so appealing—is she very independent?"

"How do you mean?"

"Does she need a group, or can she do things alone?"

"They have a group."

"And are you in the group?"

"Not exactly."

"Then she may choose the group," her mother counseled, as though grasping her daughter's problem. "And what about Jocelyn?" she pursued, asking as usual about the black girl. Hearing no response, she concluded, "Well, there's always Sabrina's girls."

Of course Alice would have been willing to go to Sabrina's house, though the girls were somewhat older and presumably had other things to do; but her mother was just delaying, it seemed, caught up in Peace and Freedom and the Cleaver campaign. She was also doing the choosing, as always; indeed, she was so gushing on the subject of Sabrina's daughters—Helen and Maggie—that it seemed as though she were the one pining for companionship. By comparison, Alice was feeling overwhelmed and could hardly say how impossible Jocelyn had really become, or why she found Tammy appealing; that was why her mother had the chance to say so much. And so her imagination kept replaying someone else's hopes, as her own could barely be heard. There should have been a response regarding Tammy—but her mother had moved on. Tammy had been judged; if the girl had measured up, her mother would have been more willing to ferry Alice around.

She resolved to see Tammy somehow, with no one's help.

IN CLASS, THE morning dragged through its final half hour as Mrs. Whitman waded rudderless through the room, pausing here and there, coaching the others. Her face flushed, her blouse dusted with chalk, she offered encouraging words that calmed the group as a lullaby would, though leaving Alice feeling more keyed-up than before. She could have read more if only Mrs. Whitman had assigned more reading. For now, though, Alice was daydreaming away the hour, imagining going home with Tammy. If only she'd joined her early on—but Tammy was far away, in the row by the door, where she was showing off her green Girl Scout uniform and giggling with Debra. The uniform had lapels and a sash and gave her a foreign look, as though she'd come from an Iowa 4-H club. Even Debra was admiring the badges on the sash. Tammy was so confiding and amusing that she could make Debra giggle, though Debra was sour and judgmental with everyone else. Unfortunately, she was always hanging around the group, clinging for safety under Nora's wing. Nora enjoyed her role as leader and Tammy, refusing to conceal her fears as Alice would, showed no shame in following. Envying the other girl's freedom, Alice resolved to become a Girl Scout. Her mother made fun of such things—badges, uniforms, troop leaders—but Tammy's house was far away, and badges and uniforms were the price of seeing her after school.

Nearby, Jocelyn and Nora were jealously eyeing Alice's paper. Though they'd been doing well enough so far, the reading was new, and nearly everyone was confused. Jocelyn and Nora had begun teaming up in class, if only for the shared goal of beating Alice.

When the bell rang, Alice ignored the group as Nora joined Tammy and Debra and headed for the door. She would go her own way, passing up lunch and reading in the school library. There were safe ways of moving alone through the halls. She would drop Nora's group and manage on her own.

Away from the lunchroom, the long hallway echoed as she walked. Just being there was asking for problems, as someone much worse than Nora or Jocelyn could come along. Feeling lonely and scared in the abandoned space, Alice changed her mind. Nora's group would be on the bench soon enough.

The schoolyard was in full sun. Only a maple tree rose through the asphalt, shading an overflowing garbage can.

On the bench were Nora and Tammy and Debra. They eyed Alice as she came up, and though Tammy waved, Nora and Debra were looking her over with cool displeasure. Soon they were joined by Sharon, Nora's pal from another class. Nora and Sharon had houses in the hills and had always known each other. Sharon's plump arms and droopy curls gave her a puppy-dog demeanor, while Nora's gossipy sense of humor always made her laugh. These days Tammy and Debra grouped with them, forming a foursome.

As usual, they were comparing preferences and family outings and grumbling about class. That week they'd heard a lesson on the presidential campaign.

"Of course everyone's for Humphrey," Tammy said, giggling, as though conformity should be seen as inherently funny.

Alice saw an opening, a way of impressing them. Surely she'd heard as much from her mother as anyone and could join in. She'd had enough of hearing the girls gossip about unfamiliar local parks, knowing she would have nothing to say. In the beginning, she'd assumed her parents would help her learn the ropes, but with her father away on weekends and her mother reading or going to Party gatherings, there'd been no chance. And there were so many new things she could be doing.

A pause came. In a rush of energy, Alice glanced at Tammy and announced that her mother would not be voting for Humphrey, along with everyone else, but for Cleaver. The pause dragged on; then someone—Debra, whose father was a nuclear something-or-other—demanded, in a humorless tone, "Who?" She glared for a moment from pale eyes, made ugly by blonde, nearly bare lashes.

"Eldridge Cleaver. He's—"

"I thought so," Debra responded, snapping like a Venus fly trap. Then she added, "I'm sorry to say, but your mother is dangerously wrong."

Nora and Sharon leaned away, laughing. For a moment Alice was dumbfounded, then embarrassed by Debra's dry judgment. But soon she was angry they would shun her for something her mother planned to do. She was simply informing them. In any case, Cleaver had no chance of winning. Her mother was merely protesting. Was there something wrong with that?

On the other hand, if everyone else was for Humphrey, why was her mother dumping him for Cleaver?

The sun shone. Sharon and Nora were whispering, then giggling. Finally Tammy spoke up.

"Well, I'm sure your mom has her reasons."

Tammy was looking around the playground as she spoke, so who could say if she approved of Cleaver, or was merely showing sympathy for someone—anyone—condemned for an idea. Tammy defended nonconformity. Her family was from Philadelphia, and they'd come to Berkeley the year before. Her father was a professor, like Debra's; he researched what Tammy called the psychology of "doing what They say, even when you know it's wrong." Beyond that the explanation grew hazy and Alice was wary of probing, for fear of showing her ignorance. After all, when she'd asked the meaning of "nuclear," Debra had glared from those lashless eyes and then changed the subject.

Tammy had found a way of resolving that problem, too.

"Even her mother has no idea, I'm sure," she'd murmured to Alice as they were heading for class. The thought was amusing and sly; it made Alice laugh.

The only people Tammy condemned were those who never refused commands. They were the dangerous ones, she was always saying. She felt sympathy for Vaughan and Michael, the rambunctious bad boys, for the same reason everyone else found them annoying: they refused to comply. Tree Frog had escaped, becoming a running joke for Tammy, but Vaughan and Michael had no such hopes. They impressed her by being glum or buoyantly rude. Vaughan could be heard laughing when he should have been reading, and if anyone objected, he would say something demeaning and saucy. Though they were pushing as far as they could, Mrs. Whitman hung in, pleading and cajoling or ignoring them so the class could go on. The unruly boys had the run of things; Tammy had dubbed Mrs. Whitman's class "The Vaughan and Michael Hour." Unable to share Tammy's sympathy, Alice felt a pang of envy thinking of how her brother could do as he pleased, even when it made her mother angry. Vaughan and Michael were far more daring, responding with open contempt. Once Mrs. Whitman had commanded Vaughan, and he'd responded, cool and surly, "Try and make me."

These were new phrases, new ideas, and suddenly her group was learning them. Alice wondered where they could be used.

As for Jocelyn, she was a moody presence; though aloof if she found herself lagging, she would engage when she chose, offering commentary on the class and vaguely personal information. Jocelyn's mother was an imposing figure, they'd been informed—a schoolteacher; on bad days, when Vaughan and Michael really got going, Jocelyn would assume charge, and her glares and scoffing words could do more than the teacher's pleas.

ONE DAY, DURING a lull, as Alice was reading from her mother's book of fairy tales, Jocelyn and Nora found a subject they could share—church. Alice heard them, but there was no sense in getting drawn in, for she had nothing to say about church. She'd learned her lesson with the Humphrey-Cleaver argument. And so she immersed herself in a new tale—a girl whose brother drank from an enchanted river and became a roebuck.

Jocelyn rapped on her desk. Alice glanced up and saw Jocelyn's eyes.

"How about your family? Where do they go?"

"We never go to church."

"Oh." Jocelyn barely paused. "So you're Jewish." She glanced
over, as though something finally made sense.

"No."

Jocelyn glanced harder. "If you are, why not say so?"

"Because I'm not."

"Then how come you never go to church? How about your
mother?"

"She's an agnostic."

"A what?"

"She's not sure . . . not sure if there's a God." The words
sounded foolish even as she spoke, impossible to defend.

"Then send her on over to my church, maybe she can learn
some." Jocelyn slammed her desk, causing Ben to eye them. He'd
been ignoring Alice ever since the day in Mr. Boyd's office.

Nora had been amused by the sparring. Barely glancing over,
she proceeded to clear things up. "No way could she be Jewish."

"No?" Jocelyn shrugged. "I thought maybe she was."

"My family is Protestant, but we never go—"

"I heard you before. And Sunday school?"

"Well—"

"When do you read the Bible?" Jocelyn demanded. She
paused, her eyes narrowing. "And you say you were for Dr. King."

"Oh, no," came Nora's helpful commentary. "Her mom's for
Cleaver."

Jocelyn glared, uncomprehending. "You're foolin' me."

Alice was stung: she'd imagined Jocelyn would be impressed.

"You're bad," the girl concluded. "You're gonna burn." She
waved her hands, as though conjuring up the flames. "Good
thing you been baptized—"

"No . . . maybe . . ."

Jocelyn's jaw dropped. "You mean you ain't never been baptized?" Leaning away, she surveyed the other with steady, smoldering eyes. She'd found the clue she needed.

Alice's mother had grown up going to church and could
clear things up. For now, though, Jocelyn had found Alice vulnerable and there would be no more tangling with her.

COMING HOME FROM school, Alice found her mother in the bedroom, reading.

"Of course I had you baptized! You've always belonged to the Church!" she gasped, as though denying some outrageous lapse. "Whatever made you think otherwise?"

The claim was surprising, maybe false. Baptism conferred some belonging, it seemed, some place in the Church, yet her mother had rejected such things and chosen to keep her in ignorance. Her mother should have informed her; then she could have belonged, she could have defended herself.

"How come we never go to church?" she demanded, growing annoyed.

"You've never asked to go!"

"But—"

"I've always thought you should choose for yourself—and you've never shown any interest."

They'd never gone to church; Alice knew nothing of what happened there. She was angry to hear her mother blaming her.

"Are you feeling a real impulse?" her mother asked soothingly, closing her book, her words carefully chosen. "If so, I'm sure we could find—"

"No, please."

Her mother's eyes were steady, full of suggestion; she paused, inhaling deeply. "I've always seen you as a true nonbeliever, like your father. And I've always thought you should choose for yourself."

There had never been any grounds for choosing. Yet Alice had been deemed an outcast by her classroom neighbor and would now be dealing with the consequences. Moreover, Nora and Debra had heard the argument, and something would surely come of that.

Her mother was peering closely. "I hope nothing happened to offend the other girl—what was her name?"

"Jocelyn."

"Oh my—Jocelyn!" she gasped. "Well, there's no use in showing contempt for her religion."

"I never showed contempt."

"Are you sure? What made her so angry, then?"

"How should I know?"

"Sometimes you have to be careful in conversation; you can't always say whatever you please."

Alice was dumbfounded. Why was her mother accusing her and defending Jocelyn? She fled the room before her outrage could show.

THE OTHERS WERE never as openly rude as Jocelyn, yet the Cleaver remark and the church argument hung over the bench. Alice's anger was growing. The others were merely parroting what they heard at home—so why should they censure her for doing the same?

Soon Alice began following her own commands. Choosing to keep away from the bench, she would go her own way on the playground or, if nothing good came of that, she could read in the school library.

One day, bored by the lunch-hour playground and daydreaming away from the crowd, Alice wandered through the large, gloomy building. The lunch hour was nearly over—there would be no chance for browsing books. She passed her classroom on the second floor and paused, hoping the bell would ring, for the hallways were somber and abandoned. Beyond her classroom was an announcement board and then more classrooms. Sounds came from the far end of the hall, as several black boys slammed through some double doors, laughing and scuffling with each other. The group was coming her way; they neared, closing the gap, and the joking ceased. As they approached she veered away, regarding the floor, wondering why she'd come here when there were safer places to go. Even so, she knew why—there was something galling in being pushed around by other people, by fear.

A boy spun loose from the edge of the group. He was long-limbed and angular, with a loping walk and sober eyes. Alarmed, and with the boy heading her way, she glanced over the group; one waved, grinning falsely. A smile formed uncomfortably on her face as the boy sauntered up, murmuring softly in her ear, "Gimme some pussy," as one dangling hand made a sly movement and snagged her between the legs. Barely aware of the words' meaning but lashing out against the grabbing arm, she shoved the boy's shoulder and, unable to repel him, became entangled in a clumsy embrace. For a moment the group surrounded her, laughing mirthfully; then they swaggered on down the hall. A new feeling spread beneath her suddenly snug jeans —a grotesque merging of rage and pleasure.

She heard the boys slam through more double doors just as the bell was ringing. Others were coming, and she had nowhere to go. Longing to leave and go home, she found a back stairway down to the schoolhouse door, where lawn and flagpole formed a no-man's-land. Beyond was a black neighborhood. She could go up Ashby Avenue; she would be safe on a large street. But then there was her mother, and how would she judge what was happening? She would blame someone; there would be probing. Who were the boys and why had she been in the hallway? Why had they shamed her, if that's what they'd done? And why— though of course no one would ask—had her body responded?

The following day, when Tammy found her alone on the playground, Alice was feeling ashamed. Things were happening; boys were choosing her. She was not choosing for herself, as her mother supposed, or even accused her of doing. She wondered if these things were happening to Tammy and the others, but there was no way of asking. If only her mother could help—but so far the conversation was unimaginable. What if her mother blamed her, as she'd done with Jocelyn? In any case, the boys had faded away among many others, so what could anyone do? No, her mother was from somewhere else and could be of no help. She imagined what her mother would say: something about how she would grow up and love a boy someday. For her mother, that was the all-important thing—what she should feel someday. Before those things could happen, however, her anger would command her. She would choose, and she would refuse these boys.

If anyone could help, it would be Tammy. Maybe Tammy would have something to say, though things would go on happening. Tammy would say something real now, as she had before. Tammy was open; she'd been tearful and unashamed and she would understand, somehow that was clear.

As Alice emerged from her brooding, she became aware that Tammy was regaling her.

"And your brother, is he foxy?" Tammy was leaning close.

Alice shrugged, confused, and Tammy laughed loudly.

A boy ran up. Though nothing like her brother, he was handsome, with heavy eyebrows, pale eyes, and a splash of sunburn, as if he'd just come from the beach. She remembered the face; she'd seen him somewhere before.

"Hey, do you know Jason?" he asked, eyeing Alice. Of course: he hung with Jason, the shaggy, piano-playing boy from Mrs. Whitman's class. He'd been looking for her; maybe she would choose him.

Tammy moved away, as though on cue.

"Yeah, from class."

"Oh." The boy came closer. "Where do you live?"

"Forest Avenue."

The boy nodded and said, "Jason's on Garber."

The boy had some unannounced purpose. She'd heard the rumors: Jason's father played the banjo and owned a guitar store off Telegraph Avenue, and he was known around the Bay Area for sponsoring folk concerts. Feeling a pang of envy, she'd even dropped by the store. Jason rode her bus, and though they rarely spoke, she could probably see the house on Garber Street from her brother's room or from the bathroom they shared.

"Jason's having a slumber party on Saturday," the boy said, grinning. "He says you can come by." And he laughed and ran off.

Tammy came closer. "Maybe he has a crush on you," she murmured. "But my God, what a jerky thing for him to say." Her laugh was overlapped by the bell.

SATURDAY MORNING CAME. Alice remembered the party, though surely the boy had been teasing, because no girl would ever go to a boy's slumber party. The suggestion was confusing and ambiguous, a demeaning compliment. Even so, she couldn't help wondering what the boys would be doing. Opening the telephone book, she learned that Jason's house was just around the corner from her own.

In the evening, before going to bed, she searched from the sunporch for Jason's house but saw only a corner of the roof and some trees overhanging glowing house lights.

On Sunday morning, as she was in the bathroom lounging in the tub, she remembered the party once more, and wondered what games the boys had played.

That afternoon, the phone rang. Feeling an odd foreboding, Alice answered the call. There was a boy on the other end.

"How was your bath?" he demanded.

"What do you mean?"

"We saw you through the window, a whole bunch of us."

She was dumbfounded. The boy must be from Jason's party. "I never had a bath today."

"You had a bath this morning, we saw you."

"Who are you?"

The boy laughed. "Are you going out on Halloween?" he wanted to know.

"None of your business."

"If you go out, we're gonna rape you."

She hung up hard. Warmth rose up her face in a fever of shame and rage. Her mother called from the living room, "Who was that?"

"No one—just a boy from school."

"A boy?"

She would have to regroup, fast. If she confessed one thing, then there would be another and another—who could say where things would end? Life was suddenly overwhelming. Her mother appeared in the doorway.

"That reminds me," she began. "Have you made plans for Halloween? It's coming on Thursday."

"No."

"Are you planning on going out?"

"Not sure."

"Curt's going with Sammy. I suppose you could go with them—"

"No way."

"—or we could see about Sabrina's daughters. Helen's too old but maybe the younger one—"

"I've never met them."

"Maybe there's a group—"

"No."

She should reveal nothing—that much was clear. Things had already gone way beyond where they should be. Her mother glanced at her, wary and vaguely annoyed, as though finding her hard to fathom. Back in Washington, Alice would have followed the plan and gone with family friends. But Sabrina's daughters had seemingly come from nowhere; even her mother hardly knew them. They were older and had no reason for wanting her along. She'd been counting on going with Tammy but then learned that Tammy would be one of Nora's group. They planned to dress as characters from *The Wizard of Oz*. In theory Alice could go along, but the good characters had already been chosen, leaving only the Scarecrow. As she thought of the Scarecrow and Nora and Jason's house and the phone call—altogether too much—she was no longer interested in playing dress-up.

When Halloween came, Alice hung around the nearby playground before going home from school; she was in no hurry to see her brother getting ready. When she came through the door, he was in the living room, wearing boxing gear. From the school gym he'd somehow borrowed boxing gloves, and he wore a gold-colored warm-up jacket and matching gold sweatpants, borrowed from another boy. Engaged and focused, he was adjusting the laces on the gloves as she came in. He glanced up.

"Mom says you're staying home," he remarked. He'd grown a head of wavy blond hair, unshorn for months and bleached by the sun. Wearing jeans, he would have resembled the local boys, or maybe someone from an album cover.

"Yeah. So?"

"How come?"

"Because."

Curt glanced up, encountering her eyes. He was in a surly mood. "I'm going with Sammy. You're not coming along."

"I know. Whoever said I was?"

"Mom was asking me."

"Well, I'm staying home."

"As long as you leave me and Sammy alone."

He glanced away.

Alice passed through the living room and dining room. In the kitchen, her mother was playing the news.

"Your brother's looking so grown up," she commented. Then she added, "Are you sure you don't want to go with him and Sammy?"

"I'm sure."

"Then would you mind turning up the radio? There's some breaking news."

"What's happening?"

"Let's hear what they say."

Indeed, something big was happening. Lyndon Johnson's

slow Texas vowels were coming through the speaker, announcing that because of progress in the Paris peace negotiations, he had ordered a bombing halt over North Vietnam, and the bombardments would be ending the following day. The words made her mother gasp, and then as the American leader was concluding the speech she sighed, "If only there could be peace."

Curt came through the doorway, boxing gloves dangling by his thighs. He'd heard everything. "Soon as the election's over," he shrugged, a gleam of humor, or anger, playing in his eyes, "he's gonna bomb them back to the Stone Age."

Her mother's eyes clouded. "Let's hope he means what he says."

Election Day was coming soon. There would be much news, and though it would be confusing, they could be on the verge of some momentous change. The war would end . . . if only . . .

Remembering an image of a burning girl—it was an image from the war; the girl had been napalmed, and her suffering flashed appallingly on the evening news—Alice sought refuge in the yard. Images from Vietnam were everywhere, even in her mind; yet the girl's suffering was unimaginable. Alice lay on the grass, eyes closed, her flesh recoiling from her thoughts. She had an impulse to flee—but no, the house and yard were safe. She wondered why she should be safe, or safe enough, when so many others were in such danger. True, some boys had phoned saying they'd seen her bathing and claiming they would rape her, but how could they? As long as she stayed home for Halloween, there was nothing they could do.

She wondered why she should fear going out, when it was safe for Curt.

She wondered why her school was such an angry place. Some days she would pass the hours in class wondering why so many others were angry, why they enjoyed harming her, when they hardly knew her. She'd heard many things—slavery, segregation, so many evil things in the South and even the North. But now things were changing and her black peers could harm her, if they chose; they could get revenge for those humiliations. And what of the boys from Jason's party—why were they coming after her? Though it was unimaginable, things could simply go on this way.

The sun was fading through some trees. Evening was coming.

Soothing herself, she remembered the swimming pool in Las Vegas. The place was cool and cornflower blue, and she remembered the pale stone statue of a boy, one arm dangling loose as though he'd just thrown a spear and was watching the weapon's flight.

Closing her eyes, she imagined lying by the pool. She could feel the coolness, the blades of grass by her face as a boy wandered up, holding a spear . . .

Opening her eyes in alarm, she glanced along her belly, her legs, and wondered how many girls had been ambushed in school by groups of boys.

School was going badly. She'd managed to annoy the girls, other than Tammy; bad things were flowing from that. She'd been alone and in the wrong place and was partly to blame. Even so, getting along with the girls would be challenging. They were following family, and so was she. How could she learn something new on her own? Everyone was learning from someone—that was how people were.

Then there was her father—a lawyer. The dangers of ignoring or defying the law had always seemed overwhelming, because her father's anger was more than personal; he spoke for the government, the law. Even so, many others had no such fear. She was young, only ten years old—yet already, boys had groped her body, forcing on her things she refused; they'd phoned and menaced her with worse. She'd never heard of such ambushes in her school in Washington. They were outrageous, and yet out here they were common enough—so common that boys would gather in groups for the sport. And because the boys had no fear, there was nothing that would keep them away, if they chose her. The problems would get worse as she grew older. Would she just have to endure these things?

She thought of telling her mother, but her mother would blame her. "Are you sure?" she would ask, as if Alice could be making it all up. And what of her father—had he done aggressive things to girls before he'd chosen her mother, before he'd begun enforcing the laws?

He was becoming a confusing power. He would go away on Saturdays, coming home after dinner, bringing a funny odor as though he'd been around dogs. One evening, he'd even gone around the house to the basement before coming in.

She'd been wondering why.

She stood up and crossed through the grass to the house.

Wooden slabs led down to the basement; the door was slightly ajar. Just beyond the door was a light switch and a tangle of protruding wires. She turned on the light; a bare bulb hung dimly over the room. The damp, rough floor had a sour odor of mildew. An abandoned workbench ran along one wall; nearby was a cupboard. She crossed the rough boards toward the cupboard. The handle hung loose, the hinges were red and crusty, but the door swung smoothly open, revealing cowboy boots. Apart from some sand and mud, the boots appeared new. Reaching for them, she heard clumping sounds overhead.

She carefully closed the cupboard. Moving soundlessly, she sped up and along the flower beds.

Orange clouds gleamed over the yard. She caught an animal odor as her father's image rose from the grass and then faded.

As Alice came through the house door, she heard the phone ringing and then her mother's sharp response, drowning out the radio announcer. So many things were happening: the campaign, the bombing, Johnson's speech. Only her father would be calling now; other family members were thousands of miles away.

Marian

THE PHONE WAS presumably Tom, informing her that he'd be late. Glancing at the clock, Marian heard a woman's voice: someone from the Party, then.

"Yes?"

"Oh, it's Ginger," the woman said, in a singsong voice. "Have you heard?"

"No—"

"Johnson's announced a bombing pause."

"Oh, yes—I just heard the speech."

"Is Tom home? Does he know?"

Marian felt her cheeks burning. Tom had referred to a woman named Ginger—rather warmly, she thought—but he'd mentioned her only in the beginning. They were no longer working together—or were they?

"Is there some message for him?" she demanded, more coolly than was wise.

"Just the news," Ginger responded. "I thought Tom should know. G'bye."

Marian hung up the phone, trembling. How revealing that Ginger should call before any other of Tom's colleagues.

Looking up, she saw her son, wearing boxing gloves.

"That was Ginger," she announced in a phony voice. Then, as he made a face, she fled the room.

ONE EVENING IN November, as the Raysons were passing the bookshop on Telegraph Avenue, Marian paused, scanning a bin of used books. There was no chance of browsing through them now; the others had already rushed ahead in a loose threesome, as though unaware of her. When she caught up, Marian found her daughter by a leather shop, fancying a row of cowboy boots —or was she eyeing the fringy leather jacket in the window? Marian was amused by her daughter's way of glancing around, for she rarely revealed her cravings so openly. And then, just as the girl was moving on, Tom came up close on her shoulder, nudging her.

"See something?" she heard Tom saying.

Marian knew the game: he was moving Alice along. There was no chance he would buy her a leather anything, just as there was no chance she would beg.

There was only a shrug from Alice, as she glanced over her shoulder. Marian thought there was some girlish pining in her face.

"I've always admired suede," Marian commented. Then, with an encouraging emphasis, "Would you wear one to school?"

"Wear what?"

"Weren't you admiring those fringy jackets?"

"No."

"What, then?"

"Nothing. Just the boots. What are they for?"

"Oh, they're for style, I suppose."

Marian followed her family, wondering how they would seem to her had they been someone else's. Of course, she could never see them that way; she would always be aware of so many background things. Her son was loping along, as though he'd come to Telegraph Avenue alone. He was spending weekends with Sammy and Sammy's older brother, because Tom was busy nearly every Saturday. He'd come home one day wearing some-one else's red velour pullover, saying some boys had been dump-ing clothes around the gym. She wondered if Sammy could be the problem, though that was only a hunch. There'd been an-other day when the boys had come home waving money they'd found by the bank, or so they'd proclaimed. So far she regarded Sammy as the ringleader.

There was no sense in running the problem by Tom, for he could be demeaning. She would pry her son away from Sammy, if only she could.

Even so, she was losing Curt, regardless of Sammy. He hung aloof, ignoring them, as though seeking camouflage among the fledgling young. The rebuff was wounding yet revealing, for he seemed alarmingly self-possessed. Of the Raysons, he alone was made for Telegraph: overwhelmed by an early adolescence, wav-ing a coarsening tangle of hair, he was blooming and newly muscular, and though he had a boy's smooth face, up close he had a man's odor. He would be very handsome—more hand-some than Tom—and she wondered if, growing among the freely expressive young, he would become more pleasing as well.

He was growing up much sooner than he should. For now, he should be hers.

Tom paused as they reached La Fiesta, the Mexican place Sabrina had been recommending so highly. Tom had agreed on the Mexican place because they'd heard the food would be tasty and cheap. Marian was pushing Sabrina's preferences because Tom ignored her own and the family needed something new. She enjoyed hearing how Sabrina and her husband had voyaged to faraway places. How mind-expanding that would be, Marian thought, though she'd never imagined such things before—a season under the palm trees. And Sabrina's daughters had been there, though of course they'd been very young.

On the way to Telegraph, Tom had purchased beer. Now, as the family crowded around the table, father and daughter on one side and mother and son on the other, he opened a can. A bearded and aproned man appeared bearing a glass. Tom poured carelessly, and as the glass foamed over, he leaned slurping the foam. Then he ordered some food more or less randomly. Tom's presence was changing, becoming dour and unbending. Ever since the phone call from Ginger, he'd begun dropping references to her. The references were no more than he might say about other colleagues, yet there was something meaningful in them.

Tom, sunburned and sparing of words, was peering blandly through the window, as if the passing scene were enough.

Marian regarded her son, who was bouncing a leg as he leaned over the food. Soon he'd be old enough for the army. During the campaign, Nixon had used the ambiguous code words "peace with honor" in suggesting he would end the war. Then the bombing pause announced by Johnson had fallen through. Maybe, as many supposed, there had never been an agreement and Johnson had only hoped to improve Humphrey's chances by announcing the opening of peace negotiations. Or maybe, as others supposed, Nixon's people had sabotaged the plan by promising more favorable terms, if he were to win. Sure enough, the confusion and delay had worked in Nixon's favor. Now, she was sure, the war would simply go on—no peace, no honor.

"How old is Sammy's brother?" Marian inquired.

"High school."

"Do you know what year?"

"Sophomore."

"I hope he's planning on college."

"Why?"

"Among other reasons," she responded, feeling her face flush, "college students can get draft deferrals. And college is safer than the army."

"I'm planning on college."

"Good."

She would be damned if her son would go to war. She could be reasonably sure he would never join the army—but if he were called up, would he refuse? Though the problem was years away, she pondered all the same. He'd become obsessed with the carnage, following the evening news as zealously as a new baseball season—could she really be so sure he'd never go searching for glory? He would never say if the bloodshed appalled him or pumped him up.

Marian sought Tom's gaze, wondering why he was so aloof, why he was always away. How far had things gone with Ginger?

Sabrina's husband was engaging, flamboyant where Tom was drab, humorous where he was dour—if only . . . !

If only Humphrey had won. He was drab but safe, and she'd only been angry. Of course her personal vote for Cleaver had been of no consequence in California, where Humphrey never had a chance. She'd done nothing for the more dangerous one, Nixon, whose margin in his home state had been very secure. Tom had gone for Humphrey, she was reasonably sure; he'd never do anything so unruly as she'd just done! Her son was unhappy with her, of course; he was loyal to the home team—and for the Raysons, that was Humphrey. Her daughter was also unhappy, though the reasons for that were somewhat obscure. In the ensuing days, Marian had made one thing clear—Humphrey would have been preferable, if she'd thought her vote would change anything.

The evening was cool and damp as the Raysons emerged from the restaurant. Marian led them around the corner in search of a jewelry shop she'd found on one of her forays and was hoping to browse. She'd already persuaded Alice to go, by reminding her of the turquoise rings she'd seen in Santa Fe and —was it not so?—found very alluring. Alice had forgotten the rings; but that was all the more reason to see them now. Surely she would be eager to remember something she'd so truly enjoyed.

Marian paused in the doorway, Tom by her shoulder. From the shop, a woman surveyed them through a fringe of lemon-colored bangs.

"Do come in," sang the woman.

Tom hung back as the others passed through the door. The room was overflowing with beads and hangings and glass cases showing off turquoise jewelry—rings and flashing necklaces of freer design than those they'd seen in Santa Fe. Along one wall, a row of water pipes dangled from a shelf, coyly camouflaged by several intermingling Hindu figures, gods and goddesses whose many waving arms resembled the curving hoses of the pipes. A musky fragrance embalmed the room, fed by the curl of smoke from a brass cupola of burning incense. Rumbling bass sounds underscored an edgy howl of melody, a posse of cars speeding through a tunnel.

By the glass cases, the woman's eyes shone; her long, lemony hair moved in dune-grass waves over her shoulders. Surrounded by her jeweled wares, she was clearly eyeing someone—the handsome boy-man, Marian's son.

He edged closer, as though moved by an unseen force.

"Can I show you my rings?" came the woman's siren song.

"Oh my!" Marian enthused, running her hand through a row of beads. Then she glanced up, catching the woman's eye. "Such lovely beads!"

Alice

ALICE WAS WONDERING what rings the woman had. Rings were good: they could render her unseen. If only she could slip on a ring and move freely . . .

In a glass case hung peacock feathers and abalone—blue, copper, and green. A woman was whispering in her ear. The murmur grew edgy, rebounding from the glass cases, the shudder of a passing world. The song was unnerving her senses, already flooded by incense. In the corner hung a poster of swirling words camouflaged among purples, reds, and greens, seeping over the paper in vibrant, unreadable code. Then she saw four faces smiling from the colors—for everyone and no one. Shrouded by glowing purple hair, the faces rose ambiguously from the shifting background shapes, among which she glimpsed the word "Avalon," before the letters faded in whirlpools of color.

A new song was beginning. Just as the others were leaving, Alice approached the case of turquoise rings, poring over them. The woman leaned closer, smiling as though from the branches of a tree.

"Can I see one?"

"Yes, if you show me the one you're looking for." The woman's face was a waxing, waning smile.

"Any one . . ."

"Are you sure?" The woman seemed oddly amused.

"Maybe . . . no . . ."

"You can find yours," summed up the woman, "if you look long enough."

There was no chance now, but she would come back.

Alice made her way through a rumbling, thumping din, just as her family was moving off. Under the glare of a street lamp, an unleashed dog nosed the curb. A lanky man wearing fringed leather swayed by. She passed along the curb, joining the family as they gathered at Telegraph and then moved on. Day had faded, replaced by pools of amber glare. Bushes and flowers loomed; trees cast branching shadows along the ground. Unseen birds sang a few melancholy phrases as they passed: songbirds, whose shadows lay among the lacing branches. Turning here and there they ambled on, passing from shadow to shadow, and just as she was growing sleepy they reached a brown-shingle house with a palm tree swaying in the yard.

chapter two

Marian

JANUARY WAS NEARLY gone. Everyone was away when Marian emerged from the bedroom, consoled by the lonely house where she could do as she pleased. Tom had been in San Francisco on Saturday, presumably with Ginger, though there was a vague chance he'd been working, as he'd been feigning so far. Marian imagined Ginger as young and callous—as a woman lawyer, she would be needing some hard surfaces. She would be demanding, and Tom, a dogged and uncompromising man, would soon enough grow weary of indulging her. In any case, Marian could manage her feelings and keep a phony peace, though she found so many causes for war these days—and of course, the problem was never the problem. Even so, Tom's absences had been posing a slew of minor problems: for example, he'd delayed her evening plans with Sabrina and Michael, and even when she'd dangled Michael's research—he would be in the Amazon soon, if the funding came through—Tom had been unimpressed.

So in place of evening plans, Marian would be joining them for lunch in one of the Telegraph Avenue cafes. Then Michael would show her the campus. Marian would enjoy some pampering, finally; she'd hardly seen the campus beyond Sproul Plaza, where she'd ended up sparring with the brassy young Wanda, and here she would be having a professor's tour.

She poured some coffee and glanced over the yard. Things were lush and blooming even in January. She could have fun here, Tom be damned.

The day shone warm. Marian wore a paisley dress and a handmade shawl; blonde waves bounced over her shoulders. Roses burgeoned along Forest Avenue: a lovely place.

Overhead, a sparrow made joyous song.

As Marian rounded the corner of Telegraph, she saw Sabrina under the awning of the Caffé Med. She was an elegant woman, wearing a loose dress in black and rose, resembling a Greek vase painting; on her feet were black sandals. Her bangs had changed, becoming wispy, and her eyes were deepened by a barely observable eye shadow.

"Such a lovely day," she exclaimed, "and such a foul world!"

Marian surmised that Sabrina was offering a form of bonding in the wake of Nixon's inauguration and chose a simple response. "So wonderful to see you, Sabrina."

"Michael's coming, but he's running late as always."

The glass door of the Med swung open, and four young men emerged, wearing shaggy sideburns and unruly manes and blinking in the sun as though they'd just awakened. The cafe was a gathering place for sundry groups; undergrads and hippies, professors and runaways could be found there rubbing shoulders, as Marian remembered from her early foray. Of course Sabrina would drop by the Med for coffee or lunch, and Michael would prefer the hubbub of a cafe, where he could do informal research on the counterculture overrunning Berkeley beyond the campus classrooms. Marian had been imagining having a group of people beyond the Party—women in the same circumstances as herself, with husbands and children. That was why she'd chosen Sabrina from among the Party people, so many of them underemployed ex-students who referred to marriage—slyly or carelessly, depending on the mood—as "sharing a pad." However Tom was passing his Saturdays, there was a good deal more to marriage than that.

As the women passed through the door, Marian found a heavy odor of food and tobacco and the hum of many people communing over coffee, or maybe just gossiping.

"By the window!" suggested Sabrina, shepherding Marian. "Let's have some sun."

"How lovely."

"I'm a tropical flower, I need my sun."

A young woman in a greasy apron came by for the order. Peering through a screen of bushy bangs, she seemed bored by these women who were merely professors' wives, or so she would suppose—no longer young and free, and having no place in the Telegraph scene.

"The Moroccan coffee's far-out," she said, nudging the bourgeoisie.

"Oh, regular for me, with cream and sugar. And you, Marian?"

"The same."

"Coming up. What else?"

"Nothing, thank you. Maybe when my husband comes."

"Hanging loose for now?"

"Yes."

The young woman moved on, surrounded by her bushy fringe.

"Some days I just embrace being a square," Sabrina laughed. "There's no keeping up anyway."

With her own glossy waves, Marian could afford to agree. "Such a change from a few years ago, when everyone had bobs." She glanced over Sabrina's elegant French bangs—had she been younger, she would have resembled Godard's lovely waif, Anna Karina. "Though I never had one."

"Nor I," laughed Sabrina. They exchanged a glance, and Marian saw something rueful in the other woman's eyes. "By the way, Michael's Amazon funding came through. He goes in July."

"That's wonderful."

"Yes, I'm glad for him. He's going to be researching some very unusual people, one of the few remaining hunter-gatherer groups on earth."

"He sounds so engaged. Tom says everyone would become Americans if they found themselves in America."

"Aggressive, you mean? Jealous and possessive?"

"Oh, freedom-loving, home-owning—"

Sabrina laughed. "I keep forgetting Tom's a federal employee. No, hunter-gatherers can show us where we come from, who we really are."

"How long will Michael be away?"

"A whole year. Plantains and roasted caterpillars—he's in for an eye-opener."

"I see."

"He's never been in real jungle before."

"But I thought—"

"He was in Samoa in '57, but that's a far cry. We were young and in love, and I was mad enough to go along. Imagine, a Pennsylvania girl—"

Marian eyed the other woman. Tom would have enjoyed such things; coming from Canadian farmers and lumbermen, he had some back-country longings. She was considerably less sure of herself, though.

"And how life-changing it was!" Sabrina exclaimed. "There's something in the place. And now we're real Californians." She paused and added dryly, "Every year or so, my mother asks if I'm ever coming home."

"Your daughter was born there?" Marian could hardly imagine the ordeal.

"Oh, yes. The women were so caring and generous. There's a hospital, of course, and American staff, but I refused to go. And Maggie's always been so happy. I've always thought that was one of the reasons."

"Maggie . . . I thought it was Helen."

"No, Helen was a toddler. In the local manner, we had her go nude, and she much preferred things that way. I worry she remembers the whole lovely unraveling—more confusing than we imagined. Helen's very free, but she wanders so from one thing to another."

"They all do, Sabrina."

"I suppose. And that's going to be her strength—feeling her way through the wilderness we call the future. Even now, she understands what's happening more clearly than any of us grown-ups."

Marian remembered the early gathering at Sabrina's house: Helen's bare feet and cool, assessing gaze, Shel and Dan Dupres, the announcement of Cleaver's candidacy. She paused, wondering if Sabrina had regrets about the campaign but unsure how to proceed. The subject seemed so charged, and she hardly knew Sabrina.

Before she could say anything, the young woman brought the coffee on a round tray, with a small jug of cream.

Sabrina poured some cream for them; she enjoyed doing the honors. She'd probably done much the same under the palm trees, serving up some island brew.

"Then maybe Helen can explain the Panther phenomenon," Marian suggested gently. "They seem so far removed from what King was doing."

"We're no longer needed, that's all," Sabrina said, with a shrug, "and maybe that's how it should be."

"Change has been very slow, it's true."

"Yes—gradualism. College people who were in Mississippi during the Freedom Summer were appalled by what they found there. So, imagine how blacks are feeling. Many never followed King; they've been demanding self-defense all along, though you and I were never supposed to know. Young people are forging new ways, however they can. Who's to say they're wrong?"

"I worry about groups of young men with guns." Marian was unable to untangle Sabrina's loyalties.

"So do I." Sabrina leaned in. "Everyone's so awed by black men with guns. They feel they're encountering some form of raw, male power—alarming and thrilling. The marching and waving of guns are symbolic—useful in rousing people."

"Yes, Tom was saying—"

"The cops fear these symbols—"

"They fear an ambush."

"Yes, I agree." Sabrina's eyes flashed with anger. "You know, I voted for Cleaver, but I was never impressed by him. Have you read *Soul on Ice*?"

"Of course," said Marian, though she had not.

"Everyone knows rape is political. It happens in every war, hand in glove with armed force—it's one of the things we should be opposing. I'm not surprised Cleaver should have defended the idea. But I should never have supported him."

Marian had heard vague rumors connecting Cleaver with rape but had assumed they were merely propaganda. Now she was unable to reveal her confusion to Sabrina; she too had followed along, falling for the trap.

There was a pause. A man came through the cafe door. "Things are gonna be heavy," he was saying.

"Yeah, there's a bummer coming," a woman agreed.

Looking around, Marian saw the couple: Wanda and Dan Dupres. She eyed Wanda's jeans and rough lumberman's jacket, worn over a clear vinyl bra and barely concealing her figure as she moved. Dan wore jeans and combat boots.

"We can undermine the regime," Dan was saying.

"Yeah, no sleeping with the warmongers," added Wanda.

"The warmongers say we're programmed, war is in our genes. Guys who refuse war—they say we're laggards in the evolutionary struggle."

"Laggards!" laughed Wanda.

"Yeah. Funny, huh?"

Sabrina's face reddened, as though in anger or shame. "I wonder what's holding up Michael."

Dan and Wanda were heading for the door.

Sabrina leaned in. "I oppose warmongering, but I'm also uncomfortable with some of the people being groomed as leaders." She was peering in Marian's eyes. "Dan and Wanda are up-and-coming movers."

"They're in the Party, I know." Marian was remembering the day in Sproul Plaza when she and Wanda had sparred over Tom's lawyering. Wanda was clearly up-and-coming—among other things, she'd been one of the spark plugs for the orgasm controversy. *Ramparts* had run a condescending essay on "women power," and someone calling herself "Wanda in Berkeley" had penned one of the responses, touching off a debate on women's orgasms. Groups of women had sprung up who were focusing on women's problems, but Marian would have been wary of joining such a group. Tom was already restless.

"Wanda was in anthropology, before she dropped out."

"Oh?"

"Yes, Michael found her charming." Sabrina shrugged. "Now she's moved on. You know, I was never impressed by her. I feel my husband was slumming somehow."

Feeling a pang of sympathy, Marian wondered how Sabrina could appear so calm. "Are you—do you have an open marriage?"

"Yes, I suppose we do. My husband loves me dearly, but he's always searching for new experiences. He's been pining for a research year."

"I'm sorry, Sabrina." Marian was feeling very square.

"Why? I could do the same."

"I know, but—"

"I'm planning some workshops, and then, of course, I have the girls. Helen concerns me—she always rebels when her father's away."

"I imagine she misses him."

"Of course. So do I."

There was a pause. Marian pushed her coffee away and made a sudden confession.

"Tom's been seeing someone."

"Tom?"

"Yes, a woman lawyer. There's something going on."

"Why, he seems so very regular." For once, Sabrina seemed confused. "Things are very open here, you know," she counseled. "But he's bound to get bored with her, unless it's very deep."

"Deep?" Marian was embarrassed by the image of Tom and Ginger enjoying something momentous.

"Yes, would Tom want something deep from her?"

"I assume he simply wants a fling."

"That's what I thought—he's very regular," Sabrina sighed, glancing at her watch. "Damn—where's my husband?" She was fidgeting. "Have you heard what's happening on campus?"

"What—something new?"

There was already so much. A group had been demanding new black and Chicano programs, even a Third World college. Then as demands were being made, someone had burned a campus building, Wheeler Hall—or maybe it was only the auditorium that had been engulfed in flames. Marian wondered if she would be passing by the dismaying sight. Demanding more programs was one thing; arson was another. The upheaval had begun on the campus of San Francisco State, where mobs had fought the police, closing down the campus. One young professor—or was he a grad student?—had urged black students to carry guns on campus; he'd been suspended, and now the case was among the group's unwavering demands. A semantics scholar, Professor Hayakawa, who'd been named as acting college president, had brought a harsh semblance of order: relying on armed guards, banning groups and gatherings, and clearing the campus of anyone not enrolled or employed there. Marian found herself agreeing with the man's values and pronouncements regarding the purposes of a college and was offended by the enforced coupling of those values with overweening authority. Until recently, Hayakawa had been concerned with language rather than overbearing force; why should he have been compelled to crush an uprising?

"Yes, they closed off Sather Gate yesterday. No one could pass through."

"I had no idea."

"The demands are reasonable—long overdue, in fact. If Michael had no fear of losing funding, he would have been there."

The door swung open and Michael came through, searching the room. "There you are, Sabrina. No chance of going on campus—cops are everywhere. I'm sorry, I've got to get back, they're beating people." He was young looking, in safari pants and an African tunic. "Damn those cops, they've dragged one of my students away. No one knows what's happening." He paused. "I'll call you from Kroeber Hall."

"No, I'm going with you. Marian, are you coming?" Sabrina was groping in her purse. "Oh, damn—ah, there we are!"

She slapped some bills on the table, placing her saucer over them, and then rose, reaching for Michael's elbow. Marian followed them through the door, her forehead pounding with a wary sense of emergency.

The avenue was calm, though as they neared the campus a group of large men passed by, one wearing torn jeans as though he'd just had a scuffle. As they reached Bancroft Way, bordering the campus, Marian saw a throng of people jammed by Sproul Plaza. Squads of police were grouped here and there, ready for war. Flushed and angry, Michael paused by the curb, searching the human fence that had just sprung up as the throng, arms locked together, braced to repel a police charge. Following his gaze along the line, Marian caught sight of Dan and then Wanda. As Sabrina leaned on his shoulder, Michael turned away.

"Michael, why are we here? There's nothing you can do now."

"I know."

"Oh my God, there's Dan—and Wanda!"

"Yes, I see them."

"And some of your students?"

"No, they're gone."

"Then maybe we should go."

For a moment Michael hung fast. Then a cry rose from the crowd as the police began moving in.

"Michael, we're going. Now."

"Yes, I'm coming."

Over her shoulder as they fled, Marian could see Dan and Wanda, good comrades, arm in arm on the line. A cry was wrung from the crowd as the armed police squads charged. She turned and ran along Telegraph, following Sabrina and Michael.

There was a confused goodbye near the Med, as Sabrina and Michael conferred on a new problem: whether he would go back on campus, though that meant appearing aloof from the strike, or home with her. The problem hung over them as Marian moved to go. Then she was fleeing Telegraph through streets suddenly charged with random energy. She was shaking: she'd been looking forward to a campus tour, not some armed confrontation. She could scarcely say how she'd been so nearly dragged along. It was a good thing she'd delayed enrolling in any courses; even the Pattersons were confused by the upheaval.

As she neared College Avenue, a dog ran up. He'd been lounging unleashed in someone's yard, and he rushed her aggressively, nosing her leg by way of brief preliminaries before finding her crotch.

"Down!" she commanded, smacking the animal. But he'd found her female odors and refused to go. She edged along the pavement, cursing unleashed dogs. There were so many; the city had repealed its leash laws and encouraged these roving canines, as though conferring human rights on them. Only men could dream up such schemes.

Reaching home in a fury, she found Curt splayed on the living-room rug among rows of baseball cards, obsessively scanning and arranging them. Casual as a caveman, he was gnawing on a greasy chicken leg.

"You're having dinner now, before your father gets home?" she demanded.

"Just leftovers." He tore off a chunk, testing her.

"You had lunch, I suppose?"

He shrugged, a vague and unreadable gesture.

"In any case," she continued, "you get lunch money from your father. I assume you're buying lunch with it?"

"Uh-huh."

"Are you sure? You seem awfully hungry." There was no response. "What were you doing—running laps in the gym?" she pursued, enjoying her sarcasm.

"Kinda."

"How can you 'kinda' run laps?"

"Yes, we ran some laps. And yes, I had lunch and I'm hungry anyway."

Probing would be of no use, though he and Sammy were clearly using lunch money for something else: comic books, baseball games, maybe even marijuana. He'd been coming home ravenous, as if he'd had no food all day—though when pressed, he would recap the menu and regale her with commentary on the offerings. Barely suppressing her rage at the day, and wanting to be alone, she abandoned her son for the second floor, where she slammed her bedroom door.

Curt

RESENTFUL OF HER anger, Curt scarfed the remains of chicken thigh. He was hungry—he'd been playing basketball, learning as much as he could from the guys, most of them black, who used the gym after school. He enjoyed the group, and in the close contact of a game, no one thought so much about who was black, who was white. They were just guys playing together. All the conflicts of the school day seemed to fall away; on the court, the black guys were cool.

But he was also mad—of course his mom was accusing him of spending the money on something else, even though it wasn't true. On the other hand, no way would he confess what was happening. He was a boy, he could deal. And there was a challenge in having to deal, though it made him mad that the world was shaming him and refusing him a place—demanding what no one could manage to do. He'd always been an acknowledged leader among the boys. He was already as large as his father and nearly as powerful; he could do many things. But the world was tossing out obstacles he'd never foreseen. For days now, a boy had been ambushing him by the door to the lunchroom, confronting him, demanding money. The boy was black—small but scrappy—while the ambushes were nervy and outrageous, as if he was hoping Curt would lose his cool. Then a clash involving several others would erupt, and Curt would get pounded. That was the real purpose, he knew. It would disgrace him and mess things up—just when he was getting along with the basketball group. And so he'd been ignoring the smaller boy, moving around the space he commanded rather than shoving through. Then the week before, the boy had pulled a blade—small and rusty, but a blade. That had changed things fast. The boy's eyes were gleaming with a pleasure Curt had never seen before; he would enjoy hurting someone. Curt had dug up the money and cursed the boy, who made no move but only murmured "pussy," close and rude, claiming the win, before sauntering over to the lunch line, cool as could be.

For days now Curt had been forced to skip lunch. He was becoming more and more angry, though he'd promised himself no one would ever know why.

Sabrina

ONE DAY IN early March, Sabrina passed through Sproul Plaza and crossed the border of the campus, turning along Bancroft Way. There were no more lines of students and police facing off by the plaza, as they had for weeks. She was carrying a book bag; rounding the corner, she found her car, unlocked the door, and climbed in.

As usual, the going was slow. People were jaywalking; the streets were clogged with cars; the green light was changing to red. She contemplated the passing scene, her thoughts musing over the morning's reading, Margaret Mead's book on Samoa. The book was an old standby, one she'd read over and over during her early years with Michael, along with other classics in anthropology, because she was intrigued by them and so she could be someone he would really talk to. In a general way the plan had worked, as far as Michael was concerned. The problem had come from her: she'd grown beyond her own image and begun searching for more. So she'd begun taking classes in Michael's department, some from colleagues with whom he no longer agreed. That part had been naughty and fun and had given their evenings some new charge. She enjoyed ideas and they'd engaged as real colleagues—increasingly as opponents.

Though belonging to another place and era, Mead's report of casual young love under the palm trees had rung a profound meaning for Sabrina. When the theory of a warmongering people or warmongering gene had been proposed by an Ivy League colleague, she'd been much more appalled than Michael, though he would probably never go so far as the colleague. Following Mead, she regarded human problems as largely cultural and Mead's work on Samoa as proof that the aggressive and acquisitive individualism of her own modern world was culturally programmed. Rather than a dangerous unleashing of passions under the palm trees, Mead had found the vanquishing of jealous, damaging love through the early enjoyment of earth's pleasures and one's own body. Mead's young Samoans had been spared disfiguring conflicts by the magic of enough—enough of the simple things needed for happiness: warm sun, fresh island food, tolerant elders, and ever-changing love. Young Americans, whose gadgets and perfumes far surpassed any island largesse, if freed from shame would also prune away the urge for jealous hoarding of another person—they would no longer need Plato's *Symposium* in order to learn that. The young would emerge clear-eyed from the cave of obsessive love, passing through the door of the Now, where many paths lay open for them, and where the burden would be one of choosing. Boston or Berkeley, scholar or reveler, Greek or Black English—the young would pursue and be gathered into a group harmony.

Sabrina's eyes fell on a figure, a woman. The woman was Wanda; she was walking the other way, along Fulton Street toward the campus. She was young, barely a grown-up, though she maneuvered as though in charge. Sabrina flushed; in the mirror she eyed herself, grown though not yet graying, and sped on.

As Wanda's image flooded her thoughts, Sabrina became unexpectedly enraged. Wanda had pursued Michael, her former professor, even though she'd been living with Dan Dupres: so far, so imaginable. Anthropology departments had a well-earned reputation for producing sexually experimental faculty, Sabrina was aware. But when Wanda had abruptly dropped Michael, Sabrina had been outraged by the abandonment; her pride had been wounded in sympathy. A few weeks ago her problem had been how—in what manner and through what observances—to welcome the prodigal home, wounds and all.

Then a few days before, she'd gone to Telegraph Avenue for some books. She'd no sooner rounded the corner, heading toward campus, when she glanced through the window of the Caffé Med and found Michael and Wanda in a languorous embrace. From where she gawked, Sabrina had no fear of being seen—though she'd nearly stumbled over a bedraggled girl camped on the pavement, the leash for a scruffy German Shepherd wrapped around her ankle. Wanda had come as a passing interference and Sabrina had refused to feel threatened; the young woman was only seven years older than Helen, and though her maneuverings through Peace and Freedom had shown her to be brash and sharp, she was an angry rebel whose thinking would not hold Michael for long.

But the drama in the cafe window had changed everything: it had been glaring, aggressive, voluptuous. The sun had glowed on her husband's dark mane, for thankfully she'd been unable to see his face, eyes closed in bliss, so intolerable to see; feeding on the girl's mouth he seemed to be her age. Sabrina had gathered up her day, removing herself from the reach of the German Shepherd, whose long nose was already searching her foot, before he could cause a scandal. Soon she was safely around the corner and heading along Dwight Way.

Michael had returned for dinner in the usual manner, the red beard freshly combed and—was she imagining?—the eyes blandly unmoved as he elaborated for her the inner machinations of a departmental gathering: it was an enduring assumption of the marriage that she wanted to share in the personal components of his professional life. Wanda, of course, played no role in the story, though Sabrina had grasped with barely suppressed feelings of betrayal that the departmental gathering in all its length had overlapped with another engagement in the Med and could, therefore, be presumed to be largely or wholly imaginary.

Sabrina drove along Piedmont Avenue, passing beneath the California School for the Deaf and the eucalyptus groves above. Green with spring grasses, the place was lovely and secluded; by chance she and Michael had found the fire road one day when they'd followed one impulse or another. They'd made love in the open—the only time they'd done so, other than Samoa. She'd hoped for another child but none had come . . . Sabrina glanced away just as several imaginary figures emerged dancing from the eucalyptus groves. From Ashby Avenue she turned onto Elmwood Court, parked the Volvo, and paused for several moments peering at the brown-shingle house beyond the overgrown hedge. The hedge—Michael's handiwork—had run riot, shading the lower floor and obscuring it from the street. Planted the year they'd moved into the house, it now bore soaring tendrils.

Sabrina entered the house.

"Helen! Maggie!"

There was no response; she'd expected none. Maggie would be

playing at someone else's house; moody Helen would be anywhere she pleased. Not so long ago Helen had passed her afternoons on a couch overlooking the garden, where she'd enjoyed leafing through her father's books. Helen engaged her father in long conversations about other cultures, as though they were colleagues; he responded in a humorous though teacherly way as she imagined her own family configured along the lines of one or another Amazonian tribe. Recently, though, Helen was becoming ungovernable, and Sabrina wondered if Michael's indulgence were to blame —compounded, of course, by the upcoming year in the Amazon. For example, Helen had begun complaining during dinner, saying they should refuse meat. Sabrina had assumed the girl was simply showing her concern. She knew her father enjoyed ham, beef, lamb, the foods he'd grown up with—however would he feed on caterpillars? Then one day Helen had come in from the yard, all aglow, meaning to fry up something she'd caught there. There'd been a sense of mad purpose in her, enough for Sabrina to feel a sense of foreboding as the girl had gone off laughing, leaving dead bugs on the counter.

Sabrina entered the living room. There was the heavy smell of incense: so, Helen had come and gone, and she'd been smoking grass.

Sabrina flopped on the couch, scanning a nearby shelf of photographs. In one frame she glimpsed a young Michael, standing before the Samoan commissary with an island man of indeterminate age, the men smiling so unreservedly that they seemed to be celebrating some unusual event—a wedding or a reunion. As she remembered, the man had come from another island as an interpreter. Over the years she'd woven many tales around him, so that he'd assumed a presence in her life, some manner of faraway brother-in-law, as he now seemed. He posed bare-chested in the frame, more hardy than muscular, vaguely plump. By the man's shoulder rose Michael, in trousers and a collar, a wide-brimmed hat shadowing the face. Sabrina could no longer remember the photographer, someone she'd presumably known. Michael would know; he remembered everything, a burden in a profession concerned with morphology and wholes, and became engrossed in things in themselves. When Helen put forth a theory, he probed it inch by inch.

They'd often summoned up the island in the Pacific: faded,

sun-bleached sands; heavy breeze; palm fronds lashing far above a churning sea; grass roofs perched on bare pillars; people who'd been compelled to regard themselves through the eyes of others—or so the Westerners had imagined. As a young researcher, Michael had planned on probing and confirming the Samoan work handed down by anthropological forebears. He'd passed more than a year on the opening journey, learning the language and people and sussing out webs of power among the upper class of men. From the beginning, he'd found the women charming but guarded, so far from Mead's young women of the many and unentangling loves—beneath the palm trees, he'd concluded, lay only sand and jungle. Of course, in the beginning he'd been shy of wandering under the trees by the edge of the clearing, fearful of coming upon the carefree couples of anthropological report. But when he'd asked one of the men how many of the young women were virgins, the man had repulsed the inquiry, angrily denouncing Mead's falsehoods and adding how the islanders had jeered once she'd gone. Since then, a gradual sea change had come over Michael's understanding.

Sunlight faded from the room, leaving somber evening. The photograph lay under glass, a long-ago, far-flung wave on the shore of the world. Pools of color gathered in the men's faces, changing from blue to orange to gray, an evening ocean under a receding sky. The long shadows of palm trees danced on the sand.

Sabrina headed for the kitchen, where the sun had warmed the counters and hardwood herringbone floor. Taking up a peach, she ran it under the tap until she found the damp red fur and then ate slowly, staring beyond the garden fence. She thought about the sun-drenched island in the Pacific.

As she now understood, she'd been persuaded by the promise of something new, which had entered the world for Michael and through him. That was why she'd been so undone by the image of him and Wanda: a conventional adultery, older man–younger woman, an entanglement from which he would emerge the same, following the known quest. But the lawful resolution depended on her remaining in place—here, just as she was, in hall or living room or, God knows, weeping in the bedroom.

The peach had come to an end. She dropped the pit in the garbage, wiped her fingers on a rough cloth, and took up the telephone.

chapter three

Alice

IN EARLY MAY, the mornings were sunny and warm. Playground sounds from the early lunch-hour group could be heard through the classroom window as Alice read from the book she'd brought from home, an old one of her mother's. She'd been reading it over and over for nearly a year, as the binding grew ragged. The book was amusing and seemed a way of doing something useful or maybe just keeping clear of her enemy, Jocelyn. Early in the spring, something final had happened. There had been so many things, culminating one morning in a fatal error, when Mrs. Whitman had charged Alice with explaining some math problems to Jocelyn. The problems were new, though easy enough, and because Alice had caught on fast, Mrs. Whitman had made her Jocelyn's helper as she passed by, coaching the class. That sign of seeming preference had so angered Jocelyn that she'd rebuffed the help and refused any more palling around—though of course they'd never been pals, only girls in a bad place together.

Though the class was floundering, the school year would end soon enough and everyone would go off, wherever home was. By September, when they came back and resumed the age-old conflicts, Alice would be gone . . .

There came rapping sounds and a low humming. Behind her someone's desk squeaked, then slammed shut.

She scanned the page. A boy and a girl were journeying alone through the forest, fleeing a cruel stepmother. But the woman had seen them go and so she came creeping along, for she had powers over the brooks in the forest. The day was warm, and the boy was feeling dry, when they heard a leaping brook. Just as he was leaning over, glimpsing himself in the cool waters, the girl heard a murmur. "Whoever drinks from the brook will become a wolf," she thought, "and devour me." And so they passed by and soon found a slow-moving brook. But just as he was leaning over the pool, eager for its shadowy waters, the girl heard a murmur. "Whoever drinks from the brook will become a bear," she thought, "and maul me." So they passed by, soon coming upon a babbling brook. And just as her brother was leaning over, the girl heard a murmur. "Whoever drinks from the brook will become a roebuck," she thought, "and run away from me." Kneeling on the mossy ground, the boy was enjoying the babbling sounds, and as soon as the water touched his lips, he became a roebuck, eager to join in the King's hunt.

Alice wore a turquoise ring from Telegraph Avenue. She grasped the ring, turning it round her finger as she read.

She sensed movement by her elbow. "What's that?" Jocelyn was leaning over her arm, strangely close, murmuring, "How come you're always reading some old book?"

Wondering what was brewing, Alice made no response. With summer coming up, she could ignore the other girl.

Jocelyn was leaning over, nearly pressing on her shoulder. She made the rules and assumed Alice would comply.

"That book, what's it about?"

Alice glanced up, scanning her adversary. "A boy runs away. When he's in the forest, he has some water from a brook and becomes a wild animal."

"You're foolin' with me."

"No."

"A boy gets mean and crazy, he's had something more than water." Jocelyn paused. "He went there alone?"

"No."

"Who else, then?"

"A girl." Alice eyed her enemy. "She wants to keep him from the water. He could become a wolf or a bear."

Jocelyn leaned away.

"It's a good tale."

"Sounds like someone's lying."

"If you say so."

"Uh-oh, you're messin' with me."

A page came loose, the edges brown and flaking. Alice had sloughed off her bad mood, reading in peace; but now she could feel Jocelyn's eyes moving over the book and then over her.

They'd been ignoring each other for weeks, so why was Jocelyn bothering her? Something was smoldering in them and for now, they had no hope of getting away. She leaned over the page, no longer focusing on the words.

"Teacher gave you her book?"

Alice glanced up. Though Jocelyn's mouth made a smile, her eyes were cool and roving, taking in the loose page, Alice's ring and clothing.

"Your dress looks handmade," she remarked, irrelevantly. "You made it yourself?"

"No, my mother made it."

"Oh . . ." Jocelyn folded her arms, glancing away. "Never mind then."

There was a pause. So, her dress could be jeered at, even though she preferred it to Jocelyn's fussy blouse and patent-leather shoes. Her mother had done the sewing, using a simple paper pattern, and she enjoyed wearing it. If the girl was so clever at sparring, why should she need classroom help? And why should Alice have been chosen as her helper, now her enemy? Alice was feeling angry. She closed her mother's book and spread her hands on the desk. The lunch bell would peal soon enough.

"That's a pretty ring." Jocelyn's hand reached out. "Can I see?"

"Huh?"

"I said, can I see your ring."

Jocelyn leaned close, her hand reaching across the gap and fingering the shiny band and the turquoise inlays. Alice imagined the ring's powers, how she would steal off, leaving an empty space in class. She moved her hand away.

"Lemme see it up close." Jocelyn suddenly grasped the ring and jerked hard.

"Hey! No!"

"Just lemme see—"

"What's happening over there?" Mrs. Whitman demanded.

Feeling a growing fury, Alice yanked her hand free, nearly landing a blow as Jocelyn held on, refusing to let go. Jocelyn's eyes were eager and shining; if things went her way, she would have something to scream and complain about. She was messing with Alice, but Mrs. Whitman would scold them both. There was no sense anymore; the school year would soon be over, and they would be free of each other.

Jocelyn hunched over her paper, scrawling something. The lunch bell rang. She opened her desk, slammed down the leaf, and ran from the room.

Alice wandered slowly toward the lunchroom. Though feeling fed up with everyone and aching to be alone, she found her group of girls gathered around a table. The only remaining seat faced Nora, the handball player, who'd overheard the quarrel with Jocelyn.

Nora glanced up, eyes narrowing, gauging something. Nora imagined she could handle Jocelyn, but they'd never really tangled—maybe because Mrs. Whitman had never shown a preference for her.

Nearby, Tammy leaned in. "What's with that Jocelyn?" she mouthed.

"Dunno."

"Man, she has a problem."

Nora was ignoring them, and soon she was engaged in a bun-hurling exchange with a handsome, scoffing boy with heavy eyebrows, pale eyes, and a splash of sunburn. Alice recognized him as the boy who'd suggested she drop in on Jason's slumber party; maybe he'd made the threatening phone call as well. She eyed him, and her pulse jumped as he reared up in a slow windup and hurled a bun, missing Nora. The bun bounced off Debra's head.

Debra glared and pushed away her tray. "I'd leave him alone," she warned Nora. "He has storm-trooper leanings."

"So?" Nora shrugged.

"He's a bully."

"Well, I'm not scared."

"Maybe you should be."

Debra always seemed aloof, as though judging everyone's ideas as harshly as she'd judged the Cleaver comment. Faced by the jeering boy, however, Alice found they had something in common, if only a loathing, and she would have some measure of revenge, since Debra would now engage in a running commentary.

"If he comes near me—," Debra began.

"No way!" the boy hollered.

"—he's gonna be sorry."

"Go away," Alice commanded the boy, joining Debra in the cause. "You're a creep."

"A big oaf," Debra added. "A boxer, like that what's-his-name."

"Muhammad Ali?" called the boy. "I think he's cool!"

"That figures."

At a nearby table, some black girls were giggling to hear them arguing about Muhammad Ali.

"And I'm gonna play pro baseball," bragged the boy.

"Of course. You're a bully," Debra responded dryly.

"What's wrong with baseball?" Alice asked.

"Well, if you're a dumb jock—"

"My brother plays baseball—"

"Figures."

"—and he's not a bully."

"Are you sure?"

Alice glanced away, sorry she'd made common cause.

The group emerged from the lunchroom and headed for the bench. They'd all become Girl Scouts, hanging out at weekly meetings in a church basement on College Avenue. Now and then they would meet at each other's houses in small groups; that way, Nora and Tammy had come in a group to Alice's house. Her mother had been showing them how to bake a casserole when her brother had shown up, fresh from the gym, surprised by the room full of girls. Almost before they could respond, he'd gathered himself up, wiping a sweaty forehead and assuming an aloof face. Then they'd had a good look, admiring the all-American face and unruly blond hair before he grinned and loped away. Since then, Tammy and even Nora had made a pal—sometimes a leader—of Alice.

Tammy leaned, one hand playing in her hair. "Baseball used to seem so boring," she remarked, shifting the subject. "Not anymore." Dangling one leg over the other, she scanned the playground, smiling, as though some imagined baseball game had just come to ground.

"Do you play?" Alice asked.

Tammy smothered a laugh. "Oh, I'm no good. I just watch." Gazing on a group of boys tussling by the fence, she wound a strand of hair around one finger.

Nora smiled. "I play baseball sometimes," she announced, peering past Debra to Alice, "and I'm no bully."

A scruffy boy ran by in jeans and long, tangled hair. He was followed by another of the same style. Alice was feeling keyed-up; if only she could leave the girls on the bench and run over and join them.

Debra's gaze pursued them, withering. "Some of those boys," she murmured, aghast. "I mean, look at them."

Hands propped under her chin, Nora was surveying the yard. "Look—there's another one, over by the fence!"

The boy was a new breed—pure Telegraph Avenue. Bell-bottoms, grimy jeans jacket, hair tumbling over the shoulders.

Tammy giggled. "Maybe he's on LSD."

The others paused for a moment, adjusting to the thought. Alice wondered how it could be—after all, even her brother was too young for drugs.

"Sure seems freaky enough for that," Debra concluded.

"Maybe he doesn't need it." Tammy chewed a strand of hair. "My mom says, at our age we're all naturally stoned."

"Speak for yourself."

Tammy giggled again, collapsing her head on her knees.

"What age is that?" Nora inquired.

"Oh . . ."

"Speak for yourself," Debra repeated.

Tammy gave her a gray-eyed stare. "Oh, I am."

"How freaky you are."

Nora glanced at her watch. "Hey, I need something from the library. C'mon, Tammy." Then she added, "Alice, you coming?"

They abandoned Debra on the bench and headed for the school door, passing a group of black girls grouped around a transistor radio, talking eagerly. Hovering aloof from the group, one girl swayed loosely on long thin legs, clapping to the beat, as though on the edge of a dance floor.

When they reached the door, Nora paused. "There's nothing I really want in there. I had to get away from that Debra, she's so . . ."

". . . freaky," giggled Tammy.

The bell rang. As Nora and Tammy ran off, Alice hung back, hoping for a moment alone before confronting Jocelyn again. Fingering her ring, she wandered through the hallways, dawdling, delaying, and finally reaching her classroom long after the bell. She'd never come in late before; such a random, personal moment during the school day was something new. Approaching the room, she heard the sound of Mrs. Whitman's voice, reading from *Manchild in the Promised Land*. As she slunk through the door, Mrs. Whitman looked over.

"Alice, where have you been?"

"In the library."

Tammy flashed a smile, as though colluding in the lie, and Alice heard guffaws from Vaughan and Michael. Looking around, she felt a tingling in her face; all eyes were on her as she confronted an alarmingly empty space—her seat, the way it would be if she'd gone somewhere for good, like Tree Frog. Mrs. Whitman's eyes were vaguely sad, as though concerned or even baffled by Alice's small revolt. As she resumed her reading, Vaughan was heard mumbling, "How come she never punish no white girl?" as the guffaws rose louder.

Mrs. Whitman looked up from the book.

"Vaughan and Michael!"

"Huh?"

"Whaaa . . . ?"

"Vaughan Thompson!"

Vaughan glared back at her. "That's my name," he responded, angry. "You want my address?"

"Vaughan, you know that's no way to answer."

"I do as I please. You ain't nothin' to me."

The room hushed. They'd seen Vaughan go up against Mrs. Whitman, but never so rudely, so unapologetically. Vaughan was angry and charged up by the feud with Jocelyn and the seeming unfairness, and Michael, refusing to be outdone, glowered at Mrs. Whitman and gave a sullen jeer.

"I can show you who's the manchild."

Mrs. Whitman slammed the book down and rushed from the room, her face red and clenched. The response was new and alarming; no one could say what would follow. Some among the class were enjoying the showdown; others were dismayed by the end of the reading hour. Jocelyn sat, hands folded in her lap, gazing on Mrs. Whitman's empty desk. Tammy was peering covertly at Vaughan and Michael, as if in sympathy. The moments passed in an awkward lull. Someone coughed; someone else made a drumming sound; whispering began. Nearly ten minutes had elapsed when they heard the clacking of heels and a tearful Mrs. Whitman appeared, followed by the dean, Mr.

Haynes, a large, lean black man whose head was always cleanly shaved. In one hand he grasped an aluminum yardstick, swinging it loosely.

Mr. Haynes marched before the class and faced them, heels together, shoulders squared.

"Vaughan and Michael!" he said sternly.

The boys slumped. "Yessuh."

Mr. Haynes glared down on the offenders. "How come you're talking back to the teacher?"

Vaughan hung his head; Michael scowled.

"Now, who says you can do that?"

There was no response.

"You boys gonna answer me?"

"Nobody says," mumbled Vaughan.

"Then how come you're doing it?" Mr. Haynes gave a sour-mouthed nod. "Well, young man, I'm gonna see that you stop. Now, come on up here."

Vaughan made no move as Mr. Haynes rapped the yardstick hard on Mrs. Whitman's desk. "I said come here!"

"Teacher let that white girl—"

"Come here!" Brandishing the yardstick, he bore down on Vaughan. The boy cowered, his hands over his head, as the man grasped him by the shoulder, dragging him up and through the rows to the front of the room. There they confronted each other, Vaughan staring through the man's chest. Mrs. Whitman had moved back from the fray, occupying a place by the door.

"Now get down there," Mr. Haynes commanded, grasping the yardstick and pounding the floor once, "and show me fifty pushups."

Under the admiring eyes of the class, Vaughan dropped down and, with unrepentant bravado, spread himself full length. Hands firmly planted by the man's shiny leather shoes, he began pumping wildly. "Three, four, five . . . twenty-one, twenty-two . . . thirty-eight, thirty-nine," counted Mr. Haynes.

Suddenly Vaughan collapsed. The man's legs towered over him.

"You have more to do."

"Can't do no more."

"Hurry up—you're wasting my time."

Vaughan lay gasping on the floor. Then he slowly propped

himself through several more pushups. As Mr. Haynes counted each pushup aloud, he slapped the yardstick hard on the boy's butt, as though keeping time. Vaughan was blubbering now, his face messy with tears. Michael turned from the ugly scene, angry and scowling in defeat, as the class—spellbound and ashamed—absorbed the spectacle of Vaughan's punishment.

Mr. Haynes enjoyed humiliating Vaughan and making him cry. Alice had never seen such demeaning punishment in school, and it made her queasy. She'd done something wrong and Mrs. Whitman had let it go; in any case, Mr. Haynes would never have punished her that way—she was white, and white parents would surely be outraged. But Vaughan was black, and that changed the rules. The scene was strange and repugnant, not least because Mr. Haynes was also black.

As Vaughan slunk away down the row, Mr. Haynes gave the others a sour, frigid smile, as though daring them to jump into the boxing arena for a new round. Then he addressed Michael.

"As for you, young man—come to my office tomorrow. I want to see what kind of manchild you really are." And grasping the yardstick, he marched from the room.

There was an embarrassed hush, and then the final bell rang. Jocelyn turned toward Alice, and the two girls glared at each other in smoldering rage.

THERE WAS NO reason to go home, thought Alice, where her mother would be napping or reading a novel on the couch. Her mother's involvement with the Party had ended, and she was now engaged by another group, composed only of women, whose purpose was unfathomable to Alice. So many things were becoming unfathomable. Though she'd had enough of Vaughan and Michael and the trouble they caused, she'd never imagined Mr. Haynes would choose such a degrading punishment. Mr. Haynes was a bad man, she thought; Mr. Boyd, the principal, was reasonable by comparison. Mr. Boyd had scolded her for calling Ben an ugly name; but if she'd tangled with Mr. Haynes, things could have been much worse.

The school day had been ugly. Jocelyn was a classroom neighbor, no more; yet Alice had hoped for some communication, some casual exchange, even as they went separate ways on the playground. She'd been a fool—the girl detested her. Everywhere around her was anger and conflict. Mr. Haynes was mean, and as he was humiliating Vaughan, a harmless loudmouth, other boys were getting away with worse things every day.

Lured by the presence of people who seemed safe and peaceful, Alice headed for Telegraph Avenue. Rounding a corner, she came upon a park. The park had sprung up only weeks before from a muddy lot, and though she'd heard her mother refer to it as "People's Park," she'd never seen the place.

On fresh turf, by a young tree, a group of drummers played for a surrounding throng; near them danced a girl in clown face and a long shawl. Her cheeks were painted red and yellow, and there were blue diamonds around her eyes. Flowing cloth hung from her hips as she moved around a boy who was playing a saxophone. As Alice passed by, her mind overflowing with the girl's lithe movement and the boy's reedy melody, the image of Vaughan's misery gave way before a flood of hope.

Beyond the drummers, groups of young people lounged on the grass. Alice found a bench near a flower bed, where she could see a woman watering the flowers. Opening her book, she began reading. Soon a boy and a girl her age ran up. She'd seen the boy before: he'd been on the playground, and Debra had called him "freaky."

The girl ran up, smiling. "Hey!" She and the boy may have been scruffy, but they were more welcoming than Debra.

"Hi."

"I'm Valerie," called the girl.

"And I'm Jim," added the boy. He flashed a big grin. "Our father made this park. Welcome!"

Laughing and waving, Valerie and Jim ran on.

chapter four

The Dupres

AFTER DAN DUPRES left for California, in 1965, Valerie and Jim stayed in Colorado for three years with their mother, Carol. She'd married Dan at seventeen, not long after the army school had expelled him. They'd done the ceremony before a justice of the peace, who'd frowned on Carol's maternity gown; and then the baby came. Dan soon found a machinist's job in a plant near Denver, a place called Rocky Flats. A year after Valerie was born, along came Jim.

Once the children were in school, Carol found work in a flower shop. Colorful and perfumed, flowers were easy—they never whined. Soon she could arrange and wrap them and sell them to anyone who came along. That was a blessed thing, because one payday, eight years and four days after he'd begun the rounds in Rocky Flats, Dan abandoned family and job to ramble further west. When the phone rang four months later, he had an address in a place near the Naval Supply Center in Oakland, California. He had no money, he told her. Though he left a phone number, she found no reason to call. They were through.

One day a man known as Hawk came by the shop. A large, rough man, he appeared as though he would not know an orange tulip from a poppy, but when she handed him the flowers—a bouquet of her choosing, red roses, pale lilies, and lilac—he nodded the leather cowboy hat and murmured something too low to hear. When he returned the following week, wanting another bouquet, Carol could see he was courting someone.

Dan was no flower man, Carol would always say—he dealt in army jargon and beer. The jargon had carved him a place in the army school and then the plant; beer and raucousness won a few hours of freedom. By 1965, when the war began to boom, he'd already passed the favored age; old by army standards, he was reasonably safe. He'd turned yellow anyway, grumbling about the war. Carol never understood why he'd turned so bad, so cowardly; he had a good deal, she was always saying, a government job and a suburban home in the shadow of the mountain.

Hawk had another job at the government plant. One Saturday evening, he'd purchased a bunch of red roses, held them up, and then handed them back to Carol. For a moment she thought he'd found something wrong with them, but then she understood. Before long he was hanging with her, then moving a few belongings to the house. He was another one for army jargon and beer; not a problem, Carol would shrug, so long as he was no coward, no AWOL man.

Jim and Valerie shared a room in the small suburban house. They'd always shared a room. Now Hawk was always with Carol, and he was no father. One evening when the room had gone dark, there came muffled sounds.

"Pssst!"

"What?"

"I wanna go somewhere—"

"Now?"

"Soon."

"Where?"

"Dunno. But I'm gonna go somewhere."

"On your own? How?"

"Dunno. But I know there's a way." Jim lay in the dark, hands folded on his chest. "How come he—never mind."

"What?"

"How come Dad had to leave?"

"Because he had to."

"I know, but why?"

"How should I know?" Valerie wondered when he would stop. It used to be that he would cry; now he asked unanswerable, imponderable things. She wanted to sleep.

"She's a . . . bitch," he added, barely loud enough to hear.

"So what? What are you gonna do?"

"I'm gonna leave. You coming with me, or no? Things'll be better, I promise. No Mom. No Hawk. No school."

"Oh no, I'm gonna see what happens here. 'The morning is wiser than the evening.'"

"What's that mean?"

"Dunno, but I heard it somewhere."

"Hey, Val, you sure hear some strange things."

And so they stayed with Carol and Hawk in the shadow of the mountain.

One day, the four of them went for a long walk. It was a Saturday, and when Hawk and Carol emerged from the bedroom, Hawk announced that he was going to show them how to climb the mountain. Jim and Valerie would have to learn to do more for themselves, he said. Hawk brought them in the car to the foot of the mountain, where he knew there was a path. Then they climbed up, up, up, following the path and Hawk as he forged ahead, until they had nearly reached the top of a ridge. The whole world unfolded below, or so it appeared to Valerie: slopes layered with evergreen forest, an upland valley dabbed with lakes and ponds, and, above them, gleaming peaks challenging the sky. She thought she could see the house they'd come from crouched at the foot of the mountain, near the glinting surface of a pond, gleaming like aluminum in the sun.

"Oh, no way," laughed Hawk. "Too close to the mountain. That's a house for ski bums."

"Then where?"

"See that clump of houses? Somewhere in there . . ." And he gestured carelessly, as if at a blade of grass.

There, with everything else, she thought to herself. But she was unsure what to feel; though the house was somewhere below, she was unable to find it among the heap of houses jumbled there.

Carol gave them a crust of bread and some cheese. Valerie took her bread and cheese and sat down on a rock. She was hungry. When she looked up, Hawk and her mother had found a shady ledge. Her brother had wandered down a path to a small meadow, where he was throwing crumbs to a flock of ravens. Soon he was done feeding them and came up the path, looking for something else to do.

Hawk and her mother emerged from the shady ledge onto the path, dusting themselves off. Now they were ready to go. The group began journeying down the mountain, the dappled shadows hovering on them, around them. Her mother and Hawk went on ahead, while Valerie and Jim scuffed along the path, snapping low-lying twigs from the trees as they passed and thrashing the bushes with them. Once, as they rounded a bend, they saw a stag bound onto the path. Antlers flaring, the stag turned, surveying them a moment, and then ran on through the woods.

When they came to the base of the path, the sun had gone and the shadows hung cool and damp as the gloom of a woodshed. Beyond the car rose a small wooden house, a tavern; above the door glimmered a red glass, pouring sparks of gold over those who passed through. Carol pulled Valerie by the arm and told her, "The walk was long. Hawk wants a glass. You and your brother stay by the car—you're too young to come in. The bartender says no, Hawk says." She paused long enough to frown. "No wandering off, now. We won't be long."

They went to the car. Valerie scrambled onto the front passenger seat, where her mother now usually rode. Soon her brother was slumbering in the back. She heard the cawing of ravens. She dragged herself along the seat until she was staring through the wheel, one foot pressing on a dead pedal. Her brother awoke.

"What's happening?" he yawned, then added, "I miss anything?" as though he'd fallen asleep during a cops-and-robbers program and had just tuned in again.

She touched the rearview mirror, slanting it so she could see him without turning around. She saw the small shadow along the chin: a scar from when he'd fallen from a jungle gym, before her father left.

"Well?" pursued Jim. "They coming back or what?"

"Hawk needs a glass. That's what she told me." Valerie turned, smiling. "He's quenching his thirst."

"I could do with some quenching myself. Quench, quench." Jim paused. "Those ravens sure are happy."

"That's 'cause you fed them."

"Naaah, it's not the same ones. Can't be." He opened the door. "Well, I'm going in. You coming?"

"They told us not to go in."

"Who says?"

"Hawk says."

"Hell with him, I need some quenching."

"Maybe there's a stream." Valerie turned and through the wheel she saw a meadow, and beyond the meadow a forest. "Water comes down the mountain. There's bound to be a stream."

They climbed out of the car and ran, thrashing through tall stalks of meadow grass. Soon the meadow ended in a sparse grove of aspen. It was dusk; they could enter far into the forest before coming upon a stream or small pond.

"No," she called, "I'm going back. There's enough water at home."

"C'mon, we're almost there."

"You can have some when we get home."

"No way. I'm gonna find me a stream, *now*."

And so they went on, deeper and deeper into the gloom, aspen leaves fluttering overhead, until at length they stood by the bank of a fast-flowing stream. Jim sprang forward, kneeling in the mud, but as he leaned over the rushing stream, Valerie grabbed him by one leg. He glanced up and saw where she stared warily along the far bank. There in the waning light hovered the nose and ears of a lean gray animal; the eyes shone pale yellow.

"Run," commanded Valerie, "before that dog jumps over here."

And so they ran. They ran and ran through the trembling aspen, coming at last to the forest's end, and there they stumbled from the shadowy canopy into the meadow, heavy with the last remnants of day. Soon they were near the tavern.

"What was that?" he gasped.

"Some dog—"

"Unh-unh. No way that thing was a dog."

"What, then?"

"Could be a wolf," Jim concluded. Then he stared around. "Where's the car?"

"Dunno." Valerie glanced at the tavern, chewing on her lower lip. Golden strands heavy as rope fell over her shoulders. "Maybe she's in there with Hawk."

They approached the door of the tavern and leaned, peering in. Near the door slumped a man in jeans and a full mustache. He wore a red-and-black hunting jacket; a young German Shepherd slumbered by his feet.

"Come on in."

Valerie entered the room, followed by Jim.

"Looking for someone?"

"My mother and Hawk. They've been here for over an hour."

"Hmmm. Look around then."

Valerie ventured forward, taking in the room. It was early evening and few people were there. Her mother and Hawk had gone—that much was clear at a glance. For a moment she surveyed the room, wondering what to do. Four men were gathered round a table playing cards; another leaned on the bar, smoking and jawing with the bartender. Valerie ignored the card players and approached a corner table, where someone had abandoned a jug of beer. There she found a chrome lighter: a horse galloped across the front, four red rhinestones studding the mane. The horse belonged to Hawk; he would be wanting it. Feeling the chrome cool and smooth on her fingers, she pushed it deep in her pocket.

Jim was observing the card players. He hung shyly by a man's shoulder; the man wore a cap shading his face, and he was dealing the cards, slapping them down. The other players scanned the cards one by one as they came; then they played, morose and cool, tossing them on the table. When the hand folded, the dealer glanced up, scanning Jim from head to toe.

"Oh my, what have we here."

"Hey . . ."

The man gave a raspy laugh. "How'd you come here, son?"

"Hawk brought me."

"Hawk. Oh my." He panned the room, pausing as he came upon Valerie. "He's gone now. Along with the lady . . ." There was smothered laughter from the table.

Another player, a sunburned man with heavy hands, held up a tumbler of golden rum, beckoning Jim with the other hand. "C'mon, boy, you're looking dry. Did your ma take you up the mountain?" There was more laughter from the group of players.

Jim flashed a phony grin. "Man, they took us way far."

"I see. Then you're real dry by now." A rough hand pressed the tumbler on the boy.

Suddenly the barman growled, "I warned Hawk, never bring no boy around here."

Jim grabbed for the tumbler, but the sunburned man flung it to the ground. "You heard the barman," he commanded. "Now go on, leave."

The barman was glaring, palms on the bar.

Valerie moved for the door, above which she now saw an enormous bear's head, stuffed and mounted on the wall. Followed by Jim, she rushed through the door into the unpeopled evening.

They stood in the meadow near the foot of the mountain, wondering what to do. The road curved gradually beneath a street lamp and then tapered off in the dark. Soon the headlights of a car appeared, rushing toward them in the gloom. "Maybe we can get a ride," suggested Valerie, who ran to the shoulder of the road and put out her thumb, as she'd seen people do. The car rushed past and then slammed to a halt, the door gaping open. Her mother leaned out, waving impatiently.

"Hurry and jump in," she called. "I told you to stay by the car, but what do you do?" She glared at Valerie. "You went wandering back up the mountain, I'll bet."

She shoved them in and slammed the door. The car lurched onto the pavement. Hawk gunned it, and they sped on.

"Always wandering off," Carol scolded, never turning around, "same as your father. I should send you there—have your fun with him. You're the same—always trouble, always wandering off. You want trouble, go stay with Dan."

Hawk grunted with amusement.

Jim's fingers rapped on the window. "When can I go?"

Carol turned and glared. "You can go now." Jim made her mad, for sure. She was always saying he was young Dan and growing up every day—and she'd had enough. "Tomorrow, on the bus—both of you. Gather some clothes, whatever you have, 'cause you're not coming back." She paused, as though alarmed by her own words. "You heard me," she added.

Jim had begun snuffling and refused to respond. Valerie slouched, parting a heavy golden curl as though separating the strands of a rope.

When they reached home, Carol produced a small footlocker. Valerie rounded up clothes as Jim examined an old cap gun he'd unearthed from under the bed. She heaped the clothes in the trunk, wondering if this sudden turn of events was real or if she would have to undo everything in the morning. When she was through, Jim flung the gun on top. Then he sat on the footlocker as she fastened the clamps in place.

Valerie was suddenly fed up. "Now see what you made her do."

"She'll be sorry."

"Not sorry enough."

"So what?"

"So, what's Dad gonna do when he sees us?"

"He's gonna be happy. Why?"

The following day, Carol drove them to the Greyhound terminal in Denver and put them on a bus for California. They had the footlocker and a brown paper bag with apples, bread, and jam. The bus departed in the morning; the bread and jam were gone by noon. Then there came a long, slow, rumbling ride, with nothing more to do until they pulled up in Salt Lake City at nearly nine in the evening. There they found a man who bought them ice cream and told them the Lord would be generous to those who were good. Returning to the bus, they passed a small fountain in the shape of a roebuck, with water pouring from its mouth into a shallow pool. Coins glowed dully beneath the surface. Jim leaned over and scooped up some water.

"No!"

He leaned in and drank, long and cool. A few drops splashed on his cheek, as though they were in a rainy woods. There was a jerking in his leg as though he would run. Valerie grabbed him by the arm and he looked up.

"Hey, lemme go."

"No, we're staying together."

"I've had enough of the bus. I wanna run."

"Come here."

Valerie had brought a bag of candy. She reached in her jacket and brought out a candy bar; breaking off a chunk, she dangled it for Jim.

"You can run tomorrow, when we get there."

Feeling a surge of energy, he leaped for the candy. He would be ready to run when the chance came.

Back on the bus, Valerie dozed. By morning, they'd passed the eastern slope of the Sierra Nevada, and by early afternoon they pulled into Oakland.

A large, lean man showed up for the bus. He was tardy, though not by much.

Valerie remembered her father, but vaguely; in any case, he'd changed: beads and sandals, a fringy purple vest, heavy golden strands like her own. She'd never known a man who wore no lumberjack gear but colorful cloth flowing everywhere. For some moments she was confused, then glad. But Jim was uncustomarily shy; the man who met them by the bus was no longer Hawk but the scorned and unfamiliar father, Dan Dupres.

Soon Valerie and Jim found themselves living on the second floor of a house in North Berkeley. Dan hadn't been there long, barely long enough to round up furnishings. He scrounged the beds from a woman he knew from the Movement, trading marijuana for them. Some rough army wool soon appeared along with the beds, though there were few other comforts. The army wool was heavy and scratchy. Valerie began sleeping in her clothes; then she would wear them wherever she had to go. Soon she'd forgotten the rhythm of changing clothes morning and evening. There was no more wondering what to wear: her corduroy jeans and Spider-Man top had become permanent, dead growth, armor against the world. When she was hungry, she searched the cupboard for tea bags and honey. Tea and honey made a warm syrup.

When they reached California, school had already begun. Dan enrolled them in fourth and fifth grades. Her brother had always been a handful: he fought with other boys, he needed management. Dan was busy on Telegraph Avenue; he had the jeans shop to run, he had the Movement, he had a woman named Wanda—enough to do every day, and more. In the evening, Dan and Wanda gathered around the table, smoking and peeling oranges and talking about the campus war. The country beyond was gearing up for the 1968 election: the farce of democracy, another turn of the wheel. There was war everywhere, and much to do.

FROM THE EARLY days, Jim managed to follow the father's unfamiliar ways. He'd never followed anyone's ways; but Dan demanded only that they care for themselves, not interfering with him or Wanda. Jim was happy for once, free to come and go from the North Berkeley apartment and the jeans shop on Telegraph Avenue. Even so, in the beginning he had no other boys to run with while Dan and Wanda were endlessly rapping, planning for the campus war. There was only the group that hung around near the shop on evenings when the place was closed. Soon enough, though, things were really jamming: they'd taken over Moses Hall —he'd heard of Moses—demanding that a Black Panther be made a professor; they'd closed off the border of the campus, and no one could pass unless Ray-gun and the Regents gave up the class-rooms to them.

Jim was cool with all the commotion. He had no use for the classrooms he'd seen. He was eager to hang with other boys or wander through the hallways, where he found the strange ones, who wanted to sell him oregano or do something with him in the bathroom. He would play along; he was eager to learn new things, and he could always run. On the playground, he found a handful of boys like himself, and as long as they were there, the lunch hour was fun. They saw him as a leader: he could scare the other boys by doing things they'd never do. The professors' sons could talk, but he could whup them easy. Only the black guys were ready for a hassle. Jim refused to walk away from a fight; that made him a badass, and more guys would run up to challenge him. That was becoming a real problem—black guys could do some pounding. They made fun of his unwashed jeans and lengthening hair, they shoved and taunted, sneering "cracker" or "girly." Some days he felt so mad he needed revenge, so he turned on the easy boys, the professors' sons, and made them run. Sure enough the principal would haul him in.

Jim was looking for some boys to go home with, where they would see the programs he remembered from the house in Colorado, rough men with guns, and he would urge them on and plan for when he'd become a man. For sure, he would do something dangerous. Every day in California he heard Dan and Wanda rapping about the overseas war, and he wanted to go—even though they were planning to stop it. He wondered what that meant, stopping the war—Hawk had never rapped that way. Sure enough, Jim would be a gun-toting badass in army rags; no one would end the war before he'd had a chance. One day he even hollered that in class and the teacher freaked, saying he was an angry boy. He wondered what that meant, too. Angry was just something he was, no reason for her to be so bummed.

Dan never argued about school problems, the way Carol had. He and Wanda would say school was something they used to control you, keep you down. Some of the boys in class were as good as dead—never hassled the teacher, barely moved. Jim observed them, knowing he could never be stuffed game like the black bear in Colorado, the one he remembered from the bar.

And so, it was easy, dealing with Dan. Jim and Valerie went

together to Telegraph Avenue, and when Dan was in the jeans shop, there would be people coming up and down the Avenue looking for him, looking for something other than jeans. Sometimes they would collar Jim, rapping like he was already a man, asking about Dan's side stuff. Jim wondered and observed, focused on learning what he could. He and Valerie had a good thing and no hassles. He saw the boys from the suburbs with straight, phony parents, people you'd see on TV, the father pulling the boy by the arm and the mother shielding his eyes from the likes of Jim. Why they even came to Berkeley, he would never know.

Soon he was smoking grass with some older guys on the Avenue; then he really began hearing about what went down in the back of the jeans shop.

The Avenue was a whole world, with something always happening and no one ragging on him. Whenever Valerie rapped about Colorado, he glared—that whole scene was gone. No use looking back. Now he could barely sleep for wondering what was happening on the Avenue. They'd done so much already: the bus through the mountains from Denver, awake in the dark, then through the valley and over some low mountains just like the olden days in the covered wagons. Then the bay, the Golden Gate, and far beyond the sea—China. He'd heard Wanda laugh, saying "Red China" and something about a guy named Mao—a sound like mooing, or a faraway foghorn. There was no foghorn in Colorado—only forest and snow, shining on the peaks even in summer. Hawk bragged about skiing, but they had no money for that. Now they'd found a place where things happened even when there was no money for making them happen.

EVERY AFTERNOON WHEN the school bell rang, Valerie found Jim on the playground, and together they made their way to Telegraph Avenue and Dan's shop. She was always glad to be away from school, where the other girls regarded her as outlandish. Dan had bestowed new jeans on her and Jim, but they were never laundered and soon became scuffed and grimy. Jim was proud of the shiny grunge, wearing it as a freak flag, but the schoolgirls spurned Valerie for pushing the same jeans on them every day. Soon she began maneuvering for another pair. Hanging around the shop, she learned from Wanda how to help a customer, offering suggestions or showing them to the changing room through the hanging beads in the back. And as they stood barefoot before the mirror, she learned how to close the deal, saying, "You look far-out!"

One day, when she thought she'd done enough for a reward, she told Wanda how Dan had promised more jeans. Wanda rummaged on a shelf for some bell-bottoms with colored thread on the seams. "How about these?" she said with a shrug, tossing them on the counter. The pants hung loosely on Valerie but she loved them; for three weeks she hardly removed them. Soon the girls were staring through her again and she returned to the old jeans, now fresh and clean from all the scrubbing she'd done one evening in the bathroom.

"What the hell are ya doin'?" Jim demanded, when he saw her through the bathroom doorway.

"A woman has to work for beauty," she said, and laughed, holding up the pants for him to look. "See—they're new again!"

"Wanda show ya how to wash 'em?"

"No. *I* showed me."

"You wash mine?"

"You're such a bummer."

"Does that mean yes?"

"That means no."

Holding up the soggy pants, she ran across the wooden floor and hung them by the window. Jim followed her. "Those girls are never gonna talk to you, even with clean pants," he announced.

Dan nodded and laughed. "No one on the Avenue has clean clothes. You can hang out there."

So Valerie passed many hours on the Avenue, and when there was nothing else to do, she wandered into the shop, where Dan would be, always gabbing with someone. She wanted to hear him because everyone admired him. Long and handsome, he leaned on the counter telling the freaks who dropped by how he'd come from volunteers who fought for the Republic of Texas. Ranching and anarchy were the forces they knew. He'd grown up there and gone to army school, and then he'd worked in the weapons plant in Colorado.

In army school, Dan had learned how to plan and carry out a campaign. When he'd arrived in Berkeley, in 1965, other planners were already on the scene, scheming to stop the transport of troops through Oakland. He'd always dreamed of blowing up supply lines. He remembered the opening scene from a book—an American in Spain moving among guerrilla bands, coming to blow up a bridge and then moving on.

One day, during a lull in the protest campaign, he'd landed another machinist job and suddenly the money was flowing. Running machinery and selling marijuana, he'd saved enough to open the shop. Jeans were the coming thing; jeans were everywhere, and everyone was buying them.

Though the cops regarded Dan as a rabble-rouser, he could fade away if the scene got ugly. He parlayed the shopkeeper thing into the role of Telegraph Avenue spokesman, becoming leader of the amorphous group of young people encamped on the four blocks south of campus. He'd never gone to college, but now he'd show up for the leafleting and rallies in Sproul Plaza; leaving Wanda or Valerie in the shop, he'd run to campus, weaving through the throng, hobnobbing, sharing news.

As the weeks passed, Valerie forgot her mother and Hawk. She was no longer bummed at Jim for making them leave Colorado. Soon enough, she'd be going to the Fillmore West with Arlene and Bobby, who hung around the jeans shop rapping with Dan. Then there'd be no more brushoff from the lousy schoolgirls—she'd have something over them. On the Avenue, she only had to say, "Dan is my father," and she was golden. Never before had she been found so worthy. People from the Derby Street commune were always ready to rap or offer her scraps of food or even money for carrying someone's stash. People in the flophouse rooms over the shop found her amusing, and she learned what would amuse. All afternoon she and Jim ran up and down, playing with the older group, experiencing new things, passing under the radar of undercover narcs. Then in the evening when the shop was closed, they'd grab a sandwich at the Caffé Med before heading through the campus to Dan and Wanda's.

COPS SWARMED THE Avenue and surrounding blocks, harassing the freaks for drugs and panhandling and wearing the flag in the wrong place—on the ass. Every few days there was another hassle, but then the charges would be dropped. Valerie was eleven years old and Jim a year younger; though wary of narcs, they were no runaways with nowhere to go: they belonged to Dan and the Avenue.

Jim hung with Bobby, who hung with Arlene when Marlboro Man was in Canada on a run. Bobby needed a lookout when there was a deal going down over Dan's shop, and so he showed Jim how to confuse a narc. The cops would leave him alone because he was so young, Bobby assured him; then Bobby would reward him for being so useful.

One day as Jim rambled along the block, surveying the cars for undercover narcs, he saw Bobby signaling for him. Turning, he wandered seemingly at random along the pavement, meandering finally by the doorway where Bobby lounged, thumb and forefinger pinching a cigarette.

"There's a key coming in," Bobby murmured, eyes scanning the block. "If you see anything come down, call me from the shop."

"No problem. Always ready to help."

"Hey, you're a buddy."

Then Bobby was gone. Jim had made one save so far: the narc had come sniffing around during a deal, and Jim told Dan and Dan placed a call, hanging up after one ring. That was to let Bobby know of the uncool presence. Now Bobby was very much a buddy, one moreover who gave rewards. In the beginning Jim was scared, but no more: he imagined a force or energy around them, keeping the cops from Bobby.

Jim rambled on, passing a head shop, then he wandered through the cars on Telegraph, heading for the Caffé Med. The undercover narc who hung at the Med had gone home; everyone knew him, anyway. Jim turned back, pausing to glance at some beads and pendants arranged on a small table. The woman by the table leaned over, fingering a pendant. "Aries? Sagittarius?" she inquired, as though he had money to buy something. He could grab some beads from the woman and run—but no, he'd promised Bobby.

As Jim was moving along, Valerie emerged from the doorway of the jeans shop, gnawing on an apple. Seeing her and the apple, Jim remembered he was hungry. He crossed Telegraph on the fender of a passing car, running up to Valerie.

"Hey, lemme have some!"

She was already long and gangly. "Come and get it."

He jumped and grabbed the apple and bit off a chunk.

"There's food at the Derby house!" Valerie announced triumphantly. "If you're so hungry, let's go now."

"Unh-unh, I'm spying on narcs."

"How about you go and I'll do some spying. I can eat later."

"No way, I promised Bobby."

"As long as it's one of us, Bobby won't care."

"I told you, no way."

"Then stay here," Valerie said, shrugging. "I'll bring some food from the house."

"Do that."

She ran off toward the Derby Street commune. Jim glanced after her and then the other way. Narcs could be anywhere; they could remember who they'd seen and collar him later.

Wham! The door slammed as a man appeared on the sidewalk. He was tall and lean and wearing black leather pants and a vest. He had a bushy mustache and shades, long sideburns and a ponytail. Though Jim had never seen him before, sure enough he was Bobby's man. Bobby would follow soon. The man sauntered past a head shop, as though he saw no one, as though there was no one to be seen. Jim gaped, gorging on envy. The dude swaggered, the leather taut and shiny over his ass—permanent anatomy, the leather seemed—as he waded through a lane of moving cars, lingering as the lane slowed, pausing to finger a cigarette, cupping his hands as though he would trumpet a charge and then dropping the match by the bumper of a car, exhaling, idle, as the sun rebounded from the shades. Then he sauntered on down the Avenue and through the open door of a record shop, blending into the gloom and the throbbing beat.

Soon Bobby was in the doorway, glancing around for Jim. Jim moved slowly, learning to saunter as the other had done.

"C'mon!" Bobby hissed in an urgent undertone. "Hurry up."

Jim followed him through the doorway and up several steps. Bobby turned. He pulled out some crumpled bills and thrust one into Jim's hand. "Tell Dan, no more scoring from that dude."

"No?"

"I got a bad feeling."

"He do something?"

"No, man, but I got a feeling." Bobby was angry. "Run along now. I got stuff to do."

Bobby ran up the steps.

When Jim arrived at the communal house, the dinner revel was on, something shameless.

DAN AND WANDA had much to say about the surrounding land and the people who'd been there before the coming of the Anglos. Gathered around the table, they would rap about the Costanoan Indians and the Spanish and Mexican army men who'd enslaved them on ranchos stolen from the Costanoans' old woodlands. Then the Anglos had conquered the land through warfare, and Gold Rush men had moved in, squatting on the ranchos, exploiting the land's bounty for themselves, until the US government and its courts agreed to another massive rip-off, giving them ownership of the land simply because they'd been using it.

Jim and Valerie understood only the most general flow of events. For them the story began:

Once upon a time by the bay, there was redwood forest belonging to everyone. One day a man came bearing gold by the bushel from Sutter Creek. He cleared the trees and sold the lumber and founded a town. Then as roads and houses sprang up, he founded a college for the sons and grandsons of men who made money from the wilderness. Soon enough there was no more land by the bay shore for the people who came searching for the old forest, the lumberjacks and workers and those flooding West, and so they slept on the streets by the campus. As more and more of them came, grumbling how they'd been pushed from the land, a group began planning how they would repossess the people's forest and make a new world.

The planners found some muddy turf near Telegraph Avenue— a vacant lot belonging to the people of California, but controlled by a gang of regents and professors. The people gathered there, preparing the ground for planting. The planners knew the regents and professors had control of the land; even so, they thought, *If we camp there and farm the land, there's nothing in the world they can do.*

And so one day they made a park.

They announced the plan in a local paper, naming a day for founding the park. When the day came, people flooded in from the Avenue, followed by others from the campus and the surrounding neighborhood. In small groups they worked the land by day and reveled by night, lounging on the turf and enjoying the fruits of man's labor—performed freely and willingly in the absence of bosses—sharing grass and communal meals, resolving quarrels among themselves, and planning revolution.

In the park, Jim and Valerie now ran among gardeners in colorful rags, planting and playing and feeding on roast pig. Every day they fled school for the people's land, where they wandered from group to group, foraging and doing as the others were doing. Everyone laughed because they were children, and everyone had learned long ago that children should never be doing the things that happened in the park—everyone but Jim and Valerie, who thought they'd found the real world, where they could be free and wild, where they could belong. And the more they learned from the older group, the more amusing the older group found them.

In the evenings they shared food with the others, gathered around some drummers on the grass, where Jim and Valerie lounged as they had in the playroom of the suburban home in Colorado, when they had shag rugs and television. Three women would come bearing a cauldron of soup for the park people, or a van would appear, carrying women who handed out sandwiches. The meals were fun and increasingly necessary; Dan was busy, and Jim and Valerie had no resources beyond the group from the Avenue who clung to the people's land, gardening and planning for war. They controlled the park even more than the Avenue: now, as the sun dropped below the roofs, the group had a place for themselves alone, where they could gather far from the snooping eyes of cops or suburban couples who'd heard rumors of the counterculture and come to gawk at the passing herd. Jim and Valerie had a group, a home; they camped out in the park, where a spare sleeping bag could always be found, and where someone passed them a joint before bed. Then in the morning, they would head for school.

More and more people were gathering in the park. They grew louder and louder, reveling throughout the evening, sleeping on the turf where they'd fallen, and planning for the defense of the realm. A few neighbors rushed from lonely houses to share in the work and merrymaking of those who'd gone wild and ungoverned. Others slammed their doors on the pandemonium: drugs and debauchery and the assembling of homemade gas masks.

One day a rumor was heard: armed men were coming to fence and occupy the realm. The proud founders and defenders of the park gathered round. They dug a hole in the ground for a great bonfire and hung a slaughtered pig from a pole over the flames. That evening they fed on charred and greasy pork; they soon slumbered on the turf, garments loose and unfastened.

It was May, and the nights were cool and fresh. As some made preparations for battle, Jim and Valerie lay with the people under the trees, dreaming of roast pig—the snapping and crackling fire, the aroma of burning pork. They were so far from Colorado, where nothing happened unless there was money.

Suddenly someone grabbed Jim's sleeping bag and dragged him along the turf, waking him from the sumptuous feast. Peering out, he saw a man's leg, then a length of club; nearby, Valerie was groping her way from her sleeping bag, pulling up pants, pronto. She hollered to Jim that the pigs had come and everyone was clearing out. Jim's eyes closed on a flaming pig, where someone had carved the words "No sleeping"; then he yelped as a cop shook him from the bag, roughing him up. He gaped around: the park had been overrun by uniformed men, and nearly everyone had already fled. He scrambled for the pavement just as the men were closing in, guns at the ready. Though they laughed and jeered, he escaped the park unharmed.

Jim and Valerie found a narrow passageway leading by the side of a house; from there they saw the fence go up. Then they saw the armed men tearing away at the park.

Dawn was glowing over the hills as they fled toward the jeans shop on the Avenue, for the Northside apartment was too far away now in the early morning hours with the area crawling with cops. Passing through a small doorway, they climbed to a room over the shop, where they slumped on the floor among four others who crashed there, sharing what they had. When they woke up, there was no use in heading for school; everyone knew the day had come, the day they'd planned to defend the park. Crouching by a window above the Avenue, they surveyed the scene below. People passed in groups, squads of cops had begun moving in, and up and down the Avenue roamed the park people, ready for the opening maneuvers.

The war began around noon when a throng of people appeared, marching from the campus along Telegraph Avenue toward the park. Valerie refused to budge, saying the important things could be seen from the room, but Jim was on edge as soon as he heard the throng. Bolting from the room, he was soon in the doorway by the jeans shop. Then he took off along the edges of the crowd.

Jim was running among the crowd, who moved up and down, scavenging bottles from trash cans. Soon they were confronting the enemy, crouching by cars, lobbing objects from the curb, running from tear gas exploding nearby. He followed a group of young men rounding a corner. There was pounding—a throbbing in the heart and temples. The young men he ran among had a sour odor, like Hawk; he could almost feel Hawk's hand grasping a shoulder, the way he would when he was mad. Now the odor came from men moving around him, through him, wolves of the forest opposing a common enemy.

As the group rounded the corner, a heavy droning surged in waves from the sky, pounding through the atmosphere. An ugly wind inhaled upwards, whirling debris. Craning his face toward the roar, Jim saw the deafening blades churning the sky.

"Flying pigs!" The words fell dead under the roar.

The group gazed up at the machines, hovering over the rooftops, spewing heavy gas and then moving on.

"Run from the gas!" The group stampeded forward down a street newly freed of cars: for once, it belonged to them. Something reached down, burning and scraping throat and lungs—Jim was running through tears. He slowed, coughing, as the others surged on and away.

Jim stumbled alone through the abandoned street, desperate for an escape from the tear gas. The uproar had faded to the edge of awareness. A corner opened out, carless and unpeopled; caught in the momentum, he was fully unwound, lungs heaving, one flapping rubber sole stubbing the pavement. Here was a way around the tear-gas zone.

An upended trash can lay in the street, debouching garbage. Jim rummaged for a bottle: he would be more of a man with something heavy on hand.

He ran south, planning to loop around and head for the park another way. Looking along Parker Street, he saw hordes of cops massed on Telegraph. Where was Valerie—in the room? There was no way back there now.

There came a jolt of stampeding feet. Jim lurched as a posse of older boys rounded the corner. Then as they passed he sprang into motion, nearly fouling one of them—a high-school boy who'd come out for the park, same as he had. The boys slowed, closing around him, laughing among themselves, welcoming him, and soon he was running among them toward the war on the Avenue.

Approaching the corner of Telegraph, they came upon a throng. Jim ran on, abandoning the older boys, who hung back from the gathering energy. As he entered the mob's warm vehemence there came an opening, revealing a squad car, surrounded and taken hostage. Some boys from the Avenue were bouncing on the hood as though they'd found a trampoline. Jim struggled toward them, demanding his chance; but before he knew what was happening, they'd sprung away as the mob pulled back, flinching, and flames erupted from the hood. For a moment, an enthralled hush fell over them, underscored by the gasping of flame.

Then came a shout: "Burn the pigs!"

Jim heard the roaring flames, and they surged away from the bonfire. Then he jumped at the sound of loud crackling.

There came a loud and urgent shout: "The pigs are shooting!"

They abandoned the burning car. Jim ran for cover, crouching in a doorway as the line of cops advanced, guns at the ready, firing in the air. A man appeared running, one shoulder splashed with blood. As though pulled by magnets, Jim surged headlong from the doorway, hurling something toward the advancing line. Glass burst on the pavement. He stared dumbly as one of the cops swung round; a burn scorched his thigh. He lurched toward the doorway where, crouching, he fingered the dark smudge spreading from a hole in the denim. The wound stung: he'd been branded.

The cops moved in, surrounding the burning car as though covering a fallen comrade. Jim took a chance and ran from the doorway. He'd gone about twenty feet when a hand grabbed one shoulder, reminding him of Hawk. He struggled hard but the hand was clamped on his upper arm. He turned and saw Bobby.

"What the fuck!" Bobby was wrenching Jim's arm. "They have guns!"

"I know, man." Jim held up the bloody leg.

"Come on, head for the house—there's a bunch of us there."

"No way, I'm here for good."

"You're not that tough. They have guns, man."

"I'm gonna kill 'em."

"Not now!" Bobby gripped him by the arm, and they were running.

They hauled past a used-car dealership and Willard School. The door to the gym was propped open, and through the door they saw some jocks going at it under the basketball nets. Bobby slowed.

"Look at 'em," he nodded toward the gym. "It's only a game, and they're ready to kill."

"Yeah, school's such a bummer." Jim was staring through the door. "Please God, don't make me kill anyone." Suddenly he choked up. "Maybe we're gonna have to, before it's over."

"No, we're gonna be free."

"Yeah, free." Jim gave an angry laugh.

VALERIE FOUND HERSELF alone in the Telegraph Avenue room with Arlene, one of a loose band who shared the rooms above Dan's shop. Arlene was large and vaguely regal, with sun-bleached hair and a ski-slope nose. She wore frayed bell-bottoms low around her hips and a poncho embroidered with cannabis leaves. Nearly seventeen, she'd been a presence on the Avenue for over a year, where she made some bread by dealing and dropped by the Derby commune for meals when she was hungry, bringing Valerie. The way they'd begun confiding, Valerie thought of her almost as family. Even now, as they surveyed the clashes from an open window, Arlene was confiding some of her men problems.

For a few months Bobby had been her old man, though they refused to do the monogamy thing. Bobby was a good lay, and he'd shown her how to deal. Now she had another guy, Marlboro Man. The cops called him Lawrence. She knew that because one day when they'd come by looking for Marlboro Man, they'd hassled her, saying, "Where's Lawrence?" She'd told them there was no Lawrence on the Avenue, not that she'd heard of. That was true enough. When she turned away, though, one of the cops grabbed her and snarled, "That guy you're balling, that's Lawrence." Then he shoved her around the way he would a whore, the way her father had. That was why she'd come to the

Avenue: her father had found her sleeping with a guy. As it happened, Marlboro Man had just split for Montreal, where he was scoring some kilos, so there was nothing those narcs could do. He cooled it in Montreal for almost a month, and she and Bobby were sharing a pad at the Derby Street house, but then Marlboro Man showed up with a carload of grass and he had her dealing and that ended things with Bobby for a while.

Valerie was too young for men problems—that would come soon enough. She was glad; she had her freedom. Marlboro Man was a drag: he reminded her of Hawk, when Hawk was in a bad mood. Through the window, they could see the cops moving up the Avenue, grouping to seal off the streets leading to the park, as the park people charged the clubs. So much was happening in the street; Bobby or Marlboro Man—what was the big deal?

"Look—they're fighting!" Valerie cried, feeling a sense of righteousness. "They're defending the park!"

Arlene leaned from the window. "Damn right, they're fighting. Look at those guns." She paused, chewing hard on her lip. "Oh, Val, can't you see what's going down?" She moved from the window.

"They're saving the park!"

"Saving nothing. I'm just so scared for them."

"You're scared? But why? Dan says—"

"Oh, fuck Dan and them. I just hope Marlboro Man's okay."

"I just hope we win!"

The Avenue had been busy for days; everyone knew something was about to come down around the whole park thing. Valerie had heard the rumors, how they were preparing for the war, how they would ambush the cops. Now she leaned from her veranda over the enemy line, feeling a rush. Up and down Telegraph, she could see people leaning from windows or gathered on rooftops; in the street below, armored cops swarmed like wasps, the noonday sun gleaming on ugly helmets. She hung from the window as some park people gathered in loose formation before the helmets below. One of the wasp-men broke ranks, nearing the building; her rush turned to fear as something plunged from the roof, passing her and smashing the pavement close by the cop.

"Down!" came the command from Arlene, followed by random crackling. "Away from the window!" she growled, shoving Valerie to the floor and pinning her there.

"Ow!"

"Down, girl, you wanna get shot?"

"Who says?"

"What the fuck was that?" Arlene's eyes were moving scared. "They're going for the roof."

"Something fell . . ."

"Marlboro Man's up there . . . Bobby, too."

"Uh-oh . . ." Valerie finally understood.

Arlene crawled away, taking refuge out of range of the window. Valerie lay on the floor, pinned now by fear. A strange odor pervaded the room—some skunky new incense, burning Valerie's eyes and throat. Arlene groped her way toward the window, keeping low, and then reached up, slamming it shut.

"Here comes the gas," she wheezed. "They used gas last summer . . . was Dan here?"

Valerie was coughing, and anyway, she hardly knew; she'd been in Colorado.

"C'mon," Arlene urged. "They're gonna smoke us out, same as before. There's no way out, 'cept the roof—down the fire escape."

She led Valerie along the hall, passing the open door of another room. The room was empty, the window open; Valerie fled past, coughing. Around the corner was a small ladder leading through a trapdoor to the roof. Arlene scrambled up the ladder and through the opening, as though she'd done it before. Looking up, Valerie saw Arlene's dangling flip-flops surrounded by blue sky. They too sprang through the opening, for a moment leaving only a splash of blue. Arlene's head reappeared, then her arm, reaching through the trapdoor. Imagining a jungle gym, Valerie swung up the ladder and grasped Arlene's hand. Soon she was kneeling on a tar roof above the Avenue.

Up here was another world.

Or so she thought. Then she saw how many people there were on the roof, more than anywhere else—so it seemed to Valerie. She'd found her magic carpet, and it was a popular place. Many of them were known to her from the street below, and for a moment she found no reason to worry—one more day at the park, same old gang. For sure, the group had planned where to go. They crowded away from the edge overhanging the Avenue, one of the men grasping a bloody cloth.

Arlene was nearby, eyes glancing around in fear. "Where's Marlboro Man?"

The man flung down the bloody cloth. "They're gone, those guys." He glared at her. "They got away from the firing range. No one warned us—"

"No one knew . . ."

The man spat and turned away.

Valerie was shuddering; she could feel someone by her shoulder. "I'm gonna get you out of here," Arlene was saying.

"Where's Dan? He's coming—"

"Over here, Val—"

"No. You can go. I'm staying here."

Valerie sat, hugging her knees, as Arlene moved off. She glanced along the edge of the roof. Now she saw the heaps of rubble she'd been looking for. In the park, as she'd heard them planning for what was happening now, she'd wondered how she would manage to be here. People from the park hung all around her on the roof—and on roofs up and down Telegraph. She would stay here, surrounded by her people, as long as she could. She'd been hauled from her sleeping bag and chased from the park, but she was no homeless dog. Her father had founded the park. She and Jim had unrolled sod and even planted a tree, helping anyway, going with Dan and Wanda to some man's house so they could borrow a van, riding along to the tree farm to buy the tree and bring it back to the park, and then holding the trunk steady as some guys shoveled soil around the heavy root mass. No, she belonged to the park. And for days, as everyone was planning the response to the inevitable government occupation of the park, she'd been imagining heaving something—a hunk of cement— down on the cops below.

She groped her way across the roof, glancing around at the others, wondering who would keep things rolling. Among the group gathered around the wounded man was a girl Arlene's age who'd come from Oregon with a boyfriend and was now on her own. She had blonde corn-silk hair, tangled and unwashed, and ripped jeans. Valerie had seen her on the Avenue and in the park; one day she'd even come to the Derby commune, where she'd nodded off in one of the second-floor rooms—a hanger-on, a bummer, she'd never make things happen. Usually that was Arlene's scene, but Arlene was freaking now that things were under way. If Arlene was becoming a drag, then Valerie would have to dump her, that's all.

Valerie scanned the group on the roof. Four young men hovered together, heads leaning in as though sharing a joint. The park had been home turf for them, and they'd have a rumble now, for sure. Valerie wandered over, coming up on them slowly. One of them was a fleshy young man whose face was covered in smooth beard, and he had a wild eagerness.

"They wanna fight, I'm ready," he was saying.

"Buncha pigs," grumbled a man in leather pants, eyeing the rubble. Southward along Telegraph Avenue, roofs faded in domino heaps: the earth was covered with them. Overhead was a clear, pale sky.

Wasting no more time, the leather-clad man broke from the group and crossed the roof. Crouching by a heap of rubble, he grasped a chunk and heaved it over the edge. Valerie heard a sharp thud and then the hubbub of gunfire. On a nearby roof, a man crumpled slowly. She looked, queasy with excitement and fear. He wore dark and anonymous clothing—a stranger, no one she'd seen before.

From the pavement rose a woman's scream: "Murderers!"

Everyone was now scrambling from the gunfire zone overlooking the street. Valerie heard screams coming from the nearby roof: "Ambulance!"

Arlene was shoving her along. "We're gonna find Marlboro Man," she urged. "C'mon, maybe he's up at the house."

"Hold your horses—I'm not going *now*." Valerie would have her chance; she'd heave something on those cops.

Arlene flashed her a frightened look and headed for the back of the roof, where an iron ladder dropped to the alley. Arlene swung down, hands grasping the ladder. Then she was gone.

Another volley of gunshots sprayed the front of the roof, arcing overhead. Valerie's guts lurched.

Everyone had dropped to the tar, out of the way of gunshot. Valerie scuttled toward the ladder and leaned over the edge. The alley lay far below. Soon she'd maneuvered one foot over a rung and, firmly grasping the railing, lowered herself along the wall. Looking down, she saw a trash can wavering far below. She forced her eyes to the wall—no more fooling around. Bare, weathered wood was passing along a queasy conveyor belt. Descending further, she came face-to-face with an open window, and beyond it a darkened room. She turned her head and nearly fell, one foot searching for a rung that had seemingly fled, beamed to another world. Then just as suddenly it reappeared.

Finally she was with Arlene by the back of Dan's shop. They fled through a narrow alley onto Dwight Way, then west, away from Telegraph Avenue. Valerie turned, craning to look over her shoulder, and saw a throng of cops. Then she followed Arlene back along Parker Street, approaching Telegraph again, only to find the crossroad in flames from a burning car, and jammed with cops. Oil-blackened smoke poured from the hood. They turned, running now, and fled south, beyond the range of the uproar. Soon they'd crossed Telegraph and found a passable route to the Derby Street commune.

ARLENE OPENED THE door on a somnolent atmosphere. Though the house appeared empty, sounds could soon be heard coming from a small room beyond the large communal space.

"Who's there?" a man demanded, in the tone of a sentinel.

"Arlene." She paused. "Valerie's with me. Hey, Johnny, is that you?"

A man's head appeared, unsmiling. "Come on in, then." He had eyes of blue glass and dark curls that blanched an already pale forehead. Unmoving, he surveyed them coming down the hall. The cool glance made Valerie remember the uncomfortable feeling she'd had around him on the Avenue, at least in the beginning. But no longer: now they belonged to the same people.

When they reached the room, they found Jim and Bobby as well.

"See, they're safe!" Valerie announced, nudging Arlene.

"Yeah," Bobby nodded. "Safe for now."

"I'm so glad," Arlene murmured, as Valerie rushed up to Jim. "I saw a burning car!"

"Yeah, man, the cop car. I helped them, me and Bobby."

"Sure enough," Bobby confirmed.

Valerie eyed them, mouth open. "You were there?"

"I was more than there."

They faced each other for a moment, Jim puffing his chest.

"And I heaved something on those cops!" Valerie bragged.

Then she took a step back, her foot trampling a shoebox full of small globes, each having the shape and color of a cherry and what appeared to be a heavy green stalk.

Arlene gasped. "Whoa, what a haul! My lord, Johnny, they sure could use them today."

"Hey, be careful." Johnny waved her off. "That's my stuff." He pulled another box from under the sagging sofa. "There's more. Look at these."

"Oh my God, you have M-80s."

"Yeah, enough to scare some pigs real good." Johnny fingered a cherry bomb for them to contemplate. "I can show you now," he shrugged, reaching for a match.

"What the fuck—" Arlene jumped back. Jim and Bobby laughed.

"I'm just foolin'. We're gonna need 'em. Berkeley's crawling with pigs."

Arlene was kneeling by the box. "Can I have one?"

"Now?"

"Yeah, now."

He glared at her and then at Valerie. "What, a couple of chicks?" He dropped the cherry bomb in the box.

"Oh fuck off, Johnny, you're such a bummer."

"Yeah, a real pisser," Valerie added.

Arlene leaned back, staring up at him. She rose. "Come on, Val, I've had enough of men and weapons."

Johnny regarded her, frowning, then he leaned over and fingered one from each box. "Be careful with the M-80," and he offered them to her. On the thumb was a heavy ring made from the handle of a spoon. "And God bless our army."

Arlene took them and headed for the door. "Thanks, Johnny," she said over her shoulder, smiling. "I'll remember you when it blows."

"Hey, far-out."

Arlene paused by the door. "Say, Bobby, where's the car? How 'bout taking a ride?"

The car belonged to the house, more or less, and Bobby had keys and sometimes used it for joyriding in the hills. He looked at Johnny. "You coming, man?"

"No, I'm cooling off here."

Soon the four of them were in the car. Bobby drove with

Arlene in the passenger seat and Valerie and Jim lounging in back.

"Let's go by Willard School," Arlene suggested.

Bobby rolled along Derby Street, rounding the corner onto Telegraph Avenue. It was now late afternoon. Arlene eased a box of Marlboros from her pocket and removed a cigarette. Then she pulled out the chrome lighter Valerie had given her, with a galloping horse and four red rhinestones studding the mane, and flipped open the cover. Dangling the cigarette, she held the flame to the end, inhaling in slow gasps until it burned. A thin plume of smoke escaped through the open window. No one murmured. Valerie could smell the tobacco as Arlene inhaled: a burning hayfield, only sharper and more pungent.

"I sure could use a bathroom," Arlene remarked in a honeyed, down-home drawl. "Maybe just pull up by Willard School and I'll run in . . . I can go back to school, can't I?"

"You're way beyond junior high," Bobby smiled.

"Maybe I'm just one of those fast-growing girls."

The car passed along the block. Bobby made a U-turn and pulled up by the school gymnasium. "'S open," he yawned, tapping a finger on the steering wheel. "Say, Jim, I wonder'f those boys are playing there now."

"Could be."

"More baby-killers they're gonna be someday."

Glancing up and down the street, Arlene let herself out. Valerie regarded her through the open window, as a helicopter whined overhead. A woman could be heard from the end of the block, calling for a child. Arlene approached the school building, jogged up a ramp and through the door, vanishing into the gym. Moments later she reappeared at a run, followed by a bang and then a louder one. Valerie plugged her ears.

"Ow!"

"Damn," murmured Bobby, impressed. "That was no dud."

He leaned and opened the door and Arlene leapt in, slamming it shut. The car lurched from the curb.

Arlene had dropped her smoke somewhere back in the gym. She was breathing tensely, eyes focused ahead as Bobby rushed a corner, careening right, away from Telegraph Avenue, the park, and the campus. Somewhere behind them sounded the high drone of a siren.

"Tunnel Road, Bobby," commanded Arlene. "We're done for here."

Valerie was feeling peppy. "Maybe it's an ambulance—you know, the guy on the roof."

"No way."

"Yeah," Jim said, grinning. "Pigs'r coming for us."

Bobby turned east at Ashby Avenue. They were speeding now along a thinly used thoroughfare, an off-hour commuting road, heading for the tunnel through the hills. The towers of the Claremont Hotel rose on the left, and then the car ascended a curving, tree-lined road that opened onto a freeway ramp. The siren had bled away in the flatlands below, leaving only the sounds of wind and rubber on the road.

"Hey, Arlene," Jim called out, "you sure gave those guys a scare."

"Who?"

"Those guys in the gym."

"There was no one."

"Me and Bobby saw them under the hoops."

"No more. Pigs've been there. They gassed the goddamn gym."

"That's heavy."

Bobby leaned in, flipping on the lights. "Here comes the tunnel."

Accompanied by a deafening whine, the car plunged into the tunnel, shadowless in dull, orange light and heavy with fumes. No one spoke over the drone. The tunnel unraveled on and on, echoing and confined; then it magically purged them from its thundering confines to the common purposes of day. The car rolled along a ramp, leaving the freeway for a two-lane road that ascended the coastal mountain ridge. Bobby drove calmly now, on furlough from the world.

"Free as a bird up here." He looked at Arlene. "God damn, what a day."

Valerie leaned forward. "Where are we?"

"Grizzly Peak."

Through the trees she could see the shimmering surface of the bay.

"You wanna see the park? I can pull over."

Bobby rolled the car along the shoulder of the road and

stopped. From the glove compartment he drew forth a pair of binoculars.

"Come on."

They tumbled from the car and crossed the road in a group. There was nothing near them but trees. Bobby peered through the binoculars. "Whoa . . . Looka the motherfuckers." He handed the glasses to Valerie.

She had some trouble finding the park, but then through the glasses she saw, one by one, the cops along the fence, uprooted trees and shrubs, overturned benches.

"What's goin' on?" Jim demanded.

She handed the glasses to him and he stared, sobbing loudly.

"Let's go, Bobby, there's no use." Arlene ran back to the car.

They drove slowly along the road, Jim slumped against the door, eyes covered by a corner of cloth from the sleeve of his pullover. The road wound along the summit and then began gradually sloping down, heading for the canyon. Soon they were passing among the fantasy buildings and gated roads of the Lawrence Laboratory, then came a steep drop along the border of the research gardens belonging to the university. Arlene tapped Bobby on the shoulder.

"There's a pullout coming up. I want to get out."

"But there's nothing here."

"Oh yes, there is—there's a path to those gardens. I want to have a look." She paused and resumed, her tone once more honeyed and down-home. "I'd love to sleep in a garden. They say it's only for those college people, but someone told me how to jump the fence. There's no patrolman, or so I hear."

Bobby laughed. "Jump the fence all alone?"

"Well, I was hoping—"

"'Cause I'm going back to the house. I'm gonna be ready tomorrow for whatever comes down."

Valerie leaned forward. "Me and Jim, we can go." She'd never heard of the garden before; but now that she had, she wanted to spend the night there.

Bobby slowed the car, crossing the oncoming lane and rolling onto the pullout. There he dropped them by the head of a path that plunged along the canyon wall through eucalyptus and madrone. Arlene led the way, followed closely by Valerie. Jim hung back, pulling at branches as he passed.

"Where's the garden?" Valerie demanded. "I thought there would be flowers."

"Oh, maybe there are. Marlboro Man showed me how to come along the path here, but I've never been in the garden."

"Then how do you know it's there?"

"He told me. Anyway, we just passed by—you can see it from the road."

"There was only a canyon."

"A canyon with a garden." Arlene turned, gazing back along the path. "Now what did Bobby have to do that was so important?"

"He's gonna save the park!"

"Too late, Val."

Jim appeared around a corner, walking slowly. For a moment Valerie watched him coming along the path, grasping a small branch and pounding the dust. Then she became aware of the funny walk, though it was camouflaged by the pounding of the branch. Jim ignored them as he approached, surrounded by a cloud of dust. Finally he glanced up, eyes shaded under the brow.

"Too many snakes in here," he announced.

"What snakes?" demanded Valerie.

"I saw 'em back there, a whole bunch." He held up the branch, antler-like. "I can scare 'em away, no problem."

"You're lying."

Arlene shaded her eyes with one hand. "And you're limping."

"Huh?"

"Your leg." She waved her hand toward the wounded thigh. "Diamondback, maybe?"

"Fuck no, I'd be dead." He flung the branch away through the bushes. "I let a pig get too close. Johnny says not to worry, it's probably just birdshot. I can have it out tomorrow."

Valerie's eyes widened. "You got shot? Show me."

Jim held up the wounded leg, propping it with both hands. Valerie leaned down and saw a tear in the jeans, crusty with dry blood.

"I can hardly feel it," he bragged.

Arlene frowned. "We should've gone back with Bobby."

"No hurry, it's just a scrape."

"Tomorrow there's gonna be pus." Valerie reached out and he jerked the leg away.

"Forget about it. I'm no chump."

"Arlene!" Valerie turned. "They shot my brother!"

Arlene drew the Marlboro box from her pocket. "They think they're dealing with a bunch of gardeners, but our guys are gonna show them a thing or two."

Jim dropped the leg, another mood overcoming him. Dust and tears darkened his face. "Oh boy."

"Tomorrow you'll see." Arlene tapped on the Marlboro box.

"I dunno . . . maybe we've been had." He turned away, smothering a sob. "They're gonna bring in the Army. That's what Dan says."

They began walking slowly down the path, descending further into the canyon. A car passed on the road above; when the sound had faded, it was replaced by the harsh chatter of crows. The path was bordered by rhododendron and madrone, and as it began curving away from the road, Arlene scanned the canyon, then turned to the others.

"Marlboro Man told me to go through some woods here, then over a fence."

They abandoned the path, bushwhacking along the canyon wall above a narrow creek. Before long they were facing a chain-link fence. Valerie stared up at it.

"Whoa, Arlene, how're we gonna jump that?"

Arlene shrugged. "Fences are for jumping."

They stood for a moment.

"Come on, have a boost."

Arlene leaned down, grasped Valerie by the legs, and helped her up and over. Then she helped Jim, who followed, wincing and groaning. Finally, Arlene climbed over on her own.

Soon they were on a paved path leading through a live-oak grove. The canyon was much the same here. *Why bother jumping a fence*, Valerie wondered, *if nothing changes?* Jim moved close by her shoulder.

"We should have the park here," he murmured. "Look how much space they have. We could live off the land."

"You're dreaming."

"Yeah, I sure am."

"And what would you eat—bark?"

"Naaah . . . I'd have me some roast pig, just like the olden days."

The path led along the canyon wall, then branched and dropped down toward the creek. Soon they entered a small redwood grove by a Japanese pond. It was early evening. Jim crouched by the pool, drinking in gulps; then he splashed water over his face. Smudged and dripping, he looked up at Valerie.

"Remember that day we went up the mountain?"

"Hawk took us."

"Yeah, Hawk. Where d'you suppose he's gone?"

"Gone? Nowhere—he's with her." Valerie was feeling spent.

"Maybe." Jim peered through the trees. "An' maybe not." He paused. "What's that sound?"

"Where?"

"In the trees."

"Nothing—just crows."

Arlene had been leaning over the pond, washing her hands. "Who's Hawk?"

Jim flashed her a snarly look. "Some guy."

"From the park?"

"No—," Valerie began, but Jim cut her off.

"Yeah, from the park. Used to go around with a woman named Carol."

"Hmmm." Arlene searched her memory. "How come I never met them? I thought I knew everyone."

"Maybe they had other names," Jim said, smiling. "You know, like Marlboro Man. That's not his real name."

"So what are they called?"

"Who?"

"Hawk and Carol. What do people call them?"

"Mr. and Mrs. Jones."

"You're joking. "

"Naaah, what's wrong with Jones? Hawk Jones—that just about fits. Right, Val?"

Valerie made no response.

Arlene was drying her hands on her legs. "I see."

"Yup—Mr. and Mrs. Jones. That's what we call 'em."

Arlene smiled. "Like in the Bob Dylan song." Then she sang softly: "*And you know something is happening . . .*"

Jim laughed.

". . . *but you don't know what it is. Do you, Mister Jones?*" Well, that's all gone," she sighed. "You won't be seeing them anymore."

"And that's just fine," Jim said, sadly.

chapter five

Alice

TAMMY, NORA, AND Debra were already members of the Girl Scout troop when Alice signed up. It was Tammy who'd pushed her to rebel, while her mother pooh-poohed the Scouts as a dreary, humdrum group for unimaginative girls, demanding, "Are you sure you're a joiner?" The word "joiner" had made Alice vaguely uncomfortable, as though she were succumbing to a dangerous contagion, but she'd gone ahead anyway, in the hope of doing something with Tammy, even if that would be confined to congregating weekly in a church assembly room and managing the school day in uniform. And so on Thursdays, she now showed up in the lunchroom as one of a group in Girl Scout array, resembling army nurses. The uniforms left Alice feeling aware of her long bare legs—by comparison, Nora enjoyed showing off her soccer legs and swimmer's shoulders; Debra's flesh bulged; and Tammy dangled her spindly limbs as though juggling umbrellas. If only Alice could be happy as a follower, she would be subsumed by the group under Nora's command.

The beleaguered foursome had formed under pressure. Being in a group had problems, especially when some of the members were less appealing than the girls they made fun of—for example, Kathleen, a lively person from a Catholic school in the neighborhood. Of course that made her an easy target for Nora and Debra.

"Her school is freaky—no boys," Nora scoffed, as she passed on the embarrassing rumor.

"And they go to chapel," Debra added.

As usual, Tammy was aloof from the group, even while enjoying its bonds. "They say she has four brothers," she shrugged, smoothing things over. "That's enough boys."

Nora gave her a cool glance. "Have you seen them?"

"No."

"They're Ken dolls. They've got crew cuts."

"Yuk," Debra concluded.

Alice had passed Kathleen's house and seen her brothers; they were handsome, square-shouldered boys, altogether a good-looking family. But by Berkeley standards, they were clearly nonconforming, boys from a 1950s family drama or an Uncle Sam ad.

"Where's her family from?" she asked Tammy, doing her best to ignore Nora and Debra.

"You mean you don't know?" Nora cried, leaning close and blinking slowly so the group could feel Alice's failing. "They came a year ago . . . from England!"

"London?"

"No, some village," Nora groaned.

"Oh."

"Oxford, maybe," Tammy suggested.

"Oxford? Are you kidding?" Debra demanded.

"Or maybe Cambridge. Her father's a professor."

"How do you know?"

Tammy giggled. "Why else would they be here?"

"Because everyone wants to be here." Nora folded her arms. "England's a has-been place. My dad says so."

"They have a queen," Tammy mused, furrowing her brow as though imagining a very faraway place.

Across the room, Kathleen appeared perky and confident in her green uniform, though vaguely formal, never slouching as the other girls would do. Alice had never seen herself as a sloucher; it was Kathleen who'd informed her, with gleaming eyes, that she was. As far as Kathleen was concerned, many Americans slouched; they were careless, casual, even slovenly. She, on the other hand, came from an orderly place, and though the girls made fun of her, she was leaning on her advantages. She could always find ways of impressing the troop leader, Mrs. Chaney. Mrs. Chaney was a middle-aged woman with grown-up daughters. Long bangs nearly covered her eyes; she enjoyed drama and singing. Kathleen could sing.

They were supposed to be choosing new badges to earn—singing badges were encouraged, and Kathleen already had one —but Alice's group preferred gossiping, and there were no badges for that. Alice had no badges so far and wondered why she should earn them by learning skills that had no appeal for her: the seafarer's knots Nora had shown them, Debra's home-made fig bars, or Tammy's embroidered jeans.

Suddenly her mother came rushing through the doorway. The out-of-place figure caught Alice by surprise. She gazed for a moment, confused by her mother's careless clothing: a shapeless old cardigan over her rumpled house dress; no earrings or makeup, only the sunglasses she now wore everywhere; bare legs and sandals. Leaving the sunglasses in place, she approached Mrs. Chaney. While the women conferred, Kathleen could be heard exclaiming, "So *you're* Mrs. Rayson!" as though she'd always wondered, as though the slovenly, impulsive woman was even more amusing than her imaginings.

Alice's mother had never come for her before. There was an odd moment of seeing her with Mrs. Chaney and Kathleen, chummy, heads together. Tammy leaned over.

"How come your mom's here?"

"Not sure."

"Your house is so close . . ." Tammy was surveying Mrs. Rayson, her face responding to the casual hurry of the clothing. Alice rarely found her mother embarrassing and was unsure what to feel. Her mother removed the sunglasses, revealing puffy eyes and a scowl that was seemingly fending off some ordeal. "Just passing by . . . maybe," Tammy added, covering for her, one arm dangling over her knee.

"It's my brother's birthday."

"Oh." Tammy paused, searching for a response. "Your mom's busy, then."

"I guess."

"You should go," Tammy concluded.

In any case, Mrs. Chaney was waving her over. She'd dropped her usual bubbly manner for an icy composure; something in Mrs. Rayson's words had annoyed her. As Alice came closer, she could hear Mrs. Chaney saying, "You're scaring my girls"; then the Scout leader's jaw clamped; her plump hands wrung each other.

Her mother made no response. The other girls were now whispering as Mrs. Rayson led Alice through the doorway. Her mother led her along a gravel path away from the church's high, sun-splashed walls. Pausing by the curb, her eyes fraught with dismay and scorn, she glanced back at the church as though passing judgment.

"That woman—your leader—was angry because I came for you. She accused me of alarming the girls. But something awful is happening, and even Girl Scouts should know." Her hands were trembling; one grasped the car keys. She gazed over the roof of the Chevy toward the campus, her face clouded by unbearable feelings. Scared and confused, Alice wondered who would come for the other girls.

"Telegraph Avenue's in an uproar," her mother continued. "How could I know you'd get home safely?"

"Telegraph Avenue?" For a moment Alice thought her mother was accusing her of planning to go there. The words hung over the suburban scene, so near the danger zone and yet so far.

"Oh, honey, I could just imagine you rushing down there . . ." Her mother grasped her shoulder, smoothing the green Girl Scout cloth, comforting herself by the warm touch. "They've destroyed People's Park. Now they're shooting people on Telegraph Avenue."

"Who?"

"The cops! They've got guns and tear gas!"

"But why would I go there?"

"Oh, how do I know where you go these days?"

Her mother's vehemence made Alice feel ungrounded, as though she just might do as her mother feared. The calm, tree-shaded neighborhood was confusing and false. A breeze blew in the phony peace, wafting a sour odor. If she rounded a corner, and then another . . .

The news seemed unreal as they climbed in the Chevy. Alice eyed her green hem and bare knees. The uniform seemed confining.

In the warm lull, her mother adjusted her sunglasses and turned the key, starting the car. "The cops came in the dead of night. Then they fenced off People's Park and trampled the lovely flowers."

The park had remained a fantasy: Alice had been there only once, the day she'd gone after school. Even so, as they headed up Forest Avenue, serene, barely urban, and only blocks from People's Park, she was plagued by images that jumbled her thoughts

—mangled trees, armed men in uniforms savagely uprooting flower beds.

"When people heard what had happened, they came marching down Telegraph Avenue." Her mother's hands clenched the wheel as the car moved slowly along. "The park was a lovely, peaceful thing. Sabrina and I were planning to take you girls someday. But now I'm appalled by everyone—the cops, the university administrators, and the demonstrators wreaking havoc. I thought we could do things in an orderly manner. Why must people go so far?"

Only days before, her mother had admired the park people. Now she was blaming them and everyone else.

They parked by the house in the long shadows. Her mother seemed to be resolving something in her mind. "The demonstrators have gone mad," she began, grasping Alice's hand and squeezing hard. "Why won't they leave and go home?" The cardigan hung loosely, an anonymous garment once belonging to her father. "The cops are just as crazy. They even gassed your brother in the junior-high-school gym—thank God he's safe." Then with a weary sigh, "Confronted by so many angry people, maybe I would do the same. Who knows anymore."

In the ensuing pause, droning could be heard, then a dog began barking. "Gassed him?" Alice wondered aloud, uncomprehending, though she'd heard clearly enough.

"Yes, tear gas!" her mother snapped.

"And he's okay?"

"Yes, he escaped along with the others. But how awful for them. The boys planned a game in honor of Curt's birthday. Such a lovely thing to do. And then the damn cops gassed the gym!" She yanked the keys from the ignition. "Everyone's gone mad—the cops, the mob, everyone."

Her mother opened the car door. Alice was feeling shaken. She'd always heard the people were good—and it was the cops who'd done the gassing, not the mob.

Slamming the door, her mother headed for the house, calling over her shoulder, "He was recovering when I went out. I've got to see how he's doing."

Her mother ran up the walk, cardigan flapping. She'd never run before. Alice came through the grass, feeling jealous and confused. The danger having receded, the story was more intriguing than scary: he'd been where it was happening. She imagined the scene, wondering what she would do. The Scout uniform was absurd; she would be surrounded by people wearing something resembling her brother's torn jeans and jersey, jammed together in a surging crowd. Her mother had hoped she would enjoy the park someday. Now it was gone forever. Alice was feeling rebellious—yes, she thought, glancing toward the campus, her mother's ideas were changing; only days ago, she'd been glowing when she spoke of the park, and now they were an awful mob . . .

A heavy mechanical throbbing poured from the sky. Looking up, Alice saw a helicopter swooping low over the trees, spewing gas from the belly. Fleeing through the grass to safety, she slammed the door and found herself alone in the foyer, confronting her own uniformed figure in the mirror: bangs askew over her mother's almond-shaped eyes; arms and legs slender and bare; the anonymous green of someone else's team.

As she glared, imagining tearing off the uniform, her mother appeared on the second-floor landing.

"He's coming down," she called. "He's feeling well enough for dinner."

They gathered in the living room. Curt was wearing a pajama top and old jeans he'd nearly outgrown, which made him seem older. He had puffy swellings around the eyes, under a lush, sun-bleached wave overhanging the forehead.

"What happened in the gym?" Alice asked.

Curt shrugged, rubbing a hand under the pajama collar. "We were just playing a game. Cops ran in, clearing the gym. Then before we could get out, they gassed us." The words had an angry edge.

"Oh no!" her mother cried. "I thought you boys escaped!"

"Cops lobbed some tear-gas grenades, we ran for the door. Damn gas was everywhere."

"But why would they—"

"'Cause they're crazy." Curt seemed edgy, unfamiliar—a brother who'd gone far away and come back. "I hope they get what's coming."

Her mother responded slowly. "And what do you suppose is coming?"

"Someone's gonna stomp them."

Her mother's eyes were damp. "Your father's coming home soon. Go and shower."

"One of the guys was gassed before. He was okay."

"What—one of the boys you know?"

"Don't freak out. He was okay."

Curt shrugged and was gone, leaving an unpleasant hush. Soon the hush was filled by the sound of rotors whirling overhead.

WHEN CURT CAME back down, damp-headed and wearing fresh jeans and a blue-and-gold Cal jersey, Marian was preparing dinner, a beef stew.

"Have a snack," she suggested soothingly as he came loping in.

"Not hungry."

"Honey, are you sure?"

"Can we hear the news?"

Though her mother usually enjoyed the news while cooking, she gave a weary shrug. "Right now?"

Ignoring her, Curt found KPFA, the local left-wing FM station. They heard a somber male announcer.

"*Today was worse than anything I've seen—and yes, I was in Chicago last summer during the unleashing of the police assault there. We could be reporting from the Watts uprising, August of '65, or Newark, July of '67, all over again.*"

Her mother was chopping onions. "Oh my, he was in the fray. Now we'll hear everything."

"Shhh!"

The announcer continued. "*Throughout the day cops from surrounding areas have been converging on People's Park and Telegraph Avenue. We're hearing some very scary things about the blue-uniformed Alameda County sheriffs. Be forewarned—the Blue Meanies are armed and dangerous. It's been confirmed that the Alameda sheriffs have permission to fire if they deem it necessary. The authorization is for birdshot only; but we're hearing reports of buckshot, and scores of people have been wounded, some severely. There have been hundreds of arrests in the Telegraph Avenue area, and Governor Reagan has declared a curfew for 10 p.m.*"

A second announcer chimed in. "*How have park supporters responded?*"

"*The response has been overwhelmingly peaceful, although po-lice claim that a small group surrounded and burned a squad car near the corner of Parker and Telegraph. The squad car had been abandoned. No one was harmed.*"

Her mother was no longer chopping. "Burning a squad car!" she snapped, turning toward Curt. "That's not peaceful! No wonder—"

Curt leaned closer, turning up the volume.

"*. . . tear gas was used on the grounds of Willard Junior High, only blocks from People's Park.*"

"*Do we know what happened?*"

"*Yes, gas was used in the boys' gym.*"

"*Are we hearing you correctly—the junior-high-school gym?*"

"*That's correct.*"

"*And how many of the enemy were cleared from the gym?*"

"*Eleven schoolboys, according to the Pentagon.*"

"*Presumably they were armed with basketballs and very dangerous.*"

"*Presumably.*"

Curt had a glowing smile. "Hey, we're on the news!"

They heard murmuring and then the second announcer: "*It seems we're in an undeclared state of war—*"

"*Or not so undeclared. Remember, Governor Reagan placed Berkeley under a state of emergency in early February, during Third World Liberation Front demonstrations in Sproul Plaza. That order remains in effect. And so, we've already had four months of ongoing emergency. Now it could go on much longer.*"

"*What about the shootings?*"

"*A bystander was severely wounded on a Telegraph Avenue roof. No information yet on his chances. A man has been blinded. And dozens have suffered minor injuries. The Alameda County sheriffs, the Blue Meanies—*"

Her mother snapped off the radio. "That's enough." Her eyes were shiny. "Thank God there was only gas in that gym."

Curt was grinning. "They're gonna stomp those Blue Meanies!"

Alice edged toward the door as her mother opened a cupboard, took down a bowl, then slammed the cupboard door. "Soon they'll be using guns on schoolboys!"

Through Alice's body flashed an image of Telegraph Avenue and something tearing her as she ran. She was feeling queasy.

Her body was cringing, overpowered by mangled figures from the overseas war—a napalmed body that she struggled to push from her mind. The figure seemed both compelling and unreal. A new image formed—a flaming squad car engulfing a man who struggled to flee. The image oppressed her so much that she shuddered, shaking it off.

"What's wrong?" Her mother sounded dismayed.

"Nothing."

"You're bothered by the news."

"Maybe." Alice moved away, feeling vulnerable. What was evil, anyway? Was it burning villagers with napalm, or burning a cop in a patrol car over a neighborhood park? She was supposed to refuse . . . regardless of the cause.

"What's tear gas?"

"What do you mean?"

"Why do they use it?"

"It's for dispersing a crowd. It burns the eyes—"

"Burns them?"

"Yes, it stings and—"

"Burns so bad you have to run," amended her brother, "unless you have a homemade gas mask."

There was another glare from her mother. Her brother shrugged and headed down the hallway. If the war went on and on, he would have to go and fight; then he'd be shot, or blown up, or burned . . . There was suddenly so much to learn.

"What's a curfew?"

"People have to stay off the streets."

"Off the streets?"

"Everyone has to stay home. The police can arrest anyone they find on the street."

"But what about school? Am I staying home tomorrow?"

"They want to keep people from gathering during the night. The curfew ends in the morning. Even so, I may keep you guys home tomorrow, or at least Curt. There's no reason for him to be anywhere near Telegraph Avenue." She glanced over at Alice. "Your father's coming home soon. Are you wearing that uniform for dinner?"

With an embarrassed shrug, Alice went upstairs to change out of her Scout clothes. The day's events had left her feeling agitated, her loyalties confused. The other girls had probably walked home, as usual, and been safe enough. Though the problems were real, her mother would use them to clamp down and keep her from wandering freely, or even defending herself. Just as Alice was feeling her courage rising, her mother's moods would become more confining. Surely her mother had never been in real danger—if she had, she'd know why a person must fight back. It was necessary . . . fight back or go under. If she followed her mother's ideas, people would go on pushing her around forever.

She changed into jeans, leaving her uniform on the closet floor. Why should she be caught wearing it, if by some chance she gathered with others after curfew?

In the living room, her father and Curt were standing by the hearth, conferring soberly. Her father's work clothes seemed incongruous after the day's events, reminders of a safe and orderly world that was fast slipping away, like a passing ship glimpsed from some far-off desert island by those on shore. He held a glass of red wine, cupping the bowl in a heavy workingman's hand. The pale-blue eyes had a steady look.

"About that gym," he began, engaging no one in particular, though they were seemingly gathered for some purpose—a family conference. "I'm planning to report it."

Her mother's eyes rounded. "To whom?"

"The cops."

"But they're the ones in the wrong."

"Let's see how they respond."

Curt was leaning by the window, looking skyward for the drone of helicopters. He glanced from father to mother and back again.

"But Tom," her mother objected, "we've had enough for one day. In any case, the world already knows about the gassing of the gym. They've announced it on KPFA."

"What are they saying?"

"The cops gassed a school gymnasium, clearing out eleven schoolboys, including our son."

The square jaw was damp and shiny. "Berkeley cops?"

"No way," responded Curt.

"You're sure?"

"They had blue uniforms," Curt smiled, enjoying himself.

"Oh my," her mother snapped. "And now we're going up against the infamous Blue Meanies."

"There may be grounds to sue. And from what I hear, most of the other parents may have a hard time pressing a case," her father responded, as though explaining the world to a child. "After all, they're black."

"Yes, Tom, and maybe Ginger can help," her mother announced coolly.

Ignoring her, he raised the wineglass, congratulating Curt. "Regardless of what your mother says, I'm proud of you."

"If they come back," Curt nodded, "someone's gonna stomp them."

"What on earth—"

Alice cringed as her mother rushed Curt and gave his shoulder a vehement slap. They were in startling new waters.

"You're staying home tomorrow! I won't have you down there! If these things continue, there really could be civil war."

Tom spoke, firm and level. "They need to learn what to do."

"Who—Curt and Alice?"

"Yes, they've got to be ready." In the hush, they heard a faraway drone. "Or else you'll see him in Vietnam."

"But Tom, we're a peaceful family. And anyway, what's happening now has nothing to do with the war. They're arguing over some foolish park—in a place full of parks! We've never seen so much undeveloped land. What's going on here?"

Tom wiped the dampness from his jaw. "Now there's a curfew, on top of an ongoing state of emergency. They regard us as criminals. That's what's happening."

He went down the hall for another glass of wine. Marian hung her head, crying softly, unable to look at anyone.

No one had much to say during dinner. The beef stew had been Curt's personal request, and he devoured a large second helping. Then for the presents, they grouped awkwardly on the living-room couch, as Tom stood by the fireplace, sipping wine. Curt opened the present from his father—a baseball glove—and thrust in one hand, holding it up for them to see.

"I needed a new glove," he said, smiling and fingering the laces. The smell of leather filled the room.

IN MRS. WHITMAN'S room, the class was reading. As the afternoon wound down and the class grew increasingly unruly, Mrs. Whitman called for order. She was a clergyman's wife, the girls had heard, and now she stood before them, hands clasped as though seeking rather than offering guidance.

Jason was humming to himself. He was the boy from Garber Street, near the Raysons—the one who'd had the sleepover party. Though he seemed cool, Alice had never forgiven him for the ugly Halloween call.

"Please, Jason," Mrs. Whitman urged.

The boy burst forth in a triumphal crescendo and slouched back in his chair. Mrs. Whitman looked around the classroom and began to speak.

"Many of you have heard something of what happened yesterday. When we have much controversy and conflict in our world, as we do now, then we should remember how important it is to learn from one another. By sharing our thoughts, we can come to understand our world and learn helpful ways of responding to each other." Mrs. Whitman's eyes were weary, her mood somber. "Yesterday we saw Berkeley, a peaceful place, become caught up in confrontation. We saw unnecessary suffering—assaults, tear-gassing, injured police and bystanders." There was a long hush, and then she wrung her hands. "I was hoping some of you would speak up."

Longhaired Jason waved an arm.

"Yes, Jason?"

"So many people made the park. The land belongs to everyone. What happened was wrong, to put a fence around it."

"Can you see any reason for the fence?"

"No—just greed. No one was using the land, so they made a park."

Debra's hand shot up. "They were planning on building a dorm before those park people came along. Then they were willing to come to an agreement, my father says, for a community garden, but those people from Telegraph Avenue had no committee. They didn't even think they needed one."

"My mother has roses," Tammy could be heard murmuring. "Roses for People's Park."

Jason's arm was waving. "There should be a vote. Everyone should do what the vote says."

"How come you go there?" demanded a boy from the back row. It was Vaughan.

"Who says I do?" Jason responded.

"'Cause I heard they got drugs and everything over there."

"The park was for people, that's all."

"Yeah, tramps and them."

There was smothered laughter from some of the black students, but Ben hung by himself, churchy as usual, ignoring Vaughan. Now he put up a hand—warily, at half-mast. Mrs. Whitman nodded encouragingly.

"Yes, Ben?"

"I'm not sure about that park and all yesterday. I never heard so much about it as Jason and Vaughan and everyone. But when I hear these things . . . about these arrests and shootings . . ." For a long moment he paused, floundering. Then he gathered himself up and went on: "My brother, he was at Hunter's Point when they had the problems over there. He never did anything wrong, they arrested him anyway." Ben had begun crying softly. "He's been in there over two years." The class was squirming, except for Vaughan, who'd begun exchanging glances with Michael. "They framed him. They say he had drugs but I know that's wrong. My brother never used no drugs." Ben was snuffling too hard to say any more. The bell rang, ending the day.

There was another argument about the park as Alice's school bus was passing Telegraph Avenue. From the rear of the bus, longhaired Jason hollered, loud enough to be heard over the throbbing radio, "Defend the park!" A clean-cut boy shouted back, "Trespassers go home!"

The bus chugged along. Then Jason responded, "Someone plants a flower, so you're gonna shoot him?"

"They're bums. They should go somewhere else."

"So you're gonna shoot them?" Jason demanded, coming forward.

"They're trespassers," the clean-cut boy said, glaring.

"How about the guy on the roof—"

The two boys were face-to-face. "Why was he there?" the clean-cut boy demanded. "Just throwing things down on the cops—"

"How do you know?"

"The cops say so."

"They're lying," Jason sneered.

"How do *you* know?"

The bus lurched along, reaching the corner of College Avenue and Derby Street. Alice descended, followed by the boy who'd been defending the cops. Caught up in the argument, he'd gone beyond his regular stop. Freckled and glaring, he eyed her as the bus chugged away.

"How come you know those guys from the park?" he demanded. "What do you do with them?"

"Nothing," she blurted, as though guilty of something, then added, "I never go there."

"Yeah, sure, hippie girl." He gave her a shove and ran up Derby Street.

She headed along Forest Avenue, wondering why he'd chosen her. Lingering by a neighbor's rose bushes, she grasped a stem, tearing off three plump roses. A car passed and she jumped: had she just trespassed? How easy it would be to end up in trouble—for nothing, for a flower.

If she could escape Forest Avenue, where would she go? Freedom should usher in something new. There would always be some who fled through the evening curfew along dangerous, winding paths, searching for the new, searching for what they'd lost.

THE CONFRONTATIONS WENT on for days. Angry gatherings were met by gassings and arrests and the grinding sound of helicopter rotors churning the sky. Squads of armed guardsmen enforced the curfew, even as bands of vigilantes dug new parks for them to crush. The savage cycle made Alice queasy, as if a baby had fallen in a swimming pool and the lifeguards were laughing. Every day when she came home from school, she heard left-wing announcers informing her mother of the day's gassing or roundup, and she found the announcers' feelings of outrage oddly comforting. She was feeling a similar outrage, though who could say why? People's Park was scarcely real for her. Even so, she was mourning along with the announcers.

Before the war for the park, she'd ignored the newspapers, learning of far-flung places and events through her parents or the girls at school. Even now, much of California seemed safely in the West, far from the news. Colorado, Wyoming, Nevada, Utah: spaces on a map. For all the drama, People's Park was a game; demonstrators could stage a truce in the park war by running a few blocks home. But in the real war, homes were in flames every evening on the TV, village after burning village.

In her room, Alice brooded over photographs of cops in gas masks, armed with guns, and young men in headbands, hurling rocks. She wondered where her brother was roaming. Maybe he'd joined the young men, just for fun. One evening when they were alone, he'd cornered her and bragged how he and Sammy had jumped the fence at People's Park. Then he glanced away, eyes gleaming with amusement as he frowned to keep from laughing. The story sounded so improbable, for the *Barb* showed an army camp overrun by National Guardsmen. Her brother was shamming—though who could be sure? Boys could do so many things; maybe he and Sammy had found a way. So far, she was alone; how would she know what to do, where to go?

One day, after the school bus had gone, she headed for People's Park, hoping for a glimpse of the ravaged site and the guardsmen—nothing more. Reaching the corner, she saw the fence and then, where the park had been, the army camp, a large tent looming in the center, equipment flung over the grass. Surrounding the parcel of land were men in military clothes, holding rifles, and on the rifles were unsheathed bayonets, ready to run her through. She ran, feeling her legs pumping, her hair flying.

When she reached home, her mother looked up from the couch in confusion. Her hand grasped an envelope; her face was flushed. Seeing Alice come through the door, she slipped the envelope in the pocket of her cardigan and smoothed her skirt. "I told you to come home from the bus," she reprimanded.

"I only went around the block."

"Just remember, no wandering near People's Park or Telegraph Avenue."

"I never go there, Mom."

Her mother could have wrung a confession from her easily enough, but her mother had something else on her mind.

Then on Sunday, her father asked if she would go for a walk.

"Where are we going, Dad?"

"Just for a walk. It's a beautiful day."

So, he'd learned the local commonplaces, Alice thought,

though coming from him the slogan sounded phony and jarring.

She could see they were heading for Telegraph Avenue. She wondered if they would be passing the park, but her father was an uneasy presence and there would be no asking. Contact of any kind was becoming unbearable; there was a hum whenever they found themselves alone in a room, the sound of suppressed anger. She could not remember when they'd last gone anywhere together; but here he was, on a Sunday in May, offering to lead her on a walk through the forbidden zone. Maybe the park was a sign of change, and he was responding. Maybe the adventure would forge a bond between them, the beginning of a new sympathy. She'd never been on Telegraph Avenue with her father alone. She could sense him moving alongside her, carrying her along. Why was he taking her there? Was there something he planned to show her, something he wanted her to know?

They rounded the corner by the park, the same corner she'd passed on her own before running home. They saw armed men guarding the fence, the hapless parcel of land overrun by vehicles and equipment. One hand resting on her shoulder, her father shepherded her across the street and proceeded along the edge of the park. Every few yards, they passed close by a National Guardsman as the young man's face responded, the eyes following them, human and wary. Armed with rifles and gleaming bayonets, the men were ready for combat, or for a sunny campus day.

Her father had placed himself between her and the armed men, as though forming a moving barrier—ready to block, dodge, flee. She was by a scrimmage line, and he was guarding her. They pressed on, ready for a move by one of the guardsmen. Then, as they passed a heavy-jawed man, the man shifted his weight and her father veered, bumping her hard.

The sunny day glared numbly, marred by her father's fear. If only she could run home, but her father's hand was grasping her arm.

Moving at a faster pace, they cleared the park and rounded the corner onto Telegraph Avenue. The army camp had faded, mirage-like, replaced by simmering anarchy and people in colorful garb. Her father was moving along in a bubble, barely glancing around as he paused and removed a copy of the *Berkeley Barb* from a vending machine.

"Here's the paper," he remarked, handing it over. "Don't go

anywhere—I'll be right back." Then he moved on, leaving her by the door of the jeans shop as he approached a nearby jewelers. She unfolded the *Barb*: on the cover was a photograph of a boy, younger than herself and seated in a swing. Up he smiled, sunny and joyful, at the overbearing body of an armed man, demanding that he leave or be uprooted and removed.

Emerging from a doorway, a boy dropped and crushed a smoldering cigarette before prancing on.

She moved under an awning, away from the flow of passersby. A car horn sounded as a Ford pulled up; the door swung open and several longhaired boys tumbled forth in purposeless hurry to be there.

As she lingered by the jeans shop, wondering why her father was buying jewelry, she was bumped by a young man. Pale forehead, black hair, eyes of blue glass: she'd seen him before, maybe in photographs of the park. He was lean and muscled, wearing frayed bell-bottoms slung low; beads on a leather thong hung over the bare abdomen. He paused before her, shoulders pale, and waved the lazy plume of a musk-smelling cigarette. He engaged her eyes; as he reached forth offering her a smoke, she saw the thumb, where he wore a heavy ring made from the handle of a spoon.

"I'm Johnny," he confided, holding the smoke between them. The tone was close and friendly. "I've seen you before." He put the joint to his mouth and inhaled sharply. When he spoke, a plume poured from his mouth, fading. "What's your name?"

The heavy cloth of the awning flapped near her face. "My father's in there," she said, and glanced toward the jewelers.

He moved away and was soon squandering words with a couple of boys her age. They reminded her of windup toys she'd once seen, abandoned in random movement on a store shelf.

When her father emerged from the jewelers, he was burying something in a jeans pocket. The jeans were no longer new; he always wore them now when he was home. She wondered what he'd found in the shop but never bothered asking, sure of an uninformative response.

They were passing along the park, as they'd come, when her father grasped her arm roughly and dragged her by a parked car. Then he leaned and scooped up a fragment of asphalt, balancing it loosely in his palm, as a nearby guardsman adjusted his bayoneted rifle. She would have run, but how could she abandon her father to the guardsman? She was staring at the man's rifle in the ugly noonday glare, when her father propelled her along between the parked cars and across the asphalt no-man's-land to the far side of the street. There they passed an overgrown rhododendron.

He tossed the rock in the rhododendron.

"What happened?" she asked.

He made no response. When she looked up, there were damp beads under his mouth and in the lines of his forehead. "He made a threatening move," he answered, finally. She'd seen nothing—or maybe she'd been unaware of the meaning of things she'd seen. As they passed out of sight of the guardsmen, her father glanced over and then away. "Do you plan to inform your mother that we came by the park?" he demanded. "She'll be unhappy with us both."

She was feeling too confused to respond.

"Well, have it your way," he added.

Interlude

ONCE UPON A time at the edge of the forest there lived a girl. In the household were her father, stepmother, and stepsister. The father was a fur trader, often away from home. The stepmother and stepsister made jewelry of small shells they had found in the garden, selling the jewelry in town; though they were never rough with her, there was a household to run. So they found few moments to spare for the child, who would amuse herself by wandering among the wildflowers beyond the garden. Everyone called her Flower Child.

Flower Child could scarcely remember her own mother, who had passed away before the girl had reached the age of three.

Every Wednesday, the stepmother and stepsister would journey to town to sell the jewelry they had made. Then they would use the money they had earned to buy meat and vegetables. In the yard, Flower Child mended her father's clothes or gathered twigs for the evening fire. Sometimes, though, she would wander away through the woods. One day, as the stepmother was preparing to leave for town, she commanded, "Never go to the woods, Flower Child. The woods are full of dangerous animals, such as foxes and wolves, that feed on the flowers. Keep to the house and yard. By dark we will return, and then comes your father, too."

Flower Child pledged to stay by the house. But no sooner had the two gone down the path to town than she opened the back door and wandered down an unruly path into the forest.

Vast groves bordered the path. Tree branches rose densely, obscuring the sun. Under the branches sprouted wildflowers of red, purple, and blue; as she passed them, Flower Child thought sadly how they would soon be devoured by foxes and wolves. But she had never even seen a fox or a wolf, and because the wildflowers she found on the path were far more marvelous than the animals conjured by her imagination, she soon forgot all about foxes and wolves as she gazed on the wonders of the forest plants. A wild rose reached over the path, and she leaned to inhale its musky perfume. From the upper branches of a beech tree came birdsong; she paused to hear the honeyed sounds overhead. "What a lovely song!" thought Flower Child aloud to herself, for there was no one to keep her company. She had begun to feel lonely in the deep forest, and so she sat down beneath the beech tree in the hope of hearing the bird. "The song was for me," she thought; "I'm the only one here. No one could sing so beautifully for herself alone."

As soon as she had spoken, there came a rustling by the path, under a lilac bush, and a small, red-furred creature came gliding smoothly forth until he stood before her, sniffing her foot. She withdrew her foot, too startled to speak, for she suddenly knew he was a fox. The red fox crouched low to the ground and turned his eyes toward her.

"And why are you here in the forest today, my daughter?" he asked. "Has your mother not warned you of bears?"

"Oh yes," she responded, though she was somewhat puzzled to hear a dangerous fox warning her of bears. "I know how the dangerous animals eat the wildflowers, and it makes me sad to see all the lovely wildflowers that will soon be gone, for I'm sure the animals need supper, just as we do."

"Ah," sighed the fox, as Flower Child gazed around at the lilacs and roses, "so must it be. The wildflowers will soon be gone, and then where will you be?"

"I? With father and mother, there I will be," she replied. "We make our home by the forest edge. The afternoon has grown late, and I can no longer tarry under the green beech tree. I do not want to be scolded when I get home."

When he heard her words, the fox turned with a simper to smell a deep-red velvety rose that lingered by the path.

"Oh no!" moaned the girl, starting to her feet. "Please don't eat the roses while I'm here—I couldn't bear to hear them weep." And she fled down the path the way she had come, only an hour before.

When she had come to a bend in the path, she paused, wondering whether she could spy the fox feasting on the red rose. As she turned, he was only smelling the rose; he lay crouched on the ground as though made of stone. But then, with a sudden pounce the fox caught and devoured the rose down to the last trembling red petal; for a moment it shone against the fur like ruby-red blood, before vanishing altogether.

Flower Child gasped in horror and hastened down the darkening forest path.

When she had run a long way, she found herself by a riverbank. She had made no river crossing in the forest, she was sure; but there were many paths home and she was resolved to reach the other shore, where she could continue on her way before seeing the red fox again. The river was broad, the current fast; she paused by the bank wondering what to do. When some moments had passed, she became aware of a large animal standing by her on the bank. He was covered with brown fur. "He must be a bear," she thought. Though larger and far more stout than the fox, he looked on her with welcoming eyes, the huge mouth curling in a smile. For a moment she drew back; but remembering that it was the fox who had warned her of bears, she relented, turning to him as though meeting a new comrade.

"Oh, Bear!" she murmured. "How glad am I to see you!"

The bear never moved, but only looked at her.

Flower Child stammered on. "I know the hour of your supper approaches—if you delay any longer, alas! Fox will eat all the poor flowers of the forest—but before you go I ask your help in a small way, and then you may leave."

The bear gazed at her over the dark, damp muzzle; she was too unnerved to hear a reply but went on, pouring out her thoughts.

"I ask a very small favor of you," she continued, "but an important one for me. I must cross the river and find my way through the forest, for my home is on the path through town. Perhaps you have been to town and passed the house. It's near the old oak tree that burned many years ago, though never dying, for new leaves appear every spring. My father calls it a live oak. If you would carry me to the far shore, I will take the largest blossom from the live oak and send it through the forest to you. Then tomorrow, you will dine much more splendidly than the red fox."

The bear turned toward the water and spoke at last. "I can carry you across," he replied. "However, the land you see is not the far shore but only a sandbar. The current is so strong that I must stop there and rest. We will go there; and when I have recovered my strength, we will continue on to the far shore."

Flower Child was alarmed by the thought of reaching a sandbar in a fast-moving river, at evening, and in the company of a large brown bear. But then she gazed across the darkened water and saw that the sandbar was covered with flowering rhododendrons, though in the dusk they could barely be seen, a vague and purple glow. *It is best*, she thought to herself. *When we reach the island, Bear will leave me in peace and devour the poor rhododendron blossoms, replenishing his strength. Then, as he has promised, he will carry me to the far shore.*

"Very well," she said aloud to the bear. "May we go now? For it is growing late."

And with that, the bear crouched down in the sand, and Flower Child clambered up the strong, broad back, grasping the coarse fur as she pulled herself up onto the shoulders of the bear. Then he rose on two legs. She had never before clambered on a bear's shoulders and was fearful of looking down from so high a place.

The bear lumbered down the sand and waded through the fast current to where he could no longer stand. Then he headed upstream, allowing the current to carry him nearer and nearer the sandbar. When he could finally touch the muddy shore, he rose up the sand until they had cleared the water. Flower Child dropped from the bear's shoulders, landing in dune grass that grew everywhere. All around them, rhododendrons reached forth like jungle growth, forming a dense and seemingly impenetrable wall. *No harm will come if he devours a few of these flowers*, she thought to herself, *for there will always be more, and new ones will grow so soon that we will leave no damage.*

As she was musing on the fate of the flowers, the bear gave a great yawn, revealing two rows of long sharp teeth. Then, hurtling forward, he crashed through the rhododendron brush and was seen no more. Flower Child paused, gaping at the crushed and tangled bushes, as the sound of snapping branches faded slowly away. She was alone.

Part III

the emperor sleeps

chapter one

Alice

FOLLOWING THE PARK turmoil, the Raysons were enjoying some rare camaraderie—an evening at the Patterson home. Now that Michael would be leaving for the Amazon, the women were growing closer, and the families were coming together in a show of support. The park had given everything an added urgency, even the car ride over—of course walking would be imprudent, Marian argued, with the guardsmen running around.

"As long as we're back by curfew," Tom objected, "there's nothing they can do."

Marian glanced in the foyer mirror and grasped her keys. "Then I can go in the car, and you do as you please," she responded.

Tom shrugged, and so they drove together, with Curt humming a droning song.

The door was opened by Sabrina's barefoot daughter, whose assessing gaze roved over the group. She must be Helen, Alice concluded, the one who'd gone along as a baby during a research year—or so she'd heard from her mother. If only the Raysons would go on a research year! Glancing at Curt, Alice could see he was amused by the girl's freely judgmental manner even if he was feigning the usual boredom, as though he'd rather be playing baseball.

Helen hung wordlessly in the doorway, seemingly wondering where they'd come from, as Sabrina emerged from the hall.

"Why, here they are!" Sabrina made up for her daughter's meager welcome. "Come, we're opening champagne."

There came a pop, and Michael appeared bearing long, thin-stemmed glasses. "To the Amazon!"

As the grown-ups clinked glasses, Helen poured some champagne for herself. "Plantains and caterpillars!" she cheered, gulping it down. The women shared a glance.

"Good chaser for those caterpillars, eh?" Tom deadpanned. Caught off guard, Helen made no response.

Sabrina had made hors d'oeuvres and Tuscan panini, served on heavy ceramic plates, with red wine for the grown-ups and sparkling cider for Curt and the girls. The younger daughter was away in Marin, escaping the guardsmen, so Helen was hanging around the grown-ups. That was just as well, thought Alice: Helen and Curt were already eyeing each other, as though she were a tagalong. The three of them sat on a woven bamboo rug, secluded from the grown-ups' chairs and couches, though close enough to hear the conversation, if they chose. There would be only one event of real concern: the war over the park. Alice wondered what Sabrina and Michael would have to say. Surely they would know more than her parents; even Helen would know more.

The Raysons sat apart from each other on a couch, Alice's father coolly sizing up the other couple as her mother murmured admiring words over the Tuscan panini and wine. Helen lay on the floor, her dark hair draping over the bamboo rug as she nodded to a faraway rhythm, seemingly unaware of anyone.

"These are scary days," Tom announced, in his usual impassive tone. "Be glad you'll be far away."

"Oh, there's real fascism down there," Michael responded.

"And why are you going?"

"I'm an anthropologist."

"Have you been to Cuba?" Tom demanded, as though playing a game.

"No. Why?"

"You're an organizer, aren't you? For your people in the Amazon?"

"Oh dear me, they've never been anyone's people. That's the whole point. Anyway, I'm a researcher. They're among the few remaining hunter-gatherers—" Michael poured some more wine. "Of course," he went on, "many of the so-called hunter-gatherers have never depended solely on hunting and gathering; they tend gardens, they're also growers. But our imaginations conjure up bands of savages roaming the earth, feeding off the land, foraging as an occupying army would do. There's another anthropologist—

colleague of mine—who calls them a warmongering people, says it's programmed in our genetic code."

As Alice observed Michael's easy, communicative manner, she wondered about the faraway place where he would soon be going—a place her father had scarcely heard of.

"And you're half-persuaded," Sabrina commented.

She wore jeans, and though they seemed less casual on her than on her daughter, she was clearly undergoing a change. Alice had seen Sabrina before and found her elegant—wasn't her mother always saying she resembled French cinema's lovely waif, Anna Karina? Alice had never seen Anna Karina and couldn't say; even so, the jeans and her husband's flying off seemed to go together.

"I'm a researcher—half-ignorant. They were bypassed by rubber only to be overrun by gold and uranium. Soon they'll be gone," Michael concluded mournfully.

Suddenly an angry droning poured from the sky, the sound they'd learned to dread.

"They're back," Sabrina announced, glancing toward the window.

The droning loomed closer, as though ready to whirl the house away and fling it askew on a Kansas prairie. The grown-ups glanced around in annoyance and dread, except for Alice's father, who was chewing colorlessly on a chunk of Tuscan panini.

Helen plugged her ears. "Flying fucking pigs," she muttered through the roar.

As the thing swooped by, seemingly grazing the roof, the sound pounded a rhythm, gathering them in its ugly and deafening embrace. And then as abruptly as it had come, the jackhammering moved off, leaving a vacuum.

Michael wagged his head, smiling ruefully. "They're calling it a 'people's war,'" he remarked.

"Who?" Sabrina demanded.

"The people at the *Barb*."

"Yeah," added Helen. "Hey, everyone, welcome to Hanoi." She lay on the bamboo rug, her bare feet in need of washing, the soles leathery. Alice, who'd never seen anything so wild and free, eyed them, impressed.

"Oh my, Hanoi." Alice's mother smoothed her blouse, her eyebrows rounded in doubting indulgence. Compared with Sabrina, she seemed formal and humorless. Curt made a scoffing face, as though passing judgment on her, or maybe conspiring with Helen. Alice glanced at her mother, feeling vaguely condemned by the condescending tone she'd begun to assume when referring to those people—park supporters, Peace and Freedom members, *Barb* journalists. They'd suddenly become "the Peace and Freedom kids," a gang of naughty—and dangerously foolish—schoolboys and schoolgirls. Just as Helen was sounding off freely, Alice found herself cringing.

"Everyone knows the cops have guns," her mother was saying. "If you push hard enough on men with guns, eventually they shoot. It's awful, but what was everyone thinking—that the University would just hand over its land? Soon parks would be springing up everywhere—"

"Far fucking out," murmured Helen.

"And why not?" Sabrina said, with an indulgent smile. Alice wondered if her mother would argue with Sabrina, but she paused, as though uneasy. Sabrina pressed on. "Why not have urban farms, if people are willing to work the land? Just look at Frank Madigan, of the Alameda County sheriffs—"

"Mad Dog Madigan, you mean," interjected Helen.

Curt guffawed. "Sure is some mad dog."

"Madigan is from one of those farms in Napa," Sabrina resumed, "where people bought up cheap land—poor people who'd come West, working for others and then one day buying land for a farm. Now he's a good ol' boy, defending home turf."

"Yes," Michael nodded, "and now we have people crowding in here, when there's no more land to be parceled out. Even so, they keep coming, like the '49ers. Where are they going to go?"

"That's easy," Helen laughed. "Every muddy lot in America's gonna have a People's Park."

Michael wagged a finger in refusal. "Governor Reagan and the Chancellor would never suffer a hobo jungle in People's Park. And why should they?" He paused as though wary of her mood, then plunged on, annoyed. "Some of those people are choosing to be poor. There's nothing wrong with that; but groups that follow vows of poverty usually have leaders, rules, discipline. Here we have a mob on psychedelic drugs. And you say give them free land? Any cop who went near the place would be in danger. Imagine a squad car pulling up—in a moment, they're surrounded by hundreds of angry people. No, we'd have a modern-day Sherwood Forest, with the neighborhood kids playing among the bummers and pig roasts."

"Wow," Helen grumbled, "you sound worse than Ronald Ray-gun."

Alice giggled. Helen's father was lively, she thought, examining the man's dark mane and red beard, the safari pants and African tunic, as he pondered the park aloud. Her father, by contrast, was a strategist, a cipher.

Michael shrugged. "Of course we, the university community, made the problem. We pushed people from their homes—including some of our own students—and bulldozed the land, promising public improvements. Then we became careless, as lords of the manor do. For months the land lay muddy and unused, an eyesore. Then came the park—and the improvements we'd never bothered to make. In the arrogance of power, we assumed the rabble could do us no harm; and so, magnanimously, we allowed them to run free. There was alarm, but no one would play the heavy with the people from Telegraph Avenue. Now we've finally been overrun by a higher power: Governor Ray-gun and Mad Dog Madigan. And we professors are appalled by the result."

Sabrina swept back her bangs. "Oh come now, you've never played the heavy, why should the poor Chancellor? You know Governor Reagan is the problem, not your guys."

"Reagan intruded on our problems because we refused to solve them. Now we've seen how far he can go. We're the enemy now." Michael was gazing gloomily around the room. "And Reagan has no careless, magnanimous ways. He's shepherding resources for the ongoing war—on us."

Helen wagged her head. "Fucked up, man, what they're doing." She lay on her back now, her dark hair spread over the floor in a halo. "Man, that park was so beautiful . . . of course they had to make war on us."

"Were you there?" Alice whispered.

"Sure . . . weren't you?"

"Once—"

"I thought she was much too young for the park," Alice heard her mother saying, as Curt wagged his head, smirking.

"There are other arguments," Sabrina began in a commanding tone.

"Yeah, how about your women's group," Helen called out, "and what they say about orgasms?"

The mothers exchanged wary glances. Things were veering dangerously. Then Sabrina resumed, her speech clear and calm, as though they were in a meeting. "As Michael says, the University of California purchased some land, pushing people from homes to clear the way for development. Then the money ran out and the improvements never came. So people improved the land for themselves, developing gardens and so on. Now those people want control—what's the legal term?"

"User's rights." The grown-ups hung on Tom's words as if an oracle had spoken—one that could save them from rumbling anarchy.

"Ah, yes," Marian sighed.

"User's rights, of course," Sabrina said, smiling. "What a wonderful concept."

"Nonsense," Michael scoffed. "It's merely the law of the jungle, somewhat cleaned up. I grab up some land, and once I've made good money from it, I become the owner. It's only moral if you're dealing with real, uninhabited wilderness."

"Come on, there's no such thing," Helen muttered.

"I read something," Alice heard her mother musing, "about some old Spanish ranchos here, before the Gold Rush. Whatever happened to them?"

"Americans—Anglos—won the land through the courts," came her father's lawyerly response.

"But how?"

"Through war, mainly." Michael was pouring a glass of wine. "Before Mexican independence, the Spanish government chose to grant rancho land to Spanish army men, in exchange for forcing Catholicism on the local peoples."

"You mean serfdom," Helen interjected.

"Yes, of course. They thought it would produce good workers—good serfs. The whole East Bay was one huge rancho belonging to a man named Peralta. Not much farming, just the usual ranch amusements—rodeos and horse racing, cattle roundups, and so on. Then in 1848, the United States won California from Mexico, and along came the Yankees. Here in Berkeley, a man named Shattuck squatted on Peralta land, and when the courts were through the land belonged to Shattuck—known, of course, as Berkeley's founder and early developer."

Sabrina smiled. "So then, squatting's in the scheme of things."

"And how," murmured Helen.

"Only useful, enterprising squatting," Tom deadpanned. "User's rights endorses economically meaningful squatting, as opposed to mere camping. Maybe those People's Park folks improved the land, maybe not—for now, Reagan's the judge of that."

"So what you're saying, Tom," Marian summed up dryly, "is that unless we plant a garden very soon, some group could come along and occupy our yard."

"Yup," Curt nodded.

"That would be pushing the case law. However, if the yard became enough of an eyesore, the neighbors could legally compel us to do something about it."

"But what I'm asking is: Could they grow marijuana in my flower beds and gain control of our yard?"

Helen gave a war cry.

"Because when you come down to it, Tom, that's how People's Park came about."

"Not exactly," Michael corrected. "The park belongs to the people of California. So the problem becomes: Why is the people's land reserved only for the very few?"

"Even public land is governed by rules," Marian argued. "Suppose a caravan of people wanted to form a squatter's community in Golden Gate Park?"

"Oh man, they already have," Helen announced, "and it's far-out." There was an awkward pause. Helen rose on her knees. "Don't you get it? They murdered a man over People's Park— he's gone! They'd be happy to murder us all," she remarked gloomily. "Someone told the cops they had to stop shooting —'You're killing my friends,' he told them. And you know what the cop said? 'That's what you get for fucking around.'"

She rose and, giving them a withering glance, abandoned the room.

Alice was impressed by the wild, fearless girl—and scared by her. How would she manage among such peers? Helen's rebel words were exciting, but also daunting. There was danger in them; everyone in the room was feeling the moody anger, as though a fire had just caught and they were facing the leaping flames.

OVERLOOKING NEARBY YARDS and wiltingly hot, the sun-porch was secluded from the family. Through oak branches that dangled leaf-heavy by the window, Alice could see the comings and goings of young people on the neighboring veranda. She was feeling caught up in the group's camaraderie as a bearded man sang, strumming a guitar. It was already July; her brother was off playing baseball, while her mother was in the bedroom, napping as usual.

Alice was paging through the *Berkeley Barb*. Newspapers were new for her—she'd begun with the *Barb* and had no grounds for comparison as she leafed through eulogies to People's Park, outraged censure of the occupying forces, mourning hymns and rallying cries. The paper appeared regularly in the house for the enlightenment of one or another of the Raysons. It would be her way of learning how the world was changing, as everyone around her was forming groups, agendas, plans for a new order.

There were the gushing early columns on the people's Eden, evenings when *someone sounded a drum, pounding the rhythms of work and love. Soon drumming came from shovels and cans, summoning the park workers round the fire for a communal feast—the sharing of roast pig and smoking of grass.* Photographs showed a woman's form, nude and young, gleaming in the light from the bonfire's leaping flames. *The free men among us have made a homeland near Telegraph Avenue. But the pigs are planning the rape of a dream—stealing our homeland, replacing our Park with a holding pen guarded by savage dogs. And those of us who refuse to go beyond where we've gone so far will have to get out.* Another column claimed the park had founded *a strange freemasonry* —"What is freemasonry?" Alice murmured aloud—*of street people and mothers.* She thought of her mother, who'd gone to Peace and Freedom Party meetings but then dropped the group. Some mothers had been ready, it seemed; some had gone very far—in fact, *her* mother had gone very far. And why had she changed?

Glancing up, Alice saw the neighbor's veranda through the leaves, a man and a woman fondling each other, the woman's hand caressing the man's thigh. Lured by the unfolding idyll, she wondered if they could see her through the trees.

Then came the fence and the bayonets, the skirmishes on

Telegraph Avenue and photographs of the wounded, followed by days of confrontations, gassings. She'd seen the pages before and remembered the phrases: *We must build a People's Army . . . Capitalism is a deadly drag . . . Mayor Johnson, leader of the occupation force's Quisling government*—"and what is a Quisling?" she murmured again, promising herself that she would ask her mother, if her mother ever reappeared from the bedroom. *Days of marches, then an appalling finale . . . the release of gas over Sproul Plaza —CS, the standard gas used in flushing out tunnels in Vietnam . . . At Tolman Hall pigs barred the doors and stood by laughing as people squirmed in seeming suffocation.*

Reading on, Alice reveled in the camaraderie. *On any corner, people smile and nod, sharing news, candy, grass, and conjecture. We've learned to live in the flash of our shared dream and resolve. A pig car lurches up and we're clubbed and handcuffed. We're on our bloody streets planning revenge—and they'll never enclose and suppress our dream, for we are stealing everyone's children.*

Surging from a collage of People's Park photographs was a Black Panther holding a gun, and on the following page, an image of nude and laughing girls—three or four years old—playing in the grass. In the sun-drenched room, her body seemed drugged. She folded the paper, feeling confused by the ravaged Eden, the nude images, the guns and rebel words.

A presence loomed and she glanced up—her mother had appeared, a wary look on her face. Wondering what she would say, Alice surveyed the faded rug.

Finally her mother sighed, gloomy. "You're reading about all those things. Why?"

There seemed to be nothing to say. Alice glanced up at the veranda, where the couple continued the embarrassing fondling.

Her mother followed the glance. "Why do you come up here? You've read those papers already," she snapped.

Alice suddenly remembered something. "What's a Quisling?"

"A leader who serves the enemy—a puppet, a collaborator. Why?"

"Just wondered."

"And who are they calling a Quisling?" Her mother sounded annoyed.

"The mayor."

"Who can even remember the mayor's name?" her mother

said sharply. "But of course we all know he's a Quisling." She turned in fury from the doorway, leaving Alice alone in the sun-baked heat of the room.

There was a long backlog of things Alice could have been saying, as new spasms convulsed her world and old ones receded. But who would hear? Or would she go on, never bothering to say, because no one would hear? As she wondered, she heard the words in her head, forming tales: things happening, though no one would hear. Words passed in a rushing river, and as one tale ended, another began. She was feeling overwhelmed by things to say. Sometimes she rehearsed a story, changing it for the good; then she could remember it whenever she began to feel something bad.

Marian

CLOSING HER BEDROOM door, Marian glanced in the mirror. Her eyes were puffy, her cheeks flushed. She was aging; she was feeling abandoned and fearful. Ginger was becoming a formidable danger—if things continued, Marian's life would be damaged forever. Yet she'd never even seen the woman. Marian examined her own angry face, her scowling eyes, damp and glossy, and unhappy mouth. Ginger would be carefree, of course; the signs of her easy, sexy command were becoming clearer day by day. She'd rejuvenated Tom, gifted him with hope—the complacency of a man who saw things going his way.

Or was Marian imagining things? Of course California was good for Tom, freeing him from the pressures of a career in Washington. Open space, good weather, informal clothing—he'd found a personal paradise.

Nonsense. He was dallying impulsively with a loose female lawyer, leaving Marian to manage the family.

The bedroom phone rang. "Hello?" she responded, feeling weary of everyone.

"It's Sabrina. Are you coming on Wednesday?"

Sabrina had been urging her to rejoin the women's group. So far Marian had begged off, fearing Tom would respond by becoming even more aloof. "Oh, Sabrina. I'm sorry."

"We're reading the essay," Sabrina cajoled.

"The essay?"

"Yes, the one about orgasms. I assume you've seen it?"

"Yes." Orgasms were a phenomenon Marian would never feel comfortable discussing in a group—even a group of women.

"And?"

"Every couple has problems, I imagine."

"Some problems are general."

"Maybe."

"How's Tom?" Sabrina asked, lowering her voice.

"Oh, nothing's changed."

"Maybe the group can help."

"I'm sorry, Sabrina. Could we just have lunch?"

"Good idea."

They rang off.

Marian opened a dresser drawer and removed an envelope. The card from Charles, Tom's law-school roommate, had come in May, during the People's Park uproar. Even so, she'd been pleased to hear from Charles, who was in Los Angeles. When they'd last heard from him, in Washington, he'd been working for an aerospace company—bombers and spacecraft, presumably. That could be awkward—among other things, he would argue for the war, and under Nixon, he'd probably gone Republican. Even so, Tom and Charles had once agreed on many things, at least in the legal world. During the years in Washington, however, geography had been a problem. And then Charles' wife had passed away, leaving him and the boys alone, and he'd fallen out of touch. Marian remembered him with a yearning fondness.

Now Charles was suggesting coming up to Berkeley for a few days and bringing the boys. So far Tom and Marian had made no response. How regrettable—poor Charles would feel they'd forgotten him.

She was feeling an unaccustomed surge of energy. She should be enjoying things—why should that woman Ginger be given the reins? She and Charles would make plans, and Tom would have to agree. Company—another family—would cheer her up and soothe Charles as well. He would bring good French wine, and the house would have energy. They would help each other by remembering when they'd been happy.

chapter two

Alice

THE SCHOOL BUS dropped the girls on College Avenue. It was January, and the group, now in Mrs. Donnelly's sixth-grade class, was heading for a Girl Scout meeting—all but Alice, who'd quit the Scouts. She had regrets; she'd imagined replacing the group, but now, months later, found herself spending afternoons alone while the other girls were at meetings. They gossiped, and though gossip made her uncomfortable, she was aware of missing out. After People's Park, however, the green uniform and badges seemed wrong, an ugly getup for aspiring guardsmen. She could never be a guardsman, one of the enemy. And so her uniform lay on the floor for weeks. Then one day she came home and it was gone—washed and folded, in a drawer. Though she'd enjoyed the Scouts and leaving made her sad, she'd already chosen, and there could be no going back.

Tammy and Nora were buying beef jerky from a corner market. Debra was eyeing the candy. Alice hung back, wishing she could go with them.

"Going home?" Debra inquired. She'd grown plump, and her uniform bulged.

"Yes."

"What do you do there?"

"Read . . . play records," Alice said, with a shrug. In fact, it was her mother's birthday, and she would be scrambling around for a present.

"Sounds boring." Debra enjoyed reading about astronomy, but she made fun of Alice's books.

"So's Scouts."

"If you say so."

Tammy and Nora came up. They'd both gone vaguely hippie, wearing beads even on Scout days. The beads swayed incongruously over the green uniforms.

"Well, are you coming?" Nora asked brusquely. She asked the same thing every week, and every week Alice refused, loyal to a mirage of the park.

"I can't. It's my mom's birthday."

"Oh! What did you get her?" Tammy demanded eagerly.

"A cookbook," Alice said, lying. Even Tammy would blame her for delaying so long.

"Well, bye!"

"Bye."

The girls moved off, heading for the church and the leader her mother disapproved of, Mrs. Chaney.

Feeling blue, Alice ambled up Forest Avenue, passing the school playground near the house. There had been the usual January rains, and the yards were soggy. Looking up the block, she saw a row of London plane trees soaring damp and gray-green above her family's brown-shingle house.

Crossing the porch, she found the door ajar. In the foyer, her mother was moving the red velvet chairs, the ones she'd bought in Washington on a spree. They'd been in the foyer for over a year, gathering dust; now it seemed they were in demand again.

"Could you help me?" her mother asked. Her hair was damp from the shower, and she was wearing a new dress.

"Sure."

"Do you remember Charles?" her mother pursued, eyeing her warmly. "He was your father's law-school roommate. He came to our house in Washington."

"Maybe." Alice had a vague memory of an amusing though formal man.

"He's in Los Angeles now. We were hoping we'd see him for New Year's, but something came up."

"Oh."

"He just phoned an hour ago, and he's coming for dinner. I'm so pleased!" Marian paused. "Come, help me get ready."

"I was planning on going out. There's a present I want to get."

"Oh, then hurry. Charles is coming around five." Her mother smiled. "Don't worry. I can manage the chairs."

The day was damp. Alice grabbed her windbreaker and headed for Telegraph Avenue. There would be a jewelry store and a head shop selling incense and dangling earrings. There would be book and record shops. She ran along, imagining Charles—would he be formal, as she remembered? And would her mother send her off early, as she'd done in Washington whenever there were guests, so the grown-ups could talk? Alice was passing rambling yards, houses made of weather-worn shingle, the porches overgrown by tangled flowering plants, the windows hung with loose drapery, faded American flags, or colored glass mandalas. Random melody rang from a wind chime.

She ran along, soon coming to Telegraph Avenue. Rounding the corner of Telegraph, she paused by the door of a head shop and peered in. Speakers squawked above the doorway; the room's deeper recesses glowed with fluorescent black light, a shadowy lavender glare. There was nothing for her mother—or was there? She was contemplating candles and hookahs in the window, wondering what the hookahs were for—serving tea?— when a group in peach-colored robes passed by, and she was briefly surrounded. They were swaying randomly, mumbling chants and clanging cymbals, shuffling along in lazy parade. Smoky waves of incense rose from an orange-robed man swinging a censer. Following him, loyal among the careless pilgrims, was a woman with shaven head, her eyes mournful as a hound's.

The orange-clad zombies passed. Crossing Telegraph Avenue, Alice lingered by the jeans shop, her glance roaming over a display of low-riding bell-bottoms and Spider-Man T-shirts, Levi's jackets, concert posters from the Fillmore West and the Avalon Ballroom.

Suddenly a group her age came running up, a girl and three boys. As they entered the jeans shop, one of the boys hung back, waving. He was familiar—a hippie boy she'd seen at school. They'd spoken once on the playground, and she remembered the name: Joe. He'd come across as calm, admiring, humorously askew, as he bragged about going to concerts with an older brother. Although Alice had heard the albums and seen the concert posters, Joe had actually been to the Fillmore West, or so he claimed. They were on good enough terms—though not good enough for him to wave so eagerly.

"Hey," Joe called. Then louder, "Valerie! Come here!" Joe's group of junior hippies emerged like a single organism from the jeans shop.

"What?" Valerie demanded.

"You guys should meet," Joe proposed. He had a long, mousy nose.

"Oh?"

"Yeah, she's from school."

"School, bummer," mumbled one of the boys. "Let's go."

"No, Jim." Valerie was pleased by something.

"She digs music," Joe explained.

"Who—Jim Morrison? The Rolling Stones?" Valerie's eyes were blue and laughing and fearless, as if she'd already seen the world.

"She digs everything. Right?" Joe smiled, glancing askance.

Alice shrugged as the group leaned in, looking her over. They were very Telegraph Avenue. Valerie's face was long and cleanly made, a sculpture jolted awake; heavy ropes of red-blonde hair hung over her baggy Spider-Man tee. Jim stood staunchly by her, eyeing Alice as though wondering where she'd come from. He was smudged and rumpled, with loose, un-washed clothes, a jagged scar on the chin and the cool, watchful eyes of a big cat. The other boy had the face of a cherub—sunny and eager, as though he'd come from a fresh woodland village before the group had found him.

"So, you're on the Avenue," Joe said, nodding approvingly.

"I'm buying a present."

Joe's mouth curved in a smile. "Who for?"

"It's my mother's birthday."

"Some incense, maybe," the cherub boy suggested.

"No, Chris," murmured Joe.

"Or some jewelry," Valerie added, her eyes mocking.

Then the cherub, singing in a clear soprano, led the others in a jagged round of "Happy Birthday."

Joe laughed. "See ya." And he turned to go.

The cherub hung back, adjusting the bandana around his head. "Come with us," he suggested.

"No, Chris," Joe murmured again. "She's going home—her mom."

"Come with us," the cherub repeated, ignoring him.

"Where?"

Valerie's face was open and challenging. "Maybe you're scared?" she teased, smiling vaguely, as if she'd been there herself.

Jim was moving off. "C'mon, I wanna go somewhere," he urged.

"Come away, fly away," Chris was singing.

Then Joe leaned in close, choosing her. "I've got something in my pocket." He reached in a jeans pocket, grinning, conspiratorial. "Are you coming?"

They eyed her, wondering. Chris had a sweet, sensuous mouth, rounded brows and eager, impish eyes. Alice was intrigued by the group; she must go home soon—but soon was not yet.

"Okay."

"Then c'mon."

Joe opened a door by the jeans shop. The group jammed a small alcove, as though rushing a phone booth, and then paused, pressed together, barely breathing. Joe held up one hand, uncurling the fingers. They watched eagerly as he removed the top of a small plastic box, revealing four yellow pills.

Alice wondered if these things were really happening—if camaraderie could really be as easy as the *Berkeley Barb* had promised in the weeks following People's Park. If so, she would not be needing the Girl Scouts, or even Tammy.

"Wow, yellow sunshine!" Jim exclaimed, grinning in eager approval, his mouth forming a long, jagged arc. "Good score, my man."

Joe beamed. "From my brother Paul." Then he looked at Alice, who was leaning on Valerie's shoulder to see. "Hey, you've done acid before, right?"

Alice shrugged.

Joe eyed her. "No fooling around. When you say you're in, you're in. Okay?"

"Okay." She'd been there before, with her brother and the boys who played baseball. The challenge was to carry through—that would keep her in the game.

Joe doled out the pills, cleaving the final one with a thumbnail and offering it to the two girls.

"On the tongue," the cherub was saying. "That's the fastest way."

For a moment Alice examined her palm. The tiny chunk was surely more harmless than magical—but she could always hope. Then, carefully fingering it, she placed it on her tongue and waited for a momentous change. Seconds passed; no change came. Were they sharing in a sham? Or was she somehow immune?

Joe was by the door. "C'mon, let's go to the campus."

He opened the door and the group burst free. Tumbling along, they passed the jeans shop, a head shop, the leather-goods store. Feeling the group's energy change, Alice fought her sense that she'd swallowed a placebo—that she would be left out. Even so, she was emboldened by the group as they surged along Telegraph, weaving through the ragged burlesque of a grown-up crowd. The Avenue's murky, rambling purposes and sensory derangement had always made her uneasy; finally she could let herself go and be immersed in the flamboyance of the scene. As they neared Bancroft Way, bordering the campus, they were engulfed by a crowd milling around a leafleting table. Flowing along with Valerie, following the boys, Alice thought, *Nothing has changed, and nothing is the same.* She remembered the uprooted Eden and the *Barb*'s foreboding claim—*We are stealing everyone's children*—and laughed loudly. Valerie, who had hung back a moment, came up close. "I'm beginning to feel it," she whispered in Alice's ear, the words nearly drowned by the hum of cars and random sound. Hardly pausing for the signal, the crowd waded through the crossing as though the campus, the pounding conga drums, lay on a far shore. The ragtag group of sixth graders passed the border drums and was swallowed, anonymous, unseen, among the swarm jamming Sproul Plaza.

Soon they were flowing east from Sproul, heading for the Campanile bell tower and looming hills. As they neared the Campanile, from the sky the droning of an organ poured its sonorous fog.

"The bells!" Chris sang, gazing up, unmoored and joyful, on the echoing melody.

The sounds were still misting as Chris and Alice ran ahead, climbing a flight of stone steps leading to Gayley Road and the Greek Theatre. She'd passed the amphitheater before, though never entering. They paused by Gayley Road, aware of being alone together, as the others wandered on the path below.

"Where are we going?" Alice's voice sounded far away.

"Over there." Chris waved a hand, and the Greek Theatre loomed, glimmering in the sun.

There was another pealing of bells, though the clanging

dropped away so soon through the trees overhanging the amphitheater that she wondered if the sounds could have been real. Gayley Road appeared to her as a commingling of many random flows, a coming together of the branching streams of her world. Her path had always been leading here, from the lazy winding of Telegraph Avenue through congealing moments, metamorphosing new and forevermore unchanging.

"I'm going home soon," she remembered aloud. The idea was appalling.

"Now?" Chris laughed. "We're gonna be way stoned."

"Soon, I'm going soon." She was feeling mournful.

A man in colorful camouflage passed by. She was sure he was overhearing her thoughts—why else would he be there? She'd just become aware of why her father was away on Saturdays, where he was going: *He was in Los Angeles, rooming with Charles.* She was less sure why her father wore cowboy boots—though she'd seen them in the basement cupboard and was sure he wore them. The man in camouflage murmured in her ear as he passed, informing her of why, though the reason was overcome by more pealing bells —falling now from some eucalyptus trees on Gayley Road, falling in the wafting, twirling way of dead leaves separating forever from the branch. In any case, *why* had no single meaning but many meanings, all informing her of some formerly concealed but now glaring truth. Now *why* lay glimmering on the ground among pools of shadow—the bells would peal no more, replaced by the humming, buzzing hive of Gayley Road. Cars were coming toward them along the curve in luminous roar, passing and fading as they became caught up in trees. The campus lay below, an enormous gorge carved in the hills. She and her good comrade, Chris, had found a place merging in her mind with places she'd seen long ago from the family Chevy. The road above Santa Fe, New Mexico, foamed up through her mind, booming lavender, pulsing green and blue whenever her head moved. "Dummy, it's where they made the Bomb," she mumbled aloud to herself.

Gleams exploded in her eyes, dancing in waves. A man passed on a bicycle, and she laughed to see him gliding through the world, a swimmer in some unseen ocean. They ran up—Joe, Valerie, and Jim. Alice found a oneness in the group and in the drone of cars, as the zoom of engines filled her ears, like enormous whirling bumblebees. The sky had overflowed and changed the world forever. Chris was humming by her shoulder, joining in the hive. Though they'd never seen each other before, they were comrades now. She began laughing uncontrollably.

"Be cool," Chris murmured.

"Maintain, maintain," Joe counseled.

"But—," Alice giggled.

"No laughing," Jim commanded sharply.

She eyed him, her glance moving down the baggy clothes. He was bossing her. She giggled again.

"Let's go." Valerie grabbed her arm and dragged her across Gayley Road, as cars paused solemnly to let them pass.

Soon they were under sheer, looming cliffs—the amphitheater's towering walls surrounding a damp, shadowy stage. The group ran on, passing through a gloomy underworld, a no-man's-land or purgatory opening in far archways, then emerged onstage as on the surface of a pond before the sun-drenched benches of a grand arena: whirling rungs carved in the hillside beneath a flowing drapery of tree and sky. Heavy columns, seemingly ready to topple on them, rose from the stage wings.

The boys began an impromptu dance, gliding in arcs along the smooth surface of the stage as though defying an underworld. Valerie grasped Alice's arm, and together they ran to the edge of stage. Off they plummeted, landing in lumpy sand. From there they heard the boys' wild hooting and cawing as, caught in the sand, they crouched before an arena of sparkling, swarming fireflies, exploding for them alone.

Alice could feel the clammy sand through her jeans. The hooting and cawing echoed and faded. Above the arena rose hills of eucalyptus. Luminous in the western sun, leaves shimmered purple and green, far outshining anything she'd seen before: all was good. Upper branches waving among clouds and sky; purple fronds tossing; sun flickering as though on a lake: forever was happening, and she was seeing—Now.

The boys clambered from the ledge. Joining the girls in the orchestra pit, they dug furrows in the sand. Damp and heavy, clinging to them, the sand was a muddy, spraying surf, covering them and dragging them under.

The group struggled free and shook away the clinging sand. Then they ran through the lower arena, the rows bending away in cascades as they moved. Coming to the border of the lower arena, they found themselves on a semi-circular walkway. Lining the walkway were thrones carved in the shape of crouching tigers, facing the stage.

From one of the tiger thrones, Jim summoned an imaginary throng. "Hear me!" He glared around and snarled.

A boom rose from the Gayley Road abyss; overhead danced wild eucalyptus fronds.

"Bring in the pigs!" He paused, grinning. "Now, pigs, you're in my power—off with your heads!"

The group cheered. Alice was suddenly feeling alone.

Then they climbed through the upper rows of the amphitheater. As Chris and Jim ran up the center of the arena, Joe and Valerie and Alice were struggling up the flank toward the flowing movement of tree and sky. The group came together again on the upper walkway. For a long moment they gazed west over the amphitheater on the Campanile and the lands beyond the bay. Then they crossed a damp lawn and headed for the eucalyptus groves. The way soon became rough, a pathless scramble over branches and long strands of eucalyptus bark, among treacherous acorns and fallen leaves. Even so, moving was joyous and pulsing; when Alice looked west once more, the sun had gone, leaving a luminous splash along the lower sky. Day was passing: for a moment she remembered her mother, her family, time—glancing at her watch, she saw the hands in random poses, reading only *Now*.

She glanced again and saw that it was already five. *Charles is coming around five*. Good—her mother would be busy, she would never know . . .

Above the bay hung a shape—an amoeba cloud, its orange-gray mass surrounded by a glowing border. As she watched, the cloud was borne slowly northward, shape-shifting, purging away a plume of smoke, its gray aftermath. The cloud faded from orange through purple and gray. Below loomed the amphitheater, a shadowy stage folded in the dampness of evening.

"Can we go higher?" Alice wondered aloud.

Joe laughed, holding up useless hands. "All gone."

"No, I mean—" She paused. The boy's face had a glowing sheen. She was feeling confused—why would she want more of the drug? How could he fail so utterly to grasp her meaning?

Feeling alone, she looked west and saw clouds simmering, the ocean on fire. Beyond the looming columns of the Greek

Theatre, the sky was pulsing orange from the sulfurous candle now burning beneath the Golden Gate. An underworld had been loosed on the bay, churning the waters in a dull aluminum glow. A conclusive, dying blue, echoing ever deeper and more somber through the hum, was spreading over the sky.

Chris could be heard, hollering, ". . . down . . . !" The words seeped away. "Jim . . . running down!"

The cry had come from beyond some trees. Joe moved off, leaving Alice to stumble here and there, looking for Valerie. She crossed the clearing, gnarled roots snagging her feet, and found the other girl closely examining a eucalyptus tree, fingering the trunk and peeling gray-green bark. A rope of curling ivy leaves dangled overhead from a single clinging vine; bark lay strewn in long curls on the ground among sickle-shaped leaves. A pungent odor rose from the mess.

"They're running down the path, let's go," Joe called to Valerie.

There were shouts as Chris and Jim descended the hill, running, hands waving. Soon the others found the path and headed down the hill. Alice could feel her legs moving and let them go, winged and free, sure of landing, alighting once more on earth. Even so, the ground was damp and treacherous; now and then her feet caught among mud and leaves, though somehow she refused to fall. Then suddenly, in a slow tumble she was sliding down the path. When she'd reached level ground, she rose unperturbed: the mud pleased her.

They gathered once more by Gayley Road. She'd been meaning to leave—once upon a time, so long ago. There was no longer any rush.

"I wanna go somewhere," Jim announced. Then he shrugged, as though reaching a foregone conclusion. "Telegraph. The Caffé Med."

"Yeah," Valerie added. "Dan's there. I'm hungry."

Evening engulfed the campus. They passed by the Campanile, but the bells were sleeping. The fleeing hours had been a dream, a mirage—or had they? Alice glanced up. The clock tower rose high and oddly meaningless, though it read half past six o'clock.

Back on Telegraph Avenue the evening revelry was gathering speed. Alice had never been there in the evening without her family shepherding her through the wild and melancholy bughouse crowd, who surged around in eager welcome of Jim and Valerie and the young freaks—a joyous and infernal homecoming, even for Alice. Though just now encountering the revel, she was already Berkeley bred, immersed in the mood of madness. So easy and so soon—she'd hardly even been looking.

Orange glow poured from above, searching for her. She passed under the glare and was overwhelmed by a sense of seeing and being seen. Faces flowed laughing by, eyes honing in on her, acknowledging her: a playful hunting game had begun. Shoulders lunged toward her, then passed anonymously on. She could roam freely here . . .

A leaflet waved its message in a cone of orange glow. She wandered through the glow to read and, without warning, slammed a pole. Woozy, she stumbled on following her group, as passersby welcomed them.

Three men draped in an American flag came parading by. An oily dampness was oozing over her face, cooling her. She must go . . .

She would spend her money and go home. Anything she bought now would do. She paused, conjuring up images of the house—foyer and dining room, where a single candle concealing her mother's age would just now be exploding in fireworks. Ah, of course—by the time she got back the day would be done, and Charles would be gone. A feeling of melancholy overcame her— would she ever be her mother's age?

A man was leaning on a car, smelling a single rose. As Alice passed by, wondering sadly if she'd ever see a rose again, he plucked away some dabs of red and nibbled carefully, like a rabbit chewing on the color of blood. A dog ran up, paused in mid-growl, nosed the flower and ran on, head wagging among the odors in a random dance. For a moment the man went on nibbling; then he swayed down the pavement, leaving an odor of decomposing bloom. Caught in the eddy, Alice spun around.

Joe murmured by her ear. "We're leaving the Avenue."

"Bummer," Jim grumbled. "Dan's already gone."

They rounded the corner by a row of houses. Her legs were leaden and aching as she slogged through damp leaves. Before she could imagine a plan, the others were saying goodbye, and she was alone in the dampness, the freshness, the sweetness of evening.

She was feeling an odd euphoria as she ran along Forest Avenue, passing other people's houses. Hearing a pounding in her head, she ran on, for the joy of moving freely. A hedge, a dogwood tree . . . Rose canes and red-black flowers bobbed by her arm, luring her in. She leaned, parting the canes with her hand, and the thorns dug in; she felt a stabbing and a tearing as she struggled free.

Wind was cooling her face. She crossed the lawn. In her hand was a branch bearing four red rosebuds—her mother's present.

Soon she was in the foyer, hearing sounds coming through a tunnel from the inner recesses of the house: an echoing ocean roar, and submerged, whispering voices—her mother's, eddying in rising and diminishing waves. Alice's euphoria was flagging. Hours were meaningless, she'd done nothing wrong; even so, the foyer was a treacherous cage.

Her mother gave a cry. Then came her father's scary hush. Alice thought of the glowing underworld she'd seen, foaming up from beneath the Golden Gate. She would be herself soon—or would she? Who could say if she'd be the same girl—the one they'd known only yesterday, the one who'd gone out shopping only hours before. She'd never imagined such changes; the group had found her, so easy and so soon. She'd been hoping for camaraderie, but they'd unhinged her, they'd offered hours of madness. Who could say how long Alice would be gone—maybe she'd never come back.

Her family would be holding dinner for her. They would help, unless . . . Alarm sounds from her mother could be heard, pressing closer.

Alice rushed from the foyer. Safely on the second floor, she closed her bedroom door and headed for the bathroom. An uncanny image glared from the mirror: eyes enlarged and black, face greasy, head tousled, a body severed from a mind. Giggles were burbling up even as her mind was awash in raging fear. "No laughing," Jim had commanded. "No laughing," she gasped in the mirror.

A comb lay on a glass shelf under the mirror, offering its sharp prongs. She grasped it gingerly and pulled the prongs through her hair. On the walls, flowered wallpaper was undulating, woozy with color. She leaned over the bowl, washing her hands in the flow, then pressed sopping hands over her face. No breathing; a pulse was drumming through her forehead. Rubbing her face on a towel, she began breathing again. They'd run down a hill, she thought, feeling a wave of giddy abandon; her pants would be muddy.

She was in her underwear when the bedroom door thumped.

"I'm changing," she managed to say, feeling awed by the concept. She had changed—and now what would they do?

She pulled cleaner pants from a heap on the closet floor and yanked them on. Another thump. "Come in," she called. As she faced the door, her father's cold, assessing eyes were on her.

"Come down," he commanded, adding, "Charles is here. Your mother's been expecting you."

Of course, thought Alice, awash in unaccustomed insight and contempt, he was always pushing problems on her mother. She suppressed a surge of laughter. "I'm coming."

Her father's presence was weighing on her as he scanned the room, taking in the muddy pants on the floor, the signs of a rushed cleanup. As he was eyeing her, she began feeling an unpleasant glare of recognition.

"I have some wrapping to do," she mumbled.

"Your mother says now."

He moved away, leaving the door ajar. Once he was safely gone, she remembered the flash of awareness on Gayley Road: *Her father was away on Saturdays, rooming with Charles. And now Charles was here!* A surge of giggles overwhelmed her. "Maintain, maintain," Joe had counseled, as though they could fool everyone. And as they were saying goodbye, Valerie had assured her, "Your family will never know." That was small comfort when her mind was foaming. *Her family was dumb, but even so . . .*

Longing for a comforting face, she made her way through the house. She should never have come home so soon. *Anger was always there*, she suddenly knew—a web of censure and concealed purposes.

She passed the living room, where a man was leaning by the fireplace, one hand around a highball glass. Larger than her father and formally dressed, here was another of the day's unknowns.

"Welcome back," the man murmured, as though imparting a secret. *Here was Charles, and her father wore cowboy boots!*

Though needing an ally, she made no response. Charles eyed her glumly as she walked on.

In the cavernous dining room, a symphony was playing and

candles were dancing in readiness for the feast. *Charles was the king, or maybe the hangman. Off with her head!*

Her mother came through the doorway and paused, flushed and scowling. Her eyes had a glare Alice had never seen before. *She was the queen. Off with your head!*

"Here she comes." Her mother was gathering herself together. "You're awfully late. Where have you been?"

"Looking for a present." The response sounded lame. No one would go along with the charade—or would they? She was counting on change now—but they could cover up problems just as before.

Her mother slammed a cupboard. "And you found something, finally?"

"Yes."

"Good. I'm eager to see." Plates clanged on the sideboard. "Let's eat, then, before it gets any later."

Now her father began probing. "What happened?"

Unburdened by any sense of falseness, Alice spun a foolish tale. "I saw a girl—from my class. Tammy." Her words were coming from far away. "I thought it was early. The sun was there."

"Where's your watch?" Her father reached for her arm, but she eluded the grasp. "Lost already?" he pursued.

"No."

"Wear it from now on."

Her mother glared. "You saw Tammy where—on Telegraph Avenue?"

"On the campus. Her father's a professor." The words sounded as false as if she'd rehearsed them.

Charles was by her shoulder. She was cornered and would have to say more. "The campus was muddy." A laugh was coming on.

"Muddy?" her mother demanded. "Go and change, then. And hurry up."

"Oh, she's clean enough," Charles said, smiling. *Why was the hangman coming to her defense?*

Now her father looked her over, his mouth curving vaguely up. "She changed already. When you came in, eh?"

She made no response. He'd done the same thing—coming home, running up, changing out of the cowboy boots before anyone could see him. That's why he wore them—because of mud. He was the dangerous one; he would understand where she'd been because *he'd been running through mud.*

"Go up and do your wrapping, then," her mother sighed, barely glancing at her.

Alice went back through the foyer and up the stairs. The roses lay on the closet floor; there was nothing to do in the dimly lit bedroom. Drawn like a moth by the dancing colors from the neighbors' porch, she leaned on the windowsill. There came a sound by the door; someone had followed her up.

"Come in."

How long would the flashing colors be there, the fears and giddy abandon—how would she ever come back? There seemed to be no way of controlling the pulsing colors, the flowing sounds and uncanny knowledge, pressing in from everywhere.

Charles was in the doorway. "Everything okay?" he inquired, as though he knew her—as though she should confess. "You look as if something happened." His eyes moved down her arm.

She should conceal her arm—but where?

"What happened to your watch?"

"It came off."

"I see." Charles should be scolding her, but his eyes were shining warmly. "What happened to you today?"

There he was, formal yet forgiving, as though he could say more.

"Are you coming?" He moved away from the door to let her pass, a gesture her father never made. Then he followed her down to the dining room, where Curt joined them and a gloomy feast began.

The room was dim and reeking of food. Her mother and father faced off across the table, perched on the red thrones from the foyer. Charles, dressed in formal gray, appeared to have come for some undivulged purpose—a spy, maybe. Clearly her father regarded the man as vaguely treasonous.

"You're on the wrong side," he charged, accusingly, though Charles laughed it off. Charles was no fool; he was a spy and had a cover.

As the meal was ending, Charles opened the French wine he'd brought, poured freely, and rose to his feet. Then, collar loosened, he led a round of "Happy Birthday," singing with verve.

Suddenly the grown-ups were laughing—her mother and

Charles. Her father slouched on a red throne, seemingly aloof.

When her mother was opening presents, Alice ran up for the roses. Charles smiled and led a toast, and her mother seemed oddly pleased. A symphony played on and on, as though in honor of the sun.

As soon as she could safely leave the room, Alice headed for the second floor. Though her madness refused to go away, she would cover by doing the normal things. *Maintain, maintain.* Confused and frightened, yet remembering the hours of euphoria, she lay in bed, the covers over her head, unable to sleep. Later, after Charles had gone, her parents convened by her bedroom door, full of suspicion. Her mother was saying, ". . . and her eyes . . . and when the symphony was playing . . . and the roses . . ." Though her father had accused Charles, now he made no response.

The door opened. Light flooded from the hallway, searching, spying. Then the door closed. Mushrooming colors exploded in her eyes.

MORNING CAME. ALICE was no longer feeling woozy. She'd even dozed off just before dawn, only to be woken by the usual rapping on her door. School would be manageable, if only she could lay low and keep away from the girls during lunch; she was in no shape for fending off girl games. More of a worry was her family—though her mother would be sleeping, her father and Curt would be in the breakfast room, making an appearance necessary. There was no way of knowing how much her parents had deduced, or how they would respond to her weird, impromptu lapse—an ordeal, really. If they got angry, the disgrace would be over soon; they would scold and forgive, and she would regain a place in the family. But the family was fragmenting, and she'd gone beyond the pale—unimaginably so. There might be no response; they might give her up to the group. That would be worse than anger, because she'd be alone, and then she'd have a long, hard slog, for sure.

Wearing clean clothes, she made her way through the house. However loony her thoughts now seemed, surely they had some meaning. *Her father had been running through mud*—he'd been there before; he'd seen through her.

Her father's muscular presence was cramping the breakfast room. His body made her queasy. Curt came in, glancing her over slyly and smirking, pleased with himself. But her father was deadpan—could he even see her? Or was she beneath contempt? Alice was having forebodings of things crashing down soon enough.

The eggs had congealed, cool and rubbery. She pushed them away.

"Bad eggs?" her father demanded. The edgy snarl made her cringe.

"Not hungry," she muttered.

Her father gave a shrug. "May I?" He scraped the eggs onto his own plate and dug in. Then, barely nodding, he headed for the front door. Curt followed, barely glancing at her.

Feeling a wave of shame, she fled for the school bus before her mother could appear.

THE BUS PULLED up by the schoolyard fence. Alice hung back, wary of what lay ahead. Would she have a new group? A group should be chosen; more amorphous than a family, it would nevertheless confer bonds and a place in the world. Family groups were supposed to be defining; yet her family no longer cohered, no one any longer chose to belong.

She'd been pondering the problem for weeks. The group of girls was frustrating: always talking and playing psychological games; always gossiping about each other, about family.

As Alice was crossing the crowded playground, Tammy came up slyly from behind. Only the day before she'd been wearing a Scout uniform; now she had low-riding bell-bottoms that could have come from the jeans shop on Telegraph Avenue. She was growing up—slender and newly graceful, she was made for the look.

"How was your mom's party?" Tammy asked. She would rehearse everything normal from the day before, as though welcoming Alice back.

"Okay," Alice said with a shrug, soothed by the other girl's face.

"Really?" Tammy eyed her, suppressing a giggle. "Are you sure?"

"Yes. Why?"

"Dunno." Tammy shrugged, mimicking Alice. She was astute, responsive, and that made her dangerous.

"Well, my mom had fun." Alice expanded as well as she could, considering the events of the day before. Then, feeling that more was expected, she added, "My father's law-school roommate was there."

Tammy's glance was close and assessing. Alice began moving away, but Tammy followed. "What's your father's like?" she probed, scenting a morsel of gossip.

Alice, on guard, merely responded, "He's a government lawyer."

"So, he's a conformist," Tammy pursued. "And he enjoys arguing."

"Maybe."

"And your mother?"

Tammy had some hidden purpose.

"She enjoys arguing, too," Alice responded, freely inventing. The statement sounded absurd.

Tammy nodded, fingering the beads she always wore. "And your father's law-school roommate? Does he argue?"

"No, he sings. And he pours wine."

Tammy laughed loudly. "Good for him."

"My father says he's on the wrong side."

"Well, of course." Tammy paused. "And you—are you going to be a lawyer?"

"Maybe not."

"But that's what your father wants, right?"

"Not really." Alice was feeling sweaty.

"No? What, then?"

"Dunno," Alice said. She was dying to get away. Tammy's line of questioning, with its suggestions of teasing and sympathy, made her feel vulnerable.

The other girl's purpose seemed almost mocking as she leaned in, her face glowing in warmth and amusement, and summed up, "Oh, there's something you won't tell me!"

The bell rang. Tammy ran off across the yard.

Now Alice knew why she'd been avoiding Tammy. Tammy could always see when something was wrong—and something was very wrong between Alice and her father. They barely spoke;

the few remarks when she'd come home late were the only words they'd exchanged all week. Who could say what he thought of her—nothing good, for sure, even though she'd done no wrong, before the LSD.

She would get away before he could damage her. Even now, there was something good in her.

Her soul was on an island under a cloudy sky, surrounded by a glassy sea. The schoolyard hung all around her, an unhappy world closing in, but she longed for a faraway place of eucalyptus hills, purple in the new day.

Where was the group? *Running through mud . . .*

As though summoned by her thoughts, they appeared, running through the crowd under the playground's only tree. Laughing and wild, they passed her by; maybe she'd find them during the lunch hour.

Hearing the pealing of bells, Alice slipped through the doorway of Mrs. Donnelly's sixth-grade classroom. There was a soothing feeling in the stagnant room. The day would be undemanding—and for once she was glad. Desks slammed. Mrs. Donnelly perched on her desk, her head graced with curls and waves: a new hairdo. Her eyes were cool, commanding order. The day began.

The morning passed slowly. Tammy was by the window, poring over a book, only now and then moving her eyes from the page. Debra was busy, as usual, doing work she'd brought from home. Nora was pondering Mrs. Donnelly's new wave. And Alice was immersed in the flag that hung above Mrs. Donnelly's shoulder.

The classroom was jolted by the lunch bell. Mrs. Donnelly paused, running her jaded gaze over the students. Ignoring her former group, Alice ambled through the door alone.

Before she could get away, Nora ran up. Blonde and bouncing, she managed to make even jeans seem like a uniform.

"Are you coming to lunch today?" she demanded.

"No."

"Tomorrow?"

"Maybe."

Nora's mouth hung open. "How come you never have lunch?"

"Not hungry."

"Oh, you're saving money for something!"

Alice shrugged, annoyed by Nora's game.

"Yes, you are." Nora's face glowed, sly and smirking.

"So what?"

"Does your mom know you never buy lunch?"

"Yes."

"Do you buy candy?"

"No." Alice glared, contemptuous. "How dumb."

Nora glared back. "Then what do you spend it on?"

"Why should I tell you?"

"Oh, I just thought you'd want to tell . . . someone." The other girls were emerging from the classroom, Tammy gesturing urgently for Alice to accompany the group. Nora turned back, her glance shrewd and level.

"So—are you coming?"

"No."

Nora spun on her heels, as the group headed for the lunchroom.

Alice made her way slowly through the halls and double doors to the playground. The yard was empty: the others were jamming the lunchroom. She wandered along the fence, watching the yard, the street, the cloudy sky. She was feeling drained. A few people wandered through the lunchroom door. A group of black girls, one rolling a hula hoop, ran by. Boys appeared in groups of three and four, chasing each other. Alice could have been running free, but her group was nowhere to be seen.

Tammy appeared, coming along the fence. Alice was feeling wary—Tammy knew too much. The other girl held up a magazine and waved her over.

"I found something really cool." She opened the magazine to a color photograph of people in feathered masks and body paint, dancing on a gorgeous beach. "Here, look. So groovy." Though Tammy was joking—her usual sly and worldly humor—in her eyes lay a restless curiosity.

"More groovy than Mrs. Donnelly's class."

Tammy giggled. "And just think, we're in class all day, cramped in our desks," she scoffed, gathering momentum. "We're learning to do meaningless paperwork so when the time comes, we can take our places in the machine." She paused, surveying the response to her new performance.

Alice leaned over the photograph. She was remembering

246 | playground zero

Telegraph Avenue—the neon lights, the glowing orange cones, the three men draped in the flag, the man nibbling on a rose. "You don't need some goddamn desert island."

"Gosh darn." Tammy made a long dachshund face.

"Huh?"

"Some gosh-darn desert island." She smothered a giggle. "You were saying . . ."

"You can wear feathers and dance around here," came Alice's deadpan response. "You don't need some fucking faraway island."

Tammy burst out laughing. "No? Even in Mrs. Donnelly's class?"

"Well—"

"She'd send me to goddamn Mr. Haynes!"

"Maybe." Alice was smiling; she'd never heard Tammy swear before. "So wear your mask and feathers somewhere else."

"Such as?"

"When you're at home. They'll never know."

"Oh, I can never fool my mom." Tammy was looking at her now. "I bet your parents are cool."

"Maybe . . ."

"I'm sure they are."

"I guess," Alice said. "Well, yeah."

"My mom is cool, but she makes me mad all the same. I know she smokes pot, but she says she'd ground me for doing the same thing."

"Of course."

"Man, so crazy." Tammy nodded and closed the magazine. "How about your mom?"

"What about her?"

"Well, does she?" Tammy leaned in and whispered, even though they were alone. "Smoke pot—does she?"

"Maybe."

"Have you ever been grounded?"

"No."

Tammy nodded admiringly. "Your parents are way cool."

"Not yet, anyway."

Tammy paused, her eyes sober. "I bet you're bad sometimes."

"What do you mean?"

"Sometimes you won't follow orders. Like with Nora—or Mrs. Donnelly."

"I have no problem with Mrs. Donnelly."

"So how come you ignore her in class?"

"I don't. I just get bored sometimes."

"I'll say! Today you were staring at the flag all morning."

"I was thinking—"

"That's what I mean. Mrs. Donnelly could've been a fly on the wall."

"I have no problem with her."

"No, you just don't hear a word she says. She was looking over at you, but you just went on staring at the flag."

"I was thinking about something."

"Wow, it must have been deep, because you were in some other zone."

They wandered along the fence, approaching the gate leading to Ashby Avenue. Gazing back over the playground, they saw a playground counselor tossing softballs with some boys.

"I love baseball," Tammy sighed.

The pounding of feet made the girls wheel around. As though tagging home, the two boys hauled up as soon as they'd entered the gate. They were her group—Joe and Chris. As they came along the fence, Jim ran up from a corner of the yard.

"Hey, Joe!" he called.

"Jim, my man!"

Jim was wearing the same scruffy clothes. "Where'd you go?"

Joe was laughing. "I'm hungry as a wolf!"

"Oh yeah?"

"Yeah. Let's go."

"Bummer for you. I already had my lunch!"

Tammy pulled Alice away, making an urgent frown. "Do you know him? The one in corduroys, Chris." Her eyes had a sheen. "He was looking over here," she added.

"I may have seen him around."

"Oh, some boys get away with everything." Tammy blinked. "My mom would really ground me. You know, the basement dungeon. Oatmeal once a day."

"Sounds bad."

"Yeah."

The ball rang. The group of boys ran by. As they passed, Joe turned to wave. "See ya!" And they were lost in the crowd.

chapter three

Joe

ONCE UPON A time in a wood-shingle house in Berkeley, not far from the Red Family commune, there lived a mama bear and her four cubs. Many years ago—so long ago that no one any longer remembered just how it happened—someone told Papa bear about a pond far in the forest and the enchanted swan who made her home there. So one day Papa bear set forth to hunt the swan, and when he'd found her and bound her wings and brought her to the wood-shingle house in Berkeley, the four cubs were very happy.

Then one day when the cubs came home, the swan had flown. Papa bear was also gone. Mama bear, mad and gloomy, told them how the swan had flown away to her pond and Papa bear had followed her there.

The four cubs were growing year by year. Gregory, the oldest, remembered Papa bear well. Papa bear was fun, and when he was in the house, Mama bear was happy and everyone laughed. Then came Paul, but he hardly remembered Papa bear—and mostly he remembered what he'd heard about the pond. He would imagine the swan splashing in the water and the grasses by the border, and he played in the grasses and rolled them up and smoked them. One day Paul learned to sell pond weeds, and now he had a wonderful new . . . a wonderful new . . .

Joe woke to the pounding of bass and drums. He'd been dreaming—not of Papa bear, whom he remembered only from photographs, but of the group he roamed with, three boys and a girl, Valerie. Though Val was no Mama bear, at least she was a girl; she made the gang feel like a family. Joe was glad there was no Mama bear, always angry, always unhappy; now he had a group of boys the same age and could feel cool and proud. He was no longer a younger brother. Even so, the group needed a girl who could bring house and pond and boys all together in one place.

Joe lay in bed, eyes closed, head under rough wool, hearing the marching of ogre's feet. He'd been hearing it every Saturday for months, the trampling in the living room. There came a pause, as the ogre rolled up some weeds and fumbled for a lighter. Then he resumed the march.

Morning sun splashed on the faded rug. Joe flung off the covers, glad to be free of the heavy woolen army blanket the old man had brought home from the war. Not the war he'd heard so much about—the one happening now, far away in Vietnam—but another one, who could remember any longer why or even where: oh yes, Korea. Joe's father had fought and come home long ago, before the swan—before Joe. He'd made a world and then he was gone.

Peering through long, uneven bangs, Joe gazed down on the baggy pajamas he wore—Paul's old ones. Though he had a boy's slim arms and legs, the hands and feet were already growing. He would be big someday, like Paul, and then no one would push him around. For now, though, he was safe as long as he had a group. The school playground, Telegraph Avenue—he could manage them and do as he pleased.

Loud thumping was coming from the room below: Paul's new album, announcing that Mama bear, a nurse, had gone for the day. Paul began early on Saturdays, as soon as she left; more than anyone, he had command of the house.

As long as anyone could remember, Joe had shared the bedroom with Anthony, one year younger than himself. He glanced around and found the bed abandoned, a mess of rumpled wool and jeans. Anthony was hanging around a neighbor boy's house and would be gone for the day. Above Anthony's bed hung an American flag, brought home by Paul. Joe wondered how he'd come by the flag—Paul was cagey and would never say. He'd ripped it off from a school, for sure—but had he gone in during lunch hour, or crawled through a window at night? If Paul could do such things, so could Joe and the gang. Joe punched the bed, dreaming, planning. For weeks, Paul had been supplying him with grass. He was a buddy.

Near the flag by Anthony's bed hung a poster of the Rolling

Stones. Joe looked over the shaggy, flouncing group. The drummer wore a girl's pale leather boots; Jagger was flashing some leg. Along the lower edge read the words "Free Concert." Among the four brothers, only Paul and Joe had gone to Altamont—the wild Rolling Stones concert at a speedway south of San Francisco. Paul had gone with some guys from a band, and Joe had gone with Jim and Valerie in a van from Telegraph Avenue. They'd gone early, pushing up near the front. Jim and Valerie had a groovy dad who'd found them the ride. The dad, Dan Dupres, had planned on going, but he had so many things to do. He ran a jeans shop on Telegraph. He was organizing to stop the war. He had a room full of marijuana plants. He was some newfangled dad.

The drumming below surged in a crescendo, paused, and resumed in a slower rhythm. Joe was feeling chill—loose and daring, as if he already had a buzz. He would be running a dropoff for Paul; that done, he would find Jim and the gang. He could roam freely; his mom no longer cared where he was going or when he'd come back. The world was becoming fun and easy.

Joe pulled on jeans, socks, and a soccer jersey and headed for the bathroom. The only sound from below was the moaning of a song. Moving loosely to the music, he found an orange toothbrush, dampened the brush, and began scrubbing. The pounding rose louder, speeding up as he crossed the landing.

Or just another lost angel . . .

From the landing, Joe could see the room below. Near the doorway leaned a dying ficus tree, the only remaining houseplant. Once upon a time it had been a charmed thing shedding sap. He vaguely remembered other houseplants—geraniums and red sorrel—before they'd been alone on Saturdays, before the room had been flooded with marijuana smoke and the crying of the phonograph.

City of night . . .

Paul slumped on the couch by the window, head leaning back. He wore cutoff jeans and a paisley cowboy shirt. Though he had long muscled legs and had begun shaving, he had a girl's glossy auburn hair, falling damp and loose over hard shoulders, and long, graceful hands. As Joe descended, he could see Paul's left thumb and forefinger pinching a joint. A plume of smoke rose from his mouth, signs of a smoldering inner fire.

Paul looked up. The eyes were amused and measuring, as

though wondering how high Joe would fly before he crashed down. "Here's my man."

"Hey, Paul!" Though younger than Gregory, Paul was more daring, more fun. He had things to teach Joe.

A Berkeley High sophomore, Paul made money from the school's potheads and garage-band boys, who jammed after school and on weekends. Joe had heard how Paul and some pals rode racing bikes through the hills, smoking grass. Other days they would go by van through Marin County. Packing beef jerky, water, and grass, they would leave the van along the upper Muir Woods Road and descend through the canyon's redwood groves. Joe and the gang would do these things someday, and more: they would sleep on the forest floor at Muir Woods, under the nose of the rangers. He would learn from Paul where the canyon path began; from there they would find the way down. The famous groves would belong to them in dark night; there would be more deer than you'd ever see during the day. During those hours, they would be free . . .

When Joe lay awake, imagining daring deeds, he would see trees as huge as the Campanile.

Joe ran across the room, gliding on bare wood as he reached the couch by the window. For months, the team he'd always formed with Anthony had been dissolving, as Anthony hung around the neighbor boy's family. Lonely and at loose ends, Joe had sought out Paul, though apart from a physical resemblance—they were pale and long-nosed, and both would be large —they'd never been very close. A younger brother could be useful to Paul, who now saw that Joe was easy, undemanding, in need of fun and numbing, and less moody than the others. Dreamy and loyal, Joe enjoyed smoking grass and remembered how Paul had turned him on. Now he leaned close, bangs framing his face, eyes puffy from sleep, the ends of his full mouth curving up.

"Gimme a toke, man."

Paul had a deep drag and offered the joint, then changed his mind. "Later, Joey," he said, coughing.

"Later?" There was a phony urgency in Joe's voice. "Whaddaya mean?"

"Oh, well . . ." Arm waving by the window, teasing, Paul dangled the joint and Joe pursued, playing the chasing game.

"Gimme the joint," laughed Joe, "before Mr. Samuelson sees and calls the cops."

As Paul glanced through the window, Joe made a grab and the coal fell on the floor.

"Now you've done it, Joey," Paul scolded, smothering a giggle.

Joe kneeled. Wincing, he pressed the coal with a thumb. As he was rubbing the thumb on one knee, Paul turned back to the neighbor's house. Shades were drawn on the lower floor, and the woodwork was peeling. "Old Samuelson never leaves the house," he commented. "Probably never heard of reefer."

"Mom will know when she comes home," Joe teased. "The smoke."

"I can open a window. She comes back late, anyway."

"So then, lemme have some."

"Go ahead, Joey." Paul waved an arm magnanimously above the floor. "Finders keepers."

Ignoring Joe, Paul glared through the window at Samuelson's house, made a monkey face, and flipped off the old man.

Then he eyed Joe, suddenly sober. "You're gonna do me a favor, remember?"

"Yeah," Joe nodded, "a drop-off."

Paul dangled the roach. "Take the stuff to Conrad. He always pays up."

Joe saw Paul pinch the roach, open a red box, and drop it in. Then Paul pocketed the box. "Lemme know when you're ready."

Joe ran down the hall. The kitchen was a large room opening on a porch. In a folding chair on the porch, Gregory was reading a book. He wore glasses and Papa bear's old blazer; head framed in dark curls and a youthful beard, he could have belonged to another family. The sound of barking came from a nearby yard. Gregory glanced up, eyes concealed by the glasses. Joe, ignoring the older boy who passed for man of the house, rummaged in the cupboard for a box of cornflakes and a glass bowl, as Paul's new album made a faraway pounding. Joe poured the cereal. He'd learned to be careful around Gregory, who was no longer a buddy, one of the boys: he would finish high school in June and become a man. The summer before, Gregory had taken a job in a supermarket, working Sundays and a couple of afternoons a week. He'd also begun spending time with Caroline, playfully known among the boys as the swan. At first, Joe had enjoyed hanging around

Gregory and Caroline, but he'd learned to leave them alone. Some Saturdays she came early and they lounged in the front room. Other Saturdays she showed up for dinner, and then they passed the whole evening in Gregory's room.

Joe wondered if Caroline would be there today.

The telephone in the hallway rang. Gregory jumped up.

Gregory was not planning on college, unless it became necessary through the graces of General Hershey and the draft lottery, coming up in July. Along with the other young men born in 1951, Gregory would be an honored player as, randomly and one by one, Hershey removed the blue capsules from a glass bowl, a punch bowl laced with chance, Joe had heard. Each capsule held a slip of paper bearing a calendar day, and as each day came up, it was assigned the number that would damn you or spare you. When Joe heard about the punch bowl and the blue capsules, he thought of the strangeness of it, for he was reminded of the game shows he and Anthony used to enjoy, as they imagined winning the new house or Chevy behind Door Number 1, Number 2, or Number 3. Only now, rather than a new car, Gregory would come upon a land mine or some legless villagers. Apparently, that meant the older brother could now tell the younger ones what to do. Anthony was the youngest and had always been indulged. As rebels, that left Paul and Joe.

Gregory stood by the door, looking at Joe. "Caroline's coming over," he remarked. "Leave us alone today, eh, Joey?" And he was gone.

In the bowl of cornflakes Joe imagined a blue capsule; in the capsule a paper; on the paper a message, December 9—Gregory's day.

SOON JOE WAS on the porch. He was wearing a Levi's jacket sewn with colorful patches, and he'd tucked the soccer jersey, formerly belonging to Paul, into the jeans he always wore. Forming a bulge beneath the jersey were six bags of marijuana. Facing slightly sideways, Joe went fast down the steps and through the gate. Though it was nearly ten o'clock, the only sign of life was a faded green Volkswagen whining slowly down the block. Joe crossed the street and rounded the corner of Bateman Street, where he was soon passing a communal house. Weeds grew high in the front yard; from the roof hung a red flag, one corner gleaming with yellow stars; a poster of Che Guevara could be seen in an upper window. One day, Joe had passed the house with Paul, who glanced up and then elbowed Joe. "Fuckin' revolutionaries," he nodded. "They're gonna be ready. You know—guns, bombs, everything. Even the babes."

Joe crossed College Avenue. He'd learned the address, as usual: 2797 Webster Street. He rehearsed the number as he walked, wondering what would happen if he remembered the wrong number and went to the wrong house. One day, when he was carrying nothing, he'd amused himself by ringing a random doorbell, and an older woman had come to the door. He'd fumbled around, forgetting what he'd planned on saying. When she demanded if something was wrong, he ran away.

Paul always let him know what to expect. Today he'd be seeing Conrad, a garage-band guy. It would be an easy drop: Conrad had come by the house with Paul, so Joe already knew him. Conrad's family would be away. Joe would ring the doorbell, and then he'd see the boy's head though the glass. If anyone else opened the door, Joe should leave. Conrad played bass for Orpheus Rising, a high-school band that was already playing the local clubs. Though he wasn't dealing the way Paul was, he was supplying the band. Paul enjoyed the arrangement because he could hang with the guys when they were jamming—these boys who had money for grass and amps and soundproofed rooms in the family home. Joe was welcome as Paul's younger brother—and that was enough for now.

As Joe was nearing Conrad's house, a cop car rolled slowly down the block. Joe passed the house, hands swinging loosely as he sang, loudly and badly. The cop car glided along the lane. Joe rounded a corner and paused by a bush. Soon he was coming up on the address again. The cop had no reason to hassle him; as Paul kept saying, Joe was so young they'd leave him alone.

The house was large and gabled; ivy covered the upper story. Someone was playing Santana—Conrad, for sure. The song blared freely, as though confirming that everyone else was away. Joe enjoyed the glimpses of people's houses that came with helping Paul's deals go down. In each house, he would imagine living someday among the strange and wonderful objects he found there. With a regular buyer, he could really scope the place, get familiar. In the bedroom at home, he would stay awake replaying scenes from the houses he'd seen. Lying in the dark, he would imagine each house and the things he'd grab from there, if he ever got that far. He wondered what Paul had taken, beyond a school flag; but for Joe, it was houses, not schools, that really counted—houses had what he wanted. It was fun to have a flag hanging in the bedroom, and when boys came to the house they were impressed. But he'd seen much more enthralling things—personal things. Things that belonged in one place only, the place where he'd found them. In a fancy house on The Uplands he'd seen a parrot—a dazzling creature with a long, fluorescent plumed tail, eyes like glass beads, and a green helmeted head. It hung from a beam in the foyer by an unseen thread, seemingly perching on Joe's shoulder as he passed through. The house had a sloping, overgrown yard. The boy was bland and haughty, the money ready, the drop coldly impersonal. Joe wanted the green-headed parrot—the cool thing that came with the house.

As Joe rang the doorbell, a new song, a lover's ballad, flowed from the upper story. Conrad's curly dark head appeared in the glass as he opened the door, grinning. "Joey, come in." He closed the door as Joe entered the house. "Paul just phoned me, told me you were on the way. Come on up, man."

They went up and along a dark passageway to a bedroom in the back corner of the house. Conrad turned down the phonograph on a crooning guitar. The room was hung with concert posters from the Fillmore West. A huge Cuban flag hung overhead, the lone star forming a canopy, the white and blue bands running down one wall. By the bed was an amp reaching above the shoulder, huge enough to blow the windows of the house, Joe thought.

"Just in time, Joey. There's a jam this afternoon."

Joe unbuttoned the Levi's jacket. Under the jersey was a strange bulge above the belt loops. He felt comfortable with Conrad. He wanted to make the older boy happy with him. Joe unfastened his belt and the top button of his jeans and pulled on a corner of the jersey. Reaching in, he carefully removed a bag of marijuana from under the jersey and handed it to Conrad. "One . . ."

Conrad crouched on the bed, leaning over the bag as though

examining jewelry or gemstones. "Lush, man, dense, green. Oh wow, potent stuff. Paul never fucks around with seeds and stems."

Joe pulled out another bag, then another and another. Conrad was grinning.

"Wow, I'm gonna have some now. See what the man brought." Conrad reached for a shelf by the bed, where there was a package of cigarette papers. He took some dry, crumbled leaves from the bag and placed them in the paper crease, rolling it back and forth firm between his fingers until it rolled smoothly and then tucking the paper for the final roll. He wetted the inner edge and sealed it. Then he fumbled on the shelf for a lighter. The flame rose high, higher than the flame on Paul's lighter. Conrad inhaled on the joint, held the smoke for a long count, then released it slowly, letting it curl around his lips, flare from his nose. "Hey, man, I hope you get something outta this."

"Don't worry about me."

"Yeah, I guess you're a lucky man, having Paul for a brother."

"You can say that."

"Toke up, Joey." Conrad passed the reefer to Joe. "Now for the money thing." He pulled out a wad of bills and counted off seven ten-dollar bills and handed them to Joe.

"Six ounces by ten, plus another ten. That's for you, man."

"Far out—thanks, Conrad."

"And make sure Paul gets the rest."

Joe held the money in one hand as he drew long on the joint and then reached it toward Conrad. Conrad moved closer, grinning, pinching the joint. The older boy's blue and gold jersey was worn and comfortable, Joe could see the shoulder muscles moving under the cloth. Joe looked down at the money, fanning the paper in his palm. He peeled off one greenback and slipped it into the pocket of his jacket. Then he carefully folded the others and thrust them into his jeans.

As Conrad continued to smoke, Joe wandered toward a wall hung with an image of embedded blue squares, each one smaller and receding deeper from the surface, becoming more intensely blue as they plumbed a pulsing cavern. Joe felt himself falling toward nothingness; then he flinched and pulled away.

Conrad had approached, staring at the gathering blue. He gestured toward the wall. "I could plunge in there."

Joe stood, hands hanging loosely, dreaming. Conrad turned

and laughed, "Such an odd feeling." Then he added, "Maybe
you and some pals want to go to the Fillmore tonight. Someone
gave me some comps, and I can't use them."

"Who's playing?" Joe wanted to know.

"The Dead."

"Wow, how come you're not going?"

"I've seen them so many times, man . . . and something else
came up."

"Oh."

"You've been to the Fillmore, no?"

"Sure . . . with Paul."

Paul and some other guys had already taken Joe to the Fillmore West, where he'd seen Jefferson Airplane. That had been
months ago, even before Altamont, in early December; and for
Altamont he'd approached Jim on the playground one day, hoping by the look of the boy that he would know a way there, and
sure enough, Jim's dad had found them a van from the Avenue
to the muddy speedway. Now things were moving fast. Chris
had begun hanging with them and they wandered as a group,
leaving school together for the Avenue or some grass in Jim's
dad's apartment. And more and more, Valerie was coming along.

Conrad opened a drawer by the bed and found a small envelope. "Here you go, pal."

"Wow. Thanks." Over Conrad's shoulder, the blue squares
were plunging through the wall. Joe imagined a throng, a stage,
a rough leather angel hurling down a lightning bolt on a dark
figure squirming on the ground. He could hear the roar of guitars and motorcycles, feel the crowd churning, flinching away.
He squinted through the glare and saw a shadow prancing overhead on the stage, under the searchlights. Turning back toward
the low hills thronged with people, he saw thousands of small
flames burning, stars fallen from somewhere, anywhere . . . Joe
looked away, feeling queasy. "Conrad . . . the phone . . ."

"Oh, sure, down the hall, my parents' room. I'll show you."

Joe followed Conrad through the hall to the doorway of a
sprawling bedroom overlooking the street. The room was sunny
and lushly decorated, the bay windows forming an alcove furnished with a pillowed couch and a telephone. Bookshelves covered one wall; on the others hung woven Japanese mandalas.
Overwhelmed and pausing near the door, Joe found refuge in a

small framed photograph of a man with furrowed brows. He had the tempestuous look of someone who had just stepped from a racing car, or maybe a bomber plane. A smoke dangled from the clamped but sensuous mouth.

"Your father?" Joe wanted to know.

"No way . . . some Frenchman, an author. There was a novel about Reds in Shanghai, and another one about Spain, you know, anarchism and all that."

Joe squinted at the man in the photograph. "You saw the film?"

"No, Joey. I read the books, they're here somewhere."

"Oh." Joe glanced around the room, finally registering the wall of books. "Wow, your father reads."

"Yeah."

"One of the professor guys."

"He has a campus gig sometimes. But he's really more journalist than professor." Conrad paused, glancing over the photograph. "Now he's into something really cool, a book on Cuba."

"I saw that one . . . Fidel playing baseball."

"Yeah, that was a cool film. Man, who needs the Giants . . . You saw the flag, the one in my room? It's from Cuba. He's there now, rapping with them."

"Wow."

"Yeah. Hey, phone's over there, by the couch."

Joe knew the number by memory. He called Chris, who suggested meeting by a muddy vacant lot, not far from the former People's Park.

FROM THE CORNER, Joe could see Chris, by a clump of plum trees in the muddy lot, and Jim, scoping the bulldozer. For days Jim had been planning on trespassing on the thing, whose engine required no key, or so they'd heard—there were so many things they could tear down. The bulldozer leaned on a mound of earth, mud clinging to the treads, steel arms bearing up the shovel as though Godzilla were marching on Berkeley. Joe slowed, concealed by a parked car, and glanced down the block for any oncoming cop cars. He was carrying a large sum of money, admission to the Fillmore West for the whole gang, and enough reefers for the weekend—Conrad was generous, more so than Paul. And so for now, he refused to fool around. A wonderful day was coming and he would have it.

Crouching by a blue Mustang, Joe saw the plan unfold. Chris ambled by the curb gazing nonchalantly for cars as Jim wandered near the bulldozer. Chris moved one elbow up, slapped the other shoulder as if swatting a fly, and proceeded slowly along the curb. By the bulldozer, Jim scrambled up a ladder and through the opening of the cab. Chris moved on, glancing across the mud. Suddenly a cop car rounded the corner, cruising slowly along. As though roused by irrepressible joy, Chris made a loud yodel; Jim came vaulting from the cab and ran toward the clump of plum trees. A few yards from the trees, he slipped on mud, went down on one knee, jumped up and surged under the branches just as the squad car passed.

As the cops glided by, Jim appeared too enthralled by plum bark to remember the hour, day, or month.

Joe ran up. "Close call," he murmured.

"Where are they?" Jim's mouth barely moved.

"Gone."

Jim looked up through the plum branches. "Bummer," he groaned, "even the trees are a bummer now."

"Hey," Joe said, nudging him, "here comes that girl."

Jim glanced around, eyes narrow and wary. Chris was coming toward them, bringing a girl.

Joe looked her over: jeans and a boy's paisley shirt; long legs; a calm, regular face—a normal American girl, the way Valerie would never be. They knew her; she was the girl who'd done yellow sunshine with them. Though she was only in sixth grade, same as the boys, she looked a couple of years older.

Joe waved. Maybe she would come to the Fillmore with them—she would be a pal for Valerie.

Alice

JOE WAS MUMBLING, Jim's clothes were muddy and torn and he had a conspiratorial look—the boys were concealing something, Alice thought, pressing down a surge of eagerness, as if by doing so she could safeguard herself from the group. She would go home before they could sway her again. Yet who would care?

Who would even be there? Only her mother, enclosed in the bedroom. On the other hand, if she refused the group now, they would drop her—she would lose a chance. Moreover, nothing so very awful had come of her foray; as the weeks passed, her mother had simply ignored the Greek Theatre day, leaving the roses drooping in a vase.

So far, so good. Her fears were meaningless—she'd done no awful wrong.

She'd been yearning for a group—and Joe had ceased mumbling and was welcoming her. Chris's sunny face conjured up a memory of feelings shared on Gayley Road; surely he remembered. She'd seen the boys on the playground, and Tammy knew Chris from her neighborhood. He wore beads and a bandana, as usual—freak flags, Tammy called them—yet Chris's dad was a professor, same as Tammy's.

Alice would go along. They'd have a normal day.

"Let's go," Joe was saying.

Jim shrugged. "Why? They're gone."

"C'mon," Joe urged.

"Hey, we're safe."

"How do you know?"

"Oh, I can feel it," Jim bragged. He was scruffy and wild, more than Joe and Chris; if he'd been alone, she would have passed him by.

"Well, I'm going to the Med," Joe announced. "See ya."

The boys ran for the Caffé Med, racing each other. Alice joined them. She'd passed the cafe on her forays along Telegraph Avenue, and her mother had gone there—it was Sabrina Patterson's hangout. Though there were only a few people in the damp room, Alice could smell the sour reek of tobacco. A young woman eyed her group, vaguely judgmental; a man's glance passed over her. She was glad she had the group.

"Jimmy boy, where ya been?" demanded the counterman. He wore a greasy apron. "What's for lunch? Bacon sandwich and lemonade?"

"Sure thing." Jim drew himself up. "And these guys—"

"Oh no, Jimmy." The man wagged a stubby finger. "Dan pays only for you and Val."

Joe came forward. "I'm paying," he announced, waving a bill. "Four bacon sandwiches. Rye toast. And four lemonades."

"Cool!" Chris was smiling. "C'mon," he urged Jim, and they ran for the balcony.

The man pushed through a swinging door, calling the order. Alice absorbed Joe's presence—a man's denim jacket and baggy jeans, long bangs, a searching glance. Under the denim jacket was a hand-me-down soccer jersey, something her brother could have worn. But there was no teasing or contempt—he was welcoming her as a peer.

"I've seen you," he was saying, "by the fence during lunch."

"Oh?"

"You know some Girl Scouts." He seemed amused.

"Yeah."

"You're one of them?"

"No, they're in my class. I quit a while ago," she confessed.

"So you're cool," he laughed. "I thought so." Then, eyeing her boy's shirt, he added, "There's one who plays handball—"

"Nora?"

"Maybe." Joe had long hands, and he was drumming on the counter. "Have you seen her house?"

"No."

"I have," he said, so casually that he scarcely seemed to be bragging. "I know her big brother." Then he paused, remembering. "They have a Ping-Pong table. You play Ping-Pong?"

"No."

"No? How come?" Joe was round-eyed.

"Do you?"

"Chris plays, but I'm no good." Joe's hand was reaching in the denim jacket. Suddenly he leaned in, fanning out some tickets. "For the Fillmore, tonight—we're seeing the Grateful Dead. Wanna go?"

He'd been planning, and now he was including her in the plans. If Joe was asking her, that meant the boys would have her in the group.

"C'mon," Joe wheedled, "why not?" Then he dropped, "Valerie's going. She wants to see ya."

Alice made a leap. "I've gotta call my mom, but sure."

IN THE WANING afternoon, Alice pressed the phone to her ear. They'd gone to Joe's house, and Valerie had found them there.

262 | *playground zero*

Valerie was lying on the rug while the boys searched through record albums. Joe's family was away, it seemed. Alice took a deep breath, moving away from the blaring speaker box abandoned on the floor—a conch shell rallying them in the cause of an increasingly improbable rescue. As the sounds ebbed, she heard a pause in the ringing and then her mother's weary hello, as though confused by another demand.

"Hello, Mom, it's me."

"Where are you?"

"I ran into some friends from school."

"Are you at someone's house?"

"Yes." There was no use in saying it was Joe's house, because her mother had never heard of Joe.

"When are you coming home?"

Her mother sounded more unhappy than annoyed, thought Alice, though it was hard to gauge. In any case, her mother would be closed in the bedroom, supposedly reading books for her women's group; as for her father, he was gone for the day—no one seemed to care any longer where. Alice would lose nothing by asking, and as long as Valerie was going along, the group of boys would sound nearly normal to her mother.

Long and lanky in jeans and a Spider-Man T-shirt, Valerie lay propped on her elbows, watching the phone call with an explorer's daring smile. Alice recognized her as another tomboy—only more so because Valerie was a natural, as untamed as the boys. Roaming freely, she was an original phenomenon.

"Say there's someone with a car," she whispered.

Alice moved toward the window, away from the sounds in the room. As though on cue, Valerie groped her way to the phonograph and lowered the volume.

"They—some people from school—are going to a concert. Can I go?"

"When is it?"

"Tonight."

"And where? Your brother and Sammy are going to something at the high school."

"No, not that one. The Fillmore West."

"You mean the place in San Francisco?" There came a long pause. Her mother would be angry now.

"Say we have a car," Valerie repeated, more loudly.

"What's that?" demanded her mother through the phone.

Alice gazed around at the boys and stumbled on. "They have a car. There's someone with a car."

"Someone who?"

"Her brother." In a hurry Alice added, "Her older brother."

A long pause followed. Alice imagined walking home, spending another evening in her room. She'd done what she could—not a bad try, really.

Through the phone came her mother's tone of wary defeat. "And who are these people?"

"There's Valerie, and her brother—

"He's older and has a car?"

"Yes. And a couple of others, my age."

"What's Valerie's last name?"

"Last name?"

"Yes. You know her from school."

"Dupres," Valerie mouthed. "Do-pray."

"Dupres, Mom. "

"I see. Then, ask Valerie, does she know Dan Dupres? Maybe an uncle?"

Alice covered the mouthpiece and looked at Valerie. "She wants to know, do you know Dan Dupres?"

"Dan's my father. Why?" Valerie's eyebrows moved in half moons of amusement and surprise.

"Yes, Mom, he's her father."

"I see." Her mother's tone was slow and gloomy, as if she'd been coerced. "I know him from the Peace and Freedom Party. He seems responsible." She paused. "Well, if they're going to the concert and coming right home, then you can go to the Fillmore. Just this once, you understand." Her voice hardened for a moment, before apathy overcame her. "When they bring you home, please have them see you safely through the door."

"Yes. Thanks, Mom." She looked over at Valerie, who was holding a reefer and smiling shyly, as though they were about to become friends.

"I hope you enjoy the concert." Her mother rang off.

Alice turned to the group. "I can go."

"Gimme five!" Jim gave her a high five.

"She let you go," Valerie crowed, "because our father is Dan Dupres! That's far-out!"

"Your mom's really cool," laughed Jim, who was already dol-ing out the LSD. He held up a palm, swimming with orange dots. "You can thank my dad for the sunshine." They crowded around, cheering the win.

THE CAR SPED along Ashby Avenue, swerving around a Volkswa-gen van as they passed San Pablo Avenue on the bay end of Berkeley. The older girl with her sandal on the pedal was Arlene, and as she charged on, chasing the dying rays of day, "Papa Was a Rolling Stone" poured in stealthy rhythm from the radio. Grooving to the sounds, Arlene was bobbing and snapping her fingers, barely touching the wheel as her orange and black fin-gernails, done in ladybug designs, danced in Alice's face. The boys slumped in back, limply enjoying a lull before the upcom-ing take-off. The speed grabbed Alice; pressed by Arlene and Valerie, her gaze bounding with the car, she fled along the un-raveling lane, caught in the groove of a new world.

Arlene's sunglasses had blue star-spangled frames. Sun-bleached hair covered her shoulders; brass teardrops dangled from her ears. Rings made jewels of her fingers, and colored loops jingled on her arms as she swung the wheel. She rode the long-hooded Ford as though she and her young passengers were clinging to a horse's saddle, galloping up the sky through lanes of falling cars. Soon they were passing along the bay, where driftwood scarecrows surged from the mud. Arlene was hurry-ing. The concert would begin very soon.

"Off we go—into the wild blue!" she said, grinning and gunning the car up the ramp for the Bay Bridge.

"Go, Arlene!" Jim cheered from the back.

Alice glanced around; the other boys drooped vague and dreamy, blissful in the surging Now. Jim was the only one who seemed aware of where they were going, as if he'd been there before.

Arlene leaned over, slapping Valerie's knee as the bridge rumbled under them. "I'm ready for my road test now."

"You sure are!" Valerie laughed.

"I wanna be legal for a change."

As an alarm sounded in Alice's head, she found herself gig-gling. She'd come in the car willingly and would share the blame, if her mother ever found out—but how would she? The group had found a world where a mother's rules no longer had any meaning. Wandering freely, they had no fear of a reckoning, it seemed. And for now she'd be playing by the group's rules.

Arlene glanced over, nudging her. "Been on the Avenue long?"

"She just got here!" Valerie squealed.

"Yeah, I can see she's new."

"We found her!"

Alice made no response. Being the object of the girls' comments made her uncomfortable, but there was nowhere to go as Arlene's arm dug in, pinning her to the seat. For a moment, she wondered why she'd come along—how easy and safe to go home, saying her mother had refused. Then a spray of colors blossomed, and she laughed.

"You were such a fresh face, Val," Arlene said, smiling. "I remember seeing you by Dan's shop and saying to Bobby, 'Oh my, she's such a cherub.' So long ago, even before People's Park." Arlene's words were subsumed by the roar of traffic as they crossed a lane and headed for an exit ramp.

As they roared up Fillmore Street, green lights hung like a row of emerald suns and Arlene barreled under them one by one, and then they were bracing as the car pulled up in a sea of cars. They jumped out fast, leaving Arlene alone. A crowd was swarming, already carrying the boys away. Arlene would be parking and joining them soon, Alice thought—but no, the crowd was jamming the doors hung with Fillmore West posters and Arlene was flashing a peace sign and calling, "Bye!" Caught in the flow, the car rounded a corner, passing from the world.

Valerie was nudging Alice. "Come on," she urged, "hurry up."

"Where's Arlene?"

Valerie giggled. "She's gone. You saw her waving."

"But where'd she go?"

"I dunno," Valerie shrugged. "Maybe a commune, see some guy."

"She's coming back, right?"

Valerie gave a sly glance. "Who says so?"

"But I thought—"

"We're seeing the Dead! Are you coming or not?"

"Only if we have a ride back."

Valerie began moving away, fed up. "We can always bum a ride. C'mon, they're going in."

Valerie ran ahead, following the boys. Wondering how she would get home once the others were gone, Alice rushed after her.

The group jammed through the glass doors of the Fillmore West. In the lobby, a huge bear of a man was guarding the door, one hand grabbing left and right. "The Dead!" he brayed over a round, bulging belly, "The Grateful Dead!" Immersed in a throng, Alice and her group pushed past the jolly bear of a guard and found themselves in a passageway, borne up and up by the surge of human bodies. As the passageway leveled off, she was shrouded in heavy drapes of leopard design and then, as she struggled free, engulfed by an anonymous space reaching far ahead. Once in the performance room, she emerged in a smoky underground, as though a city of whirling souls had gathered. A feeling of abandonment flowed through her: the group was nowhere to be seen.

Alice was preparing for an end, a beginning—who could say? Unwillingly swallowed in the throng, she sought her bearings while others jammed around, hemming her in. She was submerged in an unmoving crowd—as though having reached a shore, they refused to go back even as more and more came massing on, lured by the hope of a crossing. Far away, black-box speakers rose, belching sound; above them, a huge wheel of flame surveyed the crowd. The flame surged in a dancing pulse.

Gathered in the human crush, Alice pressed her way here and there through the gaps, searching for her group, feeling the anonymous merging of so many swarming pilgrims. Then the jam loosened, carrying her along under a shadowless glare. As she came through the glare, a hand caught her sleeve and Joe appeared, pulling her through a gap. She was enormously glad to see him.

Alice followed Joe and the others. The flaming eye had ceased pulsing and was daring her to gaze deeply on the globular pools, the bleeding colors and seeping debris of its psychedelic iris. The eye beckoned, and she was becoming absorbed—but just as she was falling in, a hand grasped her arm.

"C'mon," Joe called, "we're over there!"

The belching sounds had moved far off. All around them, the crowd was settling in under the sleepy eye. Groups had formed small encampments, bands of drowsy emperors, some reposing on colored pillows, others on the bare floor. Onstage, shaggy men darted among cymbals and drums, sound equipment and guitars.

Feedback jolted the room like unseen lightning. The flaming eye was a black hole. In the darkness, the rustling of people could be heard. Then somewhere near the stage, two luminous moons flared on, brightening in colorful, undulating glows. The group pushed ahead, stumbling over limbs toward a clearing, a blob of ground where they could camp. Jammed together, they took their places under the glowing, jelly-like moons. Joe's denim jacket was by her shoulder; Valerie's arm lay nearby, among knees and jeans and someone else's sandaled feet.

A sudden crash of thunder exploded through the space, booming, roiling the depths. As the formless thunder gathered in rhythm, a few random souls washed by, swept past those splayed on the floor—nodding, nodding the cosmic pulse.

Crouched on the floor, Alice nodded along. Valerie's head was bobbing nearby. She'd removed her shoes and rolled her pants to the knee, as though she planned on wading. Joe was kneeling, peering over the sea of bobbing heads at the blossoming moons above the band. Though Alice and her group were far from the stage, the pulsing jelly moons soon overwhelmed her.

During a lull in the pounding, Valerie leaned over.

". . . warm-up band!"

Ah, where were the Dead?

Alice gave herself up to the light show, feeling her body merging and expanding in bass sounds and whinnying melody as alarms blared through the room—the ever-whirling banners of some army of the freaks. She was moving now in the flaming pulse; engulfing her in a quivering cosmos, the flaring jellies pumped and gasped above the band, sending its impulses through the crowd. One of them—fast-breathing and yellow, pumping green and purple pulses—was inhaling her in its pulpy glow when she freed herself. The oneness she'd been feeling was gone in a bursting bubble of sad-funny, lonely-absurd, as a pressure on her shoulder made her look away from the glow.

The floor was hard and cold. The room was gloomy, the low space hung with bulbs shedding a cheap, sulfurous glare. The Fillmore was a cavern, she thought, hearing the churning echo of some underground waterfall, as sounds rumbled through the dull aluminum air. A burst of orange jelly faded from the room.

Her body hung heavy in the lull. She was rearranging her cumbersome limbs when a new pulsing mass appeared. Her body jolted, as though connected by electrical impulses to the fast-breathing glow. A knee—hers or someone else's?—was ignoring commands. Beat on, oh joyous pendulum, counting, counting in vast eternity!

Valerie lay nearby on the floor. Alice's hand could feel the smooth jeans on the knee belonging to the other girl, as she slumbered on the floor. Valerie had gone away, only the body lay there. Even so, Alice found refuge; sound and pulse receded. They'd been in eucalyptus groves, far from home. They'd seen the sun drop through the Golden Gate, and now they'd gone below.

A HAND WAS tugging on her arm. Joe was kneeling, gesturing beyond the huge banks of speakers.

"Over there!" Joe was yelling. "Black lights!"

Alice commanded her limbs, but they were seemingly in thrall. She wobbled up. The group stumbled among the dead, passing a boundary. The area was for dancing; illuminated by black light, figures flickered nearby, whirling in the delayed images of some ghostly scene. Valerie was suffused in a pale-lavender glow that flared here and there—a source of unearthly light. She waved a sleeve in triumph, showing off the remnants of evening glow. Joe's jersey, too, shone in faded lavender bands. The group moved together among the dancers while fragments of moon-glow on and around them pulsed under strobe lights, as though they were being caught and let go, caught and let go in the ever-changing searchlight of a film projector. Whirling images rose through the cave, writhing bodies unable to escape or cease. Alice merged in the surrounding throbbing glow.

WHEN SHE SOUGHT her group again, they had already moved on. An image of Arlene surged up, suggesting a way back—but no. The car was gone for good. Above the stage, one of the jelly moons was pulsing to the ring of a telephone, while the other pumped a backbeat busy tone. Fleeing the fury and confusion, she passed back through the leopard drapes and found Valerie in a drab passageway leading to the lobby.

As the sounds faded, Alice sought to clear her head. Maybe the hour was less unreasonable than she feared. Maybe the evening could be fixed, maybe someone would come for them— Jim and Valerie's dad, Dan Dupres from Peace and Freedom, a responsible man. Jim would be in the lobby, already making the call. Of course Dan would come for them.

Once they were in the lobby, Valerie made no move. The glass doors were open, the boys grouped around. Dan was on the way, it seemed.

Suddenly Valerie's eyebrows rounded over huge pupils. "If your mom's so cool, maybe she can come for you," she suggested. Then came the challenge: "We got you here—you can get us home."

Alice was sweating. "My mom's sleeping."

"And your dad?"

"How about yours?"

"You mean Dan?"

"Can he come?"

"No way, he's busy. So, you should call your dad." Valerie surveyed her. "Hey, what's wrong? They have a phone, right?"

Valerie moved away as if she'd had enough. Alice was reeling from the drug. If only she could get home somehow—clearly there'd never been any plan. Her pulse was racing as she struggled to regain control of her body, hoping for release from a plague of sensory symptoms. She could call home, but what then?

They were going through mud—her dad and the group in the Chevy. Her dad was eyeing them. The group was jeering. Mud clogged her mind.

Unimaginable.

Three women were crossing the lobby. As they neared the doors, where cool evening gusts dropped an ocean smell, Jim ran up. The women eyed him and rushed through the door. They were from Telegraph Avenue, Alice supposed; Jim already knew them. If so, they were in an awful hurry to go. Then, as a man appeared and Jim swaggered up, thumb waving, she felt a tingling on her scalp: the group would be going with anyone who agreed. The boy was worldly and wild: he thought nothing of conning a ride.

Alice wandered by the open doors, feeling a wave of strangeness and dread. *The group would go one way through mud —and she would go another.* A cool, damp feeling spread over her face, calming her. Lamps shed an orange glow over a few passing cars. Peering around, she saw a telephone hanging in a corner of the lobby. Her mother would be sleeping—and her mother could rage when roused from sleep. Her father would show up, calmly contemptuous, and scoop her from the curb, a freak among freaks; they would say nothing the whole way home. *Why would they say nothing?* she wondered, and then remembered: *because she was already dead.*

Confirming the thought, her legs refused any command.

Valerie ran up, as though eagerly sharing some blessing or rumored rescue. The boys were jamming through the door, joined by two men.

"We found a van!" Valerie was urgently pulling Alice by the arm, and *wading through mud* they passed through the Fillmore doors into the slumbering gold-rush town, land of rough men and runaways.

Soon the men were leading them through a dead-end lane. The group hung together, except for Jim, who was hustling after the men, as though he feared they'd get away.

Joe was sweaty, jacket awry. He paused in the lane, murmuring, "What if—"

"What if you shut up," Valerie hissed.

"I was only saying—"

"Shhh!"

Joe gave a low warning call but Jim, engaged with the men, made no response. The others hung back, wary of the men and the dead-end lane. Joe was fingering the jacket, searching for something he'd misplaced. Soon he gave up. Alice's jaw was feeling numb, her tongue was a dead thing. Then they saw Jim waving them on and braying, "C'mon! They're cool!" Ignoring a queasy feeling, Alice began moving.

Valerie had found her swagger. "Chris," she was saying, "you think you're so great because your father's a professor!"

"And your dad?" Chris shrugged.

"He sells jeans. He's one of the people!" she declaimed loudly. "Your father's just a book man, but *my* father founded People's Park!"

Jim dropped back. "No messing around. I wanna get home."

The evening had a new aura. They would be safe: *Dan Dupres was a responsible man, a founder of parks for the people—a founding father*. They'd be home in Berkeley soon; she would go to her room, no one would see her, and by morning she would be herself. That was how things had gone before.

The men paused by a sky-blue Volkswagen van. One of them—small and red-haired, a fox—swung open the back door. The other had burly shoulders and a shaggy beard. The group clambered in the back of the van, Jim leaning on the front seats.

One arm on the wheel, the fox was looking them over. "Young rascals!" he purred, vaguely in awe. "So, where ya goin'?"

"Virginia and McGee," Jim commanded. He was easy with the men, as though he'd always known them.

"The whole gang?"

"Yeah. We're family."

"Virginia and McGee, barely out of our way," yawned the burly bear in the passenger seat, fingering his beard.

The fox glanced back. "How'd you like the Dead?"

"So cool, but I've seen them before," Jim bragged.

"Oh yeah?"

"We had to leave early," Valerie complained, "and scrounge a ride. Such a bummer."

"Yeah, bummer," Jim groaned.

Alice was contemplating the plan. She'd been hoping the men could drop her off on the way—but where was Virginia and McGee? The names were unfamiliar, the neighborhood far from her own.

"Are you going home?" she murmured to Joe. Maybe she could get out with him. Joe's house was in South Campus, she could get home from there.

"No, Jim and Valerie's. Virginia and McGee."

The evening hovered in the balance. If they were heading for Dan Dupres' house, she could go there and manage the phone call home. Dan's house would be a less scandalous place to call from than the lobby of the Fillmore. Or maybe the men could drop her off—maybe her family would be sleeping, and no one would ever know. Crouching on a low bench, she chose the faster way home—in the van.

The bridge rumbled under them. Jim, already a showman,

was easy and boasting. "When you guys were dancing," he was saying, "I was up by the stage. The Dead were coming on, and Jerry Garcia came over—"

"We know Jerry!" Valerie crowed.

"We sure do," Jim bragged. "Dan knows Owsley, and Owsley knows Jerry."

"Owsley—the acid king?" The burly man gave a howl.

"Young rascals!" laughed the fox.

Before long, the van was slowing along the ramp for Berkeley. Through the back window, Alice could see the bridge and the gloomy bay beyond. As the lanes unraveled, she imagined being left alone in the van. What would happen once Jim and the group were gone—what would she say? She was no young rascal offering amusement for the men—just a girl in the wrong place.

Joe leaned in. "Are you coming with us? Jim and Valerie's house?"

"I've got to get home."

"Why?"

"Because I do."

Joe tugged on the man's sleeve. "Can you make another stop?"

"Why not?"

A few minutes later, the van rounded a corner and rolled slowly along the curb. "Home safe!" Jim yelled, flinging open the door. The group was jumping out.

The burly bear looked around. "Who's staying?" As he saw Alice crouched on the floor of the van, he paused. "Hey there."

Her jaw had gone numb; she had no response. *Tom knows Owsley, and Owsley knows Jerry.* No, no—they'd never go for that. The space, creepy and dim, was closing in. The burly man could be anyone.

"So, where's your pad?" he murmured softly, as though coaxing a small animal.

Alice jumped up and scrambled from the van, tearing her jeans on jagged metal.

"Hey, where ya goin'?" the fox demanded as she slammed the door.

Colors were mushrooming around a porch lamp as the van jerked away, angry wheels churning up gravel. She jumped back from the curb, and though she was safe and whole so far, the evening was raging on. The group was already on the porch, moving on. A phone call, her father would come, and the ordeal would be over . . .

Coming up the walk, Alice saw a weedy rose bush waving limp buds. *Gone, all gone.*

"Hey," Valerie demanded from the porch, "are you coming in?" She sounded on guard, even wary.

Where were they?

"I've gotta get home."

"Where?"

"South Campus."

"How?" Valerie seemed annoyed by the problem.

"Yeah, how?" Jim scolded. "You just blew your ride."

"I can walk."

"You're an hour away." Joe came down the steps in a show of sympathy.

"Where's the campus?" Alice heard herself asking.

"Come in," Joe was urging.

"But—"

"Then go," Valerie shrugged, fed up.

They were somewhere north of campus in a neighborhood Alice had never seen. The journey home would be long and dangerous, if she even found her way. Jim and Valerie were becoming a bummer, but Dan's house would be safer than the street corner. Dan was a grown-up—he would help. She would go in, pull herself together, and make the call.

The house was a gray Victorian with peeling woodwork. In the bare foyer was a door leading to the ground-floor rooms. The group passed by and headed up some stairs to a second-floor landing. Valerie scrounged a key from under a mat and opened one of the doors on a long, dim hallway.

"Shhh!" Jim hissed. "Dan's here."

"Yeah," Valerie confirmed, "Dan and Wanda. Shhh!"

"Or everyone's going home, you hear?" Jim added in a stage whisper.

They paused like hunting dogs, listening—but no sounds could be heard from the apartment. Dan and Wanda were sleeping, assuming they were even home. Then, before anyone could come out, the group found refuge in a room off the hall. The door closed: gloom. Vague shadows moved; then a bulb shone dimly overhead, spreading low-wattage glare through the long, largely unfurnished room. Two steel bed frames, crammed side by side in the tunnel leading to a single window, gave the place a barracks feel. The mattresses were bare and lumpy, grungy with stains—no sheets, only rough army blankets in tangled heaps, and greasy, coverless pillows. Clothes lay on the floor. No rug, no dresser, no comforting anything—how could anyone sleep in such a place? They had no mother, clearly, only Dan—but then, who was Wanda? And why would Dan have no bedding or hangers, no window shade? The thought of the group curling up together in such a dump was depressing, even creepy. She would be glad to go home, just as soon as her father could come.

Alice could feel the walls closing around her. Morning was hours away. She had to get out soon, before the night sealed her in. Feeling woozy rather than sleepy, she rehearsed the phone call home. Her mother would demand information—an address, a phone number. Her father would come in the Chevy, he'd ring the bell—no, impossible; she'd be on the porch when he came.

But before she could say anything, before they could come and drag her from the den of Dan Dupres, she would need a telephone.

Joe and Chris were dropping shoes and socks on the floor like molting hawks shedding feathers. Jim was bouncing up and down on a sagging bed. On the other bed, Valerie was leaning on the wall, humming and winding golden strands around her fingers. New energy began flowing among the group, as though they were fired by a single impulse. Alice's family was fading dangerously from her thoughts. The room was a wayfarer's rest where she and the group could pass a few dead hours before resuming.

Resuming what?

Alice remembered the phone. "Where are we?" she heard herself saying as she opened the door, prodded by a blunted spur of fear before her will abandoned her.

Valerie seemed confused. "Why?"

"Hey," Jim hissed, "where ya goin'?" For once he seemed alarmed.

"Where's your phone? My mom—"

"No one's coming for you," Valerie bluntly informed her.

"Yeah, no way," Jim added, bouncing higher.

"I can go down. But I need to say where—"

Jim gave a scoffing grin. "Sorry, no phone."

"Yeah, bummer for you," Valerie added with vague sympathy. "They took the phone away."

"We found you a van, but you came here," Jim shrugged, as though she'd refused a pony ride.

"You can sleep here," Joe suggested, "and go in the morning."

Alice could feel her pulse pounding through her body. The world was falling away. Morning was meaningless; her family was a crumbling bridge over a chasm.

Colors overwhelmed her eyes as Valerie made room on the tangled bed. *What if day never came?* Alice lay down by the wall. The boys flopped on the other bed, claiming space like puppies. *Dan Dupres was a wolf, if only her mother could see.* Alice lay rigid, her mind flooding in fear as the room crawled with glow-worm colors. Her family was far, far away. Would they think she'd run off—would they care?

She would cling to the raft. Then, at dawn, she would go home. If she got there early enough, how could they say she'd run away?

HOURS PASSED. GRAY shadows began looming around her, signs of day, signs of a real world—a place where she could go from here, if only . . .

She lay on the grim bed. Valerie was sleeping soundly, but for Alice, sleep had never come. During the night, she'd been flooded by a drug and fear; now she was simply groggy and confused. Though her bladder was aching, her body, rigid and sore, was refusing to go anywhere. She was reeling from the half-escape: if she'd stayed in the van, the men could have done anything with her. The group had thought nothing of leaving her there, and she'd barely had the will to jump. She'd gone so far—in only one night. She'd followed along through hours of madness, doing one dangerous thing after another. Who could say what such a girl would become? Now every cesspool would be hers—she could end up anywhere, even among the runaways on Telegraph Avenue. She peered through the gloom: Were Joe and Chris runaways? Not exactly, and yet . . . soon.

No grown-ups were around, as far as she could judge, no

sound or sign of anyone. Good thing—running across Dan Dupres would be more to contend with, when she could barely get herself moving.

Alice squirmed from the bed where Valerie was sleeping. Opening the door, she edged along the hallway, coming up on a large corner room. Kitchen cupboards and bare floor could be seen, the glare of morning—but where was the bathroom? She passed through the doorway, peered around the room, and froze. Seated around a glass table near the bay window, a man and a woman had been coolly observing her. They were completely nude.

The man was peeling an orange. The woman's breasts pressed the table as her hand closed over a box of Marlboros.

Before Alice could scurry from the room, the man spoke up.

"Are you looking for the bathroom?" Prominent brown eyes glared from a long face.

She nodded.

"Around the corner, there's a door." He waved an arm, exposing a mass of blond curls in his lap.

"Thank you." Her pulse was urging her to leave, but the man's eyes held her.

"You came from the Fillmore with Valerie?" he pursued, calmly tearing away another orange peeling.

She made no response.

"Valerie and Jim, they brought you here." Undismayed by her presence, he appeared to be making casual conversation.

"Yes."

"You came with them from the Fillmore."

"Yes."

"I see." The man held her in a cool, assessing gaze. "No one told me you'd be coming here." He placed the orange on the table by the peelings, suddenly fed up. "Are your parents cool? Do what you want, but don't come here causing trouble."

"What Dan means is, we don't want anyone's parents coming down on us," added the woman, Wanda.

"When Valerie wakes up," he commanded, "have her come and see me."

"Yes." Alice scampered around the corner, found the bathroom, and closed the door. She fumbled with the lock. The bathroom was safe—she was alone, and she could breathe, maybe even plan. She was alert again and nearly normal—nor-

mal enough to go. But how would she find her way home? Dan
and Wanda would know—but they were clearly off limits. The
group would have to show her, once they were up and running.

She made her way to the room where Valerie and the boys
were sleeping. Now other problems loomed. The homecoming
would happen soon enough. Even as the room was closing in on
her, pushing her family far away, she was fumbling for what to
say about the cascade of unforeseen events. Already she feared
revealing so many outrageous and dangerous things. And yet, by
jumping from the van and sleeping among strangers, she'd done
the only safe and reasonable thing, under the unusual—unimaginable—circumstances.

Nonsense, her mom would say.

She lay on the bed, hearing Valerie's breathing. The drug
had worn off, all wonders gone, and fear was creeping up.

*. . . She was in the passenger seat of the Chevy, coming through
a loud forest, when the man at the wheel—a man she'd never seen
before—asked, "Can you work the gears?" Then before she knew
what was happening . . .*

Someone was shaking her by the shoulder.

"Ow!" Valerie was scrambling from the bed. "You whopped
me!" she exclaimed.

The others were awake and glancing around. Alice was confused—then knew she'd been dreaming and flailing around in
her sleep. She remembered her changed circumstances. On a
Sunday morning, her own father and brother would be reading
the paper, having eggs or cereal, conversing in monosyllables;
her mother would be sleeping. Today, though, Dan and Wanda
could be found in the nude, Dan peeling an orange, Wanda's
hand closing on a cigarette box.

Valerie had begun rummaging through the clothing on the floor.

"Sorry . . . I was dreaming."

Valerie paused, eyeing her humorously. "Oh—a beast?"

"No, maybe a van . . ."

"Something pissed you off, for sure."

"Oh?"

"Yeah—you nearly gave me a black eye!"

Alice remembered a van—nothing else was clear. "Maybe
the ride home last night—a man in a van, anyway."

"So, were you scared?" Valerie teased.

Suddenly Alice remembered Dan's message. "There's a man—," and she nodded toward the door.

"Dan? My father?"

"I guess so."

Valerie's smile hung on her face. "He saw you? When?"

"An hour ago. I was looking for the bathroom."

Jim began humming.

"He wants to see you," Alice added.

Jim made a face. "Too bad."

Valerie rummaged through the clothing, finally dredging up her rumpled jeans. Pulling them on, she went through the doorway.

Awake and full of sudden energy, the others began searching for clothing.

Jim held up a shoe. "And you," he demanded of Alice, "had any bummers? You know—flames and crawly things?"

She made no response.

"Hungry," Chris yawned.

"Hey, nothing here." Jim seemed to be announcing good news. "You know what that means."

"Tacos!"

"Yeah, the place on the corner. They take food stamps."

Just when the boys were ready to go, Valerie came running through the doorway. As she slammed the door, Jim began humming again.

"Bummer," he murmured.

Valerie paused, her face deadpan; then, with unconcealed triumph, she held up her hand, dangling a key on a rubber band. "The room! Dan gave me the key!"

"For keeps?" Jim demanded, wide-eyed.

"For keeps!" Valerie dangled the key higher as Jim made a grab. "Who's coming with me?"

"I am," Joe said. He was grinning at Alice. "And you?"

"I'm going home."

"You can go soon," Joe assured her. "Right, Val?"

"After we show her the room!"

They scampered through the hallway to the landing. Valerie paused before a second door.

"Dan says we can hang out in here!" she announced, unlocking the door. "That's so *far-out*!"

They entered a small apartment. Though sparsely furnished,

it had a cozy feel—a couch, bookshelves, even a rug. A splash of colored drapery hung in the doorway of what appeared to be a small bedroom.

Valerie drew the drapery, revealing a dark, windowless space. As the boys rushed in, Alice hung back.

"Scared?" Valerie goaded.

"What's in there?"

"Wow!" came Joe's cry. "We can sleep here now!"

"So cool!" Chris sang out, as the boys reemerged.

"Aren't you going in?" Valerie demanded.

Alice passed through the drapery. The room was enveloped in darkness except for a few glimmers. She moved slowly, feeling padding—or maybe bedding—under her feet. After a few steps, her head struck a beam. Reaching up, her hand touched a rough, sloping roof.

When she came back through the drapery, the group gave a cheer, as though she'd passed a final hazing and they were welcoming her as one of them.

Jim was grinning. "Now let's show her—"

"Shhh! Dan says no!"

Ignoring Valerie, Jim threw open the closet door. Alice leaned in on a brightly lit space burgeoning with plants reaching higher than her head and gleaming greenly under blazing lights.

She could feel the group's eyes on her.

The plants had saw-toothed leaves that formed a lacy canopy. Alice inhaled a dry, musky odor as her hand brushed through a fringe of leaves.

"What are they?" And as she spoke, she suddenly understood: marijuana. Of course.

The boys were laughing.

"We thought you'd know," Jim said, crowing at her ignorance.

There were so many things her parents had never told her, thought Alice, and her new pals could show her all of them.

"Let's go to the Med," Joe was saying.

"No, tacos!" Chris sang out.

"C'mon, then," Jim urged. He and Chris ran off, leaving the others on the landing.

Soon Valerie was leading them through a neighborhood of sparse trees. Alice looked around at the vaguely shabby wood-frame Victorian houses. Judging by the sun, it was before eleven.

On a normal Sunday, her mother would be just waking up. To-day, though, all bets were off.

Valerie was eyeing her. "Are you coming through the campus?"

"The campus?" She'd had enough wandering.

"Yeah, we're going to the Med."

The Med would be good enough—she could get home from there. "I'm going home."

"Why?" Valerie had a look of bemusement. "It's early. Are you supposed to hang out at home with nothing to do? You're not grounded, are you?"

"No, but—"

"That's such a pisser!"

Alice would remember the new phrase.

"She's been to the Fillmore," Joe said. "Now she's going home, before they get mad."

"She can do anything she wants," Valerie declared. "And if they're gonna be mad, then why go home?"

No one made a response. The group ran along, heading for the campus. There was a novel argument underlying Valerie's logic. Alice was beginning to envy the other girl's freedom—if only because she was dreading her own homecoming. She hoped her mother's moods and alarm could be managed; but it would be dangerous to delay any longer, beyond the chaos of an unplanned evening. The evening's confusion had been none of Alice's doing; she'd gone through the proper channels and been given her moth-er's blessing, a seal of approval for the Fillmore and the son and daughter of Dan Dupres of Peace and Freedom, a very responsible man. Then the evening had spun so desperately out of control. She could hardly be blamed for doing the only reasonable thing anyone had done in the whole muddy mess—jumping from the van, saving herself. No one would rage when they heard . . . or would they? Things had gone very far—her parents could accuse her of running away, choosing another home.

Valerie and Jim had unhampered freedom to come and go. Their father, a nude man peeling an orange, was only concerned that someone's parents might "come down on him," in Wanda's phrase. Joe and Chris had clearly been there before and posed no problem. Maybe they'd seen Dan and Wanda, the nude glare, the orange peelings and Marlboro box. If so, they'd never say—she'd seen enough of them to be sure.

"How long have you been living there?" Alice asked. She was wondering how many days or weeks they'd been sleeping in the dingy room.

"A few months." Valerie shrugged. "I bet your parents have a house. Dan prefers apartments, more than houses."

"Why?"

"You can come and go, he says."

"Come and go where?"

"When there's trouble!"

"I'm in big trouble now," Alice murmured.

"Who's mad—your mom and dad?"

"Yeah."

"Why? What happened?"

"I have to tell them something, why I stayed out."

"Tell them anything. What can they do?" Valerie demanded. "You told your mom you were coming with us, and she knows Dan. Everything's cool."

Alice was feeling exasperated. "But that's not the problem."

"Oh? Then what is?"

"She thought I was coming home last night."

"Hey, we found a van, and you came home with us. Nothing happened. So where's the problem?"

"My parents expected—"

"Do things always happen the way they want? They expect something—and *poof*, it happens?"

"No."

"I mean, who are they? Some kind of emperors of the world?"

Her family sounded so improbable in Valerie's rendering that Alice was beginning to wonder if her fears were real. In any case, Dan Dupres had power, a domain—he ruled over a realm of wild hippie kids. But her mother and father had dropped the reins—they'd given up governing anyone. They were no longer emperors of anywhere.

The group had crossed the border of the campus. Alice could see Valerie's shoulder bobbing by her own.

"Where does your mom live?" she inquired.

"Colorado."

Valerie's eyes suddenly rounded, as though an emerald city loomed before them. "There's the Eucalyptus Grove," she announced, looking across a lawn.

282 | *playground zero*

Although Alice had seen the Eucalyptus Grove before, she'd always come from the south, through Sproul Plaza. But Sproul Plaza was somewhere else, and even the Campanile was no help.

"Let's go," Valerie suggested, nodding toward the grove.

They veered from the path. The grove lay ahead—a soothing place. Alice enjoyed wandering the campus, but now the game had changed. She was no longer wandering alone.

A squirrel scampered by, pausing, glancing at them before dashing for a large fir. Joe was already ambling through the grass.

Alice wanted to resume the conversation with Valerie. "What's she like?" she asked.

"Who?" Valerie seemed mystified.

"Your mother."

"Oh . . . She's in Colorado, I told you."

"Do you go there?"

"What for?"

"You know, to see her."

"She's mean," Valerie announced. "She's strict—a real *bitch*."

The word hung in the air. Alice was feeling uneasy. She'd never heard a girl use that word against her own mother.

A song rose sharply from the Eucalyptus Grove. From the sloping lawn, Alice saw three women in long scarves gathered in a circle, chanting—the harsh sounds moving through the cool shade of the grove like the swooping of hawks.

"Let's wait," Alice suggested. Whatever the women were doing, there was no reason for intruding.

"What for?"

"Those women—let them finish."

"Our grove, our grove," Joe began chanting.

"Here we are," Valerie laughed, "as good as them."

Joe and Valerie ran down the slope, arms waving like birds of prey, whooping over the women's chanting as they descended on the grove. Alice hung back as her pals' raucous cawing rose, submerging the women's sounds.

Seeing her chance, Alice ran along the edge of the grove, seeking the creek and wooden bridge, the way home. When she was nearing the bridge, Valerie and Joe came running up, as though patrolling the borders of the realm, arms spread in wings that flapped uselessly before her.

"Hey, where ya going?" Joe demanded.

"I should maybe go home."

"You're gonna be sorry," Valerie called over her shoulder, already moving on.

The landing would be scary. "I'm going."

"Come back soon!" Valerie squawked. Waving and screaming, she and Joe ran back through the grove.

AS ALICE CAME along Forest Avenue, approaching the family home, the London plane trees formed an archway of branches rising in fragile design against a soundless blue sky. The day now impressed her as cool and windy, a February day. Her ongoing delay was beyond understanding: so, was she a rebel after all?

She opened the door and paused, but there was no sound or sign of anyone. Then, as the door closed, normal sounds could be heard: the ticking of a clock, the muffled hum of a car passing along the street. Pausing in the foyer, she sensed the lull of familiar rooms and no one home, a space for recovering her bearings. She wondered at the lucky break: her lapse would now be absorbed by the gently humming house. Feeling a clamoring release, Alice passed along the hall and through the doorway leading to the kitchen, her eyes on the red and black linoleum squares.

She looked up on a changed scene.

The family, cold and unmoving, had heard her coming. Occupying the red and black squares as though ready for her move, they formed a firm defense. A wave of dread passed through her.

"Where on earth—?" Face red, eyes wide, her mother was roused; her anger filled the room, barring Alice from rejoining the family.

She'd done something unforgivable.

"How could you?" her mother demanded, seemingly struggling with an impulse to slap her. "I thought you were going to a concert. Where *were* you?"

Her father was leaning on the counter, arms folded, eyes moving over Alice's body, coolly noting her slovenly look. By the refrigerator was Curt, contemptuously aloof, oozing a sense of predominance.

"At the concert."

"And then where? That was a whole day ago."

Alice's jaw had gone numb. The red and black squares

bound the family together, ready for another move, but Alice's chance had come and gone. The evening had been so stupefying that she'd been conscious only of her ordeal; now she began imagining how her family had passed the hours.

"We thought you were dead," her mother groaned, hearing no response. "Whatever made you do such a thing?"

As though I'm a criminal now, thought Alice, smothering an alarming spasm of laughter.

"How could you leave me wondering?" Her mother's eyes were damp. "I called Tammy's house and got everyone up; we've checked with every emergency room; your father called the police, and now they're searching for you. Why would you run away?" She paused. "I may not be the mother you want, but . . ."

Tammy's house? Emergency rooms, the police? Alice had never imagined so many people would hear of her problems. *Tammy was already wondering; no, the problems would never end.*

Her father summed up, "You owe your mother a reply."

"I was at Valerie's house."

"Valerie—you mean Dan Dupres' daughter?" her mother demanded.

"Yes."

"But you promised you'd come right home from the concert."

Alice shrugged, helpless. *She hadn't run away—but how could she tell them what had happened?*

"Why would you do such a thing?"

"No reason."

"Alice Rayson!" Her mother was shaking with rage. "What was happening there? What were you doing?"

Curt's face had a vague smile.

"What was so very compelling?" her mother demanded. And then she made a leap. "Who else was there?"

"No one. Me and Valerie."

"Then why not inform us of where you were?"

"I thought you'd be asleep."

Her mother gave a gasp of injured outrage.

"And there was no phone."

"Now you're lying," her mother glared. "You're saying Dan Dupres—?" A gray shadow was passing from her face. "Tom, is she making that up?"

"I was going to call, but there was no phone," Alice repeated.

"And no one would bring you home? Where was the brother?"

"He just dropped us off."

"And Dan Dupres?"

"He was asleep."

"I see."

"I only saw him in the morning."

"My, my."

Her mother's contempt stung. Alice could feel the change that had come over her family: in an evening she'd become just a wild, slovenly girl, a runaway who had to be dragged from some crash pad or marijuana den. Telling them how she'd ended up there would only scare her mother, who—in her mad fright—would need someone to blame.

"I'm about to collapse," her mother sighed. "No more problems, please—we have enough already." Then, gathering herself up, she left the room. In a moment Curt followed, clenching his hands.

Alice could feel her father judging her: a bedraggled Telegraph Avenue teenager. "Can I go to my room now?" she asked.

He made no response.

"Can I go now?" she demanded again. Feeling the blood rising in her face, she moved away.

"Your mother wants you home at night," he said, as though disengaged from her, as though the problem was her mother's to manage. "But as long as someone drops you off, she'll probably let you go to that place in San Francisco—what's the name?"

"The Fillmore." Alice was shamed by his seeming unconcern.

He glanced up. "As long as someone brings you home, eh?"

Marian

THOUGH FEELING WRUNG dry, Marian found no hope of sleep. She lay on the bed gazing vaguely through the windows, as branches swayed in the wind. When the problems had begun, Tom had just come from a day with Ginger in Golden Gate Park. For months he'd been fobbing them off with imaginary projects and deadlines, but during the sleepless hours he'd finally acknowledged spending weekends with Ginger. Marian had been aware of Tom's forays—even so, everything had changed around her. She and Tom had done poorly; now, as though spurred by some *deus ex machina*, she was on the verge of another chance. As for Ginger, she was apparently proving to be more of a challenge than Tom had foreseen; he'd been hoping for a simple affair, but she was clearly holding out for more.

In the hours of panic, Marian had leaned on Tom, as she had long ago, though that impulse was already fading, along with her fear. And he'd been calming, in his way. He'd been sure from the beginning that Alice would wander back; only when she'd shown up, tousled and sleepy-eyed, a girl men would regard as easy, had there been any sense of danger in his face.

Marian was running Dupres' image through her mind: shoulder-length hair, probing eyes. He'd come to Peace and Freedom meetings promptly and regularly, an unusual nod to responsibility these days. He'd been agreeable enough when they'd encountered each other in the office. He'd been among the demonstrators for new black and Chicano programs at UC Berkeley, and he'd argued against the growing police presence in South Campus in a sober, even dogged manner. As Marian remembered Dupres' condemnation of the many police abuses against not only the young people of South Campus but the Black Panthers, she began to feel ashamed of having informed the police. At least Tom had persuaded her to leave Dupres' name out of the report. But why no telephone? He was employed—manager or even owner of a Telegraph Avenue shop. Could he have come under surveillance, along with others in Peace and Freedom? And her mind placed him in People's Park . . .

She'd thought of Dupres as young and unencumbered. Apparently she'd been wrong. Now it seemed he had a daughter Alice's age and a son who was already driving. There was a shop but no telephone, outings to the Fillmore West and unplanned sleepovers, which Dan learned of only in the morning.

During the long sleepless hours, Marian had been unable to make sense of things. Even now, she had no confidence in what she'd been told. The story had so many holes. If Valerie's brother could drive them to the Fillmore, why couldn't he bring Alice home? Something was being left out. The casual reference to an older brother should have informed her that there was more than Alice was willing to say. She was becoming a head-turning girl, older in appearance than her twelve years. But when the older brother had cropped up, Marian had been calmed rather than alarmed: it sounded so normal. Even the Raysons had gone to a concert in Golden Gate Park one Sunday afternoon, before Tom had become so overwhelmed by Ginger's demands that a family outing had come to seem rarer than a moon landing. True, these were new pals never heard of before; that was something of a worry, but the name of Dupres had appeased her. In any case, Marian could not always choose for her daughter. And Marian herself was in a huge muddle; it would be preferable for them both if Alice had somewhere to go for the coming weeks, while she sought a way to resolve her problem. For a moment, Dupres' daughter had seemed a godsend.

But the presence of an older boy would be a real problem. The more she pondered, the more she concluded that the older boy was the lure, while the seeming enthusiasm for the girl, Valerie, was only a ruse. No wonder she'd never heard of Valerie before yesterday. Even so, much was obscure. When and where had Alice been so charmed by the older brother? The girl was so unforthcoming that it was hard to know what she was feeling; usually that meant a girl was becoming enamored of boys. With Alice, however, one could never tell.

There came a rap at the door and Tom appeared, annoying her with the poker face he wore these days.

"So, she showed up after all," he remarked, dryly.

"But how could we have known?" Marian was feeling repelled by Tom's lack of sympathy.

"It seems she just ran off."

"Yes, I suppose you could see it that way."

"What do you plan to do about it?"

"I?"

"You're the mother."

"Well, yes—"

"I assumed you were competent to keep her out of trouble."

"But Tom, you must be aware that she's growing up."

"Yes, and now you've given her permission to go to the Fillmore."

"Tom, she was already out. If I'd refused permission, she might have gone anyway. She's convinced she should be allowed to do whatever Curt does. I've always thought it was a bad idea to encourage her to regard herself as a boy—"

"Now you're blaming me."

"No, though she does have to learn not to behave as a boy in all things. There's her safety to consider."

"And you must keep her home. Am I asking too much?"

"Don't accuse me, Tom. She phoned and demanded that I let her go to the Fillmore. With deep reluctance, I agreed. If you feel so strongly, then maybe you should be the one to say no."

"I can't always be here, and you know it."

"But you're so rarely here that we can never even confer. I'm telling you—she's of an age where she may be needing some response from her father. I can't give her that."

Tom moved over to the window. He was glancing out as though called by something.

"It seems to me you're very able to say no," he accused sharply, "or is your daughter somehow the favored person of the house?"

"I don't know what you mean."

An uncomfortable hush came over the room. Marian felt the conversation moving into dangerous waters.

"Please, Tom, I need some sleep. If we can't agree about our daughter—and she is *ours*, after all—then leave me alone."

chapter four

Alice

ALICE FOUND HERSELF confronting a changed landscape. She'd been lonely—that was how the group had lured her. Now things had gone very wrong, and she was in limbo. Tammy knew she'd gone missing—Mrs. Rayson had phoned in the wee hours, waking everyone up, and of course Tammy was wondering what was wrong—but Alice, leery of prying, brushed her off. There were more and more things she was covering for, beginning with her father's absences and her mother's growing heedlessness regarding the family. In any case, hanging around with Tammy and a group of Girl Scouts made less and less sense for the girl Alice was becoming, one who'd smashed so many rules that there would be no easy way back. Joe and the group were wrong for other reasons; but at least they'd be making no judgments on her estrangement from the family. And now the family was angry, compounding her problems; worse, they'd begun seeing another girl in her—an unleashed rebel girl who would do anything if given the chance. A world of amorphous dangers was swirling around her, caught by her mother's eyes as though by some infrared camera. Sex. Running away. Stealing and jail. Though she'd done none of these things, her mother's fears had been aroused, and the process of allaying them would be long and dreary.

For a few weeks, Alice was careful, though no one referred to her lapse or demanded that she change her ways. That was baffling; nothing could be forgiven so fast. If she'd been grounded, she would have forced herself to comply; as things were, she could neither comply nor rebel.

And so she grounded herself, going home from the bus, spending afternoons reading books in her room. Her mother acknowledged the change by showing Alice around a nearby library and recommending some very long books that would keep her busy for days or even weeks—*The Three Musketeers*, a thousand pages long, followed by a sequel. Alice passed afternoons and weekends in her room, seemingly alone in the house with D'Artagnan and the three French guardsmen even though her mother was nearby, sleeping or reading or carrying on a correspondence—her mother was lonely, too, because her father was always away. Alice enjoyed reading; even so, the endless afternoons were becoming unbearable. Maybe Valerie had been right —why should she hang around the house with nothing to do? Moreover, being grounded—or so it seemed, though her mother refused the concept—was a shameful comeuppance for a girl who'd never caused problems before. Complying would only make things worse.

And so when Joe came looking for Alice on the playground, she made a move, leaving school with the group and going to the campus. Surprisingly enough, when she came home just before dinner, her mother never asked where she'd been; the Fillmore evening had faded away and been forgotten in a rush of new concerns. Her mother was almost encouraging, as though they were sharing in a new freedom, a new bond—as though the family was moving on.

As the days passed, Alice began walking home from school. That way, she could wander as she pleased, joining the group in roaming the campus.

Then one day on the playground, during lunch, she found the group planning a new caper: stealing a mounted bear's head from a garage in the hills. From a young age, she'd been taught that stealing was wrong, and so she refused to go along, rousing unease among the group. Things were crumbling.

That afternoon, Alice headed up Ashby Avenue alone, going home. Under one arm was *The Three Musketeers*. For days, she'd been plodding through the book during class. Rounding the corner of an overgrown lot, where a fire had raged the year before, burning a house, she made her way through clumps of crabgrass. She approached the gutted shell of the house, peering through an opening in the wall.

When she looked up, two girls were coming through the crabgrass. They were black and somewhat older—probably from the junior high, her brother's school, where she would soon be going—in sequined jeans and collarless blouses, magenta and pale blue. The girl in the magenta blouse had a permanent; the other wore the looping braids of the younger girls. They were laughing as they sauntered along, heads together, never glancing over.

Then as Alice was passing the girls, a rough slap landed on her shoulder. She stumbled forward, feeling a rush of anger but preferring to dodge a fight; against two black girls, she would lose, and lose badly. But before she could get clear of them, a punch slammed her upper back. Turning, she found the older girl waving a lanky arm and glaring from under her glossy permanent, ready for more. Though it was cowardly, Alice knew she should get away; fighting was wrong, her mother was always saying. But adrenaline charged through her, a submerged rage that had been bubbling for months. Throwing off her mother's commands and phony pacifism, she would defend herself. People made trouble for her regardless.

Words were the place to begin, and so she demanded, "What was that for?"

"You brushed me."

"When?"

"Just now, when you passed." The girl paused and added, "You wipe that innocent look from your face 'fore I smack you again."

"But that's no reason to fight."

Magenta Blouse was glowing. "Who asked you? How come you never apologize?"

"I have nothing to apologize for."

"Nothing? Huh! You hear that?" Magenta Blouse demanded of the other girl, who now moved around by Alice's shoulder, surrounding her.

"I hear you."

"Now go on," Magenta Blouse commanded, "say you're sorry and go on where you belong."

"Sure enough no one wants you around here," murmured the girl by her shoulder.

"Why are you doing this?" Alice demanded, feeling queasy.

"I do as I please."

"Then you're a fool." Alice responded as Mr. Boyd, the principal, had urged, seemingly reasonable and exact, even when angry.

The words hung heavy with seeming challenge as Magenta Blouse rushed in, her open hands slapping wherever they could. Random blows pummeled Alice's head and shoulders, and though she could parry some of them, the agile hands left no gap in her enemy's armor. She was already off balance, overpowered, when she heard the girl on her shoulder cheer in a stirring and urgent tone, "Kick her butt, Pam! Kick her butt!"

Soon a dozen black faces crowded around the girls, enjoying the fun on the way home from school.

"Get her, Pam!"

"What that white girl do?"

"Ooooh, I seen her before . . ."

They'd come from Alice's own school. Maybe she'd made waves on the playground—or maybe she was just white to them. Either way, they'd remember and make more trouble for her. Pam was buoyed by the group as they pressed in, leaving no room for Alice to defend herself. She was feeling sheer danger— who could say how far they would go, if she bumped against one of them? They could close in and smash her to a pulp.

A gap opened in the crowd. Seeing her chance, Alice ran, stumbling over clumps of crabgrass. They made way, but then came Pam's cry, loud and commanding, "Get her, before she's gone!"

Alice sprinted up Ashby Avenue, wondering how she could lose them—though fast, she'd never run from real danger before. Pausing at Grove Street for the light, her pulse pounding, she glanced back at the loose group of boys and girls straggling through the crabgrass. Only a few were running; the others had slowed, their arms flailing as though in a game or performance. Cars were speeding by, barring her way. A black man leaned from a passing Ford, frowning and surveying the scene. Soon the light changed, and Alice dodged across Ashby Avenue, racing as hard as she could. She would run along Grove Street and hope for a bus; if none came, she would just run.

Low aluminum fences lined the street, guarding faded bungalows. Shades were drawn against prying eyes and a blinding afternoon sun. The way seemed long and full of dangers, and no bus was coming. Then, as Alice was passing one of the bungalows, a black girl reached for her arm, murmuring, "In my house, before they come." Confused and frightened, Alice pulled free before glancing back and seeing that the girl was from Mrs. Donnelly's class. Even so, who was she? For months she'd been in the back row, so subdued a presence that Alice could only conjure her name, Denise, and a vague impression. Denise was now urging Alice down some cement steps and toward an open doorway, pulling her by the arm, saying, "Hurry up, they're coming." Aware of a boy running up and two more following, Alice allowed herself to be dragged through the doorway.

Denise slammed the door. They were in a gloomy garden apartment smelling of mold. The room was narrow, with a couch along one wall. The floor was covered in a gold shag carpet.

"I saw them bothering you," Denise was saying. "They're some bad kids."

Alice was gasping, her chest pounding. She was among strangers, depending on them—and why should the girl help? They hardly knew each other. Yet Denise had seen the group going after her and refused to join in. She was a loner among the black students, rarely speaking in class, holding herself apart from the small group of black girls there. She had an unusual and unfashionable way of being, as if new to California—not churchy like Ben Forman, just country. Maybe she was from the South.

"Good thing you can run," Denise was saying.

"I guess." *Cowards run*, thought Alice.

"They're so mean."

"Yes, they are," boomed a voice, as a man in jeans and a gray beret emerged from the back of the room. He came forward, filling the space.

"Don't be scared," he smiled. "I'm Denise's father." Then he added, "I hope no one harmed you."

"I'm okay."

"She's fast!" Denise announced, more of a presence than she'd ever been in class.

"That so?"

Alice made no response. Running from other people was always cowardly. So was the fear she was feeling. She wondered how soon she could leave.

"How about some Coke?" Denise's father was asking.

"Yes. Thank you." She would have a soda and go.

Denise's father brushed past the girls and headed for an area separated by a counter and holding a refrigerator and stove. He opened a cupboard, reached for a cup, and poured some Coke from a half-gallon jug.

"Here you go."

Mickey Mouse was grinning from the cup. Alice drank slowly, ashamed of needing anything.

"Are you in my daughter's class?" the man was asking.

"Yes."

"Where you from?"

Alice was confused.

"Where you living?" the man pursued. "Where's your house?"

Now she understood. "Near College Avenue."

"I see, way up there. Then how come you're walking?"

"She's always walking," Denise chimed in. "I see her going by."

"Some days I walk home," Alice confessed. If her own family learned what had happened, they would blame her for causing problems. But even though her mother had urged her to take the bus, it seemed a babyish indulgence.

"Hmmm, walk." The man was mulling things over, thoughtful under the beret. Then he poured some soda for Denise. "Your mother and father, do they know?" he pursued.

"Know what?"

"That you're walking home from school."

"Yes."

"And they're okay with that?"

"I guess."

The man eyed her. "Just be careful. What's gonna happen tomorrow, when you're out there by yourself?"

Alice had no response.

"See, you're safe on the bus."

Alice wondered why the words made more sense coming from Denise's father than from her mother. Maybe because the man knew the danger—he was responding to more than a vague fear.

He peered through the blinds. "They're gone now."

Alice placed the Mickey Mouse cup on the counter. Denise's father turned away from the window, facing them.

"You go on home now. Your mother's worrying."

The girls glanced at each other.

"Take care of yourself."

"See you."

Passing through the door, Alice glanced along the street; there was only a boy leaning on a nearby gate. She wondered how long he'd been there and if he'd seen the chase. Where had Pam's group gone? Maybe the boy by the fence had been among them, jeering and laughing. She passed the boy calmly and slowly, eyes focused ahead because any sign of fear could bring on more trouble. Then, having opened a lead, she began running. Glancing back, she saw the boy following and speeded up, struggling to hold her pace. The boy chased for a block before dropping away.

Coming upon a row of shops, she slowed—scared, panting, sweaty. Blood was pumping in her head; she was feeling weight-less and ungrounded. A throbbing had begun near her eye; she pressed the cheekbone and found a swelling. That girl Pam had landed some real punches. Alice approached a shop window and surveyed her image in the glass: rumpled hair and scowling face, one eye puffy and drooping.

As her heart stopped pounding, she weighed going home and confessing to her mother that she'd been in a fight. She was feeling in need of help, or at least sympathy, and if Denise and her father could show sympathy, then so could her own family. On the other hand, Alice was causing trouble again, and her mother would be alarmed by that. Her mother had never been pummeled for no reason and then surrounded by a cheering crowd; she would blame her daughter for fighting with black girls.

Suddenly Alice remembered *The Three Musketeers*. The book had come from the library and was gone, abandoned during the rumble in the crabgrass. She felt a new wave of panic: now there really was something her mother would have to know.

Unable to calm down enough to go home, Alice headed for the Dupres apartment. Though the group was a problem, she needed a refuge before going home. Unless the signs could be concealed, her parents would see she'd been in a fight, a bad one.

She rang the doorbell. Jim appeared in the foyer.

"Gang's all here. C'mon up."

He led her up and through the door of the smaller apart-ment. "Gimme Shelter" was blaring on the phonograph; the room reeked of marijuana. Joe and Valerie were slouched on the floor, sharing a joint.

Valerie looked up. "Where ya been?" she demanded. "Are you coming with us or not?"

She was referring to the garage, the mounted bear's head: so, they would be going through with the plan, Alice thought, feeling a growing sense of outrage at where they were taking her. Then, smoke curling from her mouth, Valerie glanced longer. "What happened to you?"

Alice shrugged.

"Hey," Valerie teased, "who beat you up?"

"Some black girls."

"Ooooh, they got you bad—"

Alice headed for the bathroom and slammed the door. Valerie was amused by someone else's problems. She could hear Jim calling, "Hurry up in there, we're going soon," and then Joe, low and whining, "Leave her alone."

Alice dampened a towel and pressed the coolness over her face. Then she dropped her hands. The mirror was clouded, her image marred. She dabbed her sore and puffy cheekbone. There was a pause, the sound of her body breathing and pumping, and then a thump on the door.

"Are ya coming?" Jim demanded, pushing on the door. They faced each other. A sharp repugnance flowed through her as she saw the hard gray eyes and laughing pug nose splashed with sunburn, the scarred chin and rumpled, unwashed clothes.

"I'm going home."

"Home?" Jim wondered. "You just got here."

"Yeah."

"Too bad for you," Valerie taunted.

Joe was by the apartment door. "C'mon, Chris's gonna wonder where we are." Joe gave Alice a hapless smile of mockery and sympathy.

Alice followed them out. The group ran off, leaving her on the corner of Virginia and McGee.

Alice was home before dinner, lying on the couch on the sunporch. Though she'd cleaned up, there was no concealing the swelling under her eye. She wondered how much more school she could endure. The place was dangerous, full of people who meant her harm, and they'd be there when she got off the bus, day after day.

Valerie and the group had been no help. From the beginning

they'd made problems for her, and now she was completely through with them. Even Joe had run off, barely saying good-bye. In any case, the world was becoming a desperate challenge; if she would be safe and whole, she would have to be much more careful. As much as the Fillmore, that girl Pam had made her aware of how far wrong things could go, how hard they could be to control.

Now Alice would be alone again. Of course, she'd never belonged in the group—anyone could see that. Even so, they'd been willing to have her along. Maybe they'd wanted to see how long she would go on hanging around the world of Dan Dupres. No wonder they'd laughed—a black eye was no big deal.

And what would her family say? There would be no laughing from them, when they heard she'd been fighting.

Her mother was calling; dinner was ready. No one glanced up during the meal; and they hardly spoke, only Curt relaying some baseball scores. As they were finishing, Alice massaged the swelling under her eye. Though her face was there for the family to see, if they bothered to look, no one made any comment. Valerie's response had been more aware, even more human. For a moment, Alice imagined confessing the whole thing but then suppressed herself. What if they blamed her for the fight, or worse, what if there was no response? That would be unbearable. No—she'd rather cling to the hope that they would show sympathy, if she ever found a way of telling them.

The family cleared off, leaving Alice in tears.

SEVERAL DAYS HAD passed, when suddenly her mother's summons came, rounding the family up. She'd been dreading the moment. They had to say *something* about the Fillmore—but now, it seemed, they would demand a full accounting, and she would have to comply.

Things could change: they could simply dump her.

The other Raysons had already found places in the living room. The reason for the summons was unclear, though if the evening's unusual togetherness was for the purpose of leashing Alice, the hour had come and gone. Even so, there could be a delayed showdown regarding Valerie and her former group. Alice eyed the family: why was Curt there, unless her mother planned on confronting her? Maybe he'd seen her and the group on Telegraph Avenue and would be specifying her doings—naming the charges, so to speak.

Alice glanced along the couch and saw her brother looking smug; he would gladly inform on her. Her mother and father stood together by the fireplace, guarding some imaginary family gods.

Her mother's eyes were glowing from an inner light, more in forgiveness than anger. Remorse and hope came over Alice as she began.

"Your father and I have something to say." An odd passion flushed her mother's face. "Alice, are you there? What I'm saying involves you."

Alice glanced up. Though fearful of what was to come, she was beginning to feel a sense of relief.

"Things have gone beyond what we can endure."

Her mother looked at her so long and so unguardedly that Alice was sure a bloodletting was coming.

"We're agreed—we can no longer live together." Her mother paused, as though slightly stunned by her own words. "We're planning to separate. Your father's in love with Ginger. I'm going to marry Charles."

Laughter rose in Alice, mingled with a sense of letting go: the drugs had dredged up something unfamiliar and wild, something cruel. They'd gone on so long pretending to be a family, but she'd seen the family for what it was: a crazy charade. Now they would all be released from the nightmare. Looking at Curt, however, she was awed and shamed by the tears in his eyes. They no longer shared a world—she was smothering a laugh, he was choking back tears.

Her mother glanced around, eyes shining with resolve. "I can imagine how sad you're feeling, but we've done everything we can." There was no response, and so she resumed. "Your father and I agree—you'll both be living with me. He no longer wants the responsibility of raising children. Nor does Ginger, I rather suspect."

Her father was keeping his own counsel, seemingly unconcerned with defending himself from the dig. Alice wondered why he never had anything to say, as though he never cared what anyone thought.

"Charles?" she heard herself say.

"Yes, Charles—the man I'm in love with. You saw him a few months ago."

Curt was clenching his jaw.

"He has a job in Los Angeles. That means we'll be moving there—once we can get things arranged."

Alice had never seen Ginger and could not imagine her as a family member. Charles had shown up once. Her mother's words seemed meaningless: a story peopled by strangers. Who could say how they'd feel about her and the problems she'd just made?

Her mother's eyes were bold, buoyed by her growing command. "As you may remember, Charles has two sons. They live with him, so you're going to have new brothers. We're hoping everyone can get along."

Curt made a snuffling sound; he was crying. He'd said nothing so far—nor had her father. Her mother was in charge, it seemed; she'd found more courage than the men. Alice felt a laugh burbling up; with a gasp, she managed to stifle it.

SHE'D BEEN FEELING less confused since the announcement, because it was clear that things would be changing. Her world had become unmanageable: scary, how wrong things had gone before coming around. A new beginning would be a good thing. On the other hand, the changes could prove overwhelming. For one thing, Charles and Ginger would be judging her—now, just when she'd broken so many rules. They knew nothing of her, only her faults. Yet they would have power over her life; they would make new demands, and unless she found ways of appeasing them, they would become her enemies—or worse, push her out. Then where would she go, how would she keep from being destroyed? She was through with Telegraph Avenue; she'd seen enough runaways to know she'd never get through that world as the same girl—or as anyone.

Her father would be moving soon. Meanwhile, he was coming and going as he pleased and sleeping in the spare bedroom. He'd been showing up for dinner, as before, but gulping the meal and then closing himself in the spare room.

Sounds came from the landing; he'd just come in. He passed her door, pausing and glancing in. She lay on the rug, scanning one of her mother's books—*Nana*, a novel by the Frenchman Zola. Though she ignored the glance, she could feel her father's presence weighing on her as he moved off.

Her mother had recommended *Nana*. Lately, she'd begun supervising her daughter's reading, prodding and suggesting. Scanning the pages of *Nana*, however, Alice was unnerved by the book and by her mother's message in offering it—the ugly story of a young streetwalker who rose from the gutter by performing on stage as the Blonde Venus, and then proceeded to destroy the men who pursued her. The story made Alice feel a sense of horror and death; she wondered why her mother found her in need of the warning, if warning it was.

As Alice was pondering her mother's stratagem, a loud rap came on her door. Feeling caught, she continued reading; when she finally glanced up, her parents were coming through the doorway together. They leaned close together; her mother's face was pale, as though they'd come to announce a death.

"You've read enough for now," she sighed, her hair loose around her scowl, her eyes flashing with drama. "We need your response—and please be truthful."

They're in agreement again, thought Alice, closing the book; they have another bombshell.

"Yes?"

"Do you hear me?" Her mother demanded, sharply.

"Yes. What's wrong?"

Her mother's face contorted. "You're stealing money from your father!"

Alice was dumbfounded. "What?"

"Oh!" came her mother's cry. "How could you do such a thing?"

Alice was trembling. "But I never—"

"You're lying!"

"No, I'm not!"

"Are you absolutely sure?"

"Yes, I'm sure."

Her mother's eyes were tearing. "Why would my daughter steal a hundred dollars?" she muttered, shaking her head.

"A hundred dollars?" The sum was large—more money than Alice had ever seen.

"Yes!"

"What for?"

"Drugs," came her father's stony response.

"Drugs?"

"Yes, marijuana!" her mother snapped.

"I would never—"

"Oh! She's lying!"

Alice's pulse was racing, jolted by the baffling accusation. If drugs were the concern, why accuse her of stealing? Or could they suppose she was planning on selling the stuff and needed some seed money? She eyed them, wondering what the real charges could be.

"I've smoked marijuana." She would come clean, more or less, and maybe they would be persuaded. "But I've never bought any. And I never stole any money from you."

"Someone else, then? Who?" her father demanded, colorless and contemptuous.

"How would I know?"

"Well," her father shrugged, "you would know, if anyone would."

Alice could feel her face reddening. Her lawyer father was sure she'd done the deed as charged.

"Yes," her mother added, "you've been marauding around with your group. Who knows, maybe they broke in while everyone was away."

"They've never come here."

"So you say—but how can we be sure?"

"And I don't even see them anymore."

"Well, that's some comfort," her mother sighed, as her father began moving off. "Come down for dinner, then. Everyone's here."

Alice looked away.

"Come down—now," her mother commanded. "We're having our last dinner together before your father leaves."

Then she closed the door.

Alice closed her book and went down, feeling shaken. The others were there. Her mother's face had softened, and she put Alice to work cleaning spinach.

As Alice was rinsing the spinach, she heard Curt say, "Were you on Telegraph on Monday?"

"No. Why?"

"One of the black guys from school says he saw what's-her-name."

"Who?"

"That girl who's always hanging around Telegraph—Valerie."

"So what?"

"Gary says if you're hanging with her, you're a whore and a dope dealer."

The words hung in the room. So, guys had been groping her —and now one of them was calling her names? She glanced around, wondering why her mother and father were playing deaf and dumb, but there was no response.

Curt was smirking as though he'd made a good move. So, he'd probably been on Telegraph with Gary. Maybe Curt was using drugs—and he was clearly stealing. One day he'd come home bragging how he and Sammy had found twenty dollars near the bank. Her mother had heard him bragging and scoffing and must have known he was lying. But now that her father's money was missing, they were accusing her.

"You and Gary go there, same as Valerie," she said, glaring. "You're stealing money and blaming me. Now leave me alone."

"Alice! What's wrong with you?" Her mother's face was red.

"He's the one, and you're blaming me."

"She's the one hanging around on Telegraph," Curt said with a scowl, as though he would punch someone.

"We've asked both of you," her mother argued, "and no one can say where the money is. How should we proceed, then, if you're both blameless? As for you, Alice, we have no idea where you've been going or what you've been doing, and you're clearly never going to say."

"I never go to Telegraph anymore," Alice responded.

"Maybe. I hope so."

"And anyway, everyone else goes there."

"We're grown-ups," her mother responded flatly. "We can choose where we go. And when you come with us, we can make sure you're not running wild. Anyway, you're the one who's smoking grass. That's why we assumed you'd be stealing money."

Curt chimed in, "Gary says Valerie's a dope dealer."

Her mother's eyes rounded, aghast. "How wrong I was about Dan Dupres!" she cried. Then she peered at Alice. "Are you buying drugs from her?"

"No."

"Oh, yeah," Curt scoffed.

"Maybe you and Gary are buying drugs," Alice responded. "Maybe you stole the money, same as before, when you and Sammy found some money by the bank. Or so you claimed."

Curt was seething. "She's way out of control," he informed them coolly. Then he ducked from the room.

"Alice?" her mother probed. "What's going on?"

"I'm not a criminal."

"I know. But who—" Her words faded.

Though in a rage, Alice forced herself to be calm. Her father would be leaving soon, and she needed to see clearly how the cards were falling. She'd done enough bad things—enough for Charles and Ginger to throw her to the wolves. And now would they hear even worse? Her own mother and father might forgive her—but what about these strangers? She would be leaving Berkeley; there would be other chances if she could only hold on and keep cool. In the meantime, she would have to comply. But complying was one thing; accepting false charges was another. Curt had been eager to accuse her. Given everything that had happened to her and could go on happening, in school and elsewhere, his slander was unforgivable.

Part IV

*fire in
bohemian grove*

chapter one

Alice

HER FATHER'S SATURDAYS were no longer hushed up; everyone knew he was in Marin, riding horses with Ginger. By mid-June, he had moved from the house on Forest Avenue to a rented room nearby; how strange, then, that Alice should know more than when he'd been sleeping in the spare bedroom, or before. Now he showed up for parenting duty sunburned and unburdened, in cowboy boots and smelling of horses. Her mother had known for months, or so she informed Alice, who blamed herself for having been fooled, for never bothering to imagine, even after she'd found the cowboy gear in a cellar cupboard. For months she'd been wandering in her own world; now she learned what everyone else already knew.

"I never supposed he would find a horsewoman," her mother had begun by saying, when they found themselves alone, in the shadow of the announcement.

Her mother was equally changed—warm and gushing, unless something happened to remind her of Tom; then she would say things Alice had never heard before, about how unhappy they'd been together. It was a whole new image of her family, as a place that had never been good, rather than one that had gone suddenly bad. In any case, the family had come to an end. The past was crumbling in her mind; the house in Washington had concealed something bad, a room full of unpleasant ghosts that rushed forward, overwhelming her memory. As she now learned, nothing was the way she remembered.

Her mother had found new concerns: Charles and the boys. She prepared Alice for what was coming by informing her of these new people, who they were and how she should feel about them once they were gathered under one roof—the following summer, once the arrangements had been made. Alice was leery of her mother's monologues, because she should be choosing for herself. But no; the new people would be her family, replacing the old one, only offering more, her mother assured her—for there were so many things her father had been unable to do, and Charles could do them all.

Hearing her mother's rambling monologue, Alice knew there was no saying what these changes would mean; she would have to see. For now, her father had abandoned her world, her mother was in love, and Charles had not yet appeared. She would have to save herself.

There was the sense of a lessening burden, now that her mother was no longer always angry or sleepy—angry over some household problem that had never troubled her before; sleeping away the afternoons and emerging to pull together some dinner. There was an unaccustomed new glow and a dreamy face, spreading warmth. Even so, Alice had no power over her mother's moods and had done nothing to change them; that was spurred by someone else, the newcomer Charles. She was merely sensing the change, as some manner of bystander to a joyous turn of events far beyond her comprehension. Father and mother were madly in love, though not with each other, of course; confused by the feeling of overhearing someone else's good fortune, Alice understood that what her parents had shared had never really been love, but some barely preserved tolerance.

Now there would be the future.

She would be free of her father; maybe her world would change. She was bad for wanting any such thing. But he had some share of the blame, now that he was leaving her, or them—for she was no longer alone. Tom's abandonment bound the others together. There was an odd reassurance in hearing her mother complain about how he'd refused her an ice-cream cone on their honeymoon; hardly pausing, her mother would then announce that a man always favored a daughter. For Alice, some hope clung to the idea, followed by the foreboding that he would become a stranger. The sudden absence was oddly wounding—there would be a yearning to know the stranger, where he had gone and what he was doing. For now, though, she was glad he was away and would know nothing of her. Surely none of them approved of her.

Her father's room was near the Rayson house, on a street whose name Alice could never remember, though her mother referred to it carefully, as a place of meaning or permanence. But her father would never stay long in a cramped second-floor room having only a desk and a single bed, not even a rug—a less welcoming space than the spare room on Forest Avenue, though of course he was free of them. The purpose was clear enough.

As her mother observed from the car, her father's doorbell—camouflaged among faded wood shingles—sounded a faraway chime. The small and weather-beaten house seemed to Alice as though the one on Forest Avenue had been hurled up and flung down by whirling helicopters, losing scale in the process. She'd seen the place only once before, on her mother's demand; her mother had been arguing on the phone when she snapped, "The children should know where you're living, Tom," and ended the call. Alice had never pleaded to see the room, yet true enough, it pressed on her world as a fantasy. And so there'd been an impromptu jaunt with her father alone—her brother had been playing ball somewhere—for a glance at the room and then back to Forest Avenue, with barely a grunt from her father. She'd been hoping for more—a glimpse of a world belonging to him. Problem was, everyone knew he was already more or less living with Ginger.

Now her father was being rounded up once more on her behalf, as they headed to the Parnassus Road home of a man named Joel Cohen, who ran a school. Joel was another Harvard man. Sabrina Patterson's daughter Helen had been enrolled in Joel's school for a year already, and according to Sabrina, he had made up for Michael's absence. Now Michael was planning on spending several more months in the Amazon, and though Helen was coping badly, Joel's program was a wonderful help; the girl was performing theater, keeping a journal, reading Sartre and R. D. Laing. Alice's mother was so impressed by what she'd heard that she was considering enrolling her. The program was funded by the public schools and therefore free, and it was intended for very independent students—that was her mother's story. For herself, Alice was unsure whether she should enroll with a handful of others in some newfangled thing. So much was changing already, and she longed for something that worked—though the junior high, of course, would only be more of the same.

On the other hand, she needed a new group to replace Joe, Valerie, and Jim. The school had fewer than one hundred students, nearly all of them older; that would be challenging. Though she enjoyed the thought of being among students her brother's age, it would be sad to lose her own peers—Tammy and the other girls. But if anything new were to happen, she would have to be open. She would gladly be free—not of her peers, but of so many other things.

Joel had to approve any new student for the school, known as Other Paths Open Academy; for that, the Raysons had been summoned to Parnassus Road.

Her father appeared at the door, sunburned and wearing a black cowboy shirt and new bell-bottomed jeans. Only the worn baseball cap was familiar, though even that had changed in some absurd way, like cheap Halloween gear, sideburns draping from the edge. Bland and barely nodding, he closed the door with a slam, and they returned to the car.

Her mother was driving; that was the oddest part. Of course her mother drove nearly every day, just not when her father was in the car. Now he climbed into the back seat, while Alice remained in front. It was a strange game of musical chairs, with everyone in the wrong place, a place belonging to someone else. Saying hardly a word, they ascended the hill and parked on Parnassus Road, a narrow sloping lane leading to a dead end. For a moment they gathered by the curb, gazing over roofs and trees on a gleaming world. The house lay below, snuggled at the end of a steep path. The Raysons filed down the steps; her mother sounded the gong. Soon the door opened on a sun-splashed room. Joel Cohen, young and beaming, moved to reveal the sunscape, as though they'd come for that alone.

Though Joel and her father had gone to the same college, they were nothing alike. Alice had imagined Joel as bland, probing, deadpan; he was none of those things. Shaggy dark curls tumbled over an open collar; he wore sandals and a long strand of beads. Pale and chubby, he surveyed them, barely concealing a wave of humor that pursed the boyish mouth. For a moment, the men faced off, then with a purr of welcome, Joel ushered them through the door. They found themselves in an airy space overlooking a gleaming scene of the San Francisco Bay. Together they gazed on the day's closing glory. Wispy orange and lavender clouds laced the sky in anonymous gesture; gray shards glimmered on the bay. Fog poured through the Golden Gate, spreading over San Francisco and Marin.

Turning from the glow, Alice found several large beanbags gathered around a low glass table like frogs by the edge of a pond, amorphous shapes facing everywhere or nowhere.

From another room she heard squealing, as a toddler came running toward them through the doorway. Encountering Tom's uncompromising knee, the child paused in confusion and gazed up, laughing. Then she found Joel, grasping her father's leg in both hands, ready to shinny up in search of welcoming arms. "Come here!" she squealed.

"Can't you see I'm busy, Isabel?" he cajoled as she hung from Daddy's thumb. "Here, we have something for Ruth."

"Mommy!" the child echoed gleefully.

Joel removed the strand of colored beads and shells, dangling it for Isabel to grasp. She took the beads in one hand and ran back toward the doorway, dragging them through dense beige carpeting.

Seeing Joel's pleasure in the young girl, Alice wondered if her own father had ever shown such eagerness. Maybe she should give Joel a chance.

"That's my older daughter, Isabel," he said, as though informing them of a wondrous event. "She's learning to be more independent of her parents—creating her own play world, where she has less need of our approval. We're not there yet; you see how she comes to me for something to play with. But she can make her own game with anything I give her, even a rubber band."

"Yes, I see," Marian responded approvingly.

As Joel spoke, Tom had been eyeing one of the beanbags, leaning to assess the proper angle of repose. Now he glanced up.

"Rubber bands—they were good toys during the Depression," he remarked, poker-faced.

"So," Joel nodded encouragingly, "you remember the Depression?"

Tom made no response, as though he'd already offered more than enough. Alice glanced from one man to the other; eyeing Joel's expressive face as he assessed the family, she was feeling embarrassed by her father.

"Oh, I'm afraid some of us do," came her mother's sigh as she pondered the glowing panorama, where the bridge was vanishing in fog flowing through the Golden Gate. San Francisco rose in glass and steel from the fog. In the pause, one of the skyscrapers caught the sun's fading rays in its icy depths; only a gleam escaped.

"Well, the Depression's long gone," Joel concluded with a reassuring chuckle.

A glimmer of hope came over Alice.

Her mother was fingering the hem of her cardigan. "Oh my, yes," she enthused. Her tone suggested she'd never been so impressed before.

Joel's eyes narrowed in amusement. "Everyone ready?" He waved them magnanimously toward the beanbags.

Propped on the beanbags, they found themselves offered up to one another in embarrassing poses. Leaning back, Alice was suddenly prone; then as she lurched forward, the leather casing collapsed under her forearms. Sprawled awkwardly, she gave way under Joel's encouraging gaze to a humbling loss of control, as her parents made clumsy thrashings. Joel had assumed an easy pose: legs extended, hands laced behind the lush mane. Turning from one to the other, measuring the progress, he paused for the Raysons to come to order.

Alice could feel her family losing ground even before the conference had begun. Joel's easy mastery was revealing her parents as hopelessly square; in response, Alice was feeling unsure of herself and where she belonged. Joel could teach her something, if only she could get over her doubts; but that would be a challenge. The man's game was unknown, and being closely regarded made her uncomfortable. Her father's brooding, unspoken judgment weighed on her as Joel began, though her mother glanced over and smiled.

Joel commented that Alice would be younger than the other students, then smoothly resolved the problem by suggesting that young people should not be "cordoned off according to chronological age," but encouraged to choose a comfortable level.

Her mother agreed. "Our daughter has always been ahead of her grade level. We fear that may be causing problems."

"And you?" Joel demanded, as though Alice were a grown-up. "Do you fear there are problems?"

Alice was feeling confused. Though she had fears and problems, she could not imagine revealing them to a man she'd never seen before. In any case, her family should be the ones asking, not Joel.

He gave her a long, assessing glance before continuing. "Other Paths has some wonderful things to offer young people who are ready to move away from the dead learning." He paused for her response, but before she could weed through her thoughts, he forged on. "The old forms can get in the way of real learning, deeper learning. Our students at Other Paths choose what and how to learn; the school's role is to support the young person's own program." Smiling wisely, Joel surveyed the Raysons.

"She's a very good reader," came her mother's response. Alice could feel herself cringe—her mother had Joel all wrong.

Joel nodded sagely. "Learning encompasses many things. Of course, reading could be one focus, but at Other Paths we encourage other forms of learning as well, such as math games, guerrilla theater, exploring the wilderness. Our young people are engaged in the community, performing in nightclubs, avantgarde theaters, local political events. Empty vessels need not apply." Joel had ceased smiling.

"You're no empty vessel, are you, dear?" her mother murmured, even as Alice was feeling increasingly edgy and self-conscious.

Eyeing her, Joel pressed on. "You may be unhappy with your approach to learning. You may choose to begin by unlearning— re-thinking, re-feeling what school means. Up to now, you may have had someone else choose for you. You may doubt whether you know enough to say what and how you want to learn. 'What if I choose wrong?' So many young people bring such fears with them. Our program helps you unlearn all that . . . all that disempowering stuff."

Joel would be making new demands of her. Feeling hardly ready for them, Alice wondered why she should change, why she should need so much unlearning.

"Our daughter's more exploratory than most kids—," her mother began.

Joel waved a hand as though brushing away a fly. "Let's drop that disempowering word 'kids.' Why would we refer to young people in terms reserved for animals?" He paused for everyone to catch up. "Our language can refuse old ways of thought by encouraging young people to feel they're of value." Joel eyed her father and added, "We never learned these things at Harvard."

"No?" he responded dryly.

Joel gave a raucous laugh.

Tom lay in the beanbag, cupping the ragged baseball cap over one knee. Seeing her father's gruff poker face, Alice wondered why he'd bothered to come. She imagined he'd been bored by school, as bored as she was. Even so, following Joel's plan, he would have done nothing but play baseball and ended up in the Ford plant. On the other hand, the "dead learning" Joel was urging her to reject had gotten them both to Harvard. Though her father was seemingly unengaged, he was presumably assessing the other man and judging him a fraud, though of course he'd never say so. He'd aced school and would expect the same of her, regardless of any program or dead learning. In any case, she was no longer his problem. He had other things to do now—he'd foregone an evening with Ginger and was clearly ready to wrap things up.

Joel plunged on, seemingly amused by the confusion among the Raysons. Hands over paunch, fingertips together, he resumed the performance. As he spoke, the fingertips bounced together in rhythm, as in a game of cat's cradle. "Our students have formed a number of bands playing avant-garde rock and jazz, rehearsing together and performing in Bay Area clubs. Our program at Other Paths can free them up for rehearsal hours. Others are making theater. Helen Patterson—of course you know Helen?—and another young woman have been performing with the San Francisco Mime Troupe. They come to us already engaged in wonderful work in the arts. We can help them forge bonds with each other and the community, and we offer a place to work. For the really talented ones, we help by standing out of the way."

As Alice was wondering how she would become involved in such things or find her way among Helen's group, Joel paused, waiting for something. Like puppets on strings, the Raysons craned toward the panorama, whose fading glow had become overwhelming. Feeling in need of reassurance and sensing her father's doubts, Alice wondered why he refused to challenge Joel. But her father seemed far away, present only in the tapping of baseball cap on knee as he scanned the scene, pausing on Marin.

"Where's Mount Tamalpais?" he asked, gesturing with the cap.

Joel leaned forward, hands propped on the beanbag and head thrown back, sighting along his nose. "Can you see Angel Island? Mount Tam's north of there." He surveyed her father with amused eyes, taking in the cowboy gear and baseball cap as though they were jester's weeds. Then he turned to her mother. "That's what you see from home—Mount Tam?"

Her mother's hand smoothed the cardigan. "That would be lovely. But no, we're very happy in South Campus. Tom's with the federal government."

"Ah!" Joel nodded, absorbing the information, then turned a new face on her father. "You're with the feds? What department?"

"Health, Education, and Welfare."

"Ah, the good side. You're there to keep the home fires from burning."

"We do what we can," her father shrugged, "though there's always someone fanning the flames."

"Of course you do," Joel nodded, ignoring the jab. "There are many good people; the problems come from the system. By the way, have you gone to Angel Island?"

"A former internment camp?"

"That's where they imprisoned the Chinese who came to America. A very informative place—you should show your daughter."

"Yes, we should," her mother acknowledged.

"Good for a school outing," her father murmured as he eyed the panorama. He pulled on the cap, preparing to go, and dropped, "By the way, how do you manage the diplomas?"

Alice wondered how Joel would parry the jab, but he was ready. "As I'm sure you know, Other Paths is part of the Experimental Schools Program approved and funded by the Berkeley public schools and the feds—your own agency." Joel shrugged, clearly bored by the bureaucratic game. "The young people we enroll have grades and other records on file in the central office on Walnut Street. Our program is empowered to confer diplomas that, as far as the scrap of paper goes, are the same as common public-school diplomas."

"And the jam sessions? Are 'glee club' and 'band' dead words?"

Joel's eyelids fluttered. "'Glee club' or 'band' for some; others prefer 'jazz saxophone,' or 'solo bass improv.' The wording should encompass, as far as such phrases can, the young person's whole learning world, over months or years."

Joel was handling them, thought Alice; he was managing the terms. Her parents had never regarded a school report card as a stratagem, as Joel could do. And he was onto something: the old words were meaningless. In Washington, there had been Pilgrims and Indians, the Founding Fathers, the Declaration of Independence, and the challenge of the Confederacy. Then she'd come to California, where they learned of Spanish missions and the Mexican War, the Gold Rush and transcontinental railroad, land grants and squatter's rights, Robber Barons and People's Park.

Joel nodded, ending the conference. The panorama was fading. Regular school would be another mess, Alice concluded. Though her father was clearly unimpressed, her father was no longer in charge; he'd gone away. Joel was dangling a sanctuary and the chance for breathing room from her mother's monologues: Tom and Charles and the wonders of love. She would learn to learn—no small thing, if only she could manage, if only she was good enough. Her mother was no longer slinging accusations; she was pushing the school. Joel and Other Paths would redeem Alice, at least in her mother's eyes.

Joel

WHEN THE RAYSONS had gone, Joel stood by the window bathed in the dying rays of day flooding the room. From a pocket he drew a pair of heavy-framed sunglasses, adjusting them on his face. The sunset was unusually stunning; he was glad of a chance for the senses to revel in peace, unburdened by the problems of Other Paths. The world beyond the room shimmered in an orange glow.

Joel drew a deep breath and, removing his sunglasses, descended to the lower floor. There he had redone a bedroom as an office, adding bookshelves, an oak desk and leather reclining chair, and an elaborate tape recorder for gathering documentation on Other Paths.

Taking up a legal pad, he flopped down in the leather arm-chair, jotting impressions of the family he'd just met: "Father—boring, belly-of-the-beast Harvard man; Mother—wobbly, wants to please; Alice—unhappy, uncomfortable with both me and her parents. Maybe." He paused and added, "Recommended by Mike Patterson." Absorbed in work, Joel ignored the bay and the gathering haze. The staff of Other Paths had resolved to welcome all comers, unless they brought drug problems that endangered the school. But the Rayson girl was only twelve, younger than the others, and unforthcoming. She would be uncomfortable, he feared, unable to embrace the anarchy and energy of the group. One glance had conveyed that she was bound for college, so that Other Paths would be merely a more adventurous way of preparing for the same old role. The mother was another Berkeley woman readying her young Salomé—but for what? The role of Ibsen's Nora, alas. He was amused by the way they prodded the daughters to be loose and free in ways the mothers had never been and would never choose for themselves; they'd been taught to fear consequences. The young ones, set loose in a new world, assumed all transgressions would be forgiven.

The phone rang. Joel dropped the pen; Ruth would be bathing Isabel. Leaning back on the padded leather, he reached for the telephone. It was Raymond Connor, the young man from the school. Early on, Raymond had shown how he could romp among the young people, for he was one himself; only twenty-two, a college dropout, he made a gifted camp counselor. Yet he hungered for a leadership role and enthused about moving the school away from book learning and into the community, so Joel had brought him on board as a teacher.

Raymond hoped for a large following; Joel knew that.

"We have three more," he announced.

"Way to go." Raymond's mood sounded up. "And they are . . . ?"

"One was just here," Joel reported. "She's young, seventh grade, and shy—"

"No, Joel, no labels. You've hardly seen her. When we see her alone, no mom and dad, then we'll meet the real person. Who's her father—another professor?"

"No, a government lawyer."

"Hey, as long as he's not Harvard—"

Joel guffawed.

"Oh, man," Raymond huffed, "they're are all the same. And her mother's probably unhappy, popping Valium, sleeping around. The daughter needs something real for a change—man, I can see the whole scene."

Joel heard Raymond exhaling a long groan of anger. The phone clanged on a counter, something crashed, Santana's "Black Magic Woman" throbbed through the nasal speaker, and then Raymond resumed, "So, who else?"

"Manny's younger brother dropped by."

"Awesome. Another jazz man coming up?"

"No, he's into electronics," Joel said, eagerly. "And he has hustle, like Manny. He gathers old radios from the dump and rebuilds them at home."

"Cool. He could be useful. And number three?"

"Number three, yes." Joel paused, bothered by doubts. "Another Patterson daughter, a younger one."

"Aha." Raymond massaged the telephone. "They'll unman every boy in the school."

"Come on, now you're labeling, too. She's nothing like Helen—they're moon and sun, yin and yang."

"Yeah, how so?"

"She's all about feelings," Joel responded softly. "You know —teaching poor children."

"Good. We're doing those things."

"Of course we are."

"I'm hearing something," Raymond probed. "You're holding something back."

Joel was unprepared for Raymond; having no plan, he would have to be open. "Raymond, Helen has real problems. What happens if we take on another?"

"What do you mean?"

"You know Helen's problems—headaches, mood swings. Her father's in the Amazon. They have her on a whole pharmacy of stuff."

"Yeah, yeah, the usual." Raymond groaned loudly. "Look, we can have those girls at Other Paths, or send them away and wash our hands. You know what I'm gonna say."

"You want me responsible—" Joel's tone was rising.

"No, all of us. We work by consensus, remember?"

"We've got to be careful."

"Why?" Raymond demanded, suddenly aggressive.

"Just a hunch."

"They deserve a chance," Raymond snapped. "It's the mother playing *Peyton Place*—not the daughters."

"In any case," Joel summed up, "we need a group consensus." Joel was feeling warm; he knew Raymond was challenging him. He changed the subject. "You remember there's a meeting tomorrow—"

"We can get a consensus then."

"By all means," Joel agreed. "Remember, though, problems of curriculum are already on the agenda—"

"I've been talking with Jerome," Raymond interrupted. "We've got to have more classes on race, things the students deal with every day. Your classes may work for some, the ones pushed toward college regardless, but the problem is, you're losing the others. They're not reading *No Exit*—they're busy living it."

"Then you and Jerome should propose some classes. Of course we're open to classes on race."

"Last year, we had each group keeping to themselves. We've got to push people to deal with other groups in the school."

"When you say 'push' . . ." Joel began, doubtful.

"Come on," Raymond urged. "You know change happens only under pressure. Look what happened in China: young people held the teachers accountable, they made a revolution beyond what the leadership could ever imagine. We're here to tear down, so we can create."

"Then you and Jerome should move on it."

Some form of consensus had been reached. They hung up. Joel leaned back; fingers laced over chest, he breathed deeply. Jerome, a Black Muslim, forceful and self-taught, had been integrating yoga with basketball as a way around the usual competitive emphasis in school sports, and Joel was learning some of the techniques. Joel had been consuming alarming amounts of alcohol, but now he was replacing it with a combination of yoga and marijuana. He'd never been grounded in the body before; he'd been a head-only man. Now with Jerome's folk knowledge he would finally escape so undernourished an understanding of self —*in, hold, release*—the pounding heart subsided—*in, hold, release*—the eyes calmly beheld a mind-blowing panorama.

Joel took up the legal pad. "Headaches, depression, Valium," he wrote. He'd been there, though not in adolescence. What Helen needed was proper breathing, and maybe a lover. Joel and Ruth had brought yogic breathing into lovemaking, with marvelous results; now they were truly a body couple, rather than mostly a head-only one.

The struggle had been long. He'd graduated from Harvard, and contrary to the urging of several professors had sought a job teaching in the secondary schools. Home in New York, he'd been assigned to a special-education classroom in Harlem, where he was soon overcome by a sense of the room as a place of confinement, a holding pen. A plump, unhappy young man, he'd commanded a roomful of depressed, glaring, and angry boys. As the days passed, he no longer remembered the boy he'd been, vying eagerly for grades and honors that now appeared meaningless. The boys in Joel's classroom refused to follow him; they'd learned early on to regard school as a fraud played on them by a malevolent demon. And Joel, who for years had been enthralled by the demon, was impressed by these boys who slumped, glumly or tauntingly, in joyless classroom rows. They were enlightened, in a sense: by age eleven, they'd already thrown themselves on the gears of the machine; they would never join the Lawrence Rad Lab, or engender a nuclear bomb. Joel had much to learn from them regarding the rebel's role.

Now Joel, too, was running a lab—a lab of the modern soul, with the goal of replacing the American focus on conformity and technology with process and personal change, the process of human creators—of language, photographs, Happenings, and more. The lab he was gathering would produce the anarchy and energy for tearing down the old learning, founding new knowledge on a continuing renewal of self, the process goals of a creator. Learning would be released from the endless repetition of the same.

In the beginning, he'd gathered groups of teachers and young people in a bare storefront on Alcatraz Avenue. They brought free-floating rebel energy: he had only to offer the space and propose ways of channeling the energy, and soon he was surrounded by a core group of a dozen adolescents reveling in sound, language, and improv. The rebels were followed by black and poor youths open to some form of final chance. Then there were the sons and daughters of professors—by turns eager, angry, or complacent, for they'd been passed over by parents who managed to be both aloof and hard charging, hands-off in manner but demanding of results. The brew was dangerous; there were days when Joel was sure the school would blast off or implode. But the brew was also indispensable: rebels brought a dash of the avant-garde, useful in persuading Joel's peers, poor and black youths garnered funding from the federal government, and sons and daughters of professors could be counted on to show up. The storefront gatherings had become a school.

During Year One, Other Paths had been buoyed by hope, though frequently on the edge of collapse. Space had been a recurring problem: when the lease on the storefront had ended, no proper replacement had been found. For a few weeks, they'd gathered in the Free Church, holding a group ceremony. Come September, they would be housed on the ground floor of Finnish Hall, an old ethnic center near the bay. No one could say how the Finnish remnant would respond to the school.

Joel had begun preparing a book on the school and would be spending some days composing the book at home. He had long dreamed of such doubleness—a space of subversive conspiracy, balanced by a professor's home and family. And he'd come to possess the professor's home, though bypassing the normal hurdles—advanced degrees, scholarly research; he'd refused to be co-opted. Mornings, fog hung in the trees, exhaling a pungent odor of eucalyptus, and through the afternoon the sun shone relentlessly, drenching him in dreamy pleasure. He and Ruth had passed a summer in Barcelona; those days had returned, only more posh, for they'd been poor then. There he'd resolved to choose freely. To change the world, one needed a rebel band of one's own; now he'd founded a rebel school.

Joel's book would be a success. He knew what teachers needed to hear, what would make them feel good. They had many bad feelings, marooned as they were in classrooms of young people who desperately wanted to escape. But Joel had found ways of reshaping the school trauma as a story of hope and rescue—hope for teachers who longed to transform the classroom into a space of shared learning, a community where rescue could happen. So many teachers harbored suppressed hopes of being saved by the classrooms they ran; they would find encouragement and solace in Joel's book. And Joel, formerly programmed by the old learning, would reveal how he'd thrown it all overboard when faced with a roomful of wary, angry boys. In the schools he conjured up, anything could happen; classrooms were borne along by the energy of a spontaneous group. He would analyze the group events, drawing appealing morals for those following on the path, or simply in need of a comforting story. Joel was a purveyor of happy endings—learning found among the abandoned young, if only grown-ups would remove senseless rules and procedures.

For a long time he'd been overwhelmed, struggling to understand the young people of Berkeley, the land of free-flowing energy. He'd been so far from them as a boy in the Bronx; he'd conformed and gone complacently through school, enjoying many honors—scholarships to Harvard and even Oxford. Then one day he'd refused. Now, finally, he was no longer alone; he had only to hang a flyer, and they came running, ready for revolution.

Closing the legal pad, he removed a joint from a small chrome case and began to smoke. Then he carefully quenched the coal, returning the remnant to the case, and wandered out into the yard. The evening had turned cool and refreshing. Joel stood barefoot on the sloping lawn, surrounded by overgrown beach roses, and began to muse.

Other Paths would replace the dead learning of Joel's past. The young people would become a space of uncontrolled inner growth; through them the forms of the future would emerge, much as ever-blossoming beach roses filled the tumultuous yard. They would learn in the flowering of communal belonging that there was a heaven here.

From the yard, Joel gazed through low trees on the world, heard the murmuring of roads fanning north and south and along the garlands of crossings unfurled under a darkened sky. The hour hung heavy. The glowing lamps of fireflies flickered in random code among the beach roses. The savage war presaged confusion, and now even the Movement was abandoning the purpose of freedom.

The grass had grown cool and damp. Joel combed the blades absently with his toes and then lowered himself, so that he lay beneath the evening sky. A blade of grass brushed one ear; the sound of gnats droned and faded. He'd endured the escape from New York. Now he would make a clean break; California would be a refuge from the fray.

Alice

NOW WHEN HER mother was gone for a few breathless days with Charles and the boys, her father would spend a weekend in the Berkeley house. He passed evenings on the couch, reading a newspaper or in his cocoon, following the baseball game. They found nothing to say, even when she came through the door of the room, meaning only to make an appearance and then leave, though some compulsion urged her to the end of the couch, where she sensed her father's body though there was nothing to say. She began wondering about the stranger. Formerly, her mother had helped her understand the person who'd been her father, so long ago; for he was changed and strangely opaque, a phenomenon known only by faraway consequences. These days there was no more counting on her mother, whose story had changed, becoming full of slander and vengeance; from now on she would have to deal with the man alone.

Abandoned together as her mother played with Charles, Alice and her father measured each other. Though her father's presence seemed dreary and burdensome, who could say if he was truly unapproachable? Maybe her judgment had been clouded by slander—how would she ever know? She could hardly run the charges by her father, demanding that he confirm or deny, though she would have preferred to do so. Nor could she undo or unremember them.

In the beginning there was some squabbling—low-key and unreadable, in her father's manner—about an old canard: Telegraph Avenue. Her mother no longer cared about her going there, that much was clear; in any case, Alice rarely went to Telegraph anymore, except to drop by a record store. Even so, her father recalled the old problem, and one Sunday in August, as she headed for the door, he began probing.

"Going out?"

"Uh-huh."

"Can you say where you plan to go?"

"Just for a walk."

"Does your mother ask where you're going?"

Her mother was in Los Angeles with Charles. Was her father saying he wanted to know where she was going, or was he merely demanding to be informed, in case her mother called? There was no way of knowing.

"You can say I've gone to the campus."

"By way of Telegraph?" he pursued.

"Why do you care?"

Surveying her in the usual unfathomable way, he probed further. "Do you want me to say yes, when your mother says no?"

More and more annoyed, she made no response.

"You should learn to rely on your own judgment," he concluded, turning and leaving her alone in the foyer.

A few days later, when her mother came back from L.A., the scene changed yet again, all accusations forgotten. Her mother was in the new, dreamy mood, eyes warm, tone measured and vague, as though reading a lullaby, as she mused on about Charles, and love, and the new family. There was a sense of wonders unfolding, happiness unforeseen in the cramped spaces of the old family. Her mother's flushed and joyful face was encouraging and then crushing, even enraging: would there really be a world of love and family, Alice wondered, and if so, for whom? Maybe for mother and father, each and separately; surely not for her. Remembering her mother's false and damning accusation of theft, she was angry and confused. And what of her father—was he any longer hers? No—he was gone. He'd been persuaded of the charges; he would regard her as a thief.

Her mother's dreamy mood was making her angry; she'd heard enough for now. In the house, there would be no refusing her mother, who followed her from room to room rehearsing the story, over and over, for the pleasure of rehearsal. Volleyed from one parent to the other, from a rude hoarding of words to an overwhelming gush, Alice found no place of her own. She would have to go somewhere on her own for the day or linger in the house, hearing the woman come and go talking of Tom and Charles, as though every woman were through with Tom, as though every woman would soon marry Charles.

Alice wandered from the room even as her mother was impressing upon her the joys of love. An hour later, she passed along Telegraph following a former path, lately abandoned, hardly pausing to choose where she should go. She no longer hung around Telegraph and wondered how the group would welcome her. But they were nowhere to be found. She paused by the Med, absorbing changes in the scene.

Suddenly Valerie appeared before her, heading for the door-way of the Med. Valerie paused long enough to laugh.

"Long time no see," she goaded. "We wondered where you'd gone."

"Nowhere," Alice said. "Around."

"And now here you are. Planning to hang out?" There was a hardness in her tone.

"No."

Valerie narrowed her eyes. "Well then, see ya!" And she flounced through the cafe door.

Stung by the uncomfortable encounter, and embarrassed at being left alone on the Avenue, Alice observed Valerie moving through the scene as one who belonged. Valerie had found her out: she was an impostor, and the world of Telegraph was col-lapsing around her. Though she had no place here, she could refuse to run. She would seem to hang around, as though she belonged, as though she had no need of Valerie.

A young man—eyes of blue glass, a pale face framed by jet-black hair—had nearly passed by when he saw her, alone, or so she seemed. He'd seen her on other days, on the Avenue; surely she'd been there before. Clearly enough she was no runaway, he concluded, veering toward the door of the Med but then pausing, one hand fumbling in a charade of groping in the pouch that dangled from a worn leather thong slung over one shoulder, as he scanned her face, the full mouth and wary eyes, then perused her freshly laundered top—something a boy should wear, he thought, amused, glimpsing the open cloth over her collarbone. Her jeans were clean and unfrayed, though faded and worn. And now he remembered where he'd seen her—she was one of the group around Valerie and Jim.

She turned, responding to the young man's eyes on her. Sea-blue in a face made ashen by a halo of dark curls, the eyes glinted like colored glass in blinding sunlight. The arms were lean and pale; and as one hand probed a leather purse, she saw the thumb, where he wore a heavy ring made from the handle of a spoon.

He abandoned fumbling in the old leather purse and, lean-ing in, tapped on her arm the fingers of one hand. "Hey, have you seen Valerie?"

Alice was unsure how to gauge the space around her, for more and more she found someone leaning in on her as the man had suddenly done. "In there," she responded, barely moving her head as she nodded toward the cafe.

The man glanced through the window, paused. "Oh wow," he nodded, grooving on something. "Wow, hey, I'm Johnny." And he held up one hand, though there was hardly any room for her to offer her own. She placed her hand in the man's palm, and he grasped hard. Then he dropped her hand and leaned in.

"And you, what's your name? I know Jim and Valerie and Joe and—"

"Alice."

"Hey, so you're Alice." He nodded, regarding her closely.

She'd rarely conversed with a man, not even her father— though the man was only a boy, no more than seventeen or twenty. She'd come to Telegraph with the group, and the boy had seen and remembered her. They knew each other, maybe. Could he be from the commune on Derby Street, the one she'd heard about? She'd seen the house—a large, rambling wood-shingle place shared by many young people. The house was near her own. She'd passed by many times.

The boy was already bored with her, she thought, as he turned, eyes scanning up and down the thoroughfare. Then the blue eyes searched her once more. "So, you're hanging on the Avenue," he nodded, and she was unsure if he was assessing her or welcoming her, acknowledging her, as people on the Avenue acknowledged others they knew. That was the common way when people were sharing space—though there were other ways, as she'd learned from her father.

Then he remarked with a shrug, as though letting go of an afterthought, "Or you could come by the house, see some people. I can show you around."

Soon Johnny was leading her from the Avenue. He made plans as they walked, scheming where the cash would come from —because just before finding the babe near the Med, he'd been confronted by a dealer, Marlboro Man, demanding money. Johnny owed three hundred dollars; he would need days to pull together that much bread. He groped for a reefer, cupping it in his palm; no, man, he thought, with a rush of anger at the inter-ference, Marlboro Man could drop by the house. He opened the hand and showed her the joint, rolled in red-white-and-blue paper. He was already high from the morning toke on the porch with Arlene. They'd been on the couch in the large room, and then Arlene had held her hand to him and led him to the rear porch. They'd hung on the porch together holding hands and sharing a joint; but Arlene had pulled away, a tease as always, sashaying from him down the steps into the overgrown yard. He'd abandoned the porch, reaching angrily for the door and slamming it shut, as Arlene commenced singing loudly in the yard among the trumpet vines. Then, as usual, he'd come to the Avenue.

"Hey," he said, barely slowing, "I just remembered there's no one over the house now. Let's go somewhere else."

She'd seen him fumbling in the pouch that dangled over faded cloth hanging loosely from lean shoulders. Holding the reefer in his palm, he led her along, heading up toward the eucalyptus groves. She was glad he would be smoking. She'd begun feeling uncomfortable, wondering how she would find something to say, but now she understood how unnecessary that would be. He merely dropped a bland remark, much as her father would, whenever a pause became overly long.

As the boy rambled on next to her, she found herself losing the thread of the story that played in her head. One thing for sure, though: there was no Tom or Charles. She was beginning to enjoy strolling along. And Johnny seemed familiar in other ways, though she could not say what that meant.

They headed up an angling road of old houses and shaded yards. Leading away from a curve through the opening in a stone wall, a path wound along the shoulder of a canyon and soon faded among dry grasses and eucalyptus groves. The afternoon had turned warm; the sun engulfed her back and shoulders as they followed the path through wavering grasses. Though all words had ceased, she could hear the cawing of crows as they advanced deeper into the canyon, Johnny in the lead. She followed, fending off reeds that caught at her elbows. Soon they reached a lush, shady place greened by a nearby spring. There they found level ground, as though for a picnic.

Johnny opened the palm holding the reefer. He dampened one end and then the other in his mouth, then hung it there as he reached for some matches and tore one away, scraping sharply in a curving arc and pausing, beholding the flare. Holding the flame to the dampened paper, he inhaled as the paper browned, sending up another flare; then he began to smoke. She could smell the plume, rising sweet and pungent. Johnny smoked for a while and then reached it toward her.

Johnny was expecting her to smoke, and so she took a drag, reddening the coal, and handed off. He went on smoking; and then, when the roach was nearly down, he pinched it hard with thumb and forefinger and stowed it in the leather pouch.

She was enjoying being in the shade overlooking the bay. They'd come a long way up the slope—she'd rarely come so far, except in her parents' car. There could never be hours enough in such a place: groves and grasses, sun and gray-blue bay. The lazy eucalyptus fronds rippling overhead shed an odor of dry vinegar. Soon she was in a personal space, hardly aware of the boy, whom she could well have abandoned along the path, for now there was only herself and the place. She turned away from the boy and was moving among wavering eucalyptus leaves, green and purple and blue . . .

A large hand grasped her arm. In the heavy soundlessness, she nearly pulled away; only pausing, she remembered her father's presence and how he gripped her arm when he appeared at the house, as if to say hello though saying nothing; and then the grasses surrounded her head and a man's body pressed her in the dust, the face so near in a tangle of damp forehead and rounded sky-blue gleams black in the center, she'd never seen eyes so close . . . He lurched and pressed a hard mouth to hers, forcing her open as he fed on her tongue, a damp, smoky odor invading her nostrils. She moved her head and he followed, clamping her shoulders to the ground. She turned her head the other way and there he was, seemingly everywhere. Grasses and fronds now enclosed her, dangling above the man pressing on her in every way. When she was younger, her brother had forced her to the ground, though never so far, and when he'd won, then she could go. Johnny had changed the rules . . . Soon she'd gone under, her body no longer responding to the commands her mind was sending. She could no longer move her arms—dead branches, they seemed—as the man's thigh pressed something on hers.

Something was groping her, then there came a probing beneath her jeans, a rough grasping, a surge of power as arms pressed her against the uneven ground, one hand gripping her shoulder as the other dragged the jeans to her knees, then yanked one pant leg free, as he grappled her, prone beneath the leaden, muscled body. The shoulders above her were pale where they moved, rounded and lurching like living boulders. She'd never been overpowered in such a way, or by so formless a tangle of flesh, crushing her on the ground. She could barely breathe, and for a moment she wondered if she would be suffocated. But just as panic was overwhelming her, he braced as though preparing for something, probed her with his eyes and pressed her hard between the legs, entering her, once and then repeatedly. He was gone, a body moving on her though seemingly unaware of her. She tensed, fearing she would be torn as he leaned in; but finally a spasm loosened the heavy muscles imprisoning her and the pressure in her crotch gave way to an aching dampness. Crouching on her, he gazed away over one shoulder, then reached fumbling for what dangled heavy and subsiding between them.

There was no saying no, anymore; the chance had come and gone. Had she run away when she could, had she refused to succumb, had she hollered aloud . . . From the broad, grassy slope of eucalyptus there rose a pungent, sappy odor, as dampness flowed from her. She reached for her pants, pushing away the hand that advanced once more, as if some show of help could now be made. She hoped for none. Covered once more, she found the jeans no longer offered safeguard or defense, only a second layer of treacherous flesh, abandoned in some jarring change of form and then donned once more, an old covering of weeds and bark and mud.

She longed to be gone, but the man, Johnny, lingered there, an overbearing force or presence that had lodged some demand regarding her, as though she were a parcel of land and he'd come to squat. Throbbing with fear, she wondered how she could unsnarl the day. To go now would reveal how awful the encounter had been for her. And as she'd learned from her father and brother, refusing to cringe or show defeat was half the game; the man would never know how overpowered she'd felt, as long as she refused to show it. And so she glanced over the abandoned slope, wondering tensely what would happen next.

The man rose from the ground on one knee. He would leave; she would be alone. Her thoughts slowed, focused on a random swab of color, a daub over the bay. How she longed to fade off in the sky, leaving the man alone. But there he was, leaning over her as though some force bound them together, as though he would lead on and she would have to follow. She looked away, refusing now to acknowledge the man, though she could feel the gaze on her.

"Come on." The man's tone lacked urgency.

She looked away.

"Are you coming?" he said, still calm, assuming that she would comply.

She glanced up, dismayed, and found a bland absence in the man's eyes, as though nothing had happened. The absence confused her, for there was no possible response—no sense in showing she knew what had happened—when he'd already moved on, called to some other purpose having no bearing on what had passed between them. He had released her; he would go.

"Are you coming?" he repeated in the same toneless manner.

Then she was running hard along the path under warm sun, feeling the grass lashing her shins, wondering why the ground moved so slowly beneath her. She glanced back to see the man leaning on one hand, engulfed in grasses and fronds. As she cleared the head of the path and the stone wall, she nearly stumbled over a small boy pulling a red wagon. Nearby stood a woman, glaring sharply at her. Further on, Alice hauled up, gasping, by a juniper hedge, wondering if her jeans were undone but too scared and ashamed to touch them or look. The boy was crying now, hauling the wagon along as though it were another hand that someone would grab from him. She moved on, fumbling with her jeans; as she moved, something began pounding, heavy and hydraulic. Blood was pounding in her head. She would go now, as fast as she could, before he could come for her.

Marian

MARIAN HAD THE odd sense of having made another chance for herself, for once more she was in a college town dreaming of approaching marriage; and she'd chosen so badly before. Now there would be no danger of that; even so, the memory gnawed at her. Charles was a presence in her; every day there were calls and then weekends together. But the weekdays moved slowly, leaving her hours to brood, hours that were not always governed by the presence of Charles. There was Tom as well, hanging over her world, forcing her to manage her own feelings—hard enough—and then, at any moment, the feelings of one of the children as well. She'd found herself saying far more than she should; so the formulas had grown, ways of saying some things while concealing others, producing one formula for her son, another for her daughter. Anything would be preferable, she supposed, to her own raw feelings. Only the other day—awful to recall—she'd urged her daughter to make sure that any man she married would be appealing to her in bed. As usual, Alice had made no response, had seemingly heard the remark as a reasonable one; but that was no excuse. Marian's thoughts raced back to Tom . . .

One day from the land of aluminum rode forth a man . . .

Oh, if only she and Charles had known years ago! If only they'd understood that they were in love, if only . . . She paused, one hand on the folded towels, warm from the dryer and scenting of soap. They'd been in love, surely, when Charles had been Tom's law-school pal. They'd seen each other frequently enough in those years, and she and Tom had even gone along for several gatherings of Charles's family. That way, she'd had the chance to know them long ago, and now—hard to imagine—she would be one of them. A whole web of connections would be renewed, and she would have her own family, finally—for she'd always been lonely with Tom.

The laundry folded, Marian returned to the living room. Charles loved the baroque and Romantic composers, and she'd found some chamber recordings in the library. Schubert's "Death and the Maiden" was on the phonograph; she longed to hear it once more. As the phonograph turned, there came the mournful, yearning sound of violins: so lovely, following on the raucous heels of all that thudding stuff everyone else so enjoyed.

Without warning, her daughter was in the doorway. Mother and daughter exchanged apprehensive glances. Marian had not anticipated the girl's entrance into the room, eyes wary and wandering, face bearing Tom's flat gaze. Her daughter's appearance was unnerving, long hair tangled, head down, feet bare. Surely she was brooding on the reasons for her father's abandonment—surely that was the problem absorbing her now and for several days past. How long would she go on probing the change, Marian wondered. There had been a long conversation only the day before, with Marian carefully choosing her words, and even so, her daughter had frowned, eyes askance. The danger of her daughter blaming her for leaving Tom had spurred Marian on, and so she'd found herself going over the same ground in a thorough unfolding of her suffering during the marriage to Tom, before Charles had pleased her soul. So far, her daughter seemed oddly unmoved for a girl with much to hope for. Clearly the year following the loss of her father would be a confusing and unhappy one; but, with some encouragement, she would respond to Charles, even as her feelings regarding her father would probably fade. That shift in emotional focus would resolve many problems. In any case, Tom's own encouragement would surely be underwhelming.

"The Schubert is so lovely; it's called 'Death and the Maiden,'" Marian remarked. An unfathomable look passed over her daughter's face, pulling down the corners of her mouth and flattening her eyebrows. Taken aback, Marian paused, wondering what the girl was about to divulge; but as with Tom, there was nothing. Marian forged ahead.

"Charles has played some Schubert for me, and I'm hoping to learn more about the music he admires. That's so important—sharing in the other person's interests."

Her daughter turned away, face clouded, embarrassed by something.

"I do hope you find real companionship someday. It's so important to one's happiness."

As her daughter abandoned the room, Marian heard the throbbing of a cello. There were days when she wondered if she'd been aroused from a bad dream, and how long she'd slumbered. Had she ever been fully living during her years with Tom? There was danger in remembering only unhappiness. Worse, though, was the thought of having loved Tom and seen those feelings change so far, so fast—the danger of losing control. But none of that could be helped now; above all, there would be no mourning for Tom. No force on earth could have compelled her; a new energy drove her toward Charles. There was so much to be done, now and everlastingly, so many things to learn about Charles; for though she'd known him for years, they'd rarely seen one another. She'd always remembered how he stood one evening in the law-school quad, one hand waving a red maple leaf as he argued with Tom—over nothing, she supposed. Now there was something uncanny in the new encounters, both familiar and thrillingly strange.

Once her daughter was in the new school, Joel Cohen's Other Paths, Marian would have the days to herself. No more dreading unhappy hours; now as she thought of Charles, waves of pleasure accompanied each image of the coming weekend, when she would feel the embrace of a man she loved.

Though the faces of her son and daughter resembled Tom's, deadpan and wary, she hoped they would soon respond to Charles, as she had done. Tom would fade . . .

Alice

FROM THE DOORWAY, Alice glared at the wine-colored rug. She was angry with herself for having come down from her room. Wearing cutoff jeans and with her feet bare, she'd wandered down on impulse, resolved to unburden herself about the man who had forced her and sensing that the passing days only made the unburdening harder. Had there been no delay, her mother would have responded with dismay, even fright, but with sympathy as well. Now days had passed and there were no signs of damage, only a churning in her stomach and insomnia. The hour of sympathy had gone. Now there would be probing; maybe Charles would be informed, though who could say? That was hard to imagine, so sharp a betrayal; though it was true—anything could happen.

No, the day was all wrong for what she had to say. If she could only hang on, there would be school. The hours would no longer be dead things; she would have her own world.

chapter two

Alice

THEY PARKED BEFORE the wood-frame facade of Finnish Hall, in West Berkeley, Alice concealing her doubts. Her mother had conjured a charming lodge worthy of the Old World Finns who'd once gathered there, something grander than the weathered siding and heavy doors in the unadorned manner of a large rooming house or workingman's union hall. Nor were there any signs of a school—no lunchroom or playground. But the program was funded by the public schools, and surely Joel was doing what he could. Helen Patterson had found so much through Other Paths, or so the mothers claimed; why shouldn't Alice, too, learn to move around Berkeley freely, or regard an old workingman's club as her school?

Her mother glanced over, as though hoping for signs of enthusiasm. "Well," she began in her soothing manner, "with a man like Joel, you should never rely on appearances; a wonderful teacher could hold classes anywhere. I'm so pleased you'll be having the chance to learn from someone of Joel's competence. Usually such teachers prefer college students, but Joel has chosen you."

Alice glanced up and down, but there was no one around. Feeling confused by so many changes, she was unsure what to hear in her mother's words; Joel was an enigma so far, and she had no way of knowing how the school would go. There was no saying why she was here, though her mother had reasons, of course. In any case, Alice was feeling frayed and in need of space. Things had gone badly in regular school, then she'd found the group on Telegraph Avenue, and finally there was the awful day with Johnny. Here she would be free of Tammy and the other girls; she'd never have to see them or wonder what they would say, if by any chance they heard about Johnny. And maybe she would be camouflaged by her older peers, so her mother would no longer conjure up reasons for alarm. There was nothing so very uncommon in her adventures, she kept telling herself, though unfortunately she'd been early by a couple of years.

"Joel was a philosopher during college. You have a philosophical mind, I've always thought, so that should pose no problem for you. And you're good at math, like your father. Try to remember the good things you have from him."

The reference to her father was unnecessary, thought Alice, who'd managed to forget him all morning.

As her mother resumed, an older boy appeared loping along, singing loudly. He wore an old vest and jumper pants, and long blond curls hung from a formless derby. Waving in one hand as he loped was a large journal or pad, pages slapping one leg in rhythm.

Suddenly her mother was in Charles mode, gazing with approval on the boy. "I suppose that boy is keeping a journal. Young men who carry notebooks usually want to be authors." She hardly paused as Alice flung open the door. "I'm sure that boy—"

The door banged on the curb. "I'm going, Mom." She was clambering free.

"Honey, have a wonderful day," came the soothing response, covering for her jarring departure. "Do you know where to find the bus?"

"Uh-huh."

The older boy had gone through the door of Finnish Hall. She approached the door, hearing the car pull away from the curb. Though it was good to be away from her mother, the presence of the boy made her pause, embarrassed. She waited long enough to be sure he'd passed on, then she hauled open the heavy door and scrambled through as it swung closed, propelling her into a foyer. There she nearly bumped the boy, who was already leaving. Arms flung open and balancing on one leg like Charlie Chaplin, he sprang back, landing spread-eagled on a bench by the wall. He removed the crumpled headgear, bowed to her, and paused, scanning her up and down.

"And who are you?" he demanded. Before she could reply, he announced loudly, "You're early! No one comes before ten!" There came a happy sneer as he rounded the derby over one hand, brushing and shaping it. Then he rose and lumbered through the door, leaning with one arm and lurching from leg to leg. The door slammed, leaving her in the gloomy foyer.

Wondering when the amusing boy would come back, she advanced through an inner door and found herself in a large room housing only a grand piano, old and weatherworn as the hall itself.

The room was cool and shadowy, its high windows facing north. The walls were bare; the floor had been cleaned and shone dully of wax. There were no sounds, only the cawing of crows on the roof. She'd never been in a school alone; but here she was, early, encouraged by a sense of impending connection to search through the place, as something belonging to her. Surely there would be more rooms beyond the here and now.

Propped open in a far corner, the old grand piano gave the room order. Feeling drawn by the piano, she approached and played a chord, then ran through a door and found herself in a redwood-paneled hallway, near some stairs leading up. She'd climbed several steps when a man's voice boomed.

"Come down from there," he commanded as she froze, caught. "Are you here for Other Paths?"

She nodded. The man wore workman's clothes, and though light-skinned, he had African features. Waving her down, he led her toward the rear of the building, where they entered a storage room furnished with a gas stove and a large tub. There was only one window; glancing over, she saw a jumble of classroom desks and a ruddy young man, who was slumped in one of them. Wearing greasy jeans, tangled curls, and a bushy red mustache, he was staring at her as though he'd been aware of her long before she'd entered the room.

Lanky and even older than the boy she'd encountered in the foyer, he rose from the wobbly desk. The image of Johnny rose in her mind; but no—the ruddy young man clearly belonged to the school.

"Come on in. I'm Raymond Connor," he nodded, holding out a hand. "Hey, I'm a teacher," he added, as she held her ground. "But no one's gonna make you shake my hand."

"I knew she'd never shake mine, so I never asked," declared the other. "I'm Jerome," he drawled, "and I was teaching when Ray here was being born."

She heard a merry laugh as another man came through the door. Plump and dark, in a trim Afro beneath a tan fedora, a trench coat, and leather shoes, he resembled Raymond and Jerome in only one way: he, too, seemed to have appeared for duty somewhere other than a school.

"You have no manners, Jerome, man," he teased. "We have a young lady here, and I can see she comes to learn—why, here she comes on Day One and she's even early—and you're gonna welcome her, man, let her know she belongs. Now, young lady," he pursued, "I would love to hear your name."

"Alice."

"Why, that's a lovely name. I'm Reggie Pryor. And I'm so proud to have you here. We have a wonderful day planned, so you should stay around. No runnin' around on your own—do as your mama says, come to school every day. That's the real revolution: learn, baby, learn!" Reggie pumped an arm, while Jerome faded through the doorway.

Though enjoying Reggie's outgoing presence, Alice wondered why he thought she needed a pep talk just to show up. She'd been going to school every day for years. Maybe he assumed she was feeling in such need of "unlearning" that she was in danger of wandering off.

"We have fun here, you'll see," Raymond added. He paused, clearly taking her measure. She found herself feeling uncomfortable. "Everyone here has the same problem as you—bored to death by regular school."

"Oh my, yes," Reggie chuckled.

"But there's no need to be bored here," Raymond assured her, smiling vaguely as though he had some goody up his sleeve. "We can help you learn the things you want to learn. And you'll be in good company. Everyone who comes here wants a change from the status quo in the schools."

She made no response.

"No, not everyone. Some go back," Reggie said sadly. "Some refuse to be free. I say, let them go."

"Yeah, if you're happy at Berkeley High, then you should be there," Raymond added, folding his arms in a posture of command. "But chances are you're here for a reason."

"Oh yes, I'm sure she's here for a good reason," Reggie said, nodding, as Raymond surveyed her. "And may I say, young lady," Reggie added, "I hope to see you in class. I want to hear what you have to say about urban geography."

She was unsure of the meaning. Raymond was smiling as though amused by her. "He means the modern American city— you know, the older urban core and the ring of suburbs—"

"Yes," Reggie beamed, opening his arms for emphasis, "that's what we're gonna rap about. You're here to change the world, not just keep on keepin' on, same old same old. And how are we gonna change things unless we analyze the things we're here to change—how they came to be, what keeps them going, who profits, who gets hurt? Can you help us understand?"

"I guess so," Alice shrugged, feeling growing bemusement regarding how she should respond.

"Good!" Reggie said, laughing. "No being shy, now."

From the large meeting room, there suddenly came a blaring saxophone riff, followed by shouts of male revelry. Amid the clamor could be heard a wavering soprano, singing a Laura Nyro song. *Uptown, goin' down, old life line . . .* Beckoning Alice to follow them, Reggie and Raymond headed through the door of the large room, where young people were bonding and regrouping in surges of enthusiasm, loudly welcoming each other. Among them was the boy from the foyer, now playing a saxophone. Dancing around him was a girl wearing a leotard, clown-face makeup, and a many-colored skirt. Long flowing hair bounced against her hips as she weaved around the boy with the saxophone; her face shone ghostly white, and she had a blue diamond around each eye and a clown's red nose and mouth. The girl seemed older, the same age as most of the boys, some of whom had beards. Alice had imagined blending in; after all, everyone thought she was older than seventh grade. But among the high-school group, she was feeling out of place. Wishing Helen would show up, Alice regarded the dancing girl, wondering where she'd come from, how she'd become so free—if that was the word for her performance. The girl weaved around one boy and then another, engaging in teasing badinage, laughing in a rippling flow of sparrow song. Then when she'd danced long enough around her chosen boys, she abandoned them for Raymond and Reggie.

"Ray! Reggie!" she giggled with theatrical joy. "Other Paths, here in the Finnish Meeting Hall!"

"Maya, welcome back!" Reggie said, applauding.

"What a wonderful place for rehearsals! Me and Manny—we can already feel it. Let's get going!" And there came another ripple of laughter, seemingly spontaneous but maybe just flawlessly performed. As Maya's laughter rose, Manny jumped up on the piano bench and blew a long, honking riff around a submerged melody.

Before long, he was blowing, squealing his way through "The Star-Spangled Banner."

Two boys made a Nazi salute in honor of the anthem, as someone else hollered, "Burn, baby, burn!"

The room had begun pulsing with anarchy as more people came in. There were now forty young people jammed in the large space. Helen came from the foyer, leading a group of girls along the edge of the crowd, passing Alice as though unaware of her presence. The girls looked about her brother's age—early high school—and elegantly hippie, in clean bell-bottoms and scarves and clogs. Helen wore a floppy sombrero; as she pulled it off, mussing her dark mane, Alice had an uncanny feeling—Helen had become a young woman. No longer barefoot and contemptuous, she'd changed her style; like her mother, Sabrina, she had self-assurance, dangling earrings, a woman's casual grace. By comparison Alice, in jeans and sneakers, resembled one of the boys.

Helen's group rushed the teachers, sending up girlish mating calls.

"Ray! Reggie!"

"Welcome back, young lady," Reggie said, grinning, arms open to hug one of the girls, as the others mobbed Raymond. Alice eyed the scene, consumed by feelings of uneasy embarrassment. She was too shy for mobbing male teachers—it hardly seemed normal, even for girls who knew these men. She wondered how soon these people would demand such eagerness from her, as reassurance of her engagement with the group. The school day was becoming an anthropological foray—performances, group bonding, fervor. Or maybe her age was the problem. These people were older, they'd been together for a year; someday she, too, would learn to jump in and feel what she was supposed to feel. Or would she?

Suddenly the place was booming. "Joel! Joel! Joel! Joel!"

The saxophone blared the anthem's closing bars, then hung on a fading blue note. Alice peered along the edge of the crowd. Through the foyer doorway came a plump man with dark curls: Joel had arrived. The man's half-moon eyebrows rose in bashful pleasure as he balanced a large whiteboard panel on the floor. Though she'd seen Joel before, he seemed a stranger as he bubbled with laughter in the warm glow of applause. Then, touching one hand to his pursed and youthful mouth, as though pondering an enigma, he remained for a long moment unmoving, suspended in a sunbeam that landed on one shoulder and draped over the paunch. The clamor ceased.

Joel grasped the panel and made his way through the group to the grand piano. The boy with the saxophone, Manny, clambered down from the bench to make way for Joel, who now rose above the gathering bearing the panel aloft. It was emblazoned with a symbol and the words "Destroy in order to create." Joel wore blanched jeans slung low and cowboy boots, more than ample for the legs that rose from them. Rocking gently to and fro in the boots, he began to speak.

"Wonderful to see everyone," he began. "Other Paths is a large and generous family; each and every one of you belongs among us. We come here to argue, and reject, and learn, and love each other, in all the ways our culture has suppressed—"

"Ooooh, baby!"

"—and we come here to heal from the dead learning of a culture gone mad."

"Dig it!"

Joel paused as the energy flowed, then declared, "Our purpose is: Destroy in order to create! So, yes, we come here to destroy what's bad, or simply no longer useful. Some of you may feel scared or saddened by some of the work we do. But remember: mostly we come here to make something new, something in and of our moment. We come here to learn in and from the Now."

A sound of whooping filled the room, underscored by the swanking of the saxophone. Joel handed the panel to one of the boys. Rocking loosely in the hips, he closed his eyes and began swaying back and forth, thumbs hooked in the jeans. Suddenly Helen passed near Alice; leaning in, she murmured, "Joel's such a phony." Then she sashayed from the room, waving her sombrero. An odor of patchouli hung in the doorway, heavy as Southern magnolia.

The group was already coming undone. Some were heading for the foyer even as Joel resumed; others surged around Joel or one of the teachers, full of eager demands. Raymond was surrounded by several older guys, while Reggie moved around the room, working the floor, laughing and paying compliments to the girls. Jerome was near the door, conferring with a young man. As for Joel, he'd been commandeered by a group of boys of varying ages and vogues. Caught up in the confusion, Alice wandered through the room, wondering where and how to begin.

Helen came from the hallway. Brushing a wave from her temple with careless grace, she surveyed the group around Raymond and then made her move.

"Oh, Ray!" she cried, tossing a wounded glance. "You promised to lend me a book, remember?"

Raymond eyed her. "Oh yeah?"

A black guy clapped a hand on Raymond's shoulder. "Lend me a book, Ray man," he laughed. "Lend me a book, white Jesus, and save me!"

Helen glanced around, curling the wave by her temple and then flipping it over her shoulder.

"What's the book?" Raymond pursued, one hand fingering his bushy mustache.

"You remember, of course you do," she said, pouting. "You know, the one you're always carrying around—the one about Trotsky."

"Which one?"

"Oh, come on, Ray—it's your missionary bible," she taunted.

A gleam appeared in Raymond's eyes as his thumb and forefinger massaged his mustache. Helen held the glance for a moment and then, face aglow from her obscure purpose, dropped him for Joel.

Surrounded by a group of boys, Joel was fully engaged. Several of the boys had an incongruous college look; clean-cut and respectful, they leaned in, hanging on Joel's words. Helen approached and regarded them, biding her time; then in a lull, she caught Joel's eye.

"Welcome back, Helen."

"I'm planning on taking your classes, Joel—all of them."

"Oh?" Joel was nodding soberly. "Last year you were wonderful in the Happenings—"

"Yes, and now I'm ready for more. I want to learn everything."

"That's very eager of you."

"I mean it, Joel. I want you to see me as a real person."

Joel's raucous laugh burbled from the depths.

Now one of Joel's boys placed a hand on Helen's arm, then whispered in her ear. She leaned in, touching the boy's shoulder, and murmured a response before disengaging herself from him and the group. The boy glanced after her as Joel resumed, once again the focus of his eager disciples.

Without warning, Raymond could be heard announcing that the school day was ending, and informing them that they would be choosing classes the following day.

"So, make sure you come by," he commanded.

As he concluded, young people began bounding for the door, joyful at the change of plans. As far as Alice could see, she was the only one left feeling empty-handed by the early dismissal. Soon she was alone in the large meeting room. Why was everyone so eager to leave? The day would be long, and where would she go? There could be no going home now, even before noon. Her mother would be angry—or maybe she would merely resume the endless conversation about Tom and Charles, Tom and Charles . . . Oh no, surely there was someplace else she could go for a few hours.

Wondering what had happened and hoping someone would come back, Alice wandered through the room. There was no singing or saxophone, only the sound of crows cawing on the roof. Maya and Manny had gone off; they had plans, rehearsals, places to go. Even Helen had been unapproachable.

Overcome by uncanny feelings brought on by the echoing room, Alice suddenly remembered the stairway to the upper floors. They'd forbidden her, but now they were gone.

The old grand piano crouched in the corner. Feeling emboldened by a yearning for belonging, she ran over and played a few chords. The sounds rose, giving her courage, then hung in the room before slowly fading. Enjoying her freedom, she passed through the hallway, running her hand along the redwood paneling. There were the steps to the second floor: they seemed to beckon her. She began climbing and soon found herself in an upper foyer, warm and musty, garret-like. Wandering across the scarred wooden floor, she entered a damp room containing only a few books and a large leather trunk. The trunk was peeling with age; the lock had been torn away. Gingerly, she opened the cover.

In the moldy recesses lay a faded gray-green jacket, the color of eucalyptus bark. The cuffs were frayed; the shoulders bore colored insignia, marking it as a military uniform. Under the army jacket was an album of old photographs.

Lifting the album from the trunk, she leafed through a few pages of photographs labeled in an unfamiliar language. There were snowy village scenes, sleighs and dogs and figures leaning against the wind. Then came summer woods, a woman in the grass, a picnic. Turning the page, she saw a cafe table, men in army uniforms. *Were they in Finland,* she wondered; *if so, who were they fighting for?* She thought of Finland as a minor player long under the sway of larger powers. So maybe they'd been fighting under compulsion—but maybe, against the odds, they'd made a grab for freedom. Or maybe they'd fought other Finns.

Her imagination caught by the unknown, she hung the jacket over her arm. Then she made her way down the steps and through the workingman's hall to the street.

When she'd rounded the corner, she paused long enough to pull on the jacket. The sleeves hung loosely over her hands, seeming to offer camouflage. If her mother wondered, she would say she'd found it hanging on a fence.

Continuing along the block, she found herself on the corner of University Avenue, near a barber shop and a liquor store. A bus came and she boarded it. The noonday bus was nearly empty; she took a seat near the door. Motels and car dealerships rolled by as they rumbled through the Berkeley flatlands. Far ahead rose the campus and hills, seeming small and faded, as though in a photograph. Usually they were up close, looming over her house. Slumped in the seat, she began contemplating her morning at Other Paths.

She'd been unprepared for the place and the people—and the strangely free schedule. She was no longer tempted by so much freedom: she was feeling bummed. She would be unlearning, Joel had promised—but what was unlearning? It must involve something more than leaving her to wander for the day. She was through with elementary school and ready for something new. She remembered envying her brother's junior-high schedule, an array of subjects such as biology, algebra, French. Today she'd been eager to get going: choosing a schedule, heading to classes, and hearing new ideas. Her brother had regaled the family during meals; now she would have the chance to regale them—even Charles, who would be coming up from Los Angeles on weekends. But when he asked about Other Paths, she would babble about urban geography, a saxophone player and a dancing clown, Helen and Trotsky and a phony man named Joel.

Her parents assumed she would go to college, but something had happened and the plan had dead-ended. Year after year, she passed the school days in boredom, anger, and growing hopelessness. Now they'd found a hangout for her, a summer camp of fun and games. Maybe these things just happened—parents wandered off. But she'd had enough of random wandering. One way or another, she would have to save herself.

The bus ground to a stop. Beyond the glass lay Shattuck Avenue, a hub of shops and department stores and the Central Library.

Suddenly she remembered her mother coming home one day, face aglow, raving about the library—the humongous card catalogue and boundless rows of books. She ran for the door.

The Campanile bells were pealing noon. Alice approached the library, whose looming sand-colored walls and arched windows could have housed a dozen Finnish Meeting Halls. The foyer was hung with paintings of wealthy donors. Glancing at the men in formal black, she passed through a door to a large reading room lined with towering bookshelves. A long table lay before her. Hearing her footsteps echo through the enormous space, she advanced several yards and grasped a wooden chair. The chair made a loud scraping sound; she sat hardly moving, aware only of the rows of books.

Near the door was a reference desk and a woman in bangs and glasses, working alone. Pausing for a moment, the woman removed her glasses to gaze at the newcomer, then resumed her work. Alice leaned her arms on the table, wondering what to do, as an annoying drone pulsed in her head—aggravating, maddening—murmuring of Tom and Charles, Tom and Charles. It was accompanied by images of Reggie's face and pumping arm; Raymond's hand as he fingered his mustache, grooving to Helen's patchouli; Maya and Manny, dancing girl and saxophone boy; and Joel's paunch and cowboy boots as he rampaged through the room, destroying in order to create. Fingering the frayed sleeve of her foreign army jacket, she suddenly wanted to cry.

Looking around at the shelves, she wondered how she would ever learn enough to escape the churning Now, where everyone in this place was seemingly eager to drown.

In the Now a woman appeared, wearing bangs and glasses. Her eyes had an impish look as they took in the young girl and the old army jacket.

"May I help you?" she asked.

Alice looked up.

"May I help you?" the woman repeated. A cloud passed over her face.

Alice was feeling misgivings. She'd wanted a peaceful place to gather her thoughts, but there would be no chance of that. The woman was leaning close, bearing down on her.

"Are you here for school?" she demanded, her mouth curling in an ambiguous smile as she eyed the army jacket.

"Yes."

"What school are you from? Have you brought your assignment with you?"

"It's called Other Paths," Alice murmured, uncomfortable, hoping the woman would be easily appeased and go away.

"Other Paths?" The woman furrowed her brow. "Never heard of it."

Alice slumped in her seat.

"Well," pursued the woman, "I thought today was the first day of school. Am I wrong?"

"No."

"And you're here."

"Yes."

"Then you should be there—at Other Paths." The woman's eyes had become warm and humorous, as if she'd just heard a marvelous, improbable story and was eager to impart it soon.

Alice squirmed in the chair, wanting to speak. But she only said, "I suppose."

"I'm sorry," concluded the woman. "Then you really shouldn't be here, should you, if they're expecting you on . . . other paths. It's the law, you know." And she peered for a moment at the army insignia on Alice's shoulder before glancing around the humongous room.

"I know," Alice said, her tones echoing oddly. She paused and then forged on, "But they sent us away early."

"Oh?"

"I went this morning. I was early, maybe, because when I got there, no one else was around. Well, I found a teacher—three of them—in a kind of storage room—"

The woman suddenly laughed.

"—and then as we were talking some others came, they were older than me, and one of them, well—"

"Please go on."

"One of them played the saxophone, and a girl in clown face was dancing—there was a lot going on, but when I thought we'd be starting classes, the teacher told us we were through for the day and should come back tomorrow."

"I see," said the woman, furrowing her brow. Alice no longer shrank from the look. "And what were you supposed to do all day?" the woman demanded.

"I'm not sure. Maybe—" But the morning's fervor had no reasonable sequel. "Just have fun, I guess," she concluded, though the idea sounded improbable.

"I see." The woman glanced at her, as though turning something over in her mind. "You could go home, you know. Maybe that would be best." As she spoke a smile warmed her face, erasing her words.

"No, please," murmured Alice. Then pulling herself together, she added, "I really can't. There's always Tom and Charles, Tom and Charles—"

"And they are—?"

"Tom is my father. My mother plans to marry Charles."

"I see."

"My mother has an awful lot to say about them both."

"I can imagine." The woman laughed loudly. "Well," she went on, "you're enrolled in school, it seems. So maybe you should spend the afternoon here. I could show you how to search for books—you know, the card catalogue and all."

"That would be very good of you."

"Come, I'll show you around, and then if you think of something you'd like to read, I can help you find it." She paused and held out her hand. "Call me Fernwood. And your name?"

"Alice."

"Welcome to the Central Library, Alice."

They shook hands.

Fernwood led her toward the stacks of books. "What do you read?"

"I've been kind of busy."

"Tom and Charles?"

"Well, and other things—"

"You need something to do, I can see," Fernwood observed. "But where shall we begin?"

"I used to read *Lord of the Rings*."

"Oh yes, everyone reads that. Hmmm . . . do you enjoy adventure books, then?"

"I'm not sure . . . yes, I suppose." Alice really had no idea what she wanted to read.

"And how old are you? I've been trying to guess."

"Seventh grade."

Fernwood frowned. "I imagined you were older. Hmmm . . . I'll round up some books, then, and you can choose." She moved off through the stacks, pausing now and then to pull something from a shelf. As soon as she had an armload of books, she returned to the table. "Have a look through these." Then, as she turned to go, "I assume you're planning to come back?"

"Yes."

"Good. If there's something you want to see again, I can hold it for you at the reference desk."

"Thank you."

Fernwood returned to her work. Alice reached for the books; on top was a magazine. She opened to the cover story, on the war, and began reading. The page blurred before her eyes. She had assumed she would be in school—now, it appeared, she would be on her own. There were many things to study—or so she'd heard. But she knew only the words: algebra, chemistry, French. She'd learned some French phrases, but only a few, and how would she continue on her own? She'd never seen a book for learning languages. She glanced over at Fernwood, who was busy sorting a stack of index cards; she would inquire tomorrow. And she'd always been good at math —Joel Cohen would teach math, her mother had promised. She would see about that.

When she reached home, she ran to her room and hung the Finnish army jacket deep in the closet, where her mother would never go. Maybe that was the problem: like the Finns, she'd always been caught up in someone else's fight. From now on, she would be fighting for herself.

OTHER PATHS HAD an unbalanced core, formed around Joel, Raymond, and amorphous groups of students. A class schedule appeared, but the classes had odd names—Philosophy of Games; Randomness and the Unconscious; Race Rap; Urban Survival— and none of Joel's staff had done much teaching before coming to Other Paths. Moreover, each class gathered weekly for only two or three hours, following a college plan—or so her mother announced when shown the weekly schedule, her face aglow as though she and her daughter would now be sharing a source of pleasure and power. Coming from her mother's glow, Alice was dismayed to see Joel, Reggie, or Jerome showing up for class and then hurrying away, like roguish uncles, in the company of a chosen young person or two, leaving Raymond to play camp counselor. The regular school would have more going on, but her mother had chosen Joel's newfangled program, and Alice had her own reasons for going along. The place seemed safe, at least, and she'd had enough of being harassed. Even so, there were days when she had nothing to do, and Other Paths had no reading room, only a girl who slumped in the foyer with a book. Alice found herself dropping by the school in the morning, in case something was happening, then passing a few hours in the Berkeley library.

During the early days, Alice clung to hopes of Joel, though he always seemed to be conferring with older students, sharing a sly camaraderie. Only by demanding something specific would she engage him, she concluded. And so one day, finding him alone in the large meeting room, she crossed the room and asked if she was old enough for the math class he offered.

"Old enough?" he asked softly. "Why are you asking me?"

"Because I'm only in seventh grade," she responded.

"And so?" Joel's eyes surveyed her, unimpressed.

"And so I'm wondering—"

"Yes, I see. But why are you asking me?"

"I don't know," she said, feeling she was annoying the Big Man.

"Because you're the one who has to choose. Do you understand?"

"Yes."

"Good." Joel paused. "If you want to see if you're ready, come to class. Then you can choose. But I'm not choosing for you."

Alice wondered if she'd just had a lesson in unlearning. Maybe—or maybe Joel was more like her father than he seemed. Though he was unimpressed by her, she could deal with that. She would call him on his bluff.

Joel's math class assembled on Wednesday mornings in a small wood-paneled room. The group around the large table had less hippie glamour than Maya, Manny, or some of the others; they were Joel's club of older boys. For a moment, Alice thought of leaving: the group was clearly over her head. But before she could go, Helen came through the door in a purple bandana, her moody energy zapping the room just as Joel appeared.

Soon Alice understood why Joel had been so casual about her level. He spoke eagerly, though incomprehensibly, about concepts and symbols she'd never heard of before, but there were no numbers or equations. Nor would there be any way of measuring her progress: there, as well, he was leaving things up to her. Having nothing to lose, she chose to stay and see what would develop.

One day Joel introduced a class project: designing a new Happening, to be known as "Asylum." Modeled on a game, but occurring as a real event, the Happening would be performed in the streets according to rules designed for Berkeley, Chicago, or Paris. Peopled by cohorts of hippies, cops, and workingmen, it would include pop-up performers empowered to transform the rules mid-game by formulating a few changes and then announcing them to a chosen cohort. The other performers would then have to deduce the changes from the cohort's subsequent moves.

Joel had a plan—he was teaching them to change the rules and choose for themselves. But as he lay the groundwork, Alice's thoughts caught on numbing images: the group on Telegraph Avenue, drugs, her defeat by Johnny. Had she chosen those experiences? Or had they chosen her? And once such things had happened, how could she unlearn them?

As she pondered the day with Johnny—he was the real reason she was here, that much was becoming clear to her—a boy waved one arm, ending her jagged daydream. Small and sharply wound, one of the younger boys in Joel's group, he had brown, sun-bleached curls and John Lennon glasses. "I remember learn-ing to play chess," he announced, leaning over the table's scarred wood surface. "I learned from my older brother. But there were some rules he never told me, and so we'd be there, playing a game, and suddenly he'd do something I had no idea could be done. And I would be, 'Man, you just cheated,' and he would be, 'Oh wow, maybe you were high and just forgot.'"

The group laughed. Joel nodded. Alice remembered how annoyed she'd been when her brother played that way with her.

"So, what I wanna say is—how do you know if they're per-forming a new rule or if they're just cheating? You dig?"

Joel was nodding joyfully; the boy had clearly scored. "Oh yes, Andy, I can dig. You're bringing up something important: When do we have a real change of rules, and when do we just have cheating? How can we know a game changer from a fraud?"

They change the rules on you—sure, they're cheating, thought Alice. She remembered how her father had probed, demanding that she remember facts and rules—but that was long ago. In Washington, the number of congressmen had seemed worth knowing; now Congress was a phantom player in a faraway game, while the real odds were unfolding here. Johnny had trampled her; he'd changed everything. She'd been taught rules, but now the game was to break them. She wandered among wolves.

In the glow of Joel's encouraging gaze, Alice remembered how she'd seen Valerie that day, before Johnny had found her. She'd been looking for someone familiar when the boy had come along and duped her . . . She could feel her face blushing with shame. If only she could go where no one would see her; but an older boy—he was named Jonathan, and he wore a pony tail—glanced over. Why was she always feeling caught?

Joel leaned on the wood and pumped, as though engaged in some form of pushup or maybe a summoning of the dead. "Well," he pursued, pondering aloud, "let's consider chess for a moment. Do we know all the rules of play?"

"We could find them—they're in a book," Andy responded. "I know, 'cause I had to go and read them."

"And what happens when someone changes them?"

"You mean my brother?" Andy paused. "No, man, you don't understand. He never changed the rules—he just never told me some of them."

"So, one day you found a book and read them for yourself."

"Damn sure. And he never won another game."

Helen leaned back and gave a mocking cheer: "Go, Andy!" Then she unbound her purple bandana and began rumpling her hair.

Joel pursed his mouth and gazed around the room. "Now let's ask: When are there rules for changing the rules?"

Another pause followed. Jonathan, the boy who'd caught Alice blushing, spoke up. "In sports. You know— rules change in overtime, or when there's bad weather, or . . ."

"Good." Joel nodded slowly around the room, letting the insight seep in. "Now, let's go back to our Happening. Someone changes the rules—are they cheating?"

Helen folded her arms. "No, as long as they're changing the rules the way we say they can. As long as they're not like Andy's jerky brother."

One of the older boys laughed. Helen eyed Joel, hoping for a nod from the Big Man, but Joel changed gears.

"Let's move on," he suggested. Helen's hand went up.

Joel frowned. "If you have something more to say, then go ahead, Helen," he responded coolly. "But no hand-waving here, remember?"

"I forgot," Helen sighed. "Never mind."

Joel folded his arms and paused. They were unlearning hand-waving, Alice concluded.

"Oh, just go on," Helen groaned.

Joel resumed. "Let's take up something more real than chess —let's make some rules for the Berkeley performance."

Alice could sense a change in Helen's mood. She glared around, flamboyantly bored, as some of the boys began by re-calling the People's Park days. Then Andy jumped in.

"Okay, so in the Happening we're gonna occupy some land."

"Where?" someone demanded.

"Anywhere. Who cares?"

Helen scoffed, "Hey, Andy's got his own commune some-where."

"Maybe," Andy shrugged, undaunted. "But anyway, here's my idea. Once we've got our land, we can choose a pop-up performer. I say we choose Helen—that way she won't be so moody. Then she can take some LSD and change *all* the rules."

"Andy, you're so lame."

"You're just mad because Joel's ignoring you."

"Oh, please."

"Let's go back," Joel said calmly. "The group is occupying some land—and you're empowering one performer to change all the rules. But when you have so many rule changes, no one can figure out—"

"Exactly. That's my idea."

"But that's anarchy." Joel paused, contemplating. Then he gave a joyful nod. "Very good!"

When the class ended, it was nearly noon. Andy and Helen announced they were heading for the campus. Off they ran, leaving Alice alone with Jonathan.

"Fences are for jumping," Jonathan remarked, perusing Alice with steady gray eyes. He had the clean, regular features of a handsome older boy. "Helen and Andy are busy changing the rules. How about you?"

"Not sure."

"No?" He paused. "You say that a lot."

She wondered how he could know. They'd never spoken before.

"We could go to the campus ourselves," he proposed, scanning her face for signs of interest. "Unless you know of something better to do."

"I'm going to the library." She was glad to have found a response. She would enjoy having someone to hang out with, but the boy's presence made her nervous.

"The what?"

"The library."

"That's what I thought I heard. Just wanted to make sure." He let forth a moody, languorous sigh. "Wow, you had me fooled." He paused. "So, how come you're here?"

"For school," she shrugged.

"Other Paths—school?" Jonathan leaned in, amused. "You sure seem young," he murmured. "Well, have a good time reading." And then he turned to go.

For a moment she stayed in the foyer alone, wondering what other response she could have made. Helen would have found something more to say—where had she learned that? And what of Andy? Maybe he was one of the group that gathered at Joel's house on Parnassus Road. There were rumors of the classes Joel held there—surely he had a role in the school beyond the rare appearances at Finnish Hall. Many days, she'd heard, he was happening in another place, on another schedule. Some of the older boys had a passageway to Joel, an open door for them alone on Parnassus Road.

That afternoon, when Alice entered the Central Library reading room, Fernwood was nowhere to be seen. Above the door hung a large clock: nearly one o'clock. Alice roamed the shelves, opening math books, searching for something she could comprehend. One book used unfamiliar symbols; another had spheres and graphs. Wondering how she could learn what they meant, she opened the book to the beginning and began to read.

Suddenly Fernwood appeared by her shoulder.

"I see you've found something new," she remarked, leaning over the page.

Alice held up the cover. Fernwood frowned, as usual; the frown expressed thought rather than annoyance. "That's a college math book," she observed. "You can look, of course, but you may not be ready for it. What kind of math do they have you doing over at . . . over at that other path?" Fernwood was forever mangling the name of Joel's school.

They had learned something today, Alice thought, wondering how to convey the Happening.

"You do have math?"

"Oh, yes, Joel had math today."

"Algebra, I would imagine. Usually that comes before . . . what do you have there? Oh yes—advanced calculus."

Fernwood was playing dense on purpose, Alice supposed.

"No, we made up a game—a Happening."

"What fun. Do tell me."

"Well, you can choose Berkeley or Chicago or Paris. There are performers and pop-up players—the pop-up players can change some rules and then everyone else has to figure out the new rules."

"Hmmm. Sounds like a playground gang. And was there an object to the game?"

"Um, occupying land and . . ." Alice was searching for a response. "Changing the rules, maybe, so the others are stumped. Then you can win."

Fernwood frowned, unamused. "I see." She was glaring, though not at Alice. "And where does the math comes in?"

"There are rules for changing the rules—otherwise you're just cheating. And sometimes too many rules change—for example, when a pop-up performer takes LSD and changes all the rules . . ." Alice gulped; she'd revealed too much. "Joel says that's a bad game, because when all the rules change, no one can figure them out."

"True enough." Fernwood glanced slyly at Alice. "You have a brother, I suppose."

"Uh-huh."

"I thought so." She frowned once more. "Come, we'll find you an algebra book." And she led the way along the shelves.

THE FOLLOWING WEDNESDAY, when Alice showed up for Joel's math class with a graph of $3x + 4y = 12 + 7y$, she learned that the class had been canceled. Coming from the hallway, Jonathan informed her that rehearsals for the upcoming Happening would now be convening on Mondays. Alice was annoyed by the impromptu change; the morning had barely begun, and she would have nothing to do. Jonathan's gray eyes engaged her; he was more handsome than she'd remembered.

"Another library day?" he inquired, coming up close.

"Maybe. They open at noon."

"Man," he sighed, whistling softly, "you even know the schedule. That's sad." And he went off, humming the opening bars of "Eleanor Rigby."

She'd heard rumors about the school's Happenings: the year before, they'd gone shopping in clown face and made merry among the women shoppers, until someone complained and the manager banned them from the store; they'd appeared in a film. Even so, day after day nothing much happened at Other Paths. Pondering where Joel could be, she wandered toward the hallway.

Jonathan was there, still humming "Eleanor Rigby." Leaning in as she passed, he murmured in a cajoling tone, "How come you're always ignoring me?" He was handsome, maybe, but he was becoming annoying. She was blushing when Raymond came from the foyer.

Raymond paused by the door, purring, "Jonathan, my man." Then he glanced over and added encouragingly, "I'm glad you're having some fun, Alice." Jonathan laughed and moved off. She found herself alone in the gleam of Raymond's eyes.

She was suddenly angry. Though Jonathan seemed harmless enough, he'd made her remember the hassling at her old school —and was she imagining things, or was Raymond joining in? A song pounded in her head—the only things she remembered these days, it seemed, were songs and songs and songs . . . Raymond hung in the doorway regarding her, and she wondered if he was surveying her and judging her as too aloof.

Raymond fingered his mustache. "I see you know Jonathan," he commented.

Confused by Raymond's purpose, she held back. There was a comradely tone in the remark, a suggestion of brotherly warmth, but she refused to play along. After all, he was supposed to be a teacher.

"Not really."

"Oh? Then who are your pals?"

She shrugged. Raymond leaned there in old jeans, unlaundered and greasy; he had gnarled, tangled hair, like moss from some dry riverbed. Though he seemed useless as a teacher, her mother had endorsed Other Paths. And so every morning she appeared in the abandoned foyer of Finnish Hall, as though sure school would be happening.

"Hey, I'm no enemy. But you've been here a month already, and no one knows you." Raymond assumed a teacherly tone. "You should hang around more, be more involved. We have some cool people here. Have you met Manny?"

She was feeling too ashamed and confused to respond.

"You know, the guy who plays saxophone? You must have seen him."

"Oh, yeah."

"He's gonna be the new John Coltrane. And he came to Other Paths because we agreed to work with him, let him learn what he wanted. So he's learning about wind instruments, rehearsing a final project with a band."

Though impressed, she had no thought of playing a saxophone.

As though reading her mind, Raymond went on. "Maybe you don't play saxophone, but you probably do something. So all I'm saying is, hang around and find what's happening that you can be part of."

356 | *playground zero*

Several older girls appeared from the foyer: Helen and her group, followed by Maya. Helen's group usually showed up for Raymond's classes. Maya, the clown from the opening day, dropped in only for Joel; other days, she was busy dancing. She found her pals among the boys.

Over the heads of the others, Maya piped up, "Hi, Raymond."

"Hey."

"Where's Joel?"

"He canceled."

"That's so Joel," she laughed. "He's on Parnassus Road, then." Maya glanced around, barely nodding to the others, then floated off, leaving them with Raymond. Confused by Maya and her easy freedom, Alice began feeling a growing anger at Joel.

Raymond gazed around at the older girls. "Hey, we're starting in a few minutes." They wandered through the doorway to the large room. Then he turned to Alice. "Maybe you should come to my class today—Race Rap. Or do you have something else to do?"

She shrugged.

"Hang around then—you should be in class. Ten-thirty, in there." He nodded toward one of the small rooms. "Oh, and on Friday, some of us are going to San Francisco—my Urban Survival class. You should come."

Though she was unsure of Raymond, he was the only one there.

A few minutes later, the class began. They had been meeting for a month already; Alice was the newcomer. Raymond's rap soon focused on Other Paths, as he harangued them for forming separate groups, white and black. Alice remembered her old school, but she no longer blamed herself for these problems.

Helen glanced at Raymond as he spoke. "But Ray—"

"No, let me finish. You guys seem to feel you've done the hard work merely by coming to Other Paths. Then everyone finds a group of people just like themselves, where they feel safe."

"That's not true, Ray—"

"Just a moment, Helen—you'll have your turn. Now, is there anyone here who honestly feels you've done what you should to reach across the color line at Other Paths?"

"Ray, I'm not sure why you're blaming me for every bad thing that happens here."

"I'm not blaming anyone, Helen. I want us to look at the problem and start dealing."

"You're saying I do nothing to reach out, and that so unfair."

Raymond leaned back, arms folded, and gazed around. "I want everyone to look around the room."

Alice exchanged an uncomfortable glance with a nearby girl. "Who do you see?"

Andy responded, "I see Helen and Don and Becky and—"

"Unh-unh, you know what I mean."

Helen tossed her head and leaned back, suppressing a laugh. Her eyes flashed at Raymond.

Raymond's face had gone red. "C'mon, someone has to acknowledge the ugly truth."

Alice was annoyed by the game Raymond was playing, censuring them for the absence of black students in a class he'd arranged. Wondering why she should care, and emboldened by a growing outrage, she responded, "Everyone in the room is white. So what?"

Raymond pressed on with the program. "And why has no one of color chosen to be here?"

Andy perked up. "Maybe you're unpopular, Raymond."

"Good. And what else?"

Andy shrugged. "A lousy dancer?"

There was laughter.

Raymond massaged his mustache. "Anyone else—any thoughts?" He paused and then flung the gauntlet. "Let me reframe. Darryl Saunders and Greg Jackson turned down the class. I want to know why. What happened?" The glance was clearly accusatory.

"Oh, Ray, of course they—," Helen began, but Andy interrupted her.

"You asked them to come?"

"I pleaded with them. Darryl was just here. Then he cut out."

"Wow. Something really gnarly must've come up."

"No, Andy, it's not only about them."

Darryl was a handsome, swaggering boy—and he'd blown Raymond off. Alice was amused, but then Raymond eyed her as he fingered a pen.

"Who knows Darryl?" he demanded.

Andy leaned forward, fingers drumming on the table. "He's enrolled at Other Paths. And he's some heavy dude."

"When have you hung out with him—ever?"

"Naaah, he's too cool for me—knows I'm a punk."

"Anyone else? Who hangs with Darryl, Greg, Clarence, Anita?"

"I see them every day," Helen said, "usually on the front steps."

"And what do you know about Clarence?"

"I saw him nodding off," murmured Helen. She lay her head on the table and closed her eyes.

Andy thought for a moment, tapping the wood with a pen. "Clarence . . . You mean the lanky dude with the big 'fro?"

Raymond slammed one palm on the table. "You're here every day—and no one knows Clarence? Man," he nodded, red-faced, "I used to be just the same—absorbed in my personal world, unaware of how anyone else was living." Raymond raked a hand through his gnarled hair. "That's enough for today," he summed up. "I hope you'll have more to say next week." Shuffling the papers that lay unused on the table, he rose, faced them down for a moment, and then strode from the room.

As the room cleared out, Alice was savoring her anger. Raymond's performance had been unreasonable—so unreasonable that it was freeing. She owed Raymond nothing; she'd come here for school, not a harangue. Even so, she blamed Joel as much as Raymond. Joel was the Big Man; Joel was why she was here.

Soon enough she would be gone.

A DOZEN STUDENTS crowded around a long oak table in one of the side rooms of Finnish Hall. Joel breathed deeply, closed his eyes for a moment, and let the words flow.

"Today we're going to try a thought experiment. Let's imagine we no longer want to speak of ourselves as objects in uniform space-time. That's how our modern Western languages teach us to see and represent the world, using a subject-verb-object grammar that gives us a subject-verb-object model of the world. 'You do something to me.' 'I do something to her.' But as we know from quantum physics, we can't fully understand the world through the dead mechanics of Newton. The real world—revealed to us by modern physics—is eternal movement, indivisible into separate objects or essences. There's no way to cleave one part from the larger movement and regard it as an object—a thing or essence—unless we're willing to generate a fragmented and therefore false model of the world. 'You do something to me' and 'I do something to her' are poor models for what really happens. And so, to speak truthfully about the world, we need a language that truly represents the world. Something along the following lines: Happening is; and happening encompasses us all. There are no doers, objects, observers—only unfragmented movement that our modern language represents through false categories, such as 'you' and 'I.'

"Now, we can imagine a language in which happening is primary. In Hebrew, for example, the root forms of many words are verbs; these verbs can generate nouns, adverbs, adjectives. By contrast, our modern English has many words that are simply nouns—things are often primary. 'Japan bombed Pearl Harbor.' We have our nouns: Japan and Pearl Harbor. Our grammar tells us that the happening belongs to Japan, the subject, the doer. Then we have the deed performed and who was impacted. Finally, we have a name for the whole: 'the attack on Pearl Harbor.' But how can we make movement primary? How can we speak of happening in terms of the whole—happening that involves the whole world, not just the big guns that conquered other big guns?"

Andy looked up, staring at Joel and then around the room. He leaned forward, ready to speak, wagging a finger in the air.

"Andy? You have something you want to say?"

In the pause Alice compared the sentences "Andy is speaking" and "Speaking is happening." She wondered why it was always Andy who had something to say.

"That's okay, Joel . . . you finish."

"Any one of us can speak here, Andy, you know that. We're no longer playing the permission game—we've given that up."

"Okay then." Andy removed his glasses and leaned back, forearms on the table, fingers drumming on the wood. "Are you saying—these are my own words—but are you saying . . . For example, me and my girlfriend, we're really getting it on." He paused, fingering the glasses, then plowed on. "And what's really happening is: fucking is happening."

"Go, Andy."

The cheer came from a bearded boy who leaned back, hands laced behind his head. Alice was feeling uncomfortable.

"I mean, maybe I could say, 'I'm fucking her,' but there's a truer way of speaking. There's both of us; fucking is happening."

Joel nodded encouragingly. "Yes, Shakespeare had a real insight when he referred to sex as 'making the beast with two backs.'"

The bearded boy laughed. Alice glanced at Andy's boyish body—was he joking? She could feel her face turning red.

"So," reasoned Andy, struggling with an idea, "in the new language we can say what's happening, but leave out the 'me me me—'"

Helen groaned. "You should try it, Andy."

"Oh man, she's so rude," Andy responded in an undertone.

"Let's try what Andy's suggesting." Joel turned with a flourish to the movable blackboard and, forming square capitals one by one, produced the word "bonding." Then he moved away. "Let's use the prompt to speak of happening—get away from the 'me me me' and focus on the whole, the happening. Remember, we're rejecting the dead forms and learning to think in a new way."

Alice was ready; she could use words and would have something to say on paper. Rustling began as the class searched for pens; then the rustling ceased. Through the window, Alice could see swaying branches, red leaves—a plum tree.

Bonding. Her mother and Charles had taken them to Spenger's Fish Grotto, near the harbor. They'd gone for fish and chips, and Charles had enjoyed the lobster tanks and the sawdust on the floor. She'd been wearing sandals and could feel the sawdust on her feet . . .

She wrote the word "bonding," but nothing came to mind. Then to her dismay she remembered a scene having no place in her day—a happening that had unfolded in the girls' bathroom of her old school. She was in the bathroom during lunch hour, examining a red blot on her underwear. Here was something new—though she'd heard such things would happen, she was unprepared. She pressed her thumb on the dampness, as though for fingerprinting; it came up covered in red swirls. A musky odor rose and hung among the common bathroom smells, the sharp reek of urine and ammonia rising from the floor and walls. Pulling some paper from the dispenser, she rubbed uselessly at the blood. There would be more during class. Feeling baffled by the new problem, she wondered what to do.

From the playground came the sound of boys arguing, then a girl came running in, feet thumping loudly. The girl would leave soon enough, Alice thought, and she would figure out what to do. For several moments the other made no sound. Then, sensing something near her feet, Alice glanced down and saw a boy's head coming through the space under the door, face peering up. Prone on the damp floor, one shoulder jammed in the gap beneath the door, a black guy was ogling her and her bloody underwear. There was no hope of eluding the boy: his face lay at her feet, daring her to respond. She made a move with one leg and he jerked away, reappearing in the other corner of the stall. No longer pausing, she pressed her sandal on the boy's head and shoved. For a moment he shoved back, before surrendering and fleeing. The sounds faded; she was alone . . .

She could have stomped the boy's head, but she'd controlled herself. Now she was simmering mad as she remembered. Joel would condemn her for having such feelings.

On Joel's blackboard, new words had appeared: "confide" and "crave." She heard one of the girls laugh; the others were scribbling. On the paper before her, the word "bonding" refused to happen, as if marooned. She added "plum trees," then "seagulls" and "blood." She thought for a moment and wrote "weeds" and "fingerprint"—things rather than happenings. Frustrated, she turned the paper over and looked around the table. The bearded boy slouched, hands laced behind his halo of curls.

Joel looked up. "Are we ready? Yes, Don?"

The bearded boy leaned forward, reading from the page he'd covered in a sloping scrawl. "Some of us are occupying the land; we're being pressured by the cops. We're bonding—with the land, with others in the group. We've got bombs, in case the cops come in, and all around, unseen by the enemy, there's a larger group harboring us. We're holed up in the woods, up in Mendocino or maybe Canada—"

"There's some incredible forest in Mendo," Jonathan said.

"Yeah, Mendo. My band is playing in a redwood canyon—"

"So amazing—"

"Yeah, the sound is happening. There's a group of us, men and women. We're getting it on in the forest—"

"Oh wow," Andy yelped, "an orgy!"

"Yeah, group bonding—"

"Let's hold that thought." Joel was pacing, his face in his hands, contemplating. "Here's the problem," he announced. "You're describing a closed group—what I would call a perverse group. Closed groups come together for refuge, for self-defense; they can become rigidly authoritarian. But when we think in terms of happening, we're dissolving rigid boundaries. What would bonding mean if we were to see it as happening?"

Helen jumped in. "A bay—water flowing in and out—a refuge, but open. Pearl Harbor—bombs—and soon there are waves everywhere. World war."

Don was drumming his fingers on the table in a syncopated beat as she spoke. "Man, that's so crazy."

Joel held up one palm. "Someone always has bombs, and someone else can always respond with more bombs. But we're not looking for world war. How can we respond to bombs—waves of sudden change—in an open way? How can we use the energy for building our world? We can run away, as you say, Don; but we can choose another way—we can use the enemy's energy for new purposes."

"Wow!" Andy exclaimed. "Destroying and creating—that's what's happening!"

"Yes, and from the crumbling old order, we can use the happening to organize our own imagining of the future."

Alice was looking through the window at the plum tree. In the pause she heard a car passing along a nearby street, and then the warbling of a bird. From the beginning, the class had made her uneasy. Bombs; sound and orgy; closed, open, and perverse groups; the crumbling old order: here was a vocabulary for ideas she'd never imagined. The others were older; they thought in terms that were beyond her. She would understand someday, she supposed, unable to imagine a metamorphosis that would prepare her for an orgy in a redwood grove. The thought was appalling. What were her father's words? "They have to learn these things." No, there would be no telling Fernwood, much less her mother—even in the moments between Tom and Charles, Tom and Charles.

As the class was breaking up, Joel proposed in a sly tone that they read something for the following week. "You can learn so much about the closed group, the perverse group, by reading some of the family case studies in R. D. Laing," he said, holding up a copy of Laing's *Sanity, Madness and the Family*. "You have the book —I gave you Laing, along with Sartre's *No Exit*, right? Well, the family is a wonderful model for understanding the perverse group."

"That's for sure," Andy agreed. "What do we read?"

"I want you to choose one family and read the case history."

"Are any of them like my family?"

"That's for you to say," Joel responded. "I don't know your family. But Laing shows us how a family can become a perverse group—rigid and authoritarian, unable to accept members who refuse to conform. I want you to tell me what that means and how it compares with what you've seen in your own family."

Helen announced, "'Happy families are all the same; every unhappy family is unhappy in a different way.'"

"Who says?" Andy demanded.

"Me."

"I thought it was Trotsky."

"Oh, Ray gets everything wrong," Helen scoffed. Then she added, "Just be glad you come from an unhappy family."

Alice wandered from the room, passing through the heavy doors of Finnish Hall and along the block. Even when she'd wandered off, her parents had made no moves beyond sending her to Joel. Now Joel was offering a Happening, a performance made from the ashes of her life.

She heard the sound of someone running.

"Hey!" Helen caught up. "I'm so glad we're out of there, aren't you?"

"I guess."

Helen shook her head. "Joel's such a phony. Last year we were doing Happenings every week, on our own. We went to supermarkets, department stores, a bank—we were nearly charged with trespassing!"

"Oh?"

"Yeah. And hey—we were even in a film!"

"I know." Alice had heard the rumors.

"Even if Joel's a phony, he has contacts everywhere." Helen tossed her head. "That's why I hang around—I want to be in another film. It's worth putting up with Ray, don't you think?"

Alice was feeling jealous—she'd missed something after all.

"What was the film?"

"Oh, something about a free school, of course. The producer was begging Joel for help. So we drove to L.A. and spent a week in the studio." Helen eyed her. "I bet you've never even seen a film studio."

Alice shrugged.

"Well, you can come see the film with us when it opens."

THE FOLLOWING WEEK, when Joel's rehearsal class for the Happening convened, slyly and knowingly he commanded a dozen young people to spread themselves on the floor, eyes closed, and imagine an asylum. He droned on in a soothing, hypnotic tone, as the room settled down, troubled only by breathing and the barely heard sound of cars on the avenue. Wearing the Finnish army jacket she'd found, Alice lay on the floor, hands on her stomach, feet splayed, her head angled uncomfortably on the hard surface as runaway thoughts flooded her mind. Johnny's figure flashed before her, captured somehow, like a man jumping a fence only to be caught in the rungs. She pushed the image away.

She sensed a presence near her shoulder, as though a hand lay there. Fingering the frayed cuff of the army jacket, she was becoming absorbed in the smooth cloth, worn by use and years, when her face tingled, unexpectedly, reminding her of grasses and fronds and Johnny's tangled hair. Her eyes opened: there lay the others, eyes closed, breathing evenly. Nearby sprawled another girl, unmoving and serene, hands open on the floor. The girl's easy abandon revealed how tense Alice was—and so she would appear to Joel, for surely her feelings were conveyed by every movement. If only she could calm herself.

There came the sound of Joel's murmur, close and fatherly. "You're in an asylum; you can choose any madness, just so long as you make the madness happen—now, here, in the room among everyone. The moment comes when everyone chooses one or another way." Joel paused, laughing. "'That way madness lies.' Now—choose your way and open your eyes!"

The others were already moving and happening. Alice rose, having found nothing she would choose and unable to purge her mind, as the others appeared to have done. Uncomfortable revealing herself to them, she was ashamed of her body, her way of moving, her boy's clothing. Helen paced the room, proclaiming a loud and rambling monologue about an imaginary lover. Andy and another boy argued in threatening tones, while one of the girls scolded them as if they were preschoolers.

"Learn to share, boys!"

Andy snarled and grabbed at the other's sleeve.

"Naughty boy! Come to Mommy!"

Hoping for a few moments to conjure some form of madness she could safely perform, Alice moved to a corner of the room.

Soon Andy appeared, hanging on her shoulder, laughing and raving and passing one hand over her face. The girl followed.

"Bad boy! Learn to share!"

Andy was now grabbing at Alice's clothing; angered, she pushed him away, but he held firmly to her arm. As they tussled, the girl wandered off, mumbling, "Oh bad, naughty!" Maya passed by, applauding and laughing; she had brought face paint and now proposed coloring Alice's face. Andy ran off, jabbering loudly.

"Close your eyes," Maya commanded. "Who are you?"

" . . . "

"What face do you want? Are you happy or sad?"

" . . . "

"Some of both, maybe. Are you a clown?"

"No."

Maya laughed. "Then what? I have to know what face to make."

"A monkey."

"Why a monkey?"

"Dunno."

"Maybe because you're watching everyone, but you never say much."

Maya worked with ease. Around them the madness unfolded apace, but the makeup now offered a screen—a one-way mirror—through which Alice could observe the gathering. Suddenly Joel approached; it was as though he'd never really seen her before. He was peering at her jacket.

"You found it in a thrift shop?" he asked, leaning to examine the collar.

"Yes," she lied.

Joel nodded joyfully. "From the Red Army!" he exclaimed.

As he spoke, there came the sound of breaking glass. They looked over to see Andy waving a chair, ready to smash another window of Finnish Hall.

chapter three

Alice

RAYMOND'S FADED BLUE Volkswagen van was hauling over the Berkeley hills toward the eastern reaches of San Francisco Bay. Early on a Saturday morning in February, the beginning of a three-day weekend, Other Paths Open Academy was beginning a winter retreat. For months Joel had been promising how, in March, the school would finally have a permanent home in a new space, a former warehouse near San Pablo Avenue. Then came the snag: the new home would be delayed, and the school would have weeks—maybe a month—of wandering. And so, as a way of preparing for the temporary homelessness, when they'd have no common gathering place, Joel and Raymond had planned what they jokingly referred to as a "Bohemian Grove weekend" on the wooded slopes near Mount Diablo. They would use the long Washington's Birthday weekend to commemorate the school's founding—two years already—and plan for the coming challenges. School-board funding had not yet been renewed, and other problems remained. Joel had convened the Other Paths adults during earlier emergencies, when they'd feared for the open-school project; now the students would have a chance to do the same.

Alice was eager to go. She would be leaving Berkeley soon and would lose her chance of ever belonging to such a group— of being among the rebels and revels. Everyone else was enjoying themselves; so could she.

Raymond had rounded up the early birds. Under a feeble morning sun, the group was yawning and subdued, though buoyed by a sense of carefree camaraderie. Jammed along the van's benches was Raymond's usual group, joined by a few others. Joel and several carloads of young people would be arriving throughout the day; but Joel was no longer enough of a leader to be there from the beginning—or so Raymond complained to the group in the van, as though the revel had already begun.

Helen's voice rose, clear and confiding; as usual, she'd grabbed the passenger seat. "Ray's preparing a palace coup," she announced, glancing back so she could gauge the response.

Andy was leaning, forearms dangling, a leather cap perched loosely on brown, sun-bleached curls. "Man, you shoulda warned me. I woulda brought my hunting rifle."

"No, Andy, nothing so banal." Helen eyed Raymond. "They should know, Ray," she prodded.

"Know what?"

Helen leaned over the seat, facing the group. Her eyes were puffy from sleep, and she wore her floppy sombrero. "Ray's playing dumb."

"Ray's always playing dumb," mumbled Jonathan. He had entered the van after Alice and found a place near her on the bench. She wore the old army jacket from Finnish Hall, a ragged cuff hanging over each knee. Whenever the van swung around a curve, there was the pressure of Jonathan's shoulder leaning on her own.

"We're facing big changes at Other Paths; we can talk later," Raymond concluded.

Soon they were on a rural road. Through the back window, they could see firs and redwoods receding in a random, curving line. In the front seats, Raymond and Helen pursued the usual verbal tussling; though the words could be heard well enough, the meaning confused Alice, whose parents had sparred, humorlessly, and who wondered how Raymond and Helen managed to make it so much fun. For they were clearly amused by each other.

The van lunged around a corner and down a gravel road. "Hey, we're here," called Raymond. He pulled the van sharply to the left, braked, and released the gears. The engine idled for a moment and shuddered dead. Raymond jumped out. The sliding door heaved open with a scrape and a thud. They found themselves in cool damp weather on the border of a lawn; beyond rose a wooden lodge. A couple of the boys dashed across the lawn, laughing and turning somersaults, as the others huddled by the van, wondering what to do. When someone proposed a walk in the nearby woods, Raymond agreed and led the way. Near the border of the woods, the ground became muddy. The boys trudged on, but Helen shuddered and flounced away toward the lodge, followed by her group of girls, complaining loudly of the mud. Alice nearly followed them, but there would be nothing to do in the lodge before Joel and the others appeared. Anyway, she enjoyed the woods and was used to groups of boys.

Soon they found a clearing. There the group slowed, as though by unspoken consensus. The clearing was damp and barely warmed by cool winter sunlight. The temperature had dropped as they'd reached the eastern slope; the boys huddled, laughing and horsing around to stay warm. She could see her breath. As Jonathan joined her by the edge of the clearing, she wondered why the others had paused. Then Andy produced a joint, and she understood—they'd entered the woods for a smoke. She was feeling removed from the group, as Andy had a toke and passed the joint along to Raymond. She'd smoked with her pals from Telegraph Avenue, but never with boys from the school. She'd assumed that Raymond would use grass; still, it was jarring to see a teacher sharing a joint among the group of boys. He glanced at her, teasing and brotherly, and waved her over.

"What's your father's name?"

"Tom." She was feeling unsure of her place in the group. "Why?"

"So, does Tom know? Is he gonna complain?"

"Why would he?" She was confused; Raymond was no longer teasing.

"Hey, no playing dumb. C'mon, we're heading back to the lodge. Anyone who's smoking for the first time, you're on your own—I'm not gonna be involved." The joint waved in his hand as he spoke, leaving a small plume of smoke.

Andy reached for it. "Ray man, you're wasting our resources."

One of the boys giggled. "'Ray man'—that's good."

Raymond's eyes flared. "Hey man, I'm—"

"Hey man Ray man, hey man Ray man!"

Andy began the chant, and soon the group was howling in the woods among the damp leaves. Jonathan jumped on a fallen log only to have the wood crumble away; he landed in a spongy bed of ferns. As Jonathan groped his way from the ferns, the shouts tapered off. Soon they were gathered once more around Raymond.

Now Jonathan produced a joint. He hung it from his mouth and, reaching for a lighter, turned to Raymond. "You can leave now, big Ray, 'cause I'm gonna see that Alice here has her share. And furthermore, I can assure you—anyone who comes to Other Paths has already found the devil weed."

"That so?" Raymond surveyed Alice, fingering his red mustache.

She shrugged. Jonathan toked and handed off to her. She would have preferred to leave the group but there they were, eyes on her; she could hardly refuse. The other girls had done as they pleased, but she'd followed the boys and here she was, no running away now. Long ago, she'd learned from her father never to be a renegade from the group. Now he was gone—and would she also be a renegade? Inhaling lightly on the joint, she huddled with the group, hearing the sounds of the woods. When the smoking was through, they headed in a slow march toward the lawn and lodge. Jonathan fell in alongside her.

"I could hang out all day in the woods," he remarked casually. "And you?"

"I don't come here much." She wondered what he was really saying.

"I spend as much time in the woods as I can," he pursued. Then suddenly, "We could go around the other way—are you game? They're just gonna be hanging out in the lodge, and that's no fun."

She was enjoying the woods, but she hardly knew Jonathan. He had been following her around all day.

"C'mon, there's another path."

"I'd rather—"

"Oh boy." He turned from her and brushed some dead leaves from one elbow, where he'd landed on the ferns. He held up the elbow for her to survey. "Clean enough for you?"

"Yeah, clean enough."

"Good." He reached a hand to her shoulder and nodded in the direction of the lodge. "C'mon, you lead the way."

They had come farther from the lawn than she remembered. As they finally approached the border of the woods, shouts rang out. Some other cars had appeared; young people were running back and forth by the lodge, trampling the muddy grass near the porch.

Raymond was leaning on a porch railing, surrounded by a group of girls. They buzzed eagerly around him, all but Helen, who was hovering by the edge of the group as though hardly aware of the others.

Jonathan eyed the group and sighed, "*Ah, look at all the lonely people.*"

"What's going on?" Alice wondered.

"Ray's having a class on men." Jonathan's gray eyes clouded with annoyance.

"Huh?"

"Oh yeah." He nodded toward the group. "Go on, there's room for one more."

"Why would I—"

"Or you could hang out with a man." The eyebrows rose as he moved closer, leaning toward her. "Something tells me you can manage on your own—no class, no Raymond."

She was searching for a good response. He was humming, no longer "Eleanor Rigby" but a song she'd never heard. The humming stopped. "You seem shy and thoughtful all of a sudden."

"Oh?"

"Yeah." Inhaling slowly, he released a long sigh. "Care to tell me more?"

"There's nothing to tell."

"That's what they all say."

She made no response.

"You seem lonesome. But hey, why hang around with me?" The eyebrows wriggled in a funny face. "I could be some creep. Your mother should warn you away." Then he shrugged. "Well —see ya." And he turned to go.

She found herself alone by the muddy forest path. Nearby, a squirrel was rummaging in a heap of leaves. The image of Jonathan hovered before her: gray eyes, full mouth, heavy pony-tail down the back. The image confused her, so she preferred to remain near the woods, hearing the rustling of the squirrel, until Jonathan was very much gone.

When a few moments had passed, from the upper branches came the harsh sound of a blue jay. The sound urged her once more to the woods, where she wandered among firs until she found the blue-jay tree. There she lingered, hearing the jay and the groaning of trees in the wind. The ground was damp and spongy; she pressed forward along another path, plunging down a gradual slope among fallen branches and beds of dead fern.

The path led across a stream and then began to climb. A fallen log lay over the stream, serving as a bridge. Placing one foot carefully before the other, using her arms for balance, she crossed the log and began following the path as it wound uphill. All around her rose fir trees, ascending the slope in a loose mass. Wearing her Finnish army jacket, she moved among them, no longer cold. Soon the climb became rough and jagged. Overhead the sky could be seen shining through; she was nearing the crest of a low ridge.

She rounded a boulder and came upon a clear overlook. Gazing down the slope, she could see where she'd come from, far below: the lodge and the lawn. On the faraway grass a group chased here and there in random play—a game having no ball, no squads, no rules. There was no use here for baseball, the game she and her brother had played.

Beyond the boulder lay a far valley. The trees swayed, as though gathering energy for a long march, before the forest fled down the slope. Noonday sun blinded her, and she closed her eyes; from the lawn rose random, joyful shouts. As she opened her eyes, there came a gust, its raw, whipping force impelling her back down the path.

Passing through the woods, she found the stream again. A dog had appeared; crouched on the far bank, forepaws wading, he was lapping from a shallow pool. As she made her way over the fallen log, the dog glanced up and then resumed, seemingly heedless of her approach. Then, stepping from the log, she landed with a snapping sound on a dead branch. The dog looked up and rushed forward, growling and barking. She ran along the path, turning to see if the dog pursued, but he was pacing by the stream, barking and lunging at shadows.

She ran from the woods. More cars had appeared. The lodge was overrun by people, who thronged the porch and upper windows, hollering to each other. Raymond was nowhere to be seen; he would be in the lodge or the woods, hanging with a group from the van. A blues melody rose from some nearby firs, and Manny emerged from the grove, playing his saxophone and followed by a girl, her eyes lowered, her hands folded over her pregnant belly. From the grove came another couple, draped in a sleeping bag. The grass was damp from days of bad weather, and the woods were worse. Of the foursome, only Manny belonged to the school; the others would be Manny's groupies. Alice paused, unsure of where to go.

From the upper windows of the lodge leaned Andy and several others, applauding Manny's advance. Manny and the girl marched slowly, passing the porch and rounding a corner of the lodge. A blaring soprano sound faded, suspended above a far grove.

Alice crossed the lawn. Something had happened during her foray in the woods—the mood had changed, for sure. As she placed one shoe on the porch, a loud boom rumbled from the lodge and then a long absence, as though the world had been quenched by some rude uproar. She jumped in alarm, but the others appeared joyfully unconcerned. Suddenly there pounded a thump and drone, the rhythm pressing up through her rubber soles, the drone surrounding her like an enveloping ocean wave or undertow, pulling her here and there. She covered her ears and lurched along the porch.

In the far corner were three girls from class. One of them, Becky, nodded and waved for Alice to join them, mouthing words submerged by the din. The other girls were engaged in an argument and merely glanced up as Alice approached, then resumed shouting. The thump had speeded up and now moved compulsively through her shoulders in shuddering syncopation, as though she were usurped by alien forces. She was reluctant to move, for that would mean revealing how her legs, as well, were under the control of some unknown rhythm. Leaning on the porch railing, she regarded the shouting girls and now understood that there was no argument; if anything, they were confiding through the ocean of sound. She glanced at Becky, who leaned, waving her nearer. Becky's mouth was moving but Alice could hear nothing, as a crashing bass-and-drum solo hammered her shoulder through the porch railing. Then the thumping stopped in a loud *nnnnnnk!* and *pop!* as the churning rhythm evaporated like bubbles rushing the surface for release. *And where has it gone?* she wondered, hearing an echo of dead sound. On the porch she moved to and fro, marveling at her recovery of muscular control.

Then a new sound came from somewhere above her head—a

human sound howling in the wilderness. She glanced up: Raymond was leaning from a window, waving one arm.

"Hey, everyone! Hey!"

"Hey man Ray man, hey man Ray man!" From another window, Andy commenced cheerleading.

"Enough, Andy—

"Yeah, Andy, shuddup!"

Raymond paused, fingering his red mustache, then resumed. "No more joking, you guys. Joel phoned—"

"The dude should get on over here, man," Andy whined. "Where is he?"

"Joel's not coming. He—"

"No way!" Andy squealed.

"—an emergency."

There was a pause. "A *what*?"

"An emergency. Joel had an emergency."

Andy slammed the window just as Helen appeared, on cue, coming through the doorway of the lodge. In bare feet and sombrero, as though she'd just straggled in from the Amazonian jungle, she stepped from the porch and sang out, "Ray, they need to know what's happening." Then she moved long-legged over the lawn.

Raymond resumed, "Joel's flying to New York, then Washington—he has funding meetings next week with the Carnegie people and the feds. It's really important—this could be our big break."

In the middle of the lawn, Helen flung open her arms. "And here we are, on our own!"

There was a murmur from the porch. Three boys hung with wire-trailing guitars stumbled through the lodge door. One of them was Jonathan. "What's the deal?" he demanded. "Ray unplugged us and—*sayonara!*"

Helen pulled off the sombrero, her dark hair tumbling on her shoulders, and flung it away. "No Joel," she announced. "And here we are."

"Wow." Jonathan gave a sour laugh. "Where's our fearless leader?"

"He's back East, meeting with some robber barons."

Raymond called from the window, "Hey, no whining. Joel has a big funding gig—something that can help us all."

Andy demanded, "But what about the Happening?"

Subdued by the news, the group on the porch had begun wandering off. Some girls rushed up to Helen, loudly complaining, while Becky made a sad face. "Poor Joel—he's missing all the fun," she remarked to Alice. "You're in the Happening, right?"

"No."

"But I thought you were in Joel's class."

"I am."

"Then you rehearsed the Happening with Andy and everyone. Or so I heard."

"No."

Becky appeared confused, then she remembered. "Oh, of course—the rehearsals were at Joel's house!" She giggled. "They were keeping it a surprise."

Alice found the revelation annoying. How had people been chosen for the Happening—and why was she always passed over by Joel? Maybe because she was younger, the only seventh grader; or maybe because she'd been such a flop during the early rehearsals, succumbing to some fear or other, unable to reveal even the corner of an underlying fantasy world. Joel encouraged them to be rebels, but the purposes were commonplace; there were only so many symbols of personal freedom: songs and drugs and sex and hobo clothes . . . These symbols belonged to someone else, many someone elses—or no one. They would never help her know what to do.

A bearded boy—he was one of Joel's group—came across the lawn. Becky moaned, "Oh no," and rushed for the door of the lodge. Alone on the porch, Alice wondered how she would become one of the people from Other Paths—there were so many hurdles. She moved toward the door, planning to survey the lodge and grab a bed before they were all gone. Already she had been running around in the woods while the others were finding a place; as Raymond had told them, they would be free to choose a room—he and Joel knew they were no longer children.

As she approached the lodge, the bearded boy rushed past her and through the door. He was familiar from Joel's classes, one of the boys planning the Happening. Then Jonathan could be heard from the lodge. "Hey, Don, looking for Becky? She's gone *adios*!" He appeared in the doorway, facing Alice. "Looking for Don?" he deadpanned, waving a hand toward the hallway. "He's gone *hasta luego*!"

She rushed forward, confused, following Jonathan's vague gesture. The hallway opened on a large kitchen. By the counter, near a mound of apples, was Maya, from the Happening class. She turned slowly, surveyed Alice, and calmly remarked, in her songbird tone, "I'm making applesauce. You can help."

Maya had removed her scarf and woven a long braid reaching nearly to her hips. For once she wore no clown makeup, only some markings around her eyes, elongated like cat's eyes. She wore a loose handmade sweater, a colorful skirt, and purple high-top sneakers. She had been peeling an apple when Alice appeared; she held up the paring knife and the apple segment, as though offering them.

"There's no peeler. You'll have to use a paring knife," she commented, seemingly aware of some symbolic meaning in her words. "Everyone uses a peeler now; no one even knows how to peel an apple anymore." Her eyes danced with laughter. "But you can learn. It's fun."

Alice grasped the paring knife and apple and began scraping awkwardly at the peel. She tore off a small strip and dropped it on a heap of peelings on the wooden counter. "We could leave the peel on; my mother usually does," she proposed.

"We're probably the only people here who've made applesauce." Maya peeled the apples effortlessly, glancing around, her hand moving in clean, graceful strokes around the curve of the apple, ending with a long, curling segment of peel hanging between thumb and knife. She suspended the peeling over the heap and released it, reaching with her other hand for another apple. "Cans and jars of phony food," she chanted, marveling, her hands working expertly. "And they've never had a real apple." She tossed another peeling on the heap and paused, turning her cool observing eyes on Alice. Still holding the same apple, Alice was feeling foolish. Maya continued, "Dancers have to learn how to breathe. Everyone imagines they know how to breathe, they say, 'Oh, of course I can do that, it's natural.' But the body barely remembers anymore where it comes from."

Maya's dogmas were new to Alice, who knew nothing of dancing. What if she focused on breathing—would she be able, for example, to peel apples while truly breathing? She inhaled, held her breath, and slowly exhaled. Her shoulders loosened, leaving her hands suspended around the apple. Suddenly sleepy, she yawned, using the half-peeled apple to cover her mouth.

Maya giggled. "Who's in your family?" she inquired.

"Who?"

"You have a mother and . . ."

"A brother." Alice pondered for a moment. "My father moved out."

"Are you happy or sad, then?" Maya had the unruffled manner of one who always asked such things. "Maybe some of both," she added, when Alice made no response. "Probably more sad than happy."

"No." Alice held up another peeling. "More the other way around."

Maya was humming now to herself. "And your brother—is he like you?"

"How do you mean?"

"Strange and quiet."

Alice was feeling warm and confused. She had no response, because no one had spoken to her that way before. She wondered if Maya was judging her. So many people she met at Other Paths seemed to be making judgments, as though they knew the way things should be.

Maya was smiling to herself. "Everyone's who they are," she concluded ambiguously, tossing another apple in a large cauldron. "Oh, look!" she exclaimed. "We're all done."

Alice gazed around at the counters. Along with the apples, there were bags of beans and potatoes. "I wonder what we're having for dinner."

Maya giggled. "Applesauce. Joel was supposed to bring the food, but he's not coming. We can have soup tomorrow." She shrugged. "My family's poor, we have bean soup all the time."

"Well—"

"You can help make soup tomorrow." Maya added some water to the apple cauldron, covered it, and turned on the flame.

Alice remembered why she'd entered the lodge. "I need a room. See ya later."

Maya frowned. "You're slow. They're all gone."

"Gone?"

"Yes, the rooms in the lodge. Where have you been?"

"I was in the woods."

"Sounds fun." Maya paused. "There are some cabins. You could go see Raymond—" She rolled her eyes. "Uh-oh, second thoughts. He's very busy. Go around by the cabins. I heard Manny has one of them, but maybe the others are free."

The cabins were near the far end of the lodge, camouflaged by a grove of low cedars. Alice had seen them from the ridge but had assumed she would be staying in the lodge. Leaving Maya and the cauldron of apples, she passed through the hallway and entered the common room, where Jonathan's band had set up. There were long bare tables and an empty fireplace. Above the fireplace hung a moose head crowned with huge antlers. In the corner of the room crouched a jukebox, flashing mutely. Leaning on one of the tables and reading a book was a boy—Francis, who was always reading the same book, *Games People Play*. He glanced up and waved. She supposed he was learning chess, or maybe poker or backgammon. If so, he was very slow in learning the rules.

She passed through the porch door as Francis resumed reading. The porch had become strangely deserted, as though everyone had packed up and gone.

In the cedar grove were four cabins. She wondered whether Manny had taken one, as Maya supposed, and whether he would have chosen a near one or a far one. A near one, she reasoned, where he would be close by the lodge in case anything happened. Not that anything appeared on the verge of happening just then; Joel's absence had proved to be a damper, and the place had gone dead. Passing the nearer cabins, she came to one shaded by a leaning cedar. Though the door was ajar, no one was there. She entered and found the room larger than appeared from the square facade, for there was space enough for two double beds.

Leaving her scarf on the bed by the door, she ran to Raymond's van and swung open the side door. Her carryall bag was stowed under the bench. The bag crumpled in her hand, as though ephemeral, holding only pajamas, clean socks and underwear, a toothbrush, and R. D. Laing's *Sanity, Madness and the Family*. No one had warned her of the colder weather, and she had no clothes warmer than those she wore—a heavy pullover and the Finnish army jacket. During the day, the woods had been damp and cool, though comfortable as long as she was moving; now the sun was fading⁻ and a sharp chill seeped through the canyon.

She ran back to the cabin, dropped her bag on the bed, and grabbed the scarf, pulling it close over her neck and hair. She thought of returning to the hill in the dark, under the moon, if only she could find some others eager to go. Maybe during dinner they would plan an adventure, a replacement for Joel and the Happening. The day so far had proved commonplace, even dull, and she was feeling left out of the fun and companionship—for surely the others were off somewhere having fun. The group was beyond her already, older and unruly, beyond the group she'd found the year before. The others were forming couples; there was no place for her. Apparently she'd come here to learn to peel apples.

For a while she remained alone in the cabin, reading, then returned to the lodge. The apple cauldron bubbled, but Maya was no longer there. Removing the lid, Alice savored the warm cloud of fragrance that rushed up. The apples had changed to a pulpy mush. She reached for a wooden spoon and stirred, releasing more bubbles from the mush.

Maya appeared. "Applesauce is done. We can serve anyone who's hungry." She brought a wooden bowl to the counter near the burners. Alice grasped the handles of the cauldron and tipped it over the bowl, pouring out steaming pulp. Bearing the bowl before her, Maya entered the common room and placed it near Francis. He had ceased perusing *Games People Play* and was arguing with another boy, who wore overalls.

"Have some applesauce," Maya suggested, as though recommending a home remedy.

The boys looked puzzled.

"Hey, where's the rest?" demanded the boy in overalls.

"There's homemade applesauce."

"Ew, kinda lumpy," Francis said. "Warm and lumpy, ew."

Maya turned, concealing a smile, her eyes dancing. "Made from real apples," she announced over her shoulder.

"Hey, man," called the boy in overalls, "we need spoons!"

"And bowls!"

Maya wafted from the room. The boys looked wonderingly at Alice. In a moment, Maya returned with a stack of bowls. On top were a dozen or so spoons. She placed the bowls on the table. Then she handed the serving spoon to Alice. "You helped cook," she remarked simply. "Go on, have some."

The four of them dined on applesauce. Hardly anyone else showed up—only Becky, who regaled them with her family's plans to move to Bolinas. When they'd had enough, the others departed one by one, leaving Alice alone.

She emerged from the lodge and found Becky on the porch, eagerly waving her over. The evening was cold, peaceful, aglow with moonshine. They had come to a wonderful nowhere. A feeling of random energy came over Alice. Everyone was alone, responsible for themselves; no one would know how they'd spent the hours before morning. She could hang around the porch or wander through the woods. In the van, she'd refused Andy's of-fer of LSD—he'd brought some and would share with anyone—and now she had nothing to do.

Becky was bored. "I imagined there'd be a dance or some-thing," she complained. "I mean, we have Manny here, and the band. Oh, well." Seated on the railing, she swung her legs loosely as one hand played in her hair, winding a long strand one way and then the other around two fingers.

The band's loud thumping had seemed false; now, however, they heard only evening sounds echoing over the lawn.

"What does your father do?" Alice asked.

"Huh?"

"Your father—what will he do in Bolinas?"

"Oh, there's nothing to do in Bolinas—that's why we're go-ing there."

"Oh."

"You look confused."

"Well—"

"He's a professor, silly. He's on leave and has a book to do and . . ." For a moment, she waved her arms as though conduct-ing a symphony, before folding her hands in her lap. "In nowhere Bolinas no one will bother him. So we're all going."

"I see." Long, racing clouds covered the moon and then tore open, glowing yellow and gray. Alice was enjoying herself. "What does he profess?"

"How should I know? Something-ology."

"You really don't know?"

"Of course I do—sociology. There, that says everything, no?"

"Not really. What's sociology?"

"Society, social, sociology. The study of people in groups."

"That covers a lot of ground."

"Yup."

"What does he tell you about it?"

"Mostly that I'm too young to understand. But he's wrong—you should see some of the books I've read. That's the great thing about Other Paths—I can stay home and read in my father's study while he's teaching."

"What do you read?"

"Oh, you name it. Margaret Mead—"

"I've heard of her."

"Everyone reads her. Do you know that on Samoa—"

"Do you know Helen's sister?" Alice interjected, remembering her mother's monologues about Sabrina and her family.

"Sure. Why?"

"Just wondered. I thought she was enrolled in Other Paths."

"Who, Maggie?" Becky seemed amused. "Oh, no, she never comes. I mean, what for? Last year we had Joel's classes, but he's hardly there anymore. And now—" She held up her hands as if to say, "All gone."

The woods glowed under the moon. Becky pulled up her collar.

"Where's everyone?" Alice wondered aloud.

Becky giggled. "Where do you suppose they are?" She giggled harder. "Gosh, everyone turned in so early."

"No one even showed up for dinner."

"Oh, so you saw that, too."

"I was looking for Raymond—"

"Raymond?" Becky was suddenly sober. "Oh, Raymond won't come out before morning. I can promise you that."

Something made Alice feel she should inquire no further. But there was no need; Becky had more to say. She leaned over.

"Do you swear?"

"Huh?"

"Swear not to tell, silly."

"I swear."

Becky closed her eyes and inhaled deeply; then she opened them, waved her head roguishly, and leaned in. "I heard he's in a cabin with someone—"

With Becky gazing into her soul—or appearing to do so—Alice fumbled for a response, but found none that seemed on cue.

"—bad girl Helen!" Becky gasped, eyelashes fluttering.

Alice rounded her eyes in the equivalent of a shrug. She should be cool and casual, for sure. In a deadpan way, she probed the rumor.

"How do you know?"

"Oh . . . I have ways."

"You mean you saw them?"

Becky pursed her mouth and nodded vigorously. "But no one's supposed to know. So if you tell anyone, I'm in real trouble."

Several moments passed as they looked out on the lawn, leaden under the moon and fading deep among the gathering trees. The woods hung before them, enclosing the lodge and its small gleaming windows in a darkened amphitheater. At the far end of the porch, the four cabins were camouflaged by the cedar grove, marked with traces of unnatural light. Was Raymond really down there, and if so, which of the cabins had he chosen? The thought of sleeping by herself in a secluded cabin gave Alice a sense of foreboding, which deepened as she contemplated the chances of encountering Raymond in or near the cedar grove. She had thought of him as a teacher—young and overly casual, but a teacher nonetheless. Images appeared in her mind of Raymond sparring with Helen, responding with pleasure rather than anger, encouraging her to assume the lead, even though he was older and a man. There was something strange in the way the quarrels led to personal confessions. By now everyone knew how Helen's father had cornered her in the yard, complaining that her mother refused him, and how her mother had bragged one day that she'd found another man—not long after Helen's father had headed for the Amazon jungle. The group had been riding in the van, and Helen had been crying and rapping to Raymond about her problems.

"It sounds so *Peyton Place*," Raymond teased, and when Helen heard the words "Peyton Place," she laughed.

The porch had become very cold. Becky glanced in her eyes and then away. "I thought everyone kinda knew, or wondered, anyway. On Samoa—"

From the woods came a round of bloodcurdling whoops—a war cry. Then the false calm of evening sounds, as though the woods had stopped breathing. In the ensuing gasp, the sky filled with the shrill clamor of a war party, as ten boys converged on the lawn, racing and vaulting and brandishing branches.

In moments, a flame appeared on the lawn, low and crouching, then dancing up, high and wild in a smoky, snapping bonfire. Alice could feel her blood surge. Around the flames, the boys clasped one another by the shoulders, lashing back and forth like a banner made of paper cutouts, ready for the flames. Then the line broke and they charged the lodge, Andy in the lead. He was waving a red flag and a peacock feather.

"The palace is ours! The palace is ours!" hollered Andy. Another war cry arose from the group as they charged the porch, rushing the door of the lodge.

The girls stared at the leaping flames. Alice knew they should be doing something; the bonfire was flaring. The Happening was in full swing, and they'd been caught clueless.

Becky laughed loudly. "Maybe Ray will show up for the finale. Oh, goody, here he comes!"

Sure enough, Raymond appeared, running from the cedar grove, wearing only jeans. He pulled up before the porch, thrashing madly and yanking a jersey over bare shoulders.

"Andy, over here! Now!"

Andy appeared in an upper window, solemnly waving the red flag and the peacock feather. "Ray man lay man, Ray man lay man!"

From the flames came hissing and crackling.

Then Andy was gone. A moment later, a large bowl hurled from the window, bouncing off Raymond's leg. He never glanced down; but the girls could see that he was covered with applesauce.

Alice ran for the door. Something was finally happening, and she refused to be a bystander any longer.

In the common room, the band had reappeared, all but Jonathan. Dodging among the early rumblings of a sonic avalanche rebounding through the room, she headed for the upper floor, where everyone would be. Raymond suddenly charged across the room and sprang up the stairs, shoving her to the wall as he passed. She heard a heavy thumping as he ran down the hall. In the room below, the band launched into a song, frothy and untethered in the absence of Jonathan's bass. Following Raymond, she turned down the hallway and encountered the dry, musky odor of grass. He had paused before a door, where he was banging loudly.

"Open up, Andy, or they'll have the cops here."

The door opened. Grabbing Andy, Raymond hauled him from the room and shoved him against the wall. Andy crumpled to the floor, where he lay propped on one elbow, shaking the other hand at Raymond.

"Raymond, you fucker, leave my woman alone!" Andy's arm was waving madly as he squirmed forward, slapping at Raymond's leg. "I want her! I want her!"

Raymond was sneering now, one hand playing in the droopy red mustache, the other propped on the wall above Andy's head. "Shove it, Andy, or you'll have the cops here. You already have the caretaker coming down on us."

"Ray, you fucker." And he lunged for Raymond's leg.

Raymond shook him off. "No, man, you're the one who's done us in. Things were fine half an hour ago."

In the room below, the band abruptly ceased, followed by the slamming of boots on the stairs. Alice turned; rounding the corner was a heavy man in a baseball cap. The stranger held a pump gun in one hand.

"What the—" He glared down the hall, sniffing the marijuana fumes. "My, my, some pajama party you folks are having."

Andy peered around Raymond's leg. "Who's there?" he demanded.

"I'm hoping you can tell me," responded the man. He spoke calmly and held up the pump gun ever so casually, coolly surveying Andy as he squirmed on the floor.

Raymond faced the man, his hand playing in his mustache. "Sorry for the trouble. Things are under control now."

"My, my." The man paused, glancing up and down the hall, then advanced on Andy. "Why, that there troublemaker's nothing but a boy." He glared at Alice as he passed. "Your brother?"

"No," she responded, aware of something familiar in the man's anger.

"I'm glad to hear." He approached Raymond. "Any more problems and you'll be in the slammer, big fella."

For a moment, he faced Raymond down, then turned and

lumbered off. They heard the thumping of boots on the stairs, and then the slamming of the porch door. No one moved; finally, Raymond pulled Andy to his feet. "You heard the man," he said.

"Yup."

"Go to sleep."

"Yup."

"See you in the morning."

"Groovy, man, how about some jump rope?"

"No more, Andy."

"I'm not for real, you know, Ray man—I'm never for real."

"I know."

"Fucked up, man, I'm so fucked up . . ."

Raymond glanced around, waving Alice away. "You'll come down, Andy—in a couple hours everything's gonna be fine."

Alice heard Andy sobbing. "You—you stole her from me, you . . . She's mine, mine." She descended the stairs, wondering how many of the others had shared the LSD. Maybe she'd found a good place for sleep, after all, far from the lodge and the madness.

In the common room, the singer from the band called to her, "Something bad happen?"

"No." She paused. "Not really."

"Anything good happen?"

"Yeah," added the drummer, "like maybe the man with the gun pumped some lead into Andy?"

"No."

"Gosh, sorry to hear." The boys were giggling.

She stumbled through the door onto the porch. No one was there. Someone had doused the bonfire; the lawn lay before her, dark and impenetrable, smelling of damp earth and the remnants of burning wood. The evening had turned languorous, untroubled, and chilly. From beyond the forest amphitheater, stars by the myriad beckoned her with the glow of other worlds. She ran for the cedar grove.

Seen from the grove, the lodge seemed to hang in the surrounding dark, a drapery that had nearly caught and tangled her in its folds. She turned the knob on the cabin door and pushed; the door opened. The darkness felt warm; closing the door, she gazed through the window on cedar branches. She'd placed her carryall on the nearer bed; now she sat there, enjoying the grove.

Suddenly she froze.

"I was wondering when you'd show up."

The words made her jump. She spun around to find Jonathan, one hand on the chain of a lamp, and the room aglow in unforgiving light.

"I was reading, but I had trouble staying awake. I thought, man, what if she comes and finds me, you know, snoring on a bed, when she's probably hoping to have the room to herself."

"I was."

"I know." He paused. "What's happening in the lodge?"

"Nothing much."

"Andy damn near burns the place down, a man comes waving a gun—and you call that 'nothing much'? Jeez, that's when I headed for the hills." Hands folded behind his head, a copy of *Mad* magazine dangling over one leg, Jonathan was having fun.

Alice shrugged. "Someone doused the fire, the man's gone away—"

"Ray should take that puny pyro and dump him in the well."

"Andy?"

"What—you mean there's more than one?"

"There seemed to be a whole group of them."

"Andy's the idea man, haven't you figured anything out?"

"I'm not spending my days figuring out Andy."

"Yeah, you're too intelligent for that." He began humming to himself, then ceased. "Imagine being in Raymond's shoes— suddenly Andy becomes your problem. I'd rather do some dumb job, have a band in my spare time."

"Raymond seems to be having fun."

Jonathan resumed humming. Alice was wondering whether there would be anywhere else to sleep, if she began looking now. Surely one of the rooms in the lodge had girls only and a spare bed. She rose from the bed and headed for the door.

Jonathan sat up, swinging his legs from the bed. "I can leave if you want. It's your room, you came before me."

She looked at him. "Then why are you here?"

"Same reason you are—nowhere else to go." He looked reasonable enough. "I'm planning to sleep in my clothes. You should do the same. There's no heat in here, by morning the room will be really cold."

He crawled under the covers of the other bed, as though to show he was harmless. She had shared rooms with her brother on family trips, and Jonathan was behaving more as a brother than as some guy she should fear. She removed her shoes and got in bed. Then she pulled up the covers and gazed through the window at the cedar grove, dimly lit by the glow from the lodge. Jonathan turned off the lamp. Soon he was breathing steadily. Unable to sleep, she pondered the day.

As usual, there had been no plan—only Andy running wild. All the same, the day had been clarifying. She'd been duped again, brought here for group bonding—some form of community or even family—and then offered anarchy. One by one, they'd made her feel she was to blame for the problem she was having at Other Paths—Raymond, Jonathan, and Maya. They'd judged her for not following along, for being uneasy in someone else's world. No, she would be losing nothing by leaving; she would be glad to go.

SEVERAL HOURS LATER, as glimmers of dawn seeped through the room, she became aware of an arm draped over her shoulder. It was Jonathan. Her head was very cold, and although she was confused to find him there, confining her, it seemed, she knew that in the absence of his body she would have woken from the cold long before. She turned her head; he was looking at her. He moved to press his mouth to hers, but she pulled away, leaving Jonathan and the bed and the room for the early-morning canyon.

The lawn lay in morning shadow; no one was up. She'd known that Jonathan would make a move and that she would refuse, but she was surprised by the sense of deliverance she was feeling, as though she'd just escaped. For a moment, she wanted to laugh: someday she would walk in the woods—but by then Jonathan would be gone, and she'd have someone else. Jonathan was a good enough guy; things were just all wrong.

By midmorning, she was in the van with the others, all but Andy, heading for Berkeley. Raymond had assembled them on the lawn and informed them of the dreadful doom: they had been commanded to leave as soon as they reasonably could. The group in the van was subdued, even chagrined. Hardly anyone spoke;

they stared uncomfortably at the floor or through the windows on ever-fleeing trees. Confused and scared of returning home, Alice pondered what she'd done wrong—though nothing had happened, she'd shared a bed with a boy, when she should have found a room in the lodge. Furthermore, what reason would she give her mother and Charles—he'd flown up, and they'd been planning a weekend alone—for coming home early? She hoped her mother and Charles would be too absorbed in each other to probe and pry; there had been so many days when she'd feared being caught, but no one had cared to know—or maybe they'd already come to conclusions and chose to do nothing.

Raymond was in full swing. "You're gonna have to learn," he was saying, "or we're gonna lose the school. They're praying we mess up. I know, you were just in the woods, doing some reefer, the girls were learning about those bulges in the boys' pants—and that's okay. But man, when you're smoking dope in the lodge, or making goddamn bonfires, then suddenly it's not so cool. There's no blaming me—everyone helped put us where we are—and I mean everyone."

They huddled speechless in the van, shoulders touching as they rounded the curves.

The van slowed. They'd come through the hills onto Tunnel Road.

"Alice, you're first," called Raymond. Then, seeming to read her mind, he demanded, "Are your mom and dad gonna be home?"

"Yes, my mother and Charles."

"Same problem. What are you gonna say?" The van rounded a corner only blocks from her house.

"I'm not sure."

"Say we were bounced out," Raymond snapped, "and soon they'll know everything. How many beds and who was in them and—you know?"

Several heads turned to survey her.

"Then your mom complains—"

Someone coughed.

"—and we're closed down."

"That would be very uncool," remarked the boy who played drums.

Raymond resumed. "Everyone's gonna fill in the blanks with

something banal—'Oh my God, Jimmy and Mary Jane having sex' or whatever they imagine we do at Other Paths. 'Oh no, they were running naked through the woods. They had an orgy in the swimming pool—'"

"There was no swimming pool," Jonathan corrected.

"I know, and even if there was, it's February. But all you need is a good rumor, and we're defunded."

"We understand, Ray." From the front, Helen managed to sound in charge, though she was fifteen and he was twenty-three.

"I have to be sure Alice knows how things are," Raymond snapped. "She's younger than you guys and newer to the school."

Jonathan turned to Alice. "Some of us were bored and came home early."

Raymond nodded. "That should be good enough."

"She's cool, Raymond."

Alice pondered the problem. She could choose: her mother and Charles would never know what had happened, unless she informed on the school. And as everyone knew, she was younger than the others and a newcomer. Though she would be moving on, how could she betray them? Anyway, there had been no naked forays in the woods, no orgy in the swimming pool—no swimming pool, even.

"I'm just saying be careful," added Raymond. "Understand how rumors can be used. Look how the government uses false rumors to harass people who challenge it."

Helen combed her fingers through her hair. "That's enough, Ray. We all fathom."

The van pulled up by the curb on Forest Avenue. Near the door, Jonathan leaned down on the handle. Alice made her way through a tangle of feet. When she was safely on the ground, she turned and glanced back.

"Take it easy," called Raymond.

"Bye." She heard the door close with a crash as the van rumbled from the curb. She reached the porch, feeling confused and scared. She'd learned from her father never to be renegade from the group. Now she would be tested.

AS ALICE ENTERED the house, just before noon, her mother and Charles could be heard in the living room. He was eagerly spinning a tale—an unusual thing for a father to do—and her mother was laughing. The laugh was new, though the mode of conversation was becoming familiar: Charles holding forth in some eager way, a glass in one hand, as her mother appeared enthralled by the performance. There was a long gasp; the laughter rose in a crescendo, broke, and tapered off. They were engaged with each other—a promising development, for that meant they would be heedless of her return, leaving her a chance to steal up to her room, make a plan, and then come down to them with some plausible story of the retreat.

But as the house door closed, Charles paused; then he resumed in a low tone, saying, "She's come home early."

"Oh my, she's here!" her mother announced loudly.

There was another pause, followed by murmuring. The murmuring was new, as well, and made her uncomfortable; more than once she'd heard enough to infer that they were speaking of her. She wondered what Charles had been told, just as she wondered how much her mother had deduced. Some days she would have preferred that they confront her, so she would know what she was dealing with; other days she was thankful for any delay. There was some hope of making a favorable impression on Charles—so far he had no reason to blame her—but only if he remained above the fray.

Then Charles addressed her in a formal tone, "Come on in and say hello."

Maybe he'd already heard about her. There was nothing to do but comply; she would have to say something—now.

As she prepared in the foyer, he resumed the interrupted story. There was the sound of her mother's laughter.

Alice advanced through the doorway. Charles was standing by the fireplace, one hand enclosed around the usual highball glass. Larger than her father though less robust, he had dark eyes and hair, and he was formally dressed, even at noon on a Sunday. An unknown and unprecedented person, he gazed at her.

"Oh, here you are," he called, as though glad to see her.

She shrugged, unsure of how to respond.

"You're back early," observed her mother.

Alice was rehearsing her story when Charles jumped in. "Yes, and that's a good thing. Your mother and I were just planning a walk in the rose garden."

"What rose garden?"

Her mother's face had a strange incandescence. "Charles has heard of a lovely rose garden in Northside. I never even knew it was there."

From Los Angeles, Charles had managed to learn more about Berkeley than her parents had learned in three unhappy years. They would be gone for the afternoon; any reckoning would be delayed. She turned to go.

"We're leaving very soon. Do you want to change your clothes before we go?" her mother wanted to know.

"Me? What for?"

"You're coming with us, I hope," Charles urged, peering warmly at her.

She wondered what the new game was. Family outings had ceased long ago, and she was too old for dragging around with her parents. Nonetheless, she was aware of encountering another mode in Charles, one that demanded response. "Some of us came back early—we were bored. Maybe I'll go and read—"

"You would enjoy the roses," her mother suggested.

"Oh yes," Charles nodded, "they're just the thing for girls your age."

So far, Charles was nowhere near as bad as she'd feared—he was even eager to have her along. All the same, she had never heard anything so daffy as the fuddy-duddy line about girls and roses. He was everything the people around her abhorred: for-mal—even stuffy—in clothes and manner, a real square. She'd never seen such a person up close, not for years. They were not leaving her to choose; the man's manner demanded her presence in the rose garden. She would have to go and take her chances with the new parental couple. If only her mother would forget to inquire about the retreat, she could use the day to observe Charles more closely. She had to know—and fast—what to do. The outing would offer some new information, and the roses would be a useful decoy. She shrugged, and they headed in a group for the door.

THE ROSE GARDEN was in the form of a small amphitheater facing the bay; hundreds of bushes grew along the terraced rungs, row upon row in full bloom, red and orange and blush and yellow. The place was uncanny, under the gray-green and purple eucalyptus branches; though as she paused, the color ceased dancing and gathered on the bushes, grounded by some unfolding event.

Charles moved up on her shoulder. "I've always loved yellow roses," he remarked, pausing to examine a blossom; then he added, "My mother had roses," as her own mother advanced ahead, wearing sunglasses, her face in an unusual glow.

Alone in the man's presence, Alice was feeling uneasy. She made no response and headed for a shaded path as Charles pursued.

"Don't wander too far," he warned.

Her mother returned and together they gazed along the rows of flowers. Alice was feeling a wild impulse to reveal the madhouse scene, but she'd promised Ray and the others.

"Tell us something about your weekend," Charles proposed, as though reading her doubts. She fought a sense of foreboding, but there was none of her father's cold probing; it appeared that Charles was hoping to be amused. As he looked in her eyes, for some reason she remembered Maya.

"I made applesauce with one of the girls," she responded. "She was the only one who could peel an apple."

Charles laughed. "When I was in the army, they had me peeling a hundred potatoes a day. I never got the hang of it." He looked at her. "You found something more than peeling apples, I hope."

"There was nothing else to do."

Charles scrunched his eyebrows. "What was her name, the apple-peeling girl?"

"Maya."

"Hmmm . . . and how was the applesauce?"

"Okay . . . good."

"What else was there?"

"Huh?"

"Ham, maybe?"

"No, just applesauce."

He was looking at her mother now. "Just applesauce . . . I knew there was a reason she came home early," he concluded.

Her mother frowned. "Oh, but there was a real dinner, I'm sure." She gazed uneasily at Alice. "There was, wasn't there?"

"Applesauce . . . and Maya was going to make bean soup today."

"But I thought you told us Maya was one of the girls."

"Yes."

"Then why was she cooking for the whole school?"

"I guess she wanted to."

"But where was Joel?"

Alice shrugged. "Busy . . . the Happening and all."

"Oh my—a Happening. And?"

"And what?"

"How was the Happening?"

Alice was feeling very warm. "That's today also." She'd promised to say nothing that could endanger the school.

Her mother frowned. "I thought you'd stay for that."

"No big deal."

Charles sighed. "We're glad you're back, Happening or no Happening."

They moved along the row of yellow rose bushes. Suddenly Alice wondered something. She turned to Charles.

"What color were they?"

"My mother's roses, you mean?"

"Yes."

"Oh, red, mostly. And a few yellow ones. Which color do you like?"

"The blood-red ones . . ."

"Royal red . . . of course."

Under the early-afternoon sun, they ascended row upon row and found the way back to the car.

chapter four

Alice

JOEL HAD SUMMONED Alice. The call came one evening, as the Raysons were having dinner—minus Tom, of course. Curt jumped up when the phone rang; with Charles far away in Los Angeles, he was the man of the house.

"Some guy for Alice," he remarked, holding the phone like a ball he was refusing to surrender.

"Some guy?" her mother demanded, frowning. "Does he have a name?"

"Guy named Joel," Curt shrugged, seemingly bemused by Alice's world.

"You mean Joel Cohen?" her mother wondered, suddenly eager.

"Maybe."

"Oh my! Speak to Joel, dear," her mother urged, eager and breathless. It was as though she'd been dreaming all her life of such a call.

Joel was summoning her to Parnassus Road. He was working on a book project about Other Paths and needed her help. He'd already met with some of the students—Maya and Jonathan and others she knew. Now he was hoping to hear from Alice as well —her voice belonged in the book. Joel's words burbled warmly as he suggested that she come by Parnassus Road on Wednesday at one o'clock. They would have a conversation; he would ask her to speak about a few things and tape-record her responses. Alice could feel her mother hovering, ready to inquire; feeling she'd finally made an impression, she agreed to go.

Heading up La Loma Avenue just before the scheduled hour, Alice was gasping for breath. La Loma sloped steeply toward

Parnassus Road; nearly there, but unable to go any further, she paused under some redwood trees and glanced over the bay to San Francisco, where her father was. He would be working; if she made her way there, as she'd made her way to Parnassus Road, she could see him. But no, she concluded, feeling the sun on her body; no, she would have nothing to say.

A car came whining up the road. She remembered the other summons to Joel's house, when the Raysons had come by car. So long ago—before Johnny. Though Other Paths had been a dud of a school, she would speak to Joel. He would hear what she had to say; her words would be in a book.

The day was warm, the hills awash in sunlight as she rounded the corner of Parnassus Road. As before, Joel opened the door and welcomed her in. Once again she found herself in Joel's living room, awed by a glass panorama hovering above the world. A gleam escaped below; feeling far away, she wondered why he'd asked her, why she'd come.

Joel came up, offering a jar of pickles.

"Go ahead, have one," he suggested, as though offering a fancy morsel. "They're imported."

The things were swimming in greenish water, so unappealing that she refused. "No, thanks."

"No?" Joel was frowning. "How come?"

"I never eat them," she responded, wondering why he cared.

"Are you feeling comfortable here?" Joel gazed on her somberly. "In many cultures, if a guest refuses food, it's because she has some fear of the food, or maybe the host."

There was a long pause as Joel eyed the panorama, leaving the message to hang in the room. She was being judged again by someone from Other Paths—this time by Joel. The whole encounter had already gone wrong.

Then he moved on. "Are you ready? Come, we can use my office."

Joel's work space was on a lower floor, away from the rest of the house. The room was cramped, and though there were glass doors facing west, toward the bay, nothing could be seen through the houses and trees. Offering her an armchair, Joel made himself comfortable in a leather recliner by the desk. He paused, giving her a moment to take in the room: books and papers all around, framed photographs and awards, young people's drawings on the walls. Then, leaning back, he fingered a large reel-to-reel tape recorder, adjusting the microphone, bringing it toward her. As if by reflex, she moved back. Joel gave her an unrevealing glance, adjusted the microphone again, and pressed a button. The reels jerked and began slowly revolving.

Joel was suddenly encouraging. "Maybe you could say something about yourself," he nodded, spreading his hands, palms up.

She was feeling unprepared.

"Maybe you could begin with your family," he prompted, head bobbing. "How are things at home?"

Joel was as much a stranger as he'd ever been; moreover, during her months at Joel's school, she'd refused to say much about her family to anyone.

"Hmmm?" Joel murmured.

The room seemed stuffy; Alice was feeling warm. "My parents just broke up."

"Oh?" He leaned in, eyes round and encouraging. "When were you informed?"

"Last summer," she managed to reply.

"I see —almost a year ago." Joel glanced down his nose, as though he'd caught her misleading him. "So, you've had a chance to adjust."

She nodded, feeling she was learning a role.

"And how do you feel now?" Joel's glance was cool and probing.

She looked away.

"Is your mother or father seeing anyone?"

She flushed and forced herself to respond. "My father . . . there's a woman from work—"

"Oh—a secretary!" Joel nodded eagerly, as though he'd heard the story before. But he had the story wrong; Ginger was no secretary. Her father—or maybe Ginger—would be angry if Alice let the error go.

"She's another lawyer in my father's office."

"Oh? Not a secretary?" Joel's eyebrows rose.

"No, a lawyer."

"So, how do you feel about that?" Joel seemed amused by the idea.

She was feeling annoyed. Following her father, she was supposed to say that a woman lawyer was preferable to a secretary, even when she ran off with someone's father. But why? The judgment seemed phony and impersonal; real feelings were less clear. Joel's response made her even more confused—if she had to know these things, then so should he. The job of informing him had fallen on her, it seemed; but Joel was a grown-up, and she was not. He would never learn lessons from her.

"Maybe it's better for him—"

"For him?" Chin up, Joel gazed on her. "And for you?"

"Maybe." She would hedge.

"How smart is she?"

"Smart enough."

"So, your father, he wants a smart woman?" Joel's eyes were laughing.

Alice's annoyance was growing—how far would he go?

"Let's see," Joel pursued. "Your father found a woman lawyer—"

She'd heard enough. "My mother's smart, too."

"Oh? So then, where was the problem?"

"They just never got along."

"Never? Not even on the honeymoon?"

True enough, her theory sounded absurd. But that was how she saw things.

"What's your mother doing now—going back to college?"

"No, she went to college already." From now on, Alice would be safe and cling to the formula she'd heard from her mother. Words unfolded before her—a clearing in the forest—and she rushed through them. "She's going to marry a man named Charles. He and my father knew each other in law school. We're moving to Los Angeles."

"Why Los Angeles?"

"Charles lives there."

"You mean he refuses to move?" Joel leaned in. "Does he love your mother?"

"Yes."

"You're sure?"

Alice grasped for her mother's formula, but the words refused to come. She blamed Joel for that—he was arguing with her, tempting her to say something wrong. She glanced at the tape recorder; she was running out of safe words.

"He works for a company in Los Angeles. So we're moving there."

"And what does he do?"

"Lawyer."

"Another lawyer? Same as your father?"

"My father works for the federal government. Charles works for a company."

"You mean he works for a big law firm?"

"No, a company that makes things—airplanes, computer chips."

Joel had been eyeing her smugly. Now he leaned forward, frowning. "And what's the name of the company?"

"North American Rockwell." She was glad she'd remembered; from now on she would need to know.

Joel's fingers were rapping on the desk. He was no longer amused.

"I see. You mean your new father works for a company that makes bombers."

Joel was no longer expecting any response; he'd made a judgment, and there would be no contesting it. The hands lay folded over his chest, fingers flexing.

"So—he's a baby-killer." Joel glared down his nose. "And what does he think he's doing?"

Her anger flamed, warming her whole body.

"Is he immoral or merely ignorant?"

There would be no use in defending Charles here. Joel had been slamming her family all along; now he imagined she would be open to slurs regarding the newcomer, Charles. Joel had found her vulnerable point—for who was Charles? Beyond the day in the rose garden, she could hardly say, while Joel was offering a clear-cut and damning image.

The tape was running out; the reels were turning at uneven speeds, like cars in parallel lanes on a freeway. As the tape passed from one reel to the other, Joel's demands and her responses were being recorded forever on a fragile length of tape. The thought that Joel would play it—maybe over and over—made her queasy. She sat staring at her hands, harboring a smoldering rage at the man who'd made her feel that way.

SHE MADE HER way back down La Loma Avenue and across the campus, heading for Raymond's house. Even in early May, the school had no home, so Helen and the group around Raymond had begun congregating in his bungalow. Alice had passed some afternoons there, as the group hung out, smoking grass. She couldn't go home right away, following the confrontation with Joel; with Charles hovering around, her mother had woken up and begun probing. There could be no purpose in revealing Joel's condemnation of Charles or the comments regarding her father's preference for a woman lawyer.

Rounding a corner, she came upon a long driveway and Raymond's dusty, sky-blue van. Beyond the van and concealed by the main house was a bungalow, a seeming relic from some long-ago frontier. The low, sloping roof was covered by a green tarpaulin; the shingles were uneven and the door crudely made, the work of a squatter or a Sunday carpenter.

The sound of the Rolling Stones' "Midnight Rambler" was coming from the bungalow; Raymond was home. Alice rapped on the glass, then—as Raymond's group was always doing—opened the door on a low room. From the doorway, she could see a sagging couch. Sound rumbled through the place, channeling the roar of her thoughts; a sour smell of marijuana hung in the air. Stepping into the room, she encountered Raymond's exasperated face in the gloom. He was wearing only jeans. Overcome by a queasy feeling, Alice saw another person emerge from the shadows—Helen.

Helen jumped up. In a moment, she was by the door.

"Come on," she commanded, leading Alice by the arm through the yard. As they reached the van, Helen sought Alice's eyes; then she looked away. "There's something you should know."

The annoyance in her tone gave an odd charge to her physical closeness. Alice wondered what would follow.

"That's why you're here, right?" Helen demanded.

Alice remembered the rumor she'd heard during the retreat, and wondered how the confession would unfold.

Helen flung down the gauntlet: "You probably already know, but Ray and I have been sleeping together."

The news was more jarring coming from Helen herself. The older girl leaned in, an odd spasm playing around her eye.

"Hey, we thought you knew."

Alice eyed the older girl. Helen was hoping she would feel dumb. "Maybe I heard something—"

"Wow, I can imagine," Helen sneered. "I know how people gossip."

"But you're saying it's true."

"So what? Why would anyone care, other than me and Ray?"

"I know, but—"

Helen glared, challenging her to complete the thought. "But what?"

"Raymond's twenty-three. He's a teacher—"

"Oh, Ray's no teacher—he's just an overgrown boy. God, you really are young."

Helen was angry now. Alice backed away.

"Where are you going?" Helen demanded.

"Home."

"You mean, now that you know about me and Ray, you won't come in?"

Alice moved away.

"Well, if that's how you feel, then you should go," Helen concluded. Turning away, she ran for the bungalow and slammed the door.

NOW THERE WAS only the library. Alice could not go home; she was vulnerable and might say anything. Her mother suddenly wanted to know things—where she had gone, who she was with. Her mother wanted to know everything about the people she knew—not only where they lived, but what they read and how they felt. These were things Alice hardly knew. Fortunately, she'd rarely spoken of Helen; now she never would. But she would need a story to overshadow the powwow with Joel, and the safest strategy would be to read something fast in the library. That would offer the necessary detour when her mother asked about Joel.

Alice entered the reading room. Fernwood nodded and then returned to his work. Alice had no trouble finding books now, and Fernwood was usually busy. There was a shelf of biology books Alice would browse, and several books about drawing. They were always on the shelf. But today she needed an engaging story, one she could remember well enough to regale her mother, if necessary. It would have to be a good story and a lively one, so she could blow off any probing by her mother. Fernwood would know what to suggest.

Alice approached Fernwood's desk.

"You do tear through those books," Fernwood remarked. "I can see you're looking for something new."

"A good story, a fast one."

"Fast?"

"Something I can read today."

"What's the rush?" Fernwood was peering at her.

"Nothing." She paused. "I feel like reading something, that's all."

Fernwood led her toward a nearby shelf, as though nothing unusual had happened.

"You could try Hemingway," she remarked. "Love and war—all the big stuff. And they're short." She paused. "How are things going on that . . . that other path?"

"Okay."

"I seem to remember . . . there was a retreat—a Walden Pond weekend, no?" Fernwood's eyes sparkled.

"Bohemian Grove, you mean."

"Oh gosh, I'm confusing it with something. Was it fun?"

"Not really."

"Hmmm. I used to love camping."

"We weren't camping. We . . . there was a lodge."

"Oh. That's easy, then. One floor for girls and one for boys. That works."

Alice flushed red.

"I suppose there were bunk beds," Fernwood remarked. "Always hard to sleep in bunk beds. I suppose you were up half the night talking with the other girls in the room."

There was an awkward pause.

"And how many teachers were there?"

"Just Raymond."

"My goodness. And you were there for how long?"

"Just one night. We had to leave—"

She blushed. Fernwood was worse than her mother.

"Want to say what happened?"

"No."

"That's up to you, then." Fernwood glanced away. "Maybe you'll like Hemingway." She made no move to go.

"There was a girl—"

Fernwood glanced at her.

"She and Raymond—"

"Go on."

"They were in one of the rooms. And one of the boys was jealous—Andy. He made a huge bonfire, a palace coup—"

"My heavens."

"A man came with a gun—and then in the morning, we had to leave."

"Raymond—he's a teacher?"

"Helen says not."

"She should know."

Fernwood was frowning.

"Helen says—" Alice caught herself. Then she blundered on. "She says he's an overgrown boy."

"I see."

"I just saw her and Raymond—"

"You mean in class?"

"No, at Raymond's house. We've been going there . . . for class."

Fernwood gave a wry smile.

"I was angry, I just needed someplace to go—"

"Who made you angry?"

"Joel." Alice's eyes were watering. "He made me so mad. He says my family—" She paused. "He says Charles is a bad man."

"Oh? Why?"

"Charles makes bombers—or his company does. Joel says he's a baby-killer."

Fernwood gave a sudden laugh. "And what about Raymond—does Joel know?"

There was a long pause.

Fernwood shook her head. "I'm sorry," she murmured. "Just remember, girl—you're moving on."

SHE'D GONE TO sleep remembering Raymond's bare chest and Helen's eyes. *She was on a beach, along with a group from Other Paths, and the day was very warm. The sand was burning her feet, and so she ran for the ocean, where she could cool off. Soon they were all jumping in the waves, Helen and Andy and Jonathan and Maya and . . . As they struggled through the waves, the beach was consumed by raging flames pushing them deeper and deeper from the shore. The water was growing hotter as the flames lapped closer, hotter and hotter . . . The Bomb had come and everyone was gone —everyone but the group in the burning waves . . .*

She awoke. Her body was damp with sweat. She'd had the dream before—more than once. She remembered Fernwood's words: "You're moving on." She wondered if the nightmare would move on with her.

Marian

ON SATURDAY MORNING when the telephone rang, for a moment Marian couldn't identify the caller; then, with a sense of shock, she recognized the gloomy tone as Sabrina Patterson.

"My God, Sabrina, what happened?"

"Have you heard?"

"No—what in the world—?"

"They're closing Other Paths."

"They're what?"

"Someone's been spreading a rumor, and now they've got a real scandal going."

"Oh, no!" Marian glanced around. Charles was safely in the living room.

"I thought we were more enlightened than that," came Sabrina's disgruntled sigh.

"But what happened?"

There was a pause, then Sabrina's oddly cheery announcement: "Helen's been sleeping with Raymond Connor."

"How awful!"

"The awful part is that they're blaming Joel and planning to close the school."

"Oh, Sabrina—"

"Helen says everyone knew. But now someone's gone to the cops and the whole thing is collapsing."

"But how could Raymond—"

"Oh, Helen's old enough to choose what to do. I must say, though, it was awfully dumb of Raymond. There are people who would just love to destroy Other Paths. He gave them the means."

"But how? Where?" Marian's hand was trembling. She scarcely knew Helen; even so, she was overcome by flashes of a sullen, half-dressed girl. As for Raymond, she had a clear image, though she'd never seen him.

"Oh, who cares! Helen and Ray are the only ones concerned."

"Yes. I suppose." Marian glanced through the living-room door. Charles was hovering, a cup of coffee in hand; there could be no probing or challenging Sabrina.

"They were together during the Bohemian Grove weekend. She came home so charged up—" Sabrina broke off. "And Joel was back East, pleading for funding."

For the first time, Marian was sorry to have Charles in the house. He would want to know what had happened before she could have any chance of smoothing over the story. He already frowned on Joel Cohen and Other Paths; now he would thoroughly condemn them—and maybe her, for sending her daughter to such a place. There were some things she would prefer Charles never know in any real way. So much had gone wrong; now she could leave those problems behind and go with Charles, if only her children could be induced to come along. That would be hard to pull off, but maybe it could be managed, as long as no one betrayed the old family to Charles. Soon enough, these recent happenings would fade.

Charles appeared in the doorway, his keen eyes round and inquiring.

"I really have to go, Sabrina—Charles is here. Please let me know if anything else happens."

She hung up the phone.

"Who was that?" he wanted to know.

"That was the mother of one of the girls from Other Paths."

"There's been a problem?"

"I'm sorry to say there has." Marian groped desperately for a way around exposing the ugly tale; but Charles gave her no chance.

"Who is Raymond, and what has he done?" he demanded, smoothing his tie. He was suddenly in lawyer mode; Marian had never seen him gear up before.

"Oh, who knows what really happened." She paused for a moment, then found she could no longer hold back. "Raymond is one of the teachers, and apparently someone has accused him of sleeping with one of the girls."

Charles glared, though not at her. "I never thought it was a good idea to send your daughter there. How could Tom do that?"

"Tom's judgment was always poor," Marian sighed, flushing at her slander. "I agreed because we knew Joel Cohen and regarded him as a wonderful man."

"Where could that Raymond have come from?"

"Who knows."

"I imagine Joel brought him in," Charles groaned. "People do the damnedest things."

"I suppose they do." Though Marian agreed, she damped a surge of loathing for both Helen and Raymond; she was feeling in need of damage control. "Fortunately, Joel had a good deal else to offer."

"How much has she seen of Raymond?" Charles pursued.

"Who—Alice?" Marian's eyebrows rose.

"Yes—how much has your daughter seen of Raymond?" he demanded bluntly.

Marian moved away. Charles, in lawyer mode, was probing the case. "Why, I suppose she's gone to a few classes."

"Maybe you should inquire."

"I'm very sure nothing's happened—"

"No, I should hope not. But who knows what she may have heard."

"Why, who would reveal such a thing?" Marian was struggling to compose herself.

"Oh, Raymond or the girl, I suppose," Charles shrugged. "People do brag, you know."

"If Joel Cohen had heard, I'm sure he would have done something." For Marian, Joel was looming larger and larger as the lone hero of an unsavory tale.

"I can assure you," Charles responded heatedly, smoothing his tie, "Mr. Joel Cohen would swear he had no idea of any improper dealings."

"And maybe he'd be telling the truth."

"Oh, perhaps."

Alice appeared in the doorway.

"There she is," Charles nodded. "Come on in, dear."

Alice

SHE'D HEARD JOEL'S name from the foyer and was already wondering which of the school's outrages had made the rounds. Her mother knew only Helen's mother, Sabrina—and Helen had every reason to conceal her connection with Raymond. But maybe she'd confessed other things—such as Andy's palace coup.

Charles' somber face was an ominous sign. "Tell us about Raymond," he commanded.

"Raymond?"

"Yes," responded her mother sharply, "Raymond and the so-called 'Bohemian Grove weekend.'"

Alice made no response. So, had they heard about the palace coup? Or worse?

"He was there, I presume?"

"Yes, he drove us in the van."

"That's all?" Her mother's eyes were glassy. "And what was everyone doing while you were there?"

"Where?"

"At the Bohemian Grove!"

"Nothing . . ." Alice gulped; she would come clean. "Someone made a bonfire."

"Of course—you were camping!" her mother snapped. "I'm asking, was there anything else I should know?"

"No." Alice was sweating. "What's wrong?"

Her mother wrung her hands in rage. "Raymond's been sleeping with one of the girls—Helen Patterson! That's what's wrong!"

"Yes!" Charles confirmed, in a novel show of grown-up agreement. "And your mother needs to know how much you've heard."

Alice lowered her eyes. "They're older . . ."

"You've heard nothing?" her mother demanded, incredulous.

"Maybe some rumors . . ."

"How long were they carrying on—have you any idea?"

"How would I know?" The room was feeling warm. Alice had wondered the same thing, though not about Helen and Raymond. Her mother, dreamy and sighing, had told her over and over how she and Charles had found each other again, but somehow the time frame never made sense—how could so many changes have happened in only a few weeks? There was nothing to do, however, but appear to honor the story of a long-ago love so abruptly renewed. Alice struggled to hold her doubts in mind as her mother pressed on.

"Raymond chaperoned the weekend, as I recall."

"Chaperoned?" The word sounded odd and incongruous, though its meaning eluded Alice.

"He was in charge of you, no? Was there anyone else—Joel, for example?"

"Joel canceled."

"And so there was only Raymond."

Alice shrugged. There was no use denying fundamental facts.

"Did Helen and Raymond share a room?" her mother pursued, unsparing.

"Maybe. I heard a rumor—"

"And what else happened?"

What else?

"Your mother's heard everything from one of the parents—," Charles said, growing impatient.

"—from Sabrina."

Alice was feeling woozy. *What more could there be?*

"You were in Raymond's van—"

"Yes."

"And what was happening once you got there?"

"Nothing much," Alice muttered. "I hardly saw Helen."

"And I suppose *you* were doing nothing wrong."

Alice glanced at Charles for help; he glanced back.

"If you'd told me these things, I would have had you in another school." Her mother was looking at her warily. "Joel's been some help, I suppose?"

"Some. When he's there."

"And when he's not?"

"I've been in the library."

"The library?" Her mother seemed mystified.

"Down on Shattuck. I go there and read. There's a librarian who helps me, recommends books—"

"You're supposed to be in school during the day."

Alice lowered her eyes.

"You've been lying to me—"

"Now, now," murmured Charles, placing a hand on her mother's shoulder. "From the sound of it, she's been in good hands."

"I know, but—"

The inquiry lapsed. They looked at each other, as though wondering how to begin anew. For a moment, Alice pondered how much to say. "I heard a rumor during the retreat . . . but I thought maybe it was just a rumor. Then last week . . ."

"Yes?" came her mother's weary sigh.

"I ran into Helen, and she told me."

Her mother folded her arms; her head drooped. "Someone went to the police about these goings-on. They're closing Other Paths."

When she'd confessed to Fernwood, Alice had broken Raymond's commandment. But she'd never imagined that Fernwood would inform on the school. The others would blame her, if they knew. She edged through the doorway, suppressing a feeling of glee.

A FEW DAYS later, Alice was ascending a fire road above the campus, close by the path where Johnny had brought her. She had no reason for coming here, beyond some internal goading—waspish and maddening—that was driving her far into enemy turf. The place was deserted; that could be good or bad. She was moving with a sense of weightlessness—as though, released from earth, she would soar far above the grasses and eucalyptus groves.

As she rounded a bend, she came face-to-face with a group of young people. One of the girls was singing; it was Maya, in her usual clown face. On her heels came Andy and Helen, followed by Jonathan. Jonathan caught up, waving at Alice. Then Andy resumed a conversation in progress.

"Such a bummer . . . someone had to be the squealer. I really wanna know who—"

"So many people," Jonathan shrugged, with a touch of contempt. "Could've been any of them."

"Yeah, Helen, you made sure everyone knew." Andy glared around, eyes blue and watery, enlarged by the glasses he wore. "Why'd you do that?"

"Oh, Andy, they knew already." Helen pulled off her purple bandana and slapped at him. "You and your palace coup—that's how. You're a jealous brat—"

"Raymond!" Andy spat. "You and Raymond!"

Jonathan came forward, eyeing Alice. "You heard?"

"Heard?"

"Other Paths," Andy snapped. "They're closing us down."

"Oh—yes." Alice glanced at Helen. "Your mom called."

"Whoa . . ." Andy was pondering. "Hey, Helen, would your mom call the cops?"

"No way, she's cool," Helen murmured.

Maya sang on, bobbing to a rhythm in her head. "*Eli's comin', hide your heart girl . . .* I know," she giggled, her laugh rising and falling like birdsong. "It was one of those girls who's always chasing Ray."

"But who?" Andy glared around through the trees. "'Cause I got something to say to her."

Jonathan wriggled his eyebrows. "Go ask Alice. She's in the loop," he teased.

"Oh, Jonathan, be real," Helen said, frowning. "Alice heard from me. She looked appalled and told me Ray was too old."

"That's a laugh."

Maya wandered on, singing. Her long shawl was dragging in the dust.

"C'mon," murmured Helen. She and Andy followed Maya down the road.

Jonathan hung back, as though he'd been hoping for a personal word with Alice. They faced each other. "How's the library these days—fun?"

"It's okay."

"How come you're not there today?"

She moved away. "Other things to do."

"Such as wandering alone on the fire road?" Jonathan's eyebrows wriggled as he followed her.

"Why not?"

"Wanna come with us?"

She shrugged, facing an uncomfortable dilemma. If she refused, she would soon be alone in that burdened place; if she agreed and the others learned what she'd done, they would blame her.

Jonathan sighed. "You know, a couple of weeks ago I went to the library . . . thought you'd be there. There was only that priggish librarian—"

"Fernwood?"

"That's her name? I asked if you were around and she glared at me, made me feel like some kind of felon."

"Fernwood's okay."

"To you, maybe." He hummed the opening bars of "Eleanor Rigby." "Now that they've closed Other Paths, you'll have even more reading days."

She moved away, gazing on the slope. "It was Fernwood," she confessed, speaking to the grasses.

"Huh?" The gray eyes were probing her.

"I told her—Raymond and Helen—"

"You what?" He approached, speaking in a murmur. She held her ground.

"Fernwood—I told her. I never imagined she'd do anything."

The others were nearing a bend; now they called out, beckoning Jonathan.

"I won't tell anyone," he breathed, leaning in.

"Go ahead." They could blame her; she would be leaving anyway.

"I wouldn't do that." Jonathan surveyed her. "Just so you know, I think Raymond's a real perv." He turned, waving to the others. "I'm coming!" Then he faced her. "Well, goodbye."

"Goodbye."

And she began running the other way along the road.

Passing a bend in the road, she came upon a grassy slope leading away through the trees. The slope—it was where Johnny had brought her, so long ago—glimmered and rippled, blurring as though in a long camera exposure. Except for the grasses, moved by an unseen force, the day was calm, the nightmare gone. She found herself remembering and judging the world and wondering what she would take with her. Once upon a time, she'd imagined that the things she learned would go with her— she'd carry them on. Now there was no saying. All through the canyon, eucalyptus fronds dangled, releasing a sharp odor. She'd endured one thing and then another; soon she would be moving on. She was hoping for some way beyond drowning in the Now, its rushing stream, its unleashing of half-forgotten, half-life scenes—things she'd once imagined would go with her anywhere. They would weaken and fade, change as her father had been changed for Charles; yet they would go on and on, becoming remnants as she journeyed through newly forming worlds.

She would have severed good from bad, if she could, but here, among the sharp odors of eucalyptus, she'd endured a mingling, and now there was no chance of carrying only the good.

BEFORE THEY WERE to leave, Tom arranged a get-together. Ginger had seen the children, though never for long. She was always in a hurry, her eyes cool and appraising even as she showed her charm. Then one Sunday in early June, he came by the house in Berkeley and drove them to San Francisco. Ginger had made plans for dinner in a North Beach restaurant that served homemade pasta.

When the Raysons arrived, Ginger had already found a table and ordered a glass of white wine. She wore peach-colored slacks and a pale blouse with a Nehru collar. Her hair had been done in waves and highlights; her long fingernails were manicured. She looked nothing like Alice's mother, who'd gone longhaired and casual. Tom grabbed the seat facing her.

"Well, lady . . ."

"Hi, Tom. No problems on the bridge?"

"No—all clear."

She gave the children a smile. "Bet you've never had dinner in a real North Beach restaurant before," she teased. "They have three grandmothers who make all the spaghetti noodles and sauces here on the premises."

Curt laughed, humoring her.

"I hear they have a wonderful lasagna—that's something you won't get at home," she added. "Have you ever had lasagna?"

Alice looked up, encountering cool gray-green eyes. "Yes," she replied, "my mom makes it sometimes."

"Oh, does she? That's very adventurous of her."

Ginger signaled for the menus, and a plump, matronly woman handed them around, making eyes at Curt. As she moved on, glancing back over her shoulder, Ginger reached across the table and laced her fingers with Tom's, the thumbs playing in the candlelight. Curt, handsome and blooming, amused himself by pouring a few grains of salt in his palm; Ginger gave him a smile.

"Looking forward to the end of school?"

"Oh yeah."

"How soon?"

"Coupla weeks."

"Same for you?" she pursued, glancing at Alice. There was an awkward pause, as Alice wondered why she was even asking. "Oh my, I completely forgot—you're already done with school, aren't you?"

"Kind of."

"I heard from your dad how they closed your school. Such a shame." Ginger paused, reaching for the bread with her free hand. "Can you say what happened?"

Curt smothered a guffaw.

"A teacher . . . trouble . . ." Alice mumbled, glancing at her father for help, but he was looking elsewhere. Ginger was making mischief by asking; surely she'd heard about Raymond.

"So shabby." Ginger made a somber face. "I know your dad was really mad. He never thought much of the place—what's it called?"

"Other Paths."

"Yes, how could I forget. And the headmaster—I mean the principal?"

"Joel Cohen."

"He really let your dad down."

Her father's eyes were roving over Ginger, absorbing her as she spoke. He mumbled vague agreement, as their thumbs played together. Ginger was showing her charm again, but the gray-green eyes were cool. She began looking over the menu, as the others followed along.

"Ready to order?" she prompted.

Tom grunted approval.

Ginger placed her menu on the table. "Tom," she smiled, "you can order the veal for me. I'll go powder my nose."

Ginger headed for the rear of the restaurant. The three Raysons sat uncomfortably together, as Tom's eyes wandered after her.

Curt began drumming on the table. "Vida Blue's gonna win the Cy Young," he remarked, eager and upbeat.

Tom nodded vaguely.

"Maybe we can see a game . . . before I go."

"Maybe . . ." He gazed off in Ginger's wake.

Eyeing her father's face, Alice ignored the baseball plans; she would not be going, if she had any say. From the sound of it, no one would be going to a game; her father was caught up in a new world peopled exclusively by Ginger. He'd never shown much enthusiasm before, and Alice was wondering what the change would mean for her.

Ginger reappeared, hair combed and fluffed, lighting his eyes. Resuming her place at the table, she cast a glance over the uncollected menus.

"Tom, I thought you were going to order," she teased.

"Well, lady, I was waiting for you."

As they clasped hands again, the plump woman waddled up. Ginger ordered veal for the grown-ups and lasagna for the kids. She turned to Curt.

"Maybe you can come horseback riding before you leave. You'd have some real fun." Then she smiled. "I know you love baseball, but it's always good to try something new."

"Maybe," Curt shrugged, adding, "I've never been on a horse. And there's the game with Vida Blue."

"Your dad's a fast learner—I bet you are, too."

"I'd rather see the game," Curt objected, turning to his father.

"Well . . ." Her father's face had become damp. "What do you say about a game, lady?" he asked Ginger.

"Oh, Tom, I just thought—"

"You and I can go to the dude ranch this summer—"

"Yeah," Curt muttered, "and I can see Vida Blue throw a shutout."

"How about you, Alice?" Ginger pursued. "Anything you're hankering for before you go, or are you someone who never looks back?"

Alice thought of the day she'd seen Joel, Helen, and Fernwood, one after the other. Then she thought of the day on the fire road. "I've said goodbye . . . in my own way."

Ginger was no longer smiling. "I'm not sure what you mean." For the first time, she seemed uneasy.

"I already told everyone goodbye. They know what it means —or they can figure it out."

"If you say so." Ginger unlaced her fingers. "Well, here comes the lasagna," she announced, as the woman came bearing a serving tray. Ginger raised her wineglass. "Cheers," she smiled.

ALICE WAS FINGERING the ragged sleeve of her Finnish army jacket. She'd been planning on wearing the jacket for the journey south. Though they would be traveling by car, as before, everything else had changed. They had come to Berkeley as the Raysons; they'd endured the loss of Tom and personal changes; now they were leaving as another family, regrouped with Charles and his sons. Alice had been hoping that her mother would be busy with Charles and say nothing about clothes; that way, she could wear the army jacket, a covering for her wound. But then the day came, a warm Sunday in June, and she suddenly understood. She could carry only so much on the journey south. Someone had abandoned the army jacket long ago; soon enough, someone else would find it hanging in her room. By then, of course, she would be long gone.

Near the army jacket hung the jeans she'd worn that day—the day Johnny took her so far she could never go back. She'd always planned on leaving the jeans. No one would ever know where they'd come from, why they'd been abandoned. And so she would go on. She would live; Johnny would die.

Then she remembered. Groping in the jeans, she found the ring she'd bought from a head shop so long ago. The ring had been there, in the jeans, since the day Johnny had changed her. She'd been scared to look; but in an hour she would escape from Berkeley, she would be safe.

Alice grasped the ring. From now on, the changes would be up to her.

In the mingling of good and bad, hope could be found—a flame. Not the world-devouring flame of nightmare, but a flame she could carry with her. She thought of trees and sandy beaches, cars and suburbs, a school.

Joel had made them see the world as an asylum; but the asylum was here, in a failed experiment. The new family was moving on, a new experiment. She hoped they would succeed. She remembered Joel's slogan: "We destroy in order to create." Back in Washington, who would have imagined the Raysons could do such things? And yet, they'd done nothing so very outrageous, only what everyone else was doing. She was glad they were going—even minus Tom. The world was a place of beauty and destruction;

but though they'd been mingled, for her they could never be the same thing.

Her mother was calling. Alice fingered the ragged cloth, wondering; then she let the sleeve go. She'd seen things go wrong, and now she was leaving, escaping Berkeley. Who could say if the others would make it: Jim and Valerie and Maya and Helen . . .

Charles had come for them. He'd come up the day before in a Ford Thunderbird, and now the four of them climbed in together, bound for Los Angeles. As the engine rumbled and they pulled away from the curb, Alice saw her mother and Charles, happy and youthful, exchange a long glance. Then Charles donned the square sunglasses he preferred.

"Here we go."

"Yes, here we go," Marian smiled, refusing to look back as they pulled away.

Curt leaned, face clenched, for a last glimpse of the handsome brown-shingle house. Alice saw the soaring palm, then the gray-green London plane trees began rolling by. The June morning was balmy though cool. She thought how odd it seemed, eagerly leaving such a beautiful place.

They'd hardly gone anywhere when Charles suddenly headed up an old road bordered by ivy-covered stone walls.

"Where are we?" Alice wondered aloud.

"Claremont Avenue," Curt murmured, "heading for Grizzly Peak." He sounded as if he'd been there more often than he could remember.

"How do you know?"

"I used to come here with Sammy." He gazed away, vaguely contemptuous. "You mean you've never been here before?"

"No more squabbling—let's just enjoy ourselves now," Marian purred, as though she imagined they'd never squabble again.

Charles gave a sigh. "Let's have a look around before we go. Your mother says she's never come up here. Hard to imagine."

Curt shrugged. "Been here with Sammy . . ."

The car roared up and up, and soon they were on Grizzly Peak Boulevard, rounding the edge of a cliff. Far below lay the shimmering surface of the bay.

"Oh, we *have* been here," Marian gasped, gazing on a Florentine villa perched on a promontory below. "That strange afternoon." She glanced back at the children. "Do you remember how scared you were? You'd never seen such hills—and the road was so winding. Do you remember how the brakes were smoking on the way down?"

So many worse things had happened, but that was how they'd be remembered, thought Alice—as a road winding along a ridge and then dropping down, faster and faster. Only the burning rubber had saved them, by slowing them down.

Charles drove calmly, peering around the slope, as though on furlough from the world. The road wound along the summit, then began sloping down toward the canyon. Soon they rounded a sharp bend, and Charles nodded toward a clump of sci-fi buildings below.

"That's the Lawrence Laboratory," he commented. "And there's the cyclotron."

He had a reason for bringing them here, Alice sensed, as her mother's voice pealed.

"Oh, look at the fog!"

Sure enough, fog was pouring through the Golden Gate.

Alice was sitting behind Charles. She leaned forward. "What's a cyclotron?" She'd heard the ominous word before, and wanted to know why he'd brought them there.

Charles smiled wryly at her mother. "You mean all they know is People's Park?"

"Just look at the fog," she sighed. "Soon enough, no one will care anymore about People's Park."

Curt leaned in. "It's where they make the nuclear fuel," he murmured, as the car dropped down Centennial Drive, past research gardens belonging to the university, toward the Greek Theatre.

For a moment, Alice remembered her dream. She would have to forgive herself for so many things, including leaving the others—Tammy and Joe and Valerie and Jonathan and . . . But she was going far away, and she would have to save herself—that would be the new experiment.

The Ford rumbled along Bancroft Way, by the border of the campus, approaching Telegraph Avenue. For a year, she'd hardly seen Telegraph; she'd been scared and ashamed. Now the whole scene loomed close: she could jump out and be there.

Charles sought Alice's gaze in the rearview mirror. "How're you doing, sport?"

"Okay." It was as though he knew.

As Telegraph Avenue was whirling by, a scruffy girl ran up alongside the Ford. She had golden ropes of hair and a ragged Spider-Man shirt, and she was ogling Charles—the close-cropped hair and square sunglasses—as though he'd come from Mars. As Charles glared back, Valerie began laughing and waving, then veered away toward the curb. With a shudder, Alice saw her go.

"Someone you know?" her brother murmured.

Alice could feel herself going warm, then cold. Telegraph Avenue passed in a blur, and soon the raucous sounds faded. The Ford was rounding a corner, heading for Ashby Avenue. Beyond the window rose the campus hills, eucalyptus trees obscuring the fire road. Who could say how, but she'd been released. That evening they would sleep in a faraway place, and in the morning, she would wake up in a new world.

Credits

Acknowledgments

My heartfelt thanks go to:

Robin Epstein, without whose encouragement and support this book would never have been written.

Everyone at She Writes Press. I am very grateful to Brooke Warner and her team, including cover designer Julie Metz and project manager Samantha Strom, for supporting this novel and for allowing me to stay true to my original purpose in writing it.

Jeff Gustavson, for his thoughtful copyediting.

Dorothy Cantwell, George Paik, Susan Sternau, and members of the Brooklyn Writers Guild (you know who you are), whose comments and suggestions made this novel richer and stronger.

About the Author

Born in Washington, D.C., Sarah Relyea left the Berkeley counter-culture at age thirteen and processed its effects as a teenager in suburban Los Angeles. She would soon swap California's psychedelic scene to study English literature at Harvard. Sarah has long addressed questions of identity in her writing, including in her book of literary criticism, *Outsider Citizens: The Remaking of Postwar Identity in Wright, Beauvoir, and Baldwin.*

With her PhD in English and American literature from The CUNY Graduate Center, Sarah has taught at universities in New York and Taiwan. She remains bicoastal, living in Brooklyn and spending time on the Left Coast.

Visit Sarah at
www.sarahrelyea.com

Photo credit: Hunter Canning Photography

SELECTED TITLES FROM SHE WRITES PRESS

She Writes Press is an independent publishing company
founded to serve women writers everywhere.
Visit us at www.shewritespress.com.

Shrug by Lisa Braver Moss. $16.95, 978-1631526381. It's the 1960s,
and teenager Martha Goldenthal just wants to do well at Berkeley
High and have a normal life—but how can she when her mother is
needy and destructive and her father is a raging batterer who disdains
academia? When her mother abandons the family, Martha must
stand up to her father to fulfill her vision of going to college.

Pieces by Maria Kostaki. $16.95, 978-1-63152-966-5. After five years
of living with her grandparents in Cold War-era Moscow, Sasha finds
herself suddenly living in Athens, Greece—caught between her psy-
chologically abusive mother and violent stepfather.

We Never Told by Diana Altman. $16.95, 978-1631525438. In the
1950s, when Sonya was fourteen, her glamorous, beautiful mother
left her two teenage daughters for months, seeking treatment for a
"stomach tumor." The secrets surrounding this event haunt Sonya
well into middle age, when she finally unravels the lies—which turn
out to be not at all what she expected.

Cleans Up Nicely by Linda Dahl. $16.95, 978-1-938314-38-4. The
story of one gifted young woman's path from self-destruction to self-
knowledge, set in mid-1970s Manhattan.

The Rooms Are Filled by Jessica Null Vealitzek. $16.95,
978-1-938314-58-2. The coming-of-age story of two outcasts—a
nine-year-old boy who just lost his father, and a closeted young
woman—brought together by circumstance.

Play for Me by Céline Keating. $16.95, 978-1-63152-972-6. Middle-
aged Lily impulsively joins a touring folk-rock band, leaving her job
and marriage behind in an attempt to find a second chance at life,
passion, and art.

9 781631 528897